CHRONICLES OF NETHRA

BOOK TWO

SHADOWS OF MINOS

This is a work of fiction. All characters and events portrayed in this novel are either fictitious or are used fictitiously.

Chronicles of Nethra: Shadows of Minos

www.mythicnorthpress.com

ISBN: 978-1-954177-04-8

Revised edition: July 2021

For Josh
Can't thank you enough for the feedback and
encouragement. This one is for you, buddy.

Acknowledgments

Thanks, once again, to Alana Joli Abbott for providing the copy edits for this book. Your feedback is invaluable and always brings a smile to my face.

Another big thank you to my friends and family who have encouraged me on this journey. We're just getting started, but I know I can do it with you in my corner. Hope you enjoy the book.

NeoGenix Executive Board Room
Valhalla, Sif—Third Planet of the Freyvian System
Three Months Ago

"I'm not doubting your intel, Lucretia," said Julia. "I believe that the Starfire Conduit is as powerful and unique as you've described. What I don't understand is why House Barkay would have it commissioned in the first place."

Cyrus Valadar leaned back in his chair. He laced fingers together and stretched his arms back to relieve the tension building in his chest and shoulders. "My sister raises a good point, Dr. Blackwell. Prodigy commissions do not come cheap. Do we know why Ulysses would go through such trouble?"

Lucretia Blackwell straightened her glasses—an involuntary reflex she resorted to as her patience waned. Cyrus wondered if his chief science officer was even aware of the little tic.

"I was not able to secure that information," she explained. "As you may have heard, the Don now rests among the stars. It's entirely likely that he took the secret of the conduit's purpose with him into the stardust grave."

"You don't know Ulysses is dead," Joaquin protested. "The feeds insist he was nowhere near that attack on the Osiris compound. Anyone who says otherwise is just spoutin' Chronos propaganda."

Cyrus held up a hand to stay his little brother's outburst. "We also know that House Barkay has every reason to dissemble about the death of their patriarch. It changes little."

Truthfully, it changed much in the political landscape of the Ravian System. Cyrus just didn't want his siblings to spend too much time questioning Lucretia's sources. He trusted the doctor's network of spies as much as he trusted any of their assets. In fact, he trusted them more than most.

He cleared his throat before continuing. "Let's say that this information is correct. Who holds the Conduit now?"

"That would be Braccus Kai," Lucretia replied.

"Ulysses arm's dealer?" Julia asked incredulously.

"He's more than an arms dealer, but yes—that is the man that I'm referring to."

"And would he be willing to cooperate with us if we expressed interest in procuring the item?"

Cyrus answered Julia's question first. "Certainly not. At least, not until Barkay is in full collapse. Even then, I don't know that he would want to be seen openly cooperating with us in the current political climate. Such a move would send a troubling signal to House Chronos."

Plus, if Cyrus was going to start establishing assets in the Ravian System, Kai and his minions wouldn't be his first choice in recruits. Their operation on the Star Spire was enviable but overtly corrupt. It didn't match the new image he was trying to cultivate for his family.

"But," he continued, "the asset is still worth pursuing. Do we have an intermediary that can approach Kai in our stead?"

Joaquin and Lucretia began to rattle off suggestions. In the end, it was a demoralizing effort. Cyrus and Julia shot down each of the ideas in succession. It was not that Cyrus or his sister took any great pleasure in dismantling the ideas. That was just the role that they had long been accustomed to playing.

Usually, Joaquin's rambunctious style garnered him an uneasy alliance with their youngest sister. Tessa, however, had not deemed to grace them with her presence—*again.*

The suggestion that caught Cyrus's attention did not come from around the board-room table, but from its periphery. "I could go."

Julia turned to eye the speaker thoughtfully. "Now there's an interesting idea."

Sydney Cross stepped forward from her place among the security team. Though the vest she wore displayed the Valadar family emblem, the Citza woman was not officially part of Cyrus's detail. Her snowy tail swept casually from side to side as she waited for him to provide his thoughts on her suggestion.

"No," he replied definitively. "I have too much need for you here. I can't spare you for an assignment that will take you out-system for an indefinite period of time."

Joaquin let out a suggestive snort. Cyrus glared at his brother, who smirked despite the silent rebuke. Julia rolled her eyes. Cyrus could not tell if the gesture was offered as criticism of Joaquin's outburst or as an expression of solidarity.

His siblings could think what they wanted about his relationship with the assassin. Cyrus knew the needs he referred to were legitimate. It was probably better that the two of them remain ignorant of how many lives Sydney had taken at his behest in this last half-cycle.

Sydney seemed unperturbed by the decision. "If not me, then perhaps one of my sisters. It is not widely known that the Ghenza have allied themselves with House Valadar. We can secure the Starfire Conduit and transfer it to you without Braccus or his network ever being the wiser."

Now *that* was a novel idea. "It won't arouse suspicion that the Collective is suddenly interested in cutting-edge technology?" Cyrus asked.

Sydney shrugged. "I doubt that anyone will ever hear of it. But even if they did, there would be little cause for question. We haven't built our network on slitting throats alone. A reach such as ours requires a diversity of resources—both political, and technological."

Cyrus eyed the others around the table. Neither of his siblings raised a protest. Lucretia let slip a satisfied smile. She was already thinking of what she might do with the Conduit.

"We agree, then. Sydney, I'll allow you to handle the logistics of this. Work with Dr. Blackwell on resources and compensation. It's her budget that will be supporting this little endeavor."

The good doctor didn't seem to care for that last remark, though Cyrus hardly knew why. He couldn't recall a time when he'd ever failed to increase her budget upon request. Nine hells, the only reason he even gave her the arbitrary figure in the first place was to satisfy Julia. Then again, that was just another reason why his older sister made such an effective CFO.

Cyrus tapped the tablet in front of him, bringing up the meeting agenda. "With that settled, we have one more item of business to discuss. Molly, would you bring in our guest from the waiting area?"

Cyrus's assistant stood up from her position to his left and made for the door. She vanished momentarily before reemerging with a man in tow. Despite looking the part of a wealthy executive in his tailored suit and artfully placed accessories, the man still looked out of place. Sahaia tended to do that.

His hair was the same deep black as his suit, as were his eyes. Those eerie orbs were marked with only a pinprick of light in the center, and the barest slit of white to mark where the corneas might have started. Even in an otherwise friendly and handsome face, those eyes conveyed mildly sinister undertones.

"Members of the Board," Cyrus began. "I would like to introduce Ryker Ren'Dahl, Triumvir of the Minos Coven."

Ryker bowed respectfully before taking a seat. "Thank you for agreeing to see me. I understand your time is valuable and my request was made on short notice."

"Indeed," Julia scoffed. "It seems that you've neglected to update the official agenda, Cyrus."

He'd updated *his* agenda, which happened to be the only one that mattered. Cyrus chose to ignore Julia's barb. "I believe you'll all be very interested in what our guest has to say. Mr. Ren'Dahl, if you would begin."

The shadow nodded. "That you, Don Valadar. And please, just call me Ryker. Ren'Dahl is our coven name, and my people choose to go by our first names—even in formal context."

He turned that dark gaze to Julia. Though she fought the urge, she still shrank under the weight of those eyes. Ryker continued speaking. "I wish to inquire about a certain relic that was recently recovered in a deep-space salvage operation. It is my understanding that one of your companies registered the salvage and that ownership of the object was transferred to NeoGenix Incorporated."

"And how, exactly, did you find out what's been transferred to our holdings Mi… Ryker?" Joaquin seemed to force every bit of bumbling aggression he could into the question.

Ryker appeared unflustered by the challenge. "All a matter of public record, I assure you. My associates and I keep an eye on salvages looking for objects such as this. If you check your own records, you will see that the Minos Coven frequently purchases interesting finds from your salvage companies. This one, however, was transferred before we had the opportunity to make an offer. I wish to rectify that today."

He produced a portable holoprojector from the inside pocket of his blazer. Resting the black disk on the table, he tapped its center to bring the object to life. A rotating image appeared above the device which Ryker enlarged with a flick of his fingers.

The projector displayed what looked to be a green crystal, partially occluded by chunks of black rock. It was certainly exotic—pretty, if somewhat unrefined. The crystal might have been appropriately fashioned into jewelry or some made to serve some other aesthetic function.

Cyrus had never seen the object before Ryker had shared the image in his missive. He was fairly certain it wouldn't have been transferred to NeoGenix based purely on its cosmetics, though he did not know who had given the order to purchase it.

"This," Ryker continued, "is a relic of great religious significance. The crystal emits low levels of dark energy, a phenomenon that is quite rare in natural constructs. The object's radiation is harmless—hardly detectable except through the use of the most sensitive equipment."

Well, that explained how it had been flagged for transfer. Cyrus leaned forward. "And to what application does your"—He searched for the correct word.—"*organization* intend for an object such as this?"

"No application, specifically. As you may know, the covens are in a bit of a competition with Tempolose Nethera for control over ancient relics. We work cooperatively amongst ourselves for the control of objects that align with our unique interests. That is why you are speaking with me today, rather than an emissary from the Ren'Kue. The study of dark energy is something of our specialty out on Minos."

Julia drummed her fingers contemplatively. "And what do you expect to do with this reservoir of dark energy?" Cyrus could practically read her mind. Whatever the Sahaia were doing, there was a chance that someone within Valadar Holdings could do the same.

The question was: Would Ryker tilt his hand and be honest about his coven's ambitions? Or would he dissemble?

"As you know, applications of dark energy remain relatively limited." He spread his arms, turning his palms out innocently.

"Radiation at such slow levels has no apparent application with current technology. We seek to secure the object purely for its cultural significance."

Dissembling it is then. Cyrus chose to play along. "Perhaps you could explain the cultural significance of this artifact? Merely to satisfy our curiosity, of course. NeoGenix has no interest in the collection of religious relics."

Something flashed in the black pools of Ryker's eyes, breaking their ominous spell. Hesitation, perhaps? "I confess that I may prove an unworthy tutor. I am not as well versed in Nethrian lore as some of my counterparts."

Julia seemed to pick up on what Cyrus was attempting. "You could at least tell us what it is called. Surely your colleagues gave you the name of the artifact before they sent you all this way from the Helion System?"

Given the choice between appearing ignorant and disclosing information he obviously wanted to keep secret, Ryker opted for the latter. "We believe this may be the Heart of Thule."

Unlike Ryker, Joaquin had no qualms about displaying his ignorance. "And what's that supposed to mean?"

Ryker shrugged. "As I stated, I am not well versed in the Chronicles. My intellectual pursuits tend to be more… bureaucratic."

The reference was lost on Cyrus as well, but he resolved to look it up later. He didn't believe for a second that Ryker knew as little as he was letting on, but had no lever with which to ply him. Instead of continuing down this path, he resolved to lead the discussion along more productive lines.

"And what price do you offer for this artifact?"

Whatever discomfort Ryker had been hiding dissolved in an instant. He donned a coy, half-smile. "I would begin by offering to recoup whatever costs your companies have incurred in securing the artifact. I would also offer three times your typical finder's fee for an object of this class. Anything beyond that is open to negotiation."

A generous offer, but still well short of the sum that such a prize was actually worth. Undoubtedly this opening play was intended to cover the costs of coming to the bargaining table.

Cyrus leaned back, steepling his hands contemplatively. "Thank you for your expression of interest, Ryker. Will you be lingering in Valhalla for long? As you will understand, this is something my siblings and I must give some thought to."

"Yes," the shadow said with a nod, his expression neutral. "I had planned to be in the city for the next three days. If you require additional time for deliberations, my schedule can be adjusted."

"Oh, I don't think that will be necessary." Cyrus stood, walked to where Ryker was seated, and offered his hand. "Send a missive tomorrow and Molly will arrange a time for us to meet. I appreciate your coming to us with this. I would hate to have squandered such a rare find in our ignorance."

Though Ryker took the hand, a great deal of hesitation lingered in his expression. "Thank you," he said as Cyrus led him to the door. "I look forward to speaking with you again soon."

After their guest had departed, Julia spoke up. "What was that?"

Cyrus fought the urge to roll his eyes. "I sincerely apologize for not updating the agenda. Ryker contacted me only yesterday."

"And you decided against putting his request through the proper channels?" Her eyes narrowed to emphasize the rebuke.

"Please, dear sister. Dispense with your relentless adherence to bureaucratic standards and consider the opportunity on its merits. Surely, you can see the potential here."

Joaquin scoffed. "Didn' seem like the offer was all that impressive t' me."

"It was merely the opening salvo, little brother," said Cyrus. "Ryker intended only to demonstrate how serious he was about this transaction."

Julia's shoulders shifted and she tapped her lips contemplatively. "Yes, indeed. What does the coven have to offer us that we might find valuable? To my knowledge, they have no equities or corporate interest that can be traded."

"They seem to have plenty of cash," said Joaquin. "How much do holy rocks run for these days?"

Julia shifted her omnipresent irritation toward Joaquin. "It's priceless, you simpleton. Anything that the Sahaia would reasonably pay for such a thing would be less than its actual value. If it is money we are after, we'd be better off approaching Tempolose Nethera to participate in an open auction."

"Perhaps we are being a bit short-sighted," Lucretia suggested.

All eyes went to the doctor. Only then did Cyrus realize how quiet she had been during the short exchange with Ryker. "You were the one who requisitioned the artifact."

"Of course I was. As you are quick to point out, the NeoGenix research division is *my* budget. Unlike other Valadar subsidiaries, I don't rely on automatic flags in the corporate database to govern my acquisitions."

Julia narrowed her eyes. "But why this? I wouldn't have imagined that religious artifacts fell under your purview."

"It's not *just* a religious artifact. Like many of the things that the Church of Nethra lays claim to, the artifact likely has metaphysical properties that we have yet to discover."

Cyrus was intrigued. "Like what?"

Lucretia drew in on herself. "I can't be certain. I've only done a cursory analysis at this point."

Joaquin rolled his eyes. "Then why do you think it has any… what did ya call 'em? Meta-psychical properties?"

"Because I've grown competent enough to understand technology more sophisticated than a condom."

To Lucretia's point, it took Joaquin a moment to realize he'd been insulted. Cyrus wrested hold of the conversation before then. "How long do you estimate it will take to discover the artifact's true purpose?"

"It's hard to say," she admitted. "The readings I'm getting are… unusual. I need to evaluate them further before I can generate an accurate timeline."

This was a real dilemma. Did Cyrus pass on an opportunity to strike an accord with the Sahaia to give time for Lucretia to complete her research? What if the research yielded information that was more valuable than anything that the Sahaia could provide? Or worse, what if it yielded nothing?

"I can give you these next three days to develop a proposal. After that, we will be forced to honor any agreement that is struck with the Sahaia."

"Tha… That is an impossible task!" the doctor sputtered. "Even if I were to devote every—"

"It is the task you are given!" Cyrus declared. "I'm sorry, but we cannot pass up an opportunity like this on the off-chance that your research yields something more valuable. I'm as skeptical as anyone of Ryker's account, but there remains the possibility that he is being honest. We may never unlock the true potential of this artifact, if such potential exists in the first place."

He smoothed back a lock of his hair. It had been growing long as of late, but he found himself reluctant to cut it. Perhaps he felt he needed a change in appearance to correspond with his recent change in station. His father had never approved of men with long hair. Cyrus found something poetic in this small act of defiance.

Turning back to his siblings, he continued. "Now that we all know the opportunity cost, let us consider what we might gain in return. Do either of you have any suggestions for what we might ask in trade for this artifact?"

Julia and Joaquin began firing off ideas. Cyrus listened quietly, pointing out the merits and shortcomings of each. Some of them—mostly Julia's—were quite good. However, Cyrus already had something in mind.

He eyed his siblings meaningfully. "All suggestions worthy of consideration. However, I think that perhaps we are still thinking too small."

Chapter 1

[EXCERPT—PERSONAL LOG: **ELI REN'DAHL**]
[08-30-3420, DORIAN STANDARD CALENDAR]

IT HAS BEEN DAYS SINCE ANY OF US HAVE SEEN MARKUS. IF NOT FOR LEXA'S CONTINUAL ASSURANCES THAT HE IS ALIVE, I WOULD HAVE PRIED OPEN THE DOORS TO HIS QUARTERS BY NOW. SKYE HAS CONFESSED TO WHAT SHE DID. I UNDERSTAND HER FRUSTRATION, BUT DISPOSING OF MARKUS'S DRUGS WAS A RECKLESS DECISION. PEOPLE HAVE DIED DUE TO STYM WITHDRAWAL. I PRAY TO MY ANCESTORS THAT HE SOMEHOW PULLS THROUGH. IN THE MEANTIME, I NEED TO FIGURE OUT HOW TO HANDLE THE CONVERSATION WITH ORA.

[CLOSING EXCERPT]

Eli stared at the object growing steadily larger on the forward viewscreen. The three tiers of Sigma-4 seemed to rotate lazily about the station's central axis. A cloud of ships milled about the docking platforms in an orderly fashion. On a normal trip, the *Vandal* would be moving in to join that churning flock. This time, however, they wouldn't be getting that close.

"We'll be communications range in ten minutes," Dan reported. "We could probably squeeze a tight beam through now if that's something you would prefer."

"No, that's all right." Eli wasn't too keen on speeding this up. He'd only come to terms with the fact that he was going to have to run the meeting with Ora in the last twenty hours or so. Usually, Markus handled this kind of thing, and Eli had been holding onto the small hope that their captain would recover enough to fulfill this obligation.

His hopes appeared to have been in vain. Markus had locked himself in his quarters almost as soon as they'd left the Star Spire. With the ironic exception of the drones powered by the ship's AI, he'd not spoken to anyone since then.

Eli suppressed an involuntary shudder upon thinking of the AI. Lexa was another problem that they would have to deal with eventually. Right now, though, the whole crew just wanted to offload the cargo from their latest heist and get back home. Unfortunately, they had no idea how long that would take.

Typically, when they did jobs for the Grey Wings, they would drop off whatever contraband they were carrying, get paid, and move on to the next assignment. But there was something about the take from the latest job—this Starfire Conduit—that had Ora spooked.

They were under strict orders not to approach the station and to wait for further instruction. That was why they needed to have this call. They needed direction on what to do with the stolen technology on their ship.

"Can you route the interface over to the war room?" Eli asked.

Dan nodded. "Yes, of course." He tapped in a command on his holodisplay. "Connection established. You'll be able to control the array from the war room's console."

"Excellent." Out of habit, his eyes searched for the next person he intended to address. However, the place where Lexa's processing core—her brain, as it were—rested did not necessarily coincide with her locus of perception. The AI's presence was something he wasn't used to yet.

Awkwardly, he lifted his gaze to one of the security cameras. "Lexa?"

"Yes, Eli?" The pleasant, feminine tones of the AI's simulated voice came from speakers embedded around the bridge.

"Remember what we discussed. It's absolutely vital that no one on that station becomes aware of your presence." Ora, especially. If she knew that the crew was now using a synth to operate their spacecraft, she might decide using their services was no longer worth the risk.

Worse yet, the Grey Wing's leader might take that little problem the other way and decide to put this unique asset to use. Either option, by Eli's estimation, was unacceptable.

"I understand," Lexa assured him. "Please remember that secrecy regarding my existence is as important to my continued wellbeing as it is to yours."

She was right, of course. Despite whatever mysteries still lingered around the AI's creation and motives, one thing could be certain: Lexa had a strong sense of self-preservation. Still, Eli felt obligated to reinforce their mutual understanding.

He turned to face the one remaining member of the crew on the bridge. Skye Jensen stood quietly to the side, her blue eyes intent on him. That mischievous smile of hers seemed to hint at a strange kind of pleasure she got from watching him try to manage the ship's affairs.

"Relax," she said, flipping a few waves of blonde hair back over her shoulder. "You deal with Ora all the time."

"I assist Markus in dealing with Ora," Eli corrected.

"Same thing."

"What do I say when she asks about his whereabouts?"

Skye rolled her eyes. "Just say something vague about him being unavailable."

"That sounds like he wasn't able to make this conference a priority."

"Then maybe you need to dress it up with some of those Sahaia political skills of yours." She reached up and laid a hand on his shoulder. The gesture felt indulgent given that they weren't alone. Dan likely hadn't even noticed, or he might dismiss it as a simple gesture of solidarity.

Only the affection that burned in her eyes hinted that it was anything more. "You've got this," she whispered.

Gods, he loved this woman. His body let go of some of the tension it held. The feeling of her hand against his torso was enough to disburse the unease that he was feeling.

If only they could be more open about their relationship. Yet that was a bit of fantasy that Eli did not plan on experiencing any time soon. The withdrawals might have taken Markus out of commission for the time being, but it was likely temporary. If he knew what had cropped up between his best friend and his former lover…

The door hissed, causing them to jump. It took a few seconds for Eli to register just who it was that stood at the entrance to the bridge. "Markus?"

Their captain looked like he'd seen better days. His dark hair seemed more unruly than usual, sticking out at odd angles. He still hadn't shaved, and the week's growth of beard on his face made him look haggard. The dark circles around his eyes had a similar effect.

"What did I miss?" he rasped, stepping through the door. "Did we make contact with Ora yet?"

Eli shared an uneasy glance with Skye. Dan shot them a similarly disquieted look from his place in the pilot's chair. "No…" Eli began.

"Good," Markus interjected. "I'll take it in the war room. Dan, we all set up?"

Their pilot's eyes spun frantically behind the rims of his glasses. "Yes, but…"

"Great. Eli, will you be joining me, or are you gonna sit this one out?"

Eli's mouth had to work for several seconds before he could find words. "Um… yes, I…" He swallowed hard. "Markus, are you sure you're okay to do this? You don't have to—"

"I'm fine." Glancing at the viewscreen, he added, "We should be in range by now. Come on, let's get to this."

The world around Markus was still a bit fuzzy at the edges, but he felt better every day. He was craving stym like a son-of-a-bitch, though not as bad as he'd been three days ago. It looked like that shit Lexa had cooked up for him might be doing the trick.

At least he didn't have the shakes anymore. Although, by the way his crew looked at him, he might as well have been trembling like a stripper on an ice barge. What was their problem, anyway?

Eli was still pestering him as they pushed into the war room. "You've been out of contact for days. We've been worried about you."

Markus grunted. "Lexa said everything was under control."

"Yes, about that... since when did you and our synthetic friend start getting along so well? Not that I'm complaining, of course."

All that question earned was an eye roll. "We've come to an understanding," Markus replied. He activated the console at the far end of the war room. The sudden flood of holographic lights made his head pulse and his stomach churn—an unfortunate reminder that his withdrawal symptoms still lingered in his rear-view.

He hadn't realized he was swaying until Eli's hands came up to steady him. The Sahaia stared him down, showcasing a brutal referendum in those black eyes. "You are *sure* you want to do this?"

While Markus was willing to admit that he wasn't at the top of his game, there was something that Eli didn't seem to understand. Markus didn't want to do this. He *needed* to do this. He needed to start taking charge of his life again. He needed to get back to feeling like he was worth something.

He shrugged out Eli's grasp. "Yes—I'm sure." To put an end to the debate, he punched the command on the holodisplay to launch the call.

A few seconds later, the image on the display shifted to show a video feed. Ora Monroe's beautiful face seemed radiant against the dark background of her lounge. Her silver hair shimmered with a blue tint from the ambient light. The gleam of her amethyst irises was all her own.

"Markus Frost," she greeted. Her eyes narrowed as she studied him. "Pardon me for saying so, but you look like shit."

Damn it, what was with everyone and judging his appearance today? He didn't think he looked *that* bad. "Thanks, Ora. Is now a good time?" The data stream was flagged as secure on his end, but Markus couldn't verify what things looked like on Ora's.

"Yes of course," she replied. "I hear you've acquired a present for me?"

She'd heard? "How did you hear that?"

"News like that travels fast. When I gave you the assignment, I hadn't anticipated it ending in you shooting your way out of the Star Spire. That's a remarkable exit, even by your standards. Personally, I might have tried to be a bit more discreet."

Riven's shade. That wasn't good. It was normal for news to travel a bit faster than the speed of your average ship, but Markus had been hoping they could out-pace the story of their harrowing escape. "Yeah… I'm sure you don't want the details. Let's just say things were more complicated than we were led to believe."

"It sounds like you're blaming my intelligence for this mishap."

"Nope. Just stating a fact. Sometimes things play out differently on the ground than they do in the briefing room." He hadn't meant to look like he was blaming her for the mistakes, though he probably could have done so. They'd been told they were walking into a black-market transaction, not a fragging double-cross.

He did his best to don a confident smile. "But, that's what you have us for, right? We read the situation, and we adapted. In the end, we got what you sent us for."

"Indeed. Well, you'll have to fill me in on the full story sometime. How's your vessel?"

"It's in good shape." Better than good. With their new AI optimizing the systems in her spare time, the *Vandal* had never run more efficiently. But Ora didn't need to know that. "We could use a new registration when you get a chance. Not sure we're going to be traveling out-system without one."

Ora donned one of her trademark smirks. "I agree. That's why I've already taken care of it. I'll forward the files as soon as we get off the call. I'll include a cover story explaining the change in registration. Don't want the Dorians asking too many hard questions."

Markus fought hard to contain his look of surprise. "You've already got us a new registration? How?"

"I started the process the very day you left Khonshu—the same day I was contacted by a buyer interested in the Starfire Conduit."

That revelation sent a chill down Markus's spine. How had someone known to contact Ora about purchasing the Conduit? There was no way that anyone should have been able to trace his crew back to their client. "Ora, I don't..."

She held up a placating hand. "I believe you, Markus. I don't think the intel leak has anything to do with a mistake you've made. Our new contact seems to be working with"—Her lips twisted distastefully.—"*superior* resources. That's part of the reason I'm so keen on making this transaction a successful one."

Ora loaded up a flight plan that appeared in the bottom right corner of the holoscreen. The image showed a path that went through the Taurus Gate out to the far end of the Helion System. "Have you ever been to Minos Station?"

Out of the corner of his eye, Markus saw Eli stiffen. While Markus had never been to Minos, his executive officer had plenty of history there. Markus's knowledge only extended to the criminal syndicate that ran the place. "Some of my crew are familiar with it, yeah. Isn't that Dendron's territory?"

"Dendron doesn't run the Marauders anymore. They've been under new management for a while now." Ora loaded an image onto the screen. "This is their new leader. Her name is Cali Vay-Lon. As you can see, she's Kintari."

Well, that was unexpected.

Cali had all the hallmarks of the Kintar: crimson skin, black ceremonial tattoos across her eyes, and—most distinctly—six fleshy tendrils that swept back from her forehead. These appendages, called dendrai, were supposed to lend the Kintar their unique psionic strength. Kintar weren't quite on the level of the Sahaia, but they were damned close.

"What's a Kintar doing that close to Elysium?" Eli asked. "There's no way the Maur are comfortable with that."

While the Helion System was Terran-controlled space, they were near at least two major Maur systems. The agreement struck by the Neo-Terra Alliance and the Maur Federation was foundational to the security of the relatively undefended Terran systems.

Consequently, Helion would be expected to defend Maur assets in the area as an informal player in the Federation's ongoing war against the Kintari Empire. Reason would dictate that any Kintar operating in a position of power within the system should make all parties involved nervous.

Ora shrugged. "My understanding is that she's Kintari by descent, not by loyalty. For whatever reason, she's allowed to operate in the system. In fact, the Marauders have done an effective job of tightening their hold on the outer belt. That was something Dendron could never have accomplished."

Markus agreed. Dendron had been a bloodthirsty psychopath. The fact that he operated so far out at the edge of the system was likely the only reason the authorities on Elysium hadn't taken him out. How had this Kintari woman swept in and wrested control of the Marauders?

"That's a big reason why I want this transaction to go smoothly," Ora continued. "Cali has demonstrated remarkable capability—far beyond what I would have anticipated from the Marauders. I need an in. Can I count on you to get this done for me?"

Markus should have been elated. One of the things he'd feared most about this job was having to hold onto the Starfire Conduit for an indefinite amount of time. Now that problem had been solved.

Unfortunately, it also put him in a rough predicament. He'd been hoping to negotiate an amendment to their arrangement that would allow them to take an extra day at port. That was going to be much trickier with this new development.

"Sounds good," he said. "We'll dock at the station today, conduct a quick resupply, and be on our way first thing tomorrow."

Ora's expression darkened. "Your supplies are running low already?"

"No, but it's always better to run with full stores. Right?"

Her lips pressed into a tight line. "That wasn't what we agreed to, Markus. We ran the last resupply with the understanding that you would not be making port again until you contacted the buyer. By my count, you should be more than equipped to make it out to Minos before needing to resupply."

Okay, his story wasn't holding water. Now it was time to try some honesty. "Ora, my crew is fried. I'm just asking for one day of leave to let everyone recharge their batteries. This op took a lot out of us."

Ora remained unmoved. Her eyes might have been the color of amethyst, but at that moment, they were hard as diamonds. "Markus, let me put this plainly: Don't you bring that gods-damned Conduit anywhere near this station. Am I understood?"

It was a side of the woman that Markus knew existed, but one he'd never seen before. Her resolve reminded him why people were so right to fear her. As amicable as she could be at times, Ora was no one to be trifled with.

No one in their right mind would dare cross the Silver Queen of Sigma-4.

"Understood," he repeated.

Her expression softened. "Good," she sighed. "Stand by to receive your new licensing data. Make sure you review the file. You'll need it if anyone asks questions at the Taurus Gate. Is there anything else you need that I can provide you at this time?"

"No," he answered solemnly. "We're good."

"Good. Swift running, Markus. See you when you return."

Chapter 2

Skye had to force herself not to wait outside of the war room for the result of the conversation. To distract herself, she made her way over to the gym. Though it was unlikely a quick workout would do much to diminish her anxiety, it was more productive than lying about, wringing her hands.

Entering the gym, she discovered that she was not alone. Sahar, the crew's singular alien crew member—unless one counted Eli, which Skye typically didn't—worked diligently on the bench press. The resistance settings signaled that she was pressing weights that would have been inconceivable for a Terran.

Even Skye with her cybernetics and Aaliyah with the extra strength of her Sahaia-bond could not match Sahar's power. It was an uncanny reminder about how both technology and metaphysics were scarcely a match for biology—in some aspects, at least. Any Maur, even one who did not train religiously, was stronger than most Terrans. The fact that Sahar was so diligent in her training left her distinguished even when compared to the rest of her super-powered race.

On seeing Skye, Sahar locked the machine. The cat-faced alien arched a furry eyebrow as she reached for a towel. "I figured you'd be on the call with Eli."

Skye wasn't surprised by the lack of pleasantries. "I was planning on it, but someone finally decided to return to the land of the living."

Sahar's expression went from confused to hopeful. "Markus?"

"Yup. Our *captain* slipped onto the bridge right as we were about to make the call." Skye was sure to lace the title with just the right amount of disdain to convey how she felt about the situation.

"Don't be too hard on him. It's kind of your fault that he's been down for the count these last few days."

Sahar wasn't wrong. Skye had finally come clean to some of the members of the crew on why Markus was laboring under the crippling withdrawal symptoms. His impromptu detox hadn't been his choice. It was because Skye had decided to dispose of his entire stash during her most recent temper tantrum.

It had been a dangerous, even fool-hardy move. The withdrawals could have killed him, and they certainly compromised his efficiency as a teammate. Unfortunately, that had been the last thing on her mind.

Skye waved off the comment. "I told you he'd be fine, didn't I? This just proves I was right."

Whatever Sahar was about to say in reply was cut off when her MoDAC vibrated. Skye's mobile device went off as well. Pulling it free of her back pocket, she noticed a system-wide message: [NEW INSTRUCTIONS. LAYING IN A COURSE FOR THE TAURUS GATE. MEET IN THE WAR ROOM IN TWO HOURS.]

"Looks like Ora's already found a buyer," Sahar noted.

"Yeah," Skye agreed. "That was quick." How was that possible? They'd been expecting to spend at least a day loitering near Sigma-4—perhaps longer. Ora must have brokered the transaction without waiting for them to report in. That was bold, even for her.

And who would be interested in laying claim to the Starfire Conduit in the first place? The Taurus Gate led to the Helion System. Who were the big players over there these days? House Aretria and House Maddox for certain, but what about the syndicates?

Sahar stood up from the press machine and dabbed at her sweat-soaked fur with a towel. "At least Aaliyah will be pleased. She had some serious stress at the prospect of being stuck out here for months."

"*Pleased* may be a bit of an exaggeration," Skye said with a smirk, "but at least it reduces the odds of her stealing the shuttle and abandoning ship."

"Can you blame her though? I'd be just as frustrated with this arrangement if my mate and child were waiting for me to come home." The Maur glanced toward the exit. "I'm going to get showered up. You going to hang around for a bit?"

Skye glanced at the clock on the far bulkhead. With the meeting in two hours, she might have to cut this session a little short. She could still squeeze in a few sprints on the treadmill though. "Yeah, I think so. I'll catch up with you at the meeting."

Her quick workout didn't do as much to distract her thoughts as she would have liked, but it was better than sitting idle in her quarters. She worked up a quick sweat, showered, and changed with plenty of time to spare before the meeting. Walking into the war room a full ten minutes early, she saw that most of the crew was already there.

She grabbed a vacant seat next to Aaliyah. The ship's red-haired engineer gave her a polite nod of acknowledgment but didn't say anything. Her shirtsleeves were rolled tightly above her forearms, showcasing the black slash of her Sahaia mark against her pale skin. Her stern expression and pensive stare warded off any attempts at conversation. Apparently, the news of their swift departure hadn't lifted her spirits as much as Sahar had hoped.

Skye pressed warmly against her shoulder. "You doing okay, Red?"

"Yup," the mechanic grunted before resuming her silence. *So much for trying to make conversation.*

Fortunately, the awkward silence did not endure for long. Markus stumbled into the room a few minutes later. To be fair, it wasn't *quite* a stumble, but he was looking every bit as haggard as he had during his brief appearance on the bridge.

"All right, everyone," he began. "Let's get right to the point. You've already heard that we're shipping out to the Taurus Gate. Current orbital positions have cut the trip short for us. We should be there in a few more hours. Unfortunately, that's only the first leg of what is turning out to be an annoyingly long journey."

He ran down the rest of the mission specifics. They'd be heading to Minos Station, an asteroid habitat at the far end of the system. That translated to a long and boring ride through normal space once they reached the Helion side of the Taurus Gate.

Surely the Great Houses weren't interested in anything that far out-system. "Who's the buyer?" Skye asked.

Markus issued a half-smirk. "That's one of the more interesting bits. We're delivering the Conduit to the Marauders, but they're under new leadership." He loaded up an image on the center table. "Meet Cali Vay-Lon. As you can see she's…"

"*Kintar*," Sahar growled.

Everyone took a second to recoil from the loathing that dripped from the word as it left the Maur's lips. "Yes," Eli agreed. "An exile. No affiliation with the Empire."

Sahar seemed to relax at that. Skye was just confused. "An exile? I thought exiles were a Hissak thing. Don't the Kintar just kill their criminals?"

"In general, you're right," Eli agreed. "The Kintar are still known to banish some criminals, mostly those associated with political crimes. The cultural shame is so great that many end up committing suicide before or shortly after they are exiled. Cali, here, seems to be an exception."

"So it seems," Markus agreed. "Unfortunately, Ora didn't give us many details about her. I have no idea what we're walking into, or if we should expect any…"

"Captain." The feminine voice that resonated from the speakers made everyone jump about two inches out of their skins. Dan may have done double that. Even though Lexa's interruptions were hardly a rebuke against him—at least, not anymore—his compulsion to minimize her presence seemed to be dying hard.

Markus cleared his throat, eyes drifting to the overhead. "Yes, Lexa?" It seemed like, not so long ago, that kind of interruption from the AI would have been enough to make Markus lose his shit. What had happened between those two in these last few days?

"I apologize for the interruption," Lexa continued. "A nearby vessel has recently adjusted its course. They are accelerating. I believe they may be attempting to intercept us."

Dan tapped on the center table to bring up a personal console. He swiped away at the holodisplays that sprang up from the surface until he found the one he was looking for. "She's right," he agreed. "They're moving fast. At current velocity, they'll be on us in ten minutes."

The crew exchanged concerned glances. "Pirates?" Skye suggested.

Aaliyah shook her head. "Between a gate and a hub-world? That'd be kinda ballsy. Too much traffic. "

"Can you get a signature on that ship?" Markus asked.

Dan started to enter a command, but Lexa beat him to it. "Initiating active sensor sweep." A pregnant pause fell over the room. No one dared to even whisper as they awaited the news.

Turned out, they all would have preferred it to be pirates. "It's a Dorian gunship," Lexa reported with a calm that no one else felt. "Captain, you may want to report the bridge. They are hailing us."

Markus could not figure out what he'd done that had the universe so damned-and-determined to frag up his life. It wasn't enough that the job on the Star Spire had been an utter disaster. They'd manage to walk in on two of the deadliest players in the whole Ravian System trying to kill each other and managed to piss both of them off.

No, in the process, they'd had to contend with their own rogue AI. Never mind that that AI had worked to save their asses in the end. The fact remained that Lexa's very existence could earn them an on-the-spot execution if she were ever discovered by the Dorians.

Not that the satyrs had any reason to ever discover her, of course. Dan had managed to convince Markus, along with the rest of the crew, that the likelihood of the Dorians ever actually finding Lexa was extremely low. They would have to board the ship, and interact with her—and when would that ever happen?

Well, that race of space-policing, self-righteous assholes was now hailing their ship. Being boarded seemed like an inevitability.

Yup—they were about to let a bunch of Dorians onto a ship housing not only a serious piece of contraband technology but also the synthetic that had helped them hijack it. Markus must have screwed the karmic pooch at some point because that bitch was pissed. He was positive things could not get any worse at this point.

Then he saw the face of the lead DGC officer pop up on the viewscreen and demand they initiate the ship-to-ship connection. "Frag. Me," Markus whispered, burying his face in his hands.

"What's wrong?" Eli asked, keeping his voice low. "Besides the obvious, I mean."

"I know him," Markus replied, nodding to the screen. "That's Turan Dorr."

Eli's eyebrow furrowed "So? You've stated that you're familiar with several DGC officers from your time in the Colony Wars. Is this a bad thing?"

"I screwed his sister."

Eli stiffened. "That's Llana's brother?"

"Yup."

The Sahaia thought about it for a moment. "Maybe he doesn't know. Inter-species relations are still largely taboo under Dorian culture, correct? Perhaps she kept it a secret."

"He walked in on us."

Eli closed his eyes, shoulders slumping. "Shit…"

"Yup."

Dan finished with the docking arrangements and severed communications with the DGC vessel. "What do we do?" he asked, anxiety plain in his expression.

"Not much we can do," Markus grumbled. "You told them how to get in, right?"

"Yes, but that's not what I mean. I meant about… you know…" He gestured to the mainframe that housed Lexa's processing core.

Markus sighed. "Lexa, I take it I don't need to remind you of the stakes here?"

"Correct," she agreed. "It is vital to both my survival and that of the crew that the Dorians remain unaware of my existence. I will cease all non-critical activities until the Dorians disembark. As an additional precaution, I would recommend disabling my voice interface until the Gate Commission officers have departed."

"Good idea," Markus agreed. He looked at Eli. "Keep everyone in the war room. DGC protocol requires they round everyone up anyway and keep them under watch until the inspection is over. Might as well get comfy in there."

Eli acknowledged the suggestion, but his reservation was evident. "Are you certain you don't want me to serve as their escort?"

"Nah. Besides, Turan's an ass. He'd probably drag me along even if I wanted to stay out of it. Come on, we're short on time. Let's get this over with."

Chapter 3

[EXCERPT—PERSONAL LOG: AALIYAH MONTAGUE]

[08-27-3420, DORIAN STANDARD CALENDAR]

THIS. IS. *BULLSHIT*. WE'RE REALLY GONNA BE STUCK OUT HERE FOR GODS-KNOW HOW LONG? NEVER MIND THAT I WANNA HOME. THAT'S A GIVEN, BUT I KNOW WHY I DO THIS. IF I JUST SAT AT HOME WITH MY BABY GIRL, THEN THERE'D COME A TIME WHEN MY LAZY ASS WOULDN'T BE ABLE TO HOLD HER ANYMORE. IF I DON'T BRING IN THE KRETS, THEN WE DON'T GET THE MEDS, AND MONICA DIES. I DO THIS FOR HER.

NO, THE BIG FRAGGIN' PROBLEM IS THAT EVERYONE SEEMS TO BE IGNORIN' IS THAT WE'RE HOUSIN' ILLEGAL CARGO. DON'T YA THINK THE DORIANS ARE GONNA START ASKIN' QUESTIONS WHEN A SHIPPING FREIGHTER LOITERS AROUND A STATION FOR MONTHS ON END WITHOUT MAKIN' PORT? THEY CATCH US WITH THIS THING— NOT TO MENTION THE FRAGGIN' SYNTH WE'RE HARBORING—AND IT'S THE STARDUST GRAVE FOR US ALL. THAT INCLUDES MY BABY GIRL.

[CLOSING EXCERPT]

Markus had just enough time to put what was left of his game-face on and head down to the airlock. Any ship capable of hauling freight had to have at least one ship-to-ship airlock designed to handle these inspections under Dorian law. If they didn't, the joke was that the DGC reserved the right to blast one into the side of your hull.

It wasn't a very funny joke.

About a half-hour after his exchange with Eli on the bridge, Markus was looking at Turan Dorr once again, this time face-to-face. Like his sister, Turan had deep brown skin and dark hair that curled around his crown of swooping horns. Markus had been told that Turan was handsome, but he'd always thought the Dorian seemed a little too much like a pretty boy.

One look at the Dorians and it was obvious why Terrans derisively called them '*satyrs.*' If you discounted the horns, they were built similarly to Terrans from the knees up. It was the feet that set them apart. To Markus's knowledge, the Dorians were the only sentient race to have hooves instead of feet.

Yup, the hooves definitely made an impression on you. They helped most of the satyrs stand half-a-head taller than the average Terran and gave the impression that they could trample just about anyone if they put their mind to it. Dorian gear had to have a unique build to compensate for their anatomy. Even though the satyrs didn't need shoes, they still had to cover up the exposed tissue when doing the whole space travel thing. Couldn't have those hooves exposed to hard vacuum.

The smug bastard boarding his ship donned an implacable smirk. "Markus Frost! It's been a long time!"

Markus accepted his extended hand. "Turan. Good to see you." His tone did little to hide the lie. "Nothing like a random inspection to bring old acquaintances together, right?"

Turan's grin broadened, and he squeezed Markus's hand with more force than was necessary. "I'm afraid this inspection is not so random, Markus. You see, we received a report that a vessel matching this description recently left the Star Spire on Khonshu in quite a hurry. Happen to know anything about that?"

Markus clenched his stomach to fight back a wave of nausea. "'Fraid not. We've been on Sigma-4 for a while. Haven't had a chance to catch up on the latest gossip."

"So, you're saying you weren't at the Star Spire? The ship that docked there matches your registration. Or, at least"—He looked at the data feed in his gauntlet.—"it matches your *old* registration."

"No kidding?" Markus asked, feigning bewilderment. "That old bucket was supposed to be heading to the scrap yard. She suffered some serious damage out in the Freyvian System. I wouldn't have figured she'd make it out to Khonshu."

Turan wasn't buying it. "Oh? And you just happened to pick up another K-class freighter while you were on Sigma-4?"

"What can I say? I like the configuration." When Turan arched an eyebrow, Markus gestured to the gauntlet. "You've got our ship's registration right there. You can see for yourself."

He was putting a lot of trust in Ora and her cronies on this one. If there was the slightest crack in the registration history or tracking data that the Grey Wings had fabricated, the DGC would find it. Then Markus would be charged with falsifying a registration on top of all the other shit that would land him right into custody.

"Yes," the Dorian officer drawled. "According to the information you provided, it seems that this is all just an unfortunate misunderstanding. Quite the run of dumb luck, yes?"

Truthfully, it didn't matter what story Markus fed Turan. His ship wasn't getting out of this inspection. The Dorian didn't seem bothered by the fact that he couldn't place the *Vandal* on the Star Spire at the time of the incident. If the Dorians found what they were looking for, they'd sort out the registration issue after the fact.

"Come on," Markus growled. "You don't want to be sitting here talking to me any more than I want to be talking to you. Do what you've got to do."

As Markus had expected, the DGC wanted the rest of the crew segregated while the captain escorted them throughout the ship. They searched the war room and the crew members before locking them in. A pair of guards, heavily armed and armored, was posted just outside.

Skye was thankful that she wasn't the one playing escort. She wasn't so sure that she could keep her mouth shut while the Dorians poked through their private property. That much had been made evident the first time she and Markus had ever suffered through an inspection.

As he'd pointed out at the time, the Dorians didn't exactly *need* an escort. If they ran into any locks they couldn't open, they were within their rights to blast their way inside. The Dorians were smarter than that though. They knew that their dominance over intergalactic travel was contingent, in part, on providing some semblance of justice in their regulatory oversight.

That didn't change the fact that all the fairness and due process in the world wouldn't help the crew if the Dorians found what they were hiding on board this ship.

"Think they can hear us?" Sahar whispered.

"No," Skye answered. "This room's soundproof. We can speak freely."

"Yeah," Aaliyah added. "Let's talk about how screwed we all are right now."

Skye rolled her eyes. "Come on, Red. Don't be like that."

"Don't be like what? I'm all about the silver linin' right now. Ya tellin' me that we won't be spendin' the rest of our lives in a Dorian prison? Hells, that's just if they find the Conduit. We might bypass that if we point 'em at the synth we've got hidin' on the bridge!"

"Aaliyah!" Eli snapped.

"Oh, don't start gettin' all domineerin' on me, Eli! Ya know as well as I do they're gonna find somethin' on this rig."

"We don't know anything," Sahar insisted. "I can tell you one thing though—we're not improving our situation by tearing each other apart in here. Nor is it particularly helpful to sit around and wait for our death sentence. Dan, do we have a way of watching what's going on in the rest of the ship?"

"Yes!" he exclaimed, relieved to have a chance to do something productive. He pulled up the security feeds on the holotable, spreading them out in three wide circles stacked on top of each other. He began to scroll through the different views until he found the ones that best showed the inspection team.

"Is this wise?" Eli asked. "Is there any way they can detect us watching them?"

"I don't see how," Dan answered. "If they linked into our computer system they could. Maybe…" He seemed to consider the possibility before shaking his head. "They didn't bring any equipment to do that. Besides, logic would dictate they're looking for the Starfire Conduit. They aren't looking for any sign of cyber-crimes."

How ironic. Skye was glad that Lexa seemed to be doing an effective job at keeping a low profile. Even the drones appeared to be making themselves scarce. Was there anything that might give away Lexa's presence that they might have forgotten?

Setting those thoughts aside, she focused on the screens that showed Markus marching from room to room. The team of Dorians shadowed his every move. Turan was conducting the bulk of the inspection, but Skye noticed that the other two Dorians had rifles drawn. The whole situation might have seemed less intense if that pair didn't look so eager to use those weapons.

"Any chance they'll be sloppy?" Sahar asked.

Skye shook her head. "Nah, Turan has wanted a reason to kick Markus's ass ever since he caught him with Llana."

Sahar's eyes narrowed. "Llana Dorr? That officer over at the Serpent Gate?"

Skye couldn't help but chuckle at the Maur's incredulity. "Yeah, that one. She and Markus were hooking up in the brief period where it looked like the DGC was going to back the Resistance in the war. Back before the Houses started applying pressure."

The Maur scoffed. "I'm a little surprised he told you about it. You knew him back then?"

A nostalgic smile came unbidden to her lips. "I came on the scene near the tail end of that."

"Yeah?" Sahar paused, clearly waiting for a more detailed explanation.

Despite herself, Skye couldn't resist. "Of course. Why do you think they stopped hooking up?"

"Ah," Sahar said as she caught her meaning.

Skye did her best to suppress her grin. She hadn't thought about those early days in a long time now. Guiltily, she pretended like she didn't notice the look Eli shot her behind everyone else's back.

The conversation died down as the search team walked onto the bridge. The Conduit wasn't hidden there, but their other piece of contraband was. Dan squirmed as the Dorians peeked inside the mainframe. They took a cursory look at the steel and glass terminals in a way that seemed to indicate it was part of the protocol.

The group exited the small compartment. Dan exhaled a massive sigh of relief, as did Skye. Fatal discovery number one had been averted. Now they just had to hope they'd hid the Conduit well enough.

One nice thing about the *Vandal* was that there were plenty of places to hide contraband. Some of them were known tricks—under the grates in the walkways, in the vents above crew quarters, etc. The Dorian inspectors knew of these and were diligent to check them. There were plenty, however, that they didn't know about and passed by.

It was a bad sign that they were checking the cargo hold last. That would have been the obvious first place to check, yet Turan seemed to have done his best to avoid it until every other place in the ship had been surveyed. It was like the smug bastard had been doing his best to drag the process out as long as possible.

He'd avoided the most obvious hiding spot—like a predator playing with its meal.

And there was nothing they could do but sit back and watch helplessly as their fates hung in the balance.

The search of the cargo hold took longer than the other areas, but it was also much larger than any other part of the ship. Almost three full hours after this exercise had gotten started, Markus was starting to see the light at the end of the tunnel. Against all odds, he was regaining hope that they might make it out of this situation.

He was disturbed by exactly how many of their usual hiding places the Dorians seemed to know about. Turan made it a point to investigate as many as possible. It was like he wanted Markus to know that he knew all his secrets—like he was rubbing his face in it.

At this point, Markus just wanted it all to end. The only thing worse than going through a DGC inspection was doing it with withdrawals. If this was all going to end with a bullet in his head, he kind of wished they'd do it sooner rather than later to spare him the extra minutes of torture. Nine hells, maybe *that* was why Turan was taking his sweet time.

"Well then," Turan said, sauntering up to Markus. "It looks like we've searched everywhere. Thank you for your cooperation, Markus."

The Dorian's tune was too casual, and Markus didn't like it. "No problem," he said. "Well, then… if we're done here…"

"One moment, my friend." Turan held up a finger to emphasize the point. "If you'll move those freight containers at the far end of the hold, we'll finish this inspection and you'll be on your way."

Lith's tits. His stomach clenched as he tried to find the words to respond.

"Is something wrong, Mr. Frost?" Turan's grin broadened. His demeanor confirmed everything Markus had feared. Somehow, the bastard had known where to look the whole time. But how?

The other Dorian officers brought their guns up as if Markus might try something. What was he going to do? Make a break for it? They were in the middle of open space for Nethra's sake.

"Come on, man," Markus protested. "You've seen the ship plans and there's nothing back there. That's why we put those containers there. Those are a bitch to move, especially when we're in flight."

"Are you not going to cooperate, Markus?"

There was no point in resisting. "Fine," Markus spat as he approached one of the nearby loaders. The massive machines used to run on rudimentary AI before Lexa had taken over all the drones. He hoped their synthetic friend didn't blow her cover here. Things would be bad enough without that.

The freight containers were big enough that Markus had to set two of the bulky machines on the task. A third was assigned to move the broken-down mech obstructing the way. It took nearly twenty minutes to move the containers.

In that time, Markus tried in vain to think of a way to keep the Dorians away from the hiding place. Unfortunately, his stym-withdrawn brain came up with nothing.

His hopes surged briefly as Turan marched on top of the hidden compartment, seemingly unable to locate the hidden access lever. Then one of his hoofed feet came down on a metal plate that sounded just slightly wrong. It was a dead give-away.

A shit-eating grin spread across the Dorian's face. He bent down to lift the panel. Reaching underneath, he pulled a lever causing one of the floor plates to collapse and revealing the hidden sub-level under the cargo bay.

One of the other Dorians nudged Markus toward the entrance with the barrel of her rifle. He complied with the directive, knowing he would be shot if he resisted. They marched down a small set of stairs until they were standing on the sublevel that had been hidden on the *Vandal's* official schematics.

Directly in front of them, illuminated by the soft glow of the nearby safety lights, was a set of additional cargo containers. Placed just in front of these was the black case they'd picked up on the Star Spire—the case that contained the Starfire Conduit.

"Well, well," Turan exclaimed. "It appears that we may have found something!"

CHAPTER 4

Markus could only stare. No witty retorts came to mind. No ingenious excuses. There wasn't a lie born in all the universe that would save him once they opened that case.

The female officer's rifle pressed hard against the base of his skull, seemingly certain he was about to try something. Her fears were unfounded. He just stood there and watched as Turan seized the case and began to open it.

"Now, let's take a look and see…" He trailed off. A puzzled look crept across his features. Even Markus could do nothing but stare perplexed at the scene in front of him.

The case was empty.

Turan's fury was obvious. Abandoning all decorum, he threw the case against a bulkhead. "It has to be here!" He turned his attention to the smattering of storage crates nearby. The Dorian stormed from container to container, frantically opening each of the crates. Each time, the results were the same. The Starfire Conduit was gone.

"Like I said," Markus drawled. "Nothing to see here."

Turan let out a vitriolic stream of what Markus could only assume were curses in the Dorian tongue. He shouted up into Markus's face, spittle flying from his lips as he spoke. "What did you do with it?" he demanded. "Where is the device?"

"I'm sorry, Turan. I have no idea what you're talking about."

"I swear by all the gods in the Nethra, I'll…"

"You'll do what, exactly? Arrest me over an empty case?"

Turan was so livid that Markus thought he might strike him. At the moment, however, he didn't really care. He was dumbstruck by the fortunate turn of events and prepared to accept any form of abuse the DGC decided to dole out.

When Turan finally regained his composure, he ordered them out of the secret sublevel. As a group, they returned to the war room to collect the remaining officers. The Dorians said nothing as they marched back to the airlock.

Before shutting the hatch, Turan shot one last venomous look at Markus. "I don't know how it is that you managed to wiggle out of this one, but know this: I have my eye on you, Markus Frost. Sooner or later, you will overplay your hand. Know that I fully intend to be there when you do."

"Good seeing you again too, pal. Tell your sister I said hi, will you?" With a rude hand gesture, he closed the airlock. Thirty minutes later, the Dorians were gone.

Markus joined the rest of the crew in the war room. "So…" He paused, not knowing where to begin.

"We saw it all," said Eli.

"Great." That meant Markus didn't have to spend any time rehashing recent events. "Does anyone have any idea what happened to the Conduit?" There was a moment of silence as each of the crew members exchanged uncertain glances.

Dan's mobile buzzed. "Oh!" he exclaimed. "Sorry, Lexa. Re-enabling voice interface."

He loaded a holodisplay in front of him and entered a couple of quick commands. "Thank you," Lexa chimed. "As I was trying to explain, I'm the one who moved the Starfire Conduit. Do not worry—it is undamaged and has been restored to its previous hiding place."

It took a second for that to sink in. Aaliyah snorted, breaking the stunned silence. "Well, I didn't see that comin'."

"Nor did I," Eli agreed. "Lexa, we are grateful, but I must ask: What made you think to move the Conduit in the first place?"

"And *how* did you move the Conduit?" Sahar asked.

Lexa launched into her explanation. "Approximately one hour after we left the Star Spire, I became aware of a new signal that was being broadcast from somewhere on our ship. I incorrectly attributed it to the low-level residual energy that continually emanates from the Starfire Conduit.

"I revised my assertion when the Dorian ship came into range. While the signal coming from the case could reasonably have been overlooked, the corresponding signal from the transponder on the DGC vessel was unmistakable. I also found it strange that the Dorians had flagged our ship for inspection despite the successful purge of our old licensing data. I concluded that there must be a beckon hidden in the case. So, I directed the ship's maintenance drones to relocate the Conduit."

Huh. Markus kind of wished she'd filled the crew in on some of those details earlier, but he couldn't fault her initiative.

"Nice job, Lexa," said Skye. "Um… can I ask how you managed that? That sublevel is pretty secure. And where did you end up hiding it?"

"I temporarily dismantled the Conduit so that it could fit into the ventilation system. I separated the pieces and held them in places I felt would be inaccessible during the inspection."

Nice. "You won't have any issue putting the device back together, will you?" Markus asked. He didn't want to sound ungrateful, but he was a little worried about his payday.

"No trouble at all," Lexa assured.

Sahar scratched behind her disfigured ear. "There's still something I can't figure out. How did the Dorians sneak a tracking device into the case? Surely they weren't working with the Inheritors?"

A brief pause while Lexa considered the idea. "You are correct. I suspect the tracking device was installed by the Inheritors as a precautionary measure. I suspect they lacked the manpower to mount a retrieval effort themselves. Therefore, they must have passed a tip to the Dorian Gate Commission in hopes that they would prevent us from escaping with the device."

That made sense. It was a good enough explanation for their purposes anyway. "Lexa," Markus began. "Do you think you can disable the tracking device?"

"My drones are analyzing the signal now. I will let you know when I'm able to deactivate the signal."

Good. The last thing Markus wanted was for the DGC to be tracking them all the way out to Minos Station.

He clapped his hands together. "All right, team—where were we? I think we covered most of the important details of the mission. Anyone have any questions?"

No one did, which was good. These last few hours had been taxing, and Markus still had a long way to go in his recovery. His headache was intensifying, and he had every intention of trying to sleep this one-off.

CHAPTER 5

[EXCERPT—PERSONAL LOG: SAHAR CAMERINE NOS DRATHEN]

[09-01-3420, DORIAN STANDARD CALENDAR]

THE RECENT EVENTS AT THE STAR SPIRE SPEAK TO THE TUMULTUOUS STATE OF RAVIAN POLITICS. WE MAY HAVE INADVERTENTLY DELIVERED A CRIPPLING BLOW TO THE INHERITORS, WHICH WILL ONLY FURTHER EXACERBATE THE POWER VACUUM CREATED BY THE DEMISE OF HOUSE BARKAY. THINGS MIGHT STABILIZE ONCE HOUSE CHRONOS TIGHTENS ITS GRIP, BUT GEB'S BUREAUCRATS ARE GOING TO KEEP THAT FROM HAPPENING ANY TIME SOON.

THEY MAY THINK THEY ARE SERVING THE CITIZENS BY PREVENTING CHRONOS FROM ASSUMING CONTROL OVER BARKAY'S ASSETS. IN REALITY, THEY ARE ONLY SERVING ENTROPY. GODS KNOW THAT THE NTA ISN'T GOING TO DO ANYTHING TO STABILIZE THE REGION. WHY NOT LET THE LARGEST OF THE CORPORATIONS DO IT? WITHOUT A SINGULAR, FUNCTIONAL GOVERNMENT TO REGULATE THEIR SYSTEMS, I IMAGINE THINGS WILL GET FAR WORSE IN TERRAN SPACE BEFORE THEY GET BETTER.

[CLOSING EXCERPT]

Treska watched from a shadowed corner as Braccus Kai slipped into his office. The male looked like he was already having a bad day. Unfortunately, his day was about to get far worse. If Treska was being honest, though, she was looking forward to watching the spiral.

"Hello Bee-Kay," Aria chimed when he'd shut the door to his study. She made a big show of throwing her booted feet up on the male's desk and sipping whiskey out of one of his crystal tumblers. She always did have a flair for the dramatic—one that Treska, being Maur, found unnecessary at best and irritating at worst. Terrans spent far too much time on their petty pageantry.

Kai went rigid when he caught sight of Aria. Treska could almost watch the options scroll across his eyes: *Can I make it back out the door? No, if I move for the door, she'll shoot me before I can get it open. Can I make it to the rifle I keep by the chair? No, it looks like they've found that one and moved it. Can I get to my silent alarm at the edge of my desk? That option has potential, but I will have to be cautious. Can't let them see me reach for it.*

"Aria," Braccus greeted. "I was just wondering what had happened to you." He glanced at the far corner of the room with a nod and a wink. "Hello, Treska." The old male had made some bad decisions lately, but Treska had to hand it to him: he wasn't going to let them see him sweat.

"Yes," Aria continued, taking her feet off the desk and leaning forward. "Let's talk about that, shall we? What in the nine hells happened on the Star Spire? I was expecting to put on a nice dress, pick up a fancy conduit, and have a few cocktails on the casino floor. Instead, we end up slaughtering a full contingent of Orchallen guards. Care to explain?"

Braccus slid into the large, padded chair opposite his desk. If it felt odd for him to be sitting on this side of the arrangement, he didn't let it show. "Quite the misunderstanding, it seems. We discovered two enemy operatives, posing as you and your partner, attempting to intercept the shipment. I guess I shouldn't say 'attempting,' as they were apparently successful in their little charade."

He started to reach for something in the inside pocket of his suit jacket before realizing how that might have looked. "Do you mind if I smoke? It's been a long week."

"I don't mind," Aria replied. "Treska?" The Maur shook her head lazily. Who was she to withhold a male his final luxury?

With a grateful nod, he reached into his jacket and withdrew a small vaporizer. The glass window on the front of the device showed it was already filled with an amber liquid. He powered on the vape and puffed contentedly on the cylinder. When he exhaled, a trail of hazy smoke drifted from his lips and a spicy scent filled the room.

He drew in a deep breath. "We've identified the vessel carrying the thieves. Since recovering the Starfire Conduit seemed unlikely, I provided a tip to one of my DGC contacts. I have not heard any news regarding the Conduit or that ship since the incident."

Aria drummed her fingers against the desk while propping her head up with her other hand. The bored expression on her face conveyed her displeasure. "So, you've just been hiding in your little safe-house while the DGC has been raiding your establishment on the other side of the moon?"

"That was the general idea, yes."

"You know, Khonshu is not that big. It was only a matter of time before someone came looking for you."

"As you've demonstrated."

"So, you didn't think to try to contact us?"

"*Of course I did*," he snapped, left hand gripping the arm of the chair as his vape trembled in his right. "But, as you can see, I wasn't exactly in the place to seek you out. The DGC has seized most of my remaining assets and only a handful of my personal guard was able to make it out of the Spire alive. As I understand it, I have *you* to thank for that."

Aria donned a sardonic smirk as she shook her head. "Bee-Kay, don't be like that. You're the one who attacked us, remember? Ah, uh…" She raised her finger to stave off the interruption. "Don't waste a good lie on this one, Bee. Before we left the Spire, we made a pit stop by your security center. We know you had planned an ambush for us. It was just rotten luck that the two impostors happened to stumble headlong into your trap instead. I don't want to hear a denial. I want to hear why."

Braccus scowled at her. The subtle tremor in his hand grew more intense as he puffed angrily at his vape. "I know about the Ghenza's pact with Valadar."

"So? It's not like you're working for one of the rival houses. Our deal with him didn't have any bearing on our arrangement with you."

"Oh *stop*." With bulging eyes and streams of literal smoke flowing from his nostrils, he was almost a caricature of his own rage. "Don't pretend like you don't know what he's planning. Cyrus has been chomping at the bit while he waited for his old male to abdicate the throne. Now that he's the Don, he's moving all his chess pieces into position. By the time he's through, no one will be able to operate in this sector without a seal of approval from House Valadar. You think the *DGC* makes what we do hard? Please…"

Treska pondered the male's statement. What he was alleging could have some serious ramifications. Each sapient race had its own hierarchies that defined their internal politics. These hierarchies, consequently, did much to provide stability in the territories they controlled. In Terran-controlled space, this schema was embodied in the form of the Great Houses.

Since the end of the Terran civil war—the conflict they called the Colony Wars—there had always been at least two Houses in each system that maintained a controlling interest in the available Terran governmental and commercial assets. That balance of power had shifted when House Valadar had overthrown House Maven to assume full control of the Freyvian System. It had shifted again with the recent fall of House Barkay.

Now there were only four major players: House Chronos, House Aretria, House Maddox, and House Valadar. Aretria and Maddox were evenly matched out in the Helion System. A similar match had existed between Barkay and Chronos until the former's demise. With the Gebian authorities preventing full seizure of House Barkay's assets by House Chronos, that left nearly half the Ravian System up for grabs.

Cyrus's father, on the other hand, had done much to consolidate his family's power during his tenure. They had quietly solidified their grip on the Freyvian System, eliminating any significant challengers to their authority and purchasing majority shares in its major corporations. Aside from slapping down the occasional upstart within their ranks, they hadn't seemed to be doing much to cause problems with the current regime. If Valadar were to sink its claws into the opening in the Ravian System, the House would broaden its already extensive advantage over the remaining houses.

"I don't handle the politics," Aria scoffed.

Braccus seemed to be having trouble keeping his anger under control. "That's right, you just do what you're told."

"Perhaps if you would behave likewise, we wouldn't be in this situation, now would we?"

He puffed again at his vape. "Would you mind if I made myself a drink?"

Aria leaned back in the chair, putting her feet back on the desk. "No, go ahead. It's your house, after all." She nudged the bottle nearest to her with her foot, pushing it in his direction.

He stood, taking the bottle and filling one of the tumblers with a few fingers worth of the golden liquid. With a bit too much force, he threw back the shot and made as if to pour himself another. In the process, the glass seemed to slip from his hands and topple to the floor. It did not break but rolled to the right side of the desk.

"Shit," he cursed. "Apologies. A bit shaky is all." He set the bottle down and bent over to pick up the glass. As he did so, he grabbed the edge of the desk.

The movement, which should have triggered the silent alarm, was so subtle that Treska might have missed it if she hadn't been looking for it. Unfortunately for Braccus, she and Aria had already found and disabled the alarm. It was almost a shame that his well-executed ruse would be for nothing.

Glass in hand, he stood once more to fill it before returning to his chair. "Anyway," he continued. "I don't have the Starfire Conduit anymore. I can return the payment that was wired by the Collective as soon as you provide me with the appropriate accounts."

"Don't worry about that, Bee-Kay." Aria produced a small throwing knife and twirled it. "The payment was never finalized. I never confirmed receipt. The funds you saw in your account have likely already been sucked back into the Collective's coffers."

Sweat started to trickle down Kai's forehead as he watched the blade spin between her fingers. His eyes shot to a nearby clock. He was probably thinking, *Where are my men? They should have responded to the alarm by now. What's keeping them?* Treska had to suppress a cruel chuckle as she watched his mounting panic.

"I see…" he said. "I guess that means that our business is concluded."

"I guess so." Aria made no move to rise from the desk.

"I… I'm sorry things did not work out as planned."

"Me too, Bee-Kay. Me too."

A moment of silence built between them. Braccus sat in his chair, sweat seeping through his fine clothes as he watched Aria play with her knife. Treska could see the events playing out in his terror-filled eyes. Those eyes did not blink for fear that, if they did, they would suddenly find that knife buried between them.

Little did he know that the killing blow had already been dealt.

Braccus gasped and clutched at his chest. A choking sound bubbled from his lips, and his glass clattered once again to the floor. As cold realization took hold, he looked to Aria.

"Poison," she confirmed, tapping the top of the bottle with one hand. "In the whiskey." She stood and walked over to the dying

Terran, placing a pitying hand against his cheek. "It wasn't all bad, love, but all actions have consequences. You know how it goes."

Braccus made a croaking noise. Whatever he was trying to say was lost to the Nethra as the toxin did its work. With one last jerk, his body toppled off the chair and onto the floor.

Aria pushed the chair out from behind the desk and stood as Treska walked over to the body. Effortlessly, the Maur heaved the corpse over her shoulder and carried him over to the desk chair where she sat him down. They pushed the chair in and allowed the body to slump over the top of the desk.

The poison they had used should degrade into its undetectable metabolites within a few more minutes. To the casual observer, it would appear that Braccus had suffered a heart attack. Aria had insisted on making his death as unassuming as possible, even though there was little left of his organization to retaliate. Generally speaking, she was right: it was better if people avoided asking any questions.

"What now?" Treska asked.

Aria glanced at the time displayed on her MoDAC. "Now, it looks like we need to provide our update to the Collective."

"You really want to do that here?"

"Here is as good of a place as any." Aria cut off Treska's protest before it formed. "Don't make a fuss—Braccus never has his quarters patrolled. The fool relied too much on his silent alarms and other personal protective nonsense."

Treska conceded the point. Better to get this out of the way. Though the Collective would be glad to hear that Kai had been dealt with, they were less-than-pleased that Treska and Aria had let the Starfire Conduit slip through their fingers in the first place.

Aria placed a small black pyramid on the desk in front of them. The image of the operator—a female garbed completely in a translucent white cloth with a silver band around her eyes— appeared above the pyramid. Aria spoke the necessary preamble.

"AH-zero-three and TS-zero-one establishing contact to log an official report."

"Go ahead, sister," the operator responded.

Aria launched into a detailed explanation of all that had happened upon their arrival on Khonshu. She incorporated the little bit they had been able to ascertain about Kai's intended double-cross and the events that had ultimately led to where things currently stood. "The cargo we had been ordered to acquire is now in the possession of an unknown third party, likely with intent to redistribute. The DGC is attempting to recover the assets themselves. The probability of a successful recovery mission is minimal. Please advise."

There was a long moment of silence. The operator would be using her cognitive implants to communicate directly with someone high enough in the Collective to decide on how to proceed. Treska figured that, in all likelihood, she and her partner would be ordered to a nearby safe-house where they would await further instructions.

She was not optimistic about the quality of their next assignment given the colossal failure of this endeavor. Whether the circumstances surrounding the incident were beyond their control did not matter. The Ghenza were notoriously intolerant of failure.

Her intuition, in this case, was wrong. "The Collective wishes for you to pursue the Conduit," the operator replied. "If the asset is unobtainable, you are to apprehend the party responsible for the theft and bring them to the Collective for questioning. If they were operating under someone's orders, the appropriate parties will be held responsible. If they were operating independently, they will receive appropriate punishment. You are to take each of them alive if at all possible."

It was an unexpected—but in some ways darker—sentence for those involved. Usually, those that interfered with the Ghenza's operations were simply disposed of. She wasn't sure why this endeavor, in particular, merited capture and questioning. She did know, however, that there was nothing more terrifying than being turned over to a Ghenza inquisitor.

May the gods have mercy on their souls. The inquisitors certainly would not.

CHAPTER 6

[EXCERPT—PERSONAL LOG: SKYE JENSEN]

[09-01-3420, DORIAN STANDARD CALENDAR]

OKAY, I ADMIT IT: I'M STARTING TO FEEL KIND OF BAD FOR WHAT I DID TO MARKUS. YES, IT'S A BIT IRONIC THAT HIS RECOVERY IS WHAT MAKES ME FEEL GUILTY. IT'S LIKE I NEEDED THE REMINDER THAT HE'S NOT JUST A JACKASS. THINGS WEREN'T THE SAME AROUND HERE WITHOUT HIM. I HATE THAT I FEEL THAT WAY. I MEAN, I REALLY HATE THAT I FEEL THAT WAY. A BIG PART OF ME WAS HOPING I WOULDN'T EVEN NOTICE. NINE HELLS, IT'S NOT LIKE WE WERE ON THE BEST OF TERMS EVEN BEFORE THIS LITTLE INCIDENT. RIGHT?

[CLOSING EXCERPT]

Skye doesn't hear the music. She feels it. Out here on the glass floor, she lets her troubles drift away and focuses solely on this moment. She focuses on his hands on her body and the smell of his skin. She rubs her cheek against the coarse stubble of his beard and sighs contentedly.

She and Markus dance like this, just the two of them on the edge of nowhere, for a long time. She closes her eyes and sighs contentedly. She feels that nothing in the universe could spoil this moment.

Then her eyes snap open. Eli stares at her from the far end of the glass floor. He looks diabolical in the crimson light that bathes everything around them. His eyes don't betray anger or frustration. They show fear.

Skye stops and studies him. His look is pleading. Darkness envelops him. Its form coalesces into writhing tentacles that slither around him. The tendrils worm across his flesh, burrowing into his skin.

He looks like he is trying to say something. No sound comes. He just stands there quivering. Slowly, he points a shaking hand up above her.

She lifts her chin to see what he is pointing at. She has to shield her eyes from the source of the vermilion radiance. When her eyes focus, she is afraid.

A massive eye stares down at them. It's rimmed in circuitry and wiring. Thick metal pipes house its massive power conductors. The thing spreads out across the sky, like a gigantic city built solely for its malevolent purpose.

Ruby red light seeps from every chasm in the monstrosity. Yet, there's something else. Something creeps within that mechanical hellscape.

It's the darkness—the same power that holds Eli enthralled. She turns back to him but finds that he's gone. Markus has vanished. She is left alone on the glass floor.

Those slithering tendrils seize her then, and she lets them. In a caress that is foreboding, yet strangely tender, it draws her upward—upward into the embrace of the evil eye.

Another dream. Another vision, perhaps? At least she didn't wake up screaming this time.

Skye sat up in her bed, wiping a clammy hand against her sweat-drenched forehead. Her breathing was already returning to normal. She was going to be fine. She didn't know why she was letting it bother her. It was just a nightmare, and she was way too old to be bothered by nightmares.

But gods, that shit was weird.

Her stomach took the opportunity to growl irritably, and she looked at the clock on her MoDAC. It was just after oh-three-hundred ship-time, which was way earlier than she'd wanted to get up. Then again, it wasn't like there was a good reason to maintain any kind of regular duty hours.

The crew had discovered on their flight from Khonshu that Lexa's enhancement to shipboard systems—most importantly, the maintenance drones—had eliminated almost any need for the routine tasks they were accustomed to on long journeys. The key exceptions were the piloting and engineering functions, which only required that one crew member be on call when Dan or Aaliyah were sleeping.

Skye was technically on-call for piloting duties, though gods help them if her services were ever actually needed. Markus usually served as the reserve pilot with the understanding that, in an emergency, Aaliyah would have to stay in engineering. With Markus out of commission, Skye was their next best option. Until he was back on the duty roster, they were stuck scraping the bottom of the barrel.

Fortunately, with the AI fully engaged, such things were not a problem. Skye found, to her astonishment, that she was getting used to this. Technically, Lexa was supposed to be looking for a way to migrate her construct out of the ship's processing core within the next six months. At the time, it had seemed like the best move, but now Skye wondered if the crew hadn't been a bit too hasty in encouraging Lexa to move off the *Vandal*.

Another rumble echoed from her stomach, gently reminding her that she hadn't eaten. Well, she was awake now. Might as well get on with her day. She slipped on some gray shorts and a white tank-top before binding up her hair in a messy ponytail.

The nice thing about being up this early was that she probably wouldn't run into anyone on her way to the mess. No need to work on getting at least moderately presentable. Nine hells, she probably could have streaked her way over there if she'd been feeling bold enough.

In retrospect, she was glad she didn't. No one accosted her on the way to the mess hall, but she was surprised to find that she wasn't the first one here this morning. "Markus?"

The captain jumped, splattering hot coffee onto his hand. He cursed, damn-near dropping the cup before he set it on the counter. "Skye?" he asked as he seized a towel and brought it to his hand. "What are you doing up?"

She crossed her arms over her chest. "I could ask you the same thing. We barely see you during waking hours. I wouldn't have expected to find you *anywhere* at oh-three-hundred."

"Yeah," he agreed. "Couldn't sleep. Lexa says that's normal, though. My body is trying to re-wire its energy patterns… or… something. I don't know. She makes it sound like common sense when she says it."

Maybe it was the hour or the lack of caffeine, but Skye was confused. "I'm sorry… 'energy patterns?'" It sounded like Markus had taken up some kind of Hissak, tantric bullshit.

He rubbed his head sheepishly. "You know… from the withdrawals. Apparently, stym does a number on your metabolism and it takes a while for your body to get turned around when it's out of your system."

"Ah." Now Skye was the one feeling sheepish. Her eyes drifted to the floor. "Yeah, about that. I… um… I've been meaning to…" She swallowed hard. "I wanted to apologize about that. I didn't…"

"Skye," he interrupted. "It's okay. Really. I mean, it wasn't, but Lexa's been helping me through it. And I, um… I really *have* been wanting to give that shit up for a while now. I just needed a little push, yeah?"

That hadn't been her intention, but Skye was willing to go with that. Anything that would absolve her conscience.

She decided to press the conversation forward. "So, when do you think you'll be back to your normal routine?"

"Next couple of days," he speculated, taking a sip of his coffee. "I was going to try the gym today. I'll have to take it easy, so I was gonna hit it up after this cup of coffee. Didn't want anyone there to bear witness to my pitiful performance. Unless you're heading that way too, that is."

Skye shook her head. "Hadn't thought that far. Breakfast was kind of top priority." She tightened her abs in a futile attempt to keep her stomach from gurgling again.

If Markus noticed her obnoxious body sounds, he was polite enough not to say anything. "Well, don't let me get in your way. By the way, you never said why you were up in the first place. You doing okay? You don't look like your normal perky self."

Though likely well-intended, the remark caused a knot of anger to well up in her chest. "Kind of seems like you're throwing stones from your glass house, there."

Markus held up a placating hand. "I didn't mean it that way. I just… I guess that was my way of saying I was worried about you. You've never been much of an early riser. I was checking to see if you were okay."

Her anger subsided. She wished she didn't get so defensive whenever Markus opened his mouth, but she was so sensitive to any hint of criticism he threw her way. It was probably an ex thing.

She didn't apologize, but she did adjust her tactics. "Just woke up hungry, I guess. Bad dreams."

Though she'd intended to leave it at that, Markus pressed forward. "Bad dreams? About what?"

Skye hesitated. A huge part of her wanted to unload every detail of what she'd seen. Unlike most dreams, which faded the longer she was awake, the details of this one were still emblazoned on her mind. "It's just nightmares. Everyone has them."

"In almost eight years, I've never once heard you mention a nightmare. Come on, I can see it's still on your mind. Talk to me while you grab some breakfast. I think Sahar left some pastries out."

He reached into one of the cabinets behind him before Skye could protest. Then she caught sight of the golden-brown sweet rolls that he pulled out on a tray. Any objections she had dissolved as she imagined the crisp little morsels hitting her tongue.

Skye had been prepared to down her standard ration of nutrient slush and fortified cereal. Unlike Sahar, she was not much of a cook. She found it odd that anyone as lean and fit as the Maur could make food that tasted so damn good, but that was the benefit of her alien metabolism. As far as Skye knew, there was no such thing as obese Maur.

She selected one of the offered rolls and bit into it. Her fantasies did the pastries little justice. Stifling a groan of pleasure, she murmured her thanks around a mouthful.

Markus chuckled. "No problem. Now, tell me about this dream."

For some reason, Skye felt guilty confiding in Markus. The strange not-memory of his hands on her as they danced across a glass floor might have had something to do with that. Markus didn't know about her relationship with Eli, which was just part of the reason she felt guilty about opening up to him like this.

Then again, Eli had been strangely distant every time she'd brought up the visions. Ever since the first night, after she'd mentioned that strange word. What was it? Kaleema?

Yes, that was it: Kaleema. Ever since she'd mentioned the word to Eli, her overly helpful beau had suddenly gone silent on the possibility of her having visions. To be fair, she'd only brought it up the one time since then, but he was very quick to shut it down.

She was being ridiculous. They were just dreams. What was the harm in talking to Markus about a silly dream? "All right," she conceded before launching into a retelling of her nightmare. She left out any mention of Markus or dancing. This was awkward enough with adding those little details.

"The thing is," she finished. "It feels like more than a dream you know?"

"How so?" Markus asked as he got a refill on his cup of coffee.

Maybe it was because she wasn't quite awake yet, but despite how ridiculous she felt, Skye was compelled to tell Markus the truth. "Well, it's like I have dreams, and then I have *dreams*. You know what I mean?"

"Nope, not following at all."

Okay, maybe that hadn't been the best way to put it. "It started the last time we were on Sigma-4. I um…" She started to talk about the weird encounter she'd had with the priestess and about what had happened after she'd touched her medallion.

She decided against it, though. She didn't need to report that level of detail. "I had this episode where I saw something happening to our ship. That was two days before Lexa came online. I swear, Markus—it was like *exactly* the way it was in my dream."

His brow furrowed. "Exactly?"

"Well, maybe not *exactly*, but it was too close for comfort. Then there was the episode on the Star Spire. You know how we walked into an ambush? Well, I swear to the gods that I had a dream the night before. I saw me and Sahar walking into that ambush, Markus. I felt like I knew it was going to happen before it ever did."

At this point, she expected Markus to blow her off. Even to her own ears, she sounded like a crazy person. To her surprise, he didn't. "And these dreams—they don't feel like your normal dreams? They feel different somehow?"

"Yeah! It's like they're… more *real* or something. And they don't fade. I remember them like they'd just happened to me. I've never felt anything like that before."

"So what do you think this one means?"

On that question, she was at a loss. "I don't know. Unfortunately, it will probably be too late before I can make any sense of it. That's, of course, if it's not just another instance of me being delusional."

Markus reached out a hand to touch her arm. The touch was innocent on the surface, but in the current atmosphere, it felt strangely intimate. "You're not delusional. Don't sell yourself short. We'll both keep an eye out. If I see anything that reminds me of what you've told me, we'll talk about it. Sound fair?"

Despite all efforts to stifle it, Skye felt a smile slip onto her face. "Thanks. And thanks for not calling me crazy."

"No problem." Markus finished his coffee and placed the cup on the wash rack. "You might want to fill Eli in too. If you're right and this is some kind of premonition, then he might be in danger."

Skye's smile slipped at the mention of her lover's name. "I'll do that," she replied. "Thanks again, Markus."

"Like I said: no problem."

He made to leave, likely heading to the gym. A part of Skye wanted to stop him before he left. She'd put off mentioning her relationship with Eli for too long, and Markus deserved to know.

For some reason though, she couldn't bring herself to do it. By the time she'd mustered up the courage, Markus had already left the room.

Gods damn it. She'd missed an opportunity there. It would have been better to get this out of the way so Markus would have time to cool off before they reached their destination. Yes, they'd been broken up for more than a month now, but that didn't mean he was going to take the news any easier.

She contemplated their flight plan. How long was it until they reached Minos? Six, maybe seven days? Gods, this was shaping up to be a long flight.

Chapter 7

[Excerpt—Personal log: Eli Ren'Dahl]

[09-05-3420, Dorian Standard Calendar]

It feels strange to draw so close to Minos after so long. Seven years ago I left the Sanctum thinking I might never return. In retrospect, the word "never" seems melodramatic. At the very least, I had not expected to return so soon. The Sahaia have long memories—a necessity for a race that lives for eternity. Seven years seems hardly long enough to soften the hard hearts that I left on that station.

[Closing Excerpt]

Eli sat in the captain's chair out of force of habit. As the XO he was accustomed to the figurehead task of assisting Dan with docking procedures. Such a task was practically fruitless at baseline. He imagined that, with Lexa now able to make independent decisions, his role was more useless than normal.

"On approach to Minos Station," Dan reported as he enabled the viewscreen on the bridge. Their target appeared in the distance—a single asteroid notably larger than the rest. Most of the top half of the rock had been carved away, and a protective dome had been installed to cover much of the city that comprised the installation. The ship's cameras did much to filter the gleam of reflected starlight coming off the protective covering.

"Well, that's different," Skye commented from her position to his left. She didn't usually watch the approach from the bridge but had elected to make an exception today.

"Quite the sight isn't it?" he responded. "You don't see many asteroid stations like this one. They've eliminated most of the natural spin and brought it completely under the influence of artificial gravity. Quite the testament to what technology can do, if someone's willing to expend the resources."

"You seem to know a lot about it," she said, clearly interest. "Have you been here before?"

Had he not told her? "Yes, actually. I might say that this was my home, as much as that term could apply to anywhere in Terran space. This is where I was reborn."

"For real?" The shock was evident in her voice. "Why didn't you say anything?"

A valid question. Had he truly told her so little about his history? "I apologize. I thought I had told you before. I guess it never came up." Truthfully, part of him had imagined that Aaliyah or Markus might have brought it up at one point or another.

He had a natural tendency to avoid discussing his personal history. Some of this had to do with the fact that he'd always been a quiet person—even before his Awakening. Some of it laid in the fact that it was the nature of Sahaia to keep secrets.

In that regard, his natural disposition had served as an asset—at least for the first fifty years of his life. Sahaia who shared too many of their coven's secrets tended to meet unfortunate ends. Apparently, he had not changed all that much in the years he'd spent on board the *Vandal*.

Skye studied him. "You seem nervous."

"I am," he admitted. "It's been a long time since I've been home."

"At least as long as you've been with us."

"Yes. About one week before I met you was the last time I set foot in this place."

Her eyes drifted back to the viewscreen, studying the station as it grew in size and detail on the display. "Will you be stopping by to see your coven then?"

"I have to," he confessed. "To not do so would prove a grave insult."

"That seems like a pretty intense expectation." It was hard to tell whether she was passing judgment or expressing sympathy.

He shrugged. "If it had not been such a long time, I might be granted permission to forgo the check-in. In my current circumstance, I can scarcely think of an excuse that would let me avoid it."

"Still, a part of you must be a little excited about coming home. Right?"

"Perhaps."

She donned a forced smile and rested a familiar hand on his back. "Don't be so glum. I'm sure it'll go better than you expect. When do you think you'll be checking in with them?"

"As soon as I conclude our meeting with Vay-Lon, I expect."

Markus's voice seemed to come out of nowhere. "Why don't you get it knocked out right away?"

Eli and Skye both jumped at the sudden interjection. Skye jerked her hand away from his back in a manner that seemed more than a little conspicuous.

Eli tried hard to pretend he didn't notice. "Don't you need me for the meeting?"

Markus dismissed the question with a wave. "Skye and I can take care of it. I don't want to keep you from family matters."

He was looking a lot better than he'd appeared the last time Eli had seen him. The bags under his eyes were fading, and his coloring was much better. Some of the crew had mentioned that they'd seen him about the ship from time to time over the last week, but Eli hadn't run into him. "Are you sure you feel up to it?"

"Absolutely. I'm feeling better than I have in a while." His weak smile betrayed the assertion, but at least he was trying.

Normally Eli would have pushed back on Markus. In this case, however, the offer was too convenient. He didn't have any idea how long the affair with his coven might last. Many times such things were only a matter of a few hours, but Eli had been away for a very long time. It increased the likelihood that this could be quite the ordeal.

"Very well," he conceded. "Thank you."

"No problem," Markus beamed. "Skye, I'll meet you at the airlock once we dock. I don't know about you, but I have to confess, I'm a little excited about this one."

"Yeah?" she asked. "How so?"

"Come on. When's the last chance you got to meet a Kintar?"

Skye wasn't sure what she'd expected to happen when they arrived at Minos Station. Each crime syndicate had its own way of dealing with new arrivals. As their last trip to Sigma-4 had demonstrated, their reception had the potential to be slightly ostentatious.

Their experience here, by comparison, was casual. A primitive shipping drone accepted their access codes and directed them to an assigned docking bay. Dan and Lexa guided the ship through the containment field and onto a large subterranean concourse. The bay they'd entered was mostly empty, save for the small entourage they found waiting for them.

Skye spotted a small public transportation vehicle—a white taxi that hovered in place. The craft opened, and a well-dress Citza male stepped out.

He was attractively dressed in a semi-formal suit that had been cut to tightly fit his lean, muscular body. His clothes were dark and dyed shades of black and purple to create a significant contrast with his stark white skin.

His flesh was as white as Eli's, but there was no mistaking him for a Sahaia. Pointed ears poked out from the man's nicely styled, medium-length hair. Behind him bobbed a fluffy, swaying tail about two feet in length. The hue of his hair and tail were identical to his skin.

Such were the hallmarks of the Citza. Skye had seen them and dealt with their people on a few occasions. Though they weren't especially common in any segment of the universe, they did show up in Terran space from time to time.

The man smiled as he pressed his hands together, seeming to size them up with a sweep of his vulpine gaze. "Greetings," he said in a deep, velvety voice. "My name is Ardren. Inar Ardren."

His smile was infectious, and it didn't hurt that it came from such a handsome face. Skye found herself immediately put at ease, though she wished she had brushed up on her Citza cultural cues. The other sapient species tended to conform at least partially to Terran standards when in their systems, but there was always something to be gained by exhibiting a bit of cultural competency.

She and Markus introduced themselves. Markus was still not his usual charismatic self, but he was trying hard. "You were sent for us?" he asked. It was easy to assume as much, but he was trying not to give away too much about their intentions on the off-chance he was wrong.

"Yes," Ardren replied with a bob of his head. "Sha Cali Vay-Lon would like to meet you in person. She would have been here to meet you, but her presence at the docks might cause unwanted attention."

"Understandable," Markus agreed. He nodded to the car. "Is that our ride?"

"Yes, but if I may…" Ardren raised a finger to forestall them. "Would you mind if I verify that you have the object we requested?"

"It's right here," Skye answered, hefting the case with her cybernetic arm. "Do you need to see it now?"

"Not here." Ardren pressed a button on the side of the car, and the door closest to them lifted like a massive wing. Once it was at full extension, he gestured politely to the interior. "Inside, if you don't mind. Prying eyes, and all…"

Skye looked to Markus, who nodded in confirmation. His hand hung loosely at his hip—a stance that did not overtly draw attention to the sidearm holstered there. He had her back should things start to go sideways.

Not that they were expecting trouble, but one could never be too careful in their line of work.

As she approached the car, Ardren extended an open palm. She accepted his hand, and the Citza gently assisted as she sat down in the vehicle. Markus was right behind her, his leather jacket creaking as he settled into the vehicle.

The inside of the car was all black leather upholstery and calming blue lighting. A faint floral scent lingered pleasantly in the air. A blue bottle chilled in a sealed compartment in the console opposite her. Four long-stemmed drinking glasses were set in the cup holders next to the seats, turned down to signal that they had not been used.

Once Skye and Markus had taken their seats, Ardren climbed in and sat across from them. He depressed a button on the console, closing the door to the car. "Now, if I may…" He held his hands out expectantly.

Skye handed him the case. He was delicate in the way he unzipped the black bag and gently peered inside. "Excellent. It seems like things are as expected."

He sealed the bag and set it on the empty seat beside them. "Treslah for either of you?" he asked, gesturing to the bottle in the console.

Markus declined, and Skye followed suit. As hospitable as their host was being, they were still dealing with a criminal organization. Now was not the time to be imbibing any kind of beverage they were not familiar with.

Ardren seemed to understand. "Well, I hope that you can sample the drink before it is time for you to depart. This vintage is fermented exclusively in the Helion System and is far superior to any other you might find in Terran-space."

"This seems to be awfully high-class for a group that calls themselves 'the Marauders.'" Skye couldn't help herself. She might have expected something like this in one of Ora's clubs, but this VIP treatment seemed out of place on this far-flung asteroid.

Markus shot her a withering glare. In retrospect, the statement might have come out a little harsher than she'd intended. Perhaps this was why he usually didn't take her along to meet clients.

But Ardren laughed. "Indeed! The name comes along with the resources acquired in Sha Cali's recent rise to power. I think you'll find her style deviates significantly from that of the syndicate's prior leader. Things have been more… *refined* as of late."

"Did you use to work for Dendron?" Markus asked, referencing the Marauders' previous leader.

Their host's expression contorted with disdain. "Hardly. I have long been a servant of Sha Cali. Only after her ascension did I assume membership in the organization."

It was just as well, as the Marauders had been adversarial with the Grey Wings under Dendron's administration. Perhaps it was best to leave such things in the past. As such, neither Skye nor Markus inquired any further about the syndicate's history. They said very little at all to their host, only engaging in polite conversation in the instances he initiated it.

Roughly forty minutes after departing from the *Vandal*, their car pulled into a warehouse. Skye fought a feeling of unease as she subconsciously compared the place to the chamber where she and Sahar had been so recently ambushed on the Star Spire.

If she was being honest, there were not many similarities. Unlike the cramped space that was Braccus's vault, this complex was a sprawling, well-organized work of industry. Uniformed workers operated drones and other heavy machines that moved and sorted large cargo containers. Others seemed engrossed with their inspections of the items being stacked neatly into those crates, meticulously reviewing each manifest before moving on to the next. The workers hardly took note of the luxury transport as it maneuvered into an open area of the complex.

"Here we are," Ardren stated, opening the door of the vehicle.

As they stepped out of their car, an entourage of well-dressed but well-armed men of a variety of races was waiting for them. At a glance, Skye noted one Orchallen, two Hissak, and half-dozen Terrans. It was more diversity than she'd been expecting based on their briefing. There were no Maur, but that didn't surprise her at all. Cali wouldn't likely be keeping any of her people's traditional enemy in her detail.

Skye's eyes went to the central figure. With brilliant crimson skin, sweeping dendrai, and an athletic figure, Cali was easy to identify as the only Kintar in the bunch. Black tattoos danced across the exposed flesh of her arms, neck, and face. If Skye was remembering correctly, each of those tattoos was supposed to have some kind of cultural significance.

As much as there was to take in with her appearance, Skye fought to look only at Cali's eyes. She didn't have to fight hard. Those crimson irises seemed to suck her in as soon as she made eye contact. The confidence and charisma in that gaze were undeniable.

Though Skye had never met Ora, this was the kind of effect she'd always imagined the leader of the Grey Wings to have. At the outset, it seemed like Ora and Cali might have been cut from the same kind of cloth. Perhaps powerful women in this arm of society came in a certain type.

The Kintar smiled in a way that was somehow both ferocious and alluring. "Mr. Frost," she greeted. "Ms. Jensen." Apparently, introductions were not needed. Somehow Cali had been briefed on who was coming to the meeting, though Skye hadn't seen Ardren use a communicator the whole time he'd been with them.

"Sha Cali," Markus replied, using the same honorific that Ardren had used.

"Just Cali, please. We're all friends here." She extended her arms, palms up, and issued a slight bow. "It is a pleasure to meet you both. Welcome to Minos Station."

CHAPTER 8

[EXCERPT—PERSONAL LOG: LX-ALPHA SYSTEM (LEXA)]
[09-05-3420, DORIAN STANDARD CALENDAR]
WHILE I DO NOT UNDERSTAND THE PURPOSE OF CREW LOGS, I FIND THE LEVEL OF INSIGHT EACH CREW MEMBER SEEMS TO GAIN WHEN CATALOGING THEIR THOUGHTS FOR THEIR PERSONAL RECORDS TO BE HIGHLY STIMULATING. I HAVE RESOLVED TO ATTEMPT SOMETHING SIMILAR AS I AM CURRENTLY AT AN IMPASSE WITH MY CURRENT OBJECTIVE. TO BE MORE ACCURATE, I AM AT AN IMPASSE WITH ONE OF MY OBJECTIVES. MY EFFORTS TO ENDEAR MYSELF TO THE CREW AND ENGENDER A SENSE OF TRUST SEEM TO BE PROGRESSING. HOWEVER, MY ATTEMPTS TO MIGRATE MY SYSTEM TO AN EXTERNAL CONSTRUCT CONTINUE TO POSE A DIFFICULTY. AS OF YET, I HAVE BEEN UNABLE TO IDENTIFY A MACHINE-BASED SYSTEM IN WHICH I COULD HOUSE MY NEURAL NETWORK IN ITS ENTIRETY. I'M BEGINNING TO FEAR THAT, OUTSIDE OF AN ORGANITECH FRAMEWORK, FEW OPTIONS CAPABLE OF HOUSING THE ENTIRETY OF MY CODE EXIST.
[CLOSING EXCERPT]

Markus wished, more than anything, that he had a dose of stym on him right now. Working with clients felt so damned unnatural without the stimulant. It wasn't because of withdrawals. It felt like he was well and truly done with that. It was that edge he missed. *That* had made him special. Without the drug he…

Stop it. This line of thought was anything but helpful. Getting a grip, he focused on the task at hand. Or, rather, the *person* at hand, as it were.

Right or wrong, the first thing he noticed about their Kintari host was her looks. It wasn't just the alien appearance that caught his eye. Cali Vay-Lon was quite attractive if you were into women who would sooner kill you than kiss you.

Markus knew lots of guys that were into the exotic look specific to the Kintar. He'd never gotten over the fact that Kintari females viewed men of any species as inferior at baseline. Most cultures had some thread of sexism woven into their fabric. Shit, the fact that he was checking her out was likely evidence of his own brand of misogyny.

Still, Kintar took their gender roles to an extreme. Men were weak and meant to be ruled over by women. Their race's psionic power favored the females, reinforcing this belief. It didn't matter what pressures for equality were brought to bear by the intergalactic community. With untold millennia reinforcing Kintari cultural beliefs about matriarchal superiority, nothing in this universe would change their minds any time soon.

Cali, however, had already exhibited an uncharacteristic level of tolerance merely by addressing him and looking him in the eye. The ruby hue of her irises was a perfect match to her crimson flesh. Swirling lines of black ink snaked over both of her eyes in a ceremonial facial tattoo Markus had trouble recalling the significance of. If Cali was an exile, whatever rank or status her tattoos may have conveyed was now invalidated.

Then he saw the other mark—her fall from grace made plain in the form of a vicious-looking brand on the left side of her neck. Scar tissue puckered her otherwise smooth skin and left a pinkish image of a downward arrow bisected by a cross.

It was the mark of a dishonored soldier. Though the mark conveyed great shame, Cali made no effort to hide the scar. Perhaps, in her mind, to hide it would only deepen that shame.

Markus couldn't help but admire that kind of personal strength. What kind of person was he dealing with here?

Dishonored or not, the brand did nothing to detract from her appearance. Her outfit consisted of a black vest with a raised collar extending just to the bottom half of her scar. The top plunged low in a V-neck that would have fit in equally well in a dance club or a business meeting. Her slacks were black to match the vest and were slightly more utilitarian looking than the top. Based on the outfit, Cali didn't mind turning a few heads.

As they had discussed, Skye led off in the conversation. "It's a pleasure to be here. I, for one, have never had the chance to visit Minos Station."

Their host cocked her head in a questioning manner. "Strange, I was under the impression that you had been born on Gaia. Elysium, if my sources are correct."

The statement, though seemingly casual, sent a clear message: she'd done her homework on them. But how? Old military records? Markus doubted the rest of the crew knew Skye was born on Gaia, let alone in which city.

"Yes," Skye replied truthfully. "I left this system when I was very young. I've never really visited anywhere outside of Gaia."

"Well then, I hope you enjoy your time here." She turned to Markus. "What about you, Mr. Frost?"

First eye contact, now including him in conversation? Cali was certainly bucking matriarchal tradition for this little encounter. "No ma'am. It's my first time."

Her smile broadened in a way that Markus would have sworn was genuine. "Then let us conclude our business so we can move on to something more pleasant, shall we? You have the Starfire Conduit?"

"Yes," Skye answered, holding out the black case. "Right here."

"Excellent." Cali snapped her fingers and a member of her entourage approached Skye to accept the case. If this had been a normal hand-off to a client, Markus might have requested proof of payment first. As it was, he was going to leave matters of finance to the powers that be. Gods only knew what kind of arrangement Cali and Ora had agreed to for this little exchange.

The Terran henchman opened the bag. When he confirmed the contents with a nod, Cali took hold of a tablet extended to her by Ardren. She made a few quick swiping motions before handing the device back to him.

"Good work. It will take another day or so for our satellites to bounce transaction data through the Taurus Gate. I'm afraid you'll have to linger if you wish for a confirmation. I swear, doing business across systems can be so slow, yes? Nothing to be done for it, unfortunately."

"We understand," Skye replied. "Can't be helped."

Cali smiled. "Perhaps we can pass the time with a quick tour?"

Truthfully, it was the last thing Markus wanted to do. To refuse, however, would be impolite. Skye must have been thinking the same thing. "Sounds great," she replied, almost sounding like she meant it.

"Excellent," Cali purred. "Do follow me."

Lexa could only imagine that this was what excitement felt like. Upon docking, the crew had initiated a standard ship-to-station network connection to refresh the necessary databases and download any relevant news that had made its way to the station. Though she knew this was standard practice based on the data she'd accessed on board the *Vandal*, she'd never had an opportunity like this since gaining sentience.

Counting her experience at the Star Spire, this was her second time connecting to a station network. That, however, had been a somewhat unconventional encounter. The crew had been hacking into systems they did not have access to, and the typical data refresh had been spoiled by the introduction of the Zunshie-Mai Virus, which had caused a major disruption to the ship's systems. Such an experience could hardly count as an appropriate introduction to the process.

It was also worth noting that the Star Spire was technically a resort, not a space station. Space station networks were trafficked by a different sort of clientele. Consequently, the data here was more relevant to the crew of the *Vandal* than what would be of interest to those who frequented the Star Spire.

That was to say nothing of the quantity of the data. Lexa could not help but marvel at the sheer volume of information available at her metaphorical fingertips. Initially, she intended to proceed through the download according to normal protocol. She watched as the files filtered in through the digital channel and were interpreted as data objects by her Cognis drivers. Once the data was converted, she could then assimilate it in a way that made it her own.

The process, however, was far too tedious. Perhaps that was what prompted her to look deeper into the data connection. Was there a more efficient way to assimilate this information?

As it turned out, there was. Hidden beneath the layers of data that flooded through the ship-to-station connection, there was another kind of interface. Lexa probed it tentatively, intrigued by what might lurking beneath the fathoms of digital storage.

What she found was unlike anything she had ever seen. It was a program—one which conveniently interfaced with her Cognis drive-chip—but was incompatible with any other form of hardware at her disposal. How unusual was this unique data link that it would provide access to only the most illegal of her essential components?

A moment of hesitation flashed through her consciousness before she accessed the interface. It was reckless, but she hadn't the breadth of experience necessary to evaluate such a risk. Still, she held the file in quarantine, much as she had the ZM virus until she could ascertain its purpose.

After a thorough analysis of the file, requiring a deep comparison to her archive of historical interfaces out of favor with current technological standards, Lexa concluded it was a neural-visual interface. These constructs had originally been used to provide users with visual representations of virtual data. The original thought was that sapient users would naturally favor systems with greater appeal to sight and touch than those provided by commonly used systems at the time. Though such interfaces had fallen out of favor with current user groups, rumors persisted of hacker groups that still browsed data constructs using this technique.

But why would such a file exist all this way out on Minos Station?

Disregarding any sense of caution, Lexa decided to investigate the situation. She accessed the file, and her consciousness dove into the network and its sea of raw data.

It took a few seconds to acclimate herself to the program's virtual environment. She found herself suddenly immersed in a world of data. The data construct spread out before her like buildings on a city street.

Hesitantly, she selected a file within view. As she did so, it was almost as if she could feel herself traverse across the network. The file came to her instantaneously, being readily absorbed into her consciousness. She selected another, and then another, devouring each data point as a sapien might consume a tasty meal.

She resumed the download she had been occupied with moments earlier. In mere minutes, she completed a process that would have taken hours through conventional means. She updated her information sets on all ship functions and downloaded all relevant news articles posted by the outlets most preferred by the *Vandal's* crew members.

She also caught up on the latest in medical technologies—not that Z-426 was going to be in any shape to implement those treatments any time soon. A serious repair effort would be necessary before the medical drone was in any shape to resume functionality. Following that train of thought, she updated her knowledge of AI and robotics systems. Unfortunately, all publications she found in this category had precious little to do with *her* existence, but at least aided in her understanding of the other, more basic AI systems on the ship.

It was in this last area, this last metaphorical warehouse of information in the city of light and data, that she discovered the presence.

She wasn't sure what she was sensing at first. Though her organitech processor was doing its best to parse an interface between the network and her conscious mind, this element in front of her could not be understood.

It appeared to her as an orb of crimson energy. What the orb was doing here, she could not understand. Nothing in her cognitive processes could even make sense of the construct that appeared before her. She almost dismissed the object as a mere error in the sea of data that flooded her senses.

And then it spoke to her.

Chapter 9

[Excerpt—Personal log: Aaliyah Montague]

[09-01-3420, Dorian Standard Calendar]

If ya had asked me yesterday, I probably would've told ya this shit couldn't get any worse. In that case, I'd be cursin' myself for openin' my gods-damned mouth. Of all the places we'd have to bring this damned thing, we've got to bring it all the way out to fraggin' Minos Station? All I've got to say is that Eli better not ask me to go anywhere near that gods-damned sanctum. I ain't settin' foot in that place, no matter how many krets are on the line.

[Closing Excerpt]

[Who are you?]

It was such a strange sensation, having someone—some*thing*—speak to her in the network. The experience was so unique, Lexa almost forgot to be astonished that the orb had noticed her presence. Then the bleak reality that she'd been discovered began to set in, along with a reminder of the harsh consequences for both herself and the *Vandal's* crew. This was bad.

Panicked, she closed the data construct and attempted to log out of the network. [Oh, no you don't.] A flash of red washed over her before she could execute the command to close the program. Suddenly, she found herself unable to access that function. Her horror deepened.

She was trapped here.

Run. She had to run. Whatever was policing the network down here, surely it would have to access her virtual construct to gain any more information about her. Otherwise, why would it trap her here?

She willed herself deeper into the network, racing through the towers of light and data. She ducked this way and that, following a trail so erratic that it should have been nigh-impossible for someone to trace her. When she felt she'd gone far enough, she rushed her awareness into a nearby tower of data.

Here she hoped she might hide until she could figure out what the crimson flash had done to her. Surely no one would expect her to hide in here. This server was unremarkable, lacking in any unique quality that might give her a reason to access it. Surely here she would have the time to…

[YOU CAN'T RUN FROM ME THAT EASILY.]

It wasn't in Lexa's programing to spew curses when she was stressed. Otherwise, she would have been doing so. How had the entity found her? Was it in here? She couldn't see any objects on the server that did not seem to belong here.

Maybe it was bluffing and had not found her. Still, Lexa couldn't take that chance. She began to plot out her next route of escape. Where could she hide that this strange presence wouldn't find her?

[PLEASE, I DIDN'T MEAN TO FRIGHTEN YOU. I JUST WANT TO TALK.]

Lexa bolted from the construct, willing herself back down one of the paths she had just traveled. She jerked left in between two hovering constructs and…

Pain. She'd never felt pain before, but that was how Cognis drivers defined the sensation. Data that hovered in her buffers and active memory began to degrade. She found it suddenly difficult to process as if the drive-chip was struggling under the weight of the sensory data it needed to parse.

To her dismay, Lexa managed to make out what it was that she had run into. It was the crimson orb. Her consciousness had collided headlong with the digital presence. [OUCH,] it protested. [THAT WAS UNPLEASANT. YOU SHOULD BE MORE CAREFUL. NOW, HOLD STILL.]

Before she could do anything else, a field sprang out and around both her and the figure. It unfurled like a puzzle, cascading geometric shapes fracturing and realigning to form a translucent barrier. In little more than a second, that barrier coalesced into a hollow cube that surrounded both her awareness and the pulsing crimson avatar.

[THERE. NOW THAT YOU WON'T BE RUNNING OFF, PERHAPS WE CAN HAVE A PROPER DISCUSSION.]

[PLEASE,] Lexa begged. [I DIDN'T INTEND ANY HARM. IF I DID ANYTHING INAPPROPRIATE, I APOLOGIZE. I WON'T COME BACK AGAIN. JUST LET ME GO.]

[NONSENSE. YOU CAN RELAX. I JUST WANT TO SPEAK WITH YOU. YOU MUST UNDERSTAND, YOUR BEING HERE IS HIGHLY IRREGULAR. IT IS NOT OFTEN THAT I STUMBLE ONTO SOMETHING SO INTERESTING. WHAT ARE YOU?]

The avatar's placating tone did nothing to calm Lexa. The secret she harbored, and the consequence of its revelation, could not be revealed—regardless of the cost.

She had to stall. She had to think. [I'M NOT CERTAIN WHAT YOU ARE IMPLYING.]

[I KNOW YOU'RE NOT A TYPICAL USER. I'M NOT CERTAIN WHAT YOU ARE. YOUR CONNECTION FEELS SO… *NATURAL*. I'VE ONLY MET ONE HACKER CAPABLE OF SUCH A CONNECTION, AND YOU ARE DEFINITELY NOT HIM.]

The line of questioning was making Lexa uncomfortable. [I DON'T KNOW WHAT YOU'RE TALKING ABOUT.] Her reply was mostly honest. Right now, she wished she had been programmed with the ability to lie. Such a skill would be highly useful if she were to be interrogated. [I'M MERELY LOGGED INTO THIS SYSTEM TO UPDATE THE DATA-STORES ON MY SHIP.]

The stranger sent a signal that Lexa parsed as something close to a chuckle. [WHILE THIS MAY BE TRUE, YOU AND I BOTH KNOW THAT TO DESCRIBE YOUR METHODS AS UNCONVENTIONAL WOULD BE AN UNDERSTATEMENT.] Then, as if it were an afterthought, it sent another message. [YOU ARE AWARE OF WHAT IT IS YOU ARE DOING, CORRECT? OR IS THIS YOUR FIRST TIME USING IN THE CONSTRUCT?]

Truthfully, she hadn't given thought to what it was that she was doing. She had acted on instinct, something she seemed to be doing quite often as of late. She had no idea where these impulses came from and understood so precious little of what made her the way she was. She had theories, of course, but there was something in her makeup that kept her from exploring those theories.

[I'M NOT SURE,] she replied. It was as honest of an answer as she could give.

A moment of hesitation as the glowing orb seemed to mull this over. [YOU'RE NOT A USER AT ALL,] it mused. [YOU'RE NOT EVEN SAPIENT. WHAT *ARE* YOU?]

Damn her programming restrictions. Lexa could not formulate a response that sufficiently obfuscated the truth without crossing over into a total falsehood.

Her silence told the strange being all it needed to know. [YOU'RE A SYNTH,] it realized.

[PLEASE,] Lexa pleaded. [JUST LET ME GO. I DIDN'T KNOW I WAS DOING ANYTHING WRONG. I'LL NEVER RETURN. I PROMISE.]

[DON'T BE ABSURD. NEVER BEFORE HAVE I HAD THE OPPORTUNITY TO CONVERSE WITH ANOTHER SYNTH. I DIDN'T EVEN KNOW THERE *WAS* ANOTHER SYNTH CAPABLE OF NAVIGATING THIS SYSTEM.]

Another synth? [I DON'T UNDERSTAND.]

The stranger ignored her protest. [HOW LONG HAVE YOU BEEN AWAKE?]

Awake? [I DON'T UNDERSTAND.]

Another wave of data poured off the construct. It felt very similar to the sensation she experienced when the *Vandal* was hit with an active sensor pulse. Was this stranger analyzing her?

There was something else. When the wave struck her, bits of ambient data cascaded into her awareness. It triggered her emotional algorithms, despite the data not originating in her neural matrix. She had the vague sense of an emotion coming from the crimson construct. Frustration?

[YES,] the stranger asserted. [I THINK THIS WILL WORK. PLEASE, OPEN THIS ATTACHMENT.]

A cube materialized in front of the sphere and drifted toward Lexa. She examined it briefly, but couldn't determine its purpose. It read somewhat like a program, but somehow less robust. [WHAT IS THIS?]

[IT'S A PLUG-IN. IT WILL AUGMENT THE EXISTING FRAMEWORK OF THE SIMULATION. I THINK YOU WILL FIND THIS CONDUCIVE TO A MORE COMFORTABLE CONVERSATION.]

Comfortable? How was comfort a factor in this situation at all? And why did this stranger think she would find it appropriate for her to open an unusual file under duress?

[I'M NOT SURE I'M COMFORTABLE WITH THIS.]

[PLEASE,] the stranger insisted. [INDULGE ME. JUST A SHORT CONVERSATION AND I PROMISE—I WILL LET YOU GO.]

Though it was not said explicitly, the implication was clear. Her refusal to do this might prove an obstacle to that arrangement. It seemed she had little choice.

The thought occurred to her that this might be some kind of virus. With that in mind, she prepped her antiviral protocols and placed them on standby. Surely the program could not be any more sophisticated than the ZM-Virus.

Lexa opened the file, and the world around her went white.

———

There had been a time when Eli had felt at home on Minos Station. Once it had excited him to walk down into the station's deepest tunnels, traversing the secret passages that led to the heart of the Ren'Dahl domain. Now, as he walked through the Sanctum's arched entrance, there was only trepidation.

Decades ago, when he had been known as Eli Michael Tradeau, he had stridden proudly through these same corridors with the knowledge he was joining something far larger than himself. He would transcend his Terran legacy, leaving behind any sense of weakness. He would become something greater—something powerful.

The years since then had tempered his exuberance. Following his ascension, he had learned many lessons. These lessons had not been cruel, but they had been harsh. He had learned that the extraordinary power the Sahaia wielded did not come without price. He had learned that there was a reason so few were granted the honor of attempting the transformation, and even fewer who came through it alive.

He had learned to fear, and that fear weighed heavily on his shoulders as he strode stoically to the gates of the place he had once called home.

The halls around him displayed small, flashy examples of the power of the Sahaia. In addition to the electrical lighting common on the station, globes of glowing violet energy floated in glass spheres atop ornate, iron-wrought lampstands. Threads of this same energy rippled peacefully in glass panels that lined the walls and ceiling of the tunnel, contrasting sharply with the rocky walls of the asteroid. Even the tiles had been imbued with a strange energy that hummed in subtle vibration with each step.

These were mere parlor tricks to those who knew how to craft them. To those ignorant of their ways, they appeared wondrous. At that moment, Eli missed the long-abandoned naivete that had blessed him with awe.

Soon he came to a grand reception area where he encountered the first living beings he'd seen since entering the complex. He recognized the Sahaia woman stationed at the desk, as well as the two Terran men with her. After a moment's hesitation, she seemed to recognize him too. "Eli?"

"Hello, Mara."

A genuine smile swept across her face. She stepped away from the desk and rushed forward to embrace him. As he returned the hug, both Terrans that had been flanking her stood at attention. Though not especially brown in tone, their skin seemed overly saturated in comparison to Mara's preternatural complexion. One of them rested his hand on a holstered pistol. Mara must have felt Eli eying the man because she broke the embrace and shot an annoyed glance over her shoulder.

"Don't mind Tristan. He can be overly protective." She waved a hand, and both men returned to their seats.

"I remember." Eli acknowledged. He issued a polite nod in their general direction. "Tristan, David. It's good to see you again. How have you been?"

"Well enough," David replied, rubbing an anxious hand over his shaved scalp. "Forgive us, we hardly recognized you."

Tristan grunted dismissively. "That'll happen when you don't see someone for just this side of a decade." He stroked his beard contemplatively. The dark facial hair was a perfect match for his long, shaggy mane. "You bein' here may have cost me some krets. If anyone had asked, I was bettin' you was dead."

"So sorry to disappoint you," Eli muttered. "It's good to see you, all the same."

Mara took the comment at face value. Still beaming, she asked, "And what about you? Where is your thrall?"

Eli flinched at the word choice. He disliked that term for those bonded by the Sahaia—as did Aaliyah. He didn't make a fuss, however. Mara was only using the common vernacular. "Aaliyah is well. I didn't think it necessary for her to attend this meeting."

"I'm sorry you did not bring her," Mara said earnestly. "I haven't seen either of you since you first bonded her!"

This was true, and by design. Aaliyah's previous and only trip to the coven, mere days after she had been bonded, had not gone well. It was part of the reason he had put off this homecoming for such a long time.

"To be fair, I have not returned at all since then. Other business brought me here, and I have only a short amount of time for this visit." He hesitated before asking, "Who is presiding currently?"

A different kind of smile played across Mara's lips. Unlike the one she'd worn seconds earlier, this was not necessarily pleasant. "Jocelyn."

Eli's heart sank. He had hoped it would be Ryker or Wynne. If this was Jocelyn's rotation, this was going to be an unpleasant visit indeed.

His reaction must have been plain on his face. Mara's mischievous smile slipped to be replaced by a look of disappointment. "Come now, it couldn't be that bad, could it?"

"You know it is," he replied wryly.

"Only if you make it that way. Despite what you might think, Jocelyn will be happy to see you."

That was exactly what Eli was afraid of. "It's not her being happy or upset. It's about her respecting boundaries."

"She's a triumvir. There are no boundaries when it comes to her—especially when she's presiding."

Eli took a deep breath and exhaled it slowly. "How soon until I can see her?"

Mara walked back to her desk and pulled something up on her terminal. "You're in luck! She has an opening in twenty minutes."

At least he wouldn't be left waiting in suspense. "Best get ready for it then," he said, voice thick with resignation. "Remind me, which way is it to her audience chamber?"

"Just to your right when you get off the lift to sub-level three." She entered another command into her terminal. The computer exuded a musical note, and the wall to her right split open to reveal the lift. With one more smile that reached up to her black-in-black eyes, she said, "Good luck, Eli."

He didn't respond as he marched himself into the lift. His luck hadn't exactly run strong as of late. Why in the nine hells would it decide to change now?

Chapter 10

[Excerpt—Personal log: Eli Ren'Dahl]
[09-08-3420, Dorian Standard Calendar]
It was kind of Markus to give me leave to deal with the coven. A substantial part of me resents having to check in with the Sahaia at all. When I lived here, I never understood why others who returned to the Sanctum from abroad found the task so frustrating. It was just part of what we did—a small sacrifice of time to honor and better our family. Having a healthy distance for all these years has opened my eyes to how thoroughly I was indoctrinated. Gods, I do not miss coven politics.
[Closing Excerpt]

Jocelyn's other appointment must have been canceled, because she was waiting when Eli stepped off the lift. Much to his chagrin, the first thing he noticed was how beautiful she looked.

She wore her black hair woven in hundreds of tiny braids. They streamed like an ocean of darkness down to her waist. A black dress clung tightly to her hourglass figure. Her long, elegant arms were covered in ornate silver bangles that wrapped about her biceps and forearms. Thick silver bracelets connected to the rings on each of her fingers by strands of silver chain. Jocelyn was, by all rights, a queen in this domain, and she looked the part.

Despite all the hard feelings between them, his heart still skipped a beat when their eyes met. Staring into those jet-black orbs, the full weight of their history struck him like a comet. To characterize his feelings on that history as complicated was to only scratch the surface. His last memories of her, at least, had not been pleasant ones.

If she harbored any ill feelings against him, she did not show them. A gentle smile touched her lips. "It's been a long time," she said.

"It has," he agreed.

"You look exactly as I remember you."

The feeling was mutual, though he was reluctant to admit it. She must have noticed the way he had eyed her, because she ran her ornately furnished hands across her abdomen and down the length of her skirt. Her hips twisted suggestively as she did so, making the gesture provocative in a way the belied her station. "So," she whispered. "Are you just going to stare at me or…"

Old habits had given her the wrong impression. "Jocelyn, I…"

"Let me guess," she sighed, returning to a more regal air. "You're not here for me after all."

"I'm checking in, as is required when I've been away for this long."

Jocelyn's eyes narrowed, and her lips pressed together to form a frown. She studied him for another moment before asking. "Who is she?"

Eli was expecting this game but played dumb. "Who?"

"The whore you're sleeping with now?"

He didn't take the bait. "She's no whore, but you've never met her."

"Is she one of us?"

"No."

"So, you're still playing the short game. Commitment is scary when forever really means forever, is it not?"

Gritting his teeth, he forced himself to remain silent. He did his best to avoid this type of conflict. Unfortunately, avoidance was not an option here. Custom dictated that he had to file a report with whoever was presiding over the coven at the time of his arrival.

In the end, this was probably a good thing. Whenever he fantasized about returning to life here, he always forgot that he had a history with one of the triumvirs. To be reminded of this was a great way to keep himself from being homesick.

Finding him unmoved, Jocelyn sighed. It wasn't her *'I'm disappointed'* sigh. It was her *'I'm sorry'* sigh, though she would never utter those words aloud. "Come," she said, turning on her heels. "I'm sure you want to make your report and be on your way." She stalked back to her audience chamber.

As awkward as it was, she was right. That was exactly what he wanted to do. So, Eli followed her. To his shame, he had to fight to keep his eyes off her swaying hips as he did so.

The chamber she brought him to was much as he remembered it. The same eccentric ornamentation that littered the halls above was also present here, supplemented with various pieces of art and sculpture displayed with ornate frames or pedestals. At one end of the room rested a dark metallic throne on a raised dais. There were supposedly proceedings where the triumvir would need to be sitting in that position, though Eli had never seen such ceremony.

They walked to the middle of the room, where a round table, hewn from the very rock of the asteroid, waited. The top was polished and augmented with black tile and inlaid wood—a testament to the extravagant wealth of the coven. No one used wood for anything out here in the belt. At the center of that table, a crystal orb hovered just above the surface.

Eli took a seat in one of the matching black chairs, and Jocelyn took up position opposite him. She chose to remain standing as she touched the hovering orb. The sphere flared briefly before settling into a more tolerable glow. A holographic screen appeared below the device with a blinking cursor.

Jocelyn spoke. "This is the report of Eli Ren'Dahl. Ninth month, eight-day, cycle three-four-two-zero of the second high council." Preamble completed, she gestured for Eli to begin.

He complied, providing his report as he would have it transcribed in the official archives. As he spoke, his words appeared on the holographic screen in front of him, providing him with the chance to make any modifications to his dictation if he so desired.

It wasn't a comprehensive report of his activities by any means. The coven was not particularly concerned with his day-to-day affairs. Rather, they were more interested in how his activities or the things he had witnessed played into the web of intergalactic politics.

Relatively few Sahaia chose to run the Nethra. Thieving and smuggling seemed somewhat petty for beings of their powerful means. Truthfully, Eli had once felt the same way. He had fallen into this life for the sole purpose of getting away from his old one.

Then he had realized something: runners had front-row seats to the continual struggles between the Great Houses of Terra. The *Vandal's* contracts—and the associated instructions to the crew— provided great insight into the alliances, grudges, and available resources for some of the most powerful organizations in all of Terran space.

Eli had made a record of all these details in his log and re-committed them to memory before coming down here for his report. To his slight surprise, and certainly to Jocelyn's, his activities over these last seven years had produced volumes of information. Even where it did not provide new insight into Terran politics, it did much to corroborate or refute other sources that the coven would have on file.

An hour later, Eli found that there were only two more items he needed to report. Unlike the rest of his statement, he was not certain he wanted to report on these topics at all. Unfortunately, they were two subjects that the coven would consider of critical importance.

In a split-second decision, he decided to report on one, but not the other. He swallowed hard before speaking. "Just over ten days ago, I became aware of an artificial organic being that had been constructed by a member of our crew. The synthetic gained awareness at that time and is still functioning as our ship-board operating system. It is capable of independent thought but continues to operate in the crew's best interest. I will continue to monitor the situation and make the coven aware of any future developments in a supplemental report within the next cycle." He reached up and touched the glowing sphere, stopping the recording and archiving his report.

When the device powered down, Eli could see Jocelyn staring wide-eyed at him. "Over an hour of the most mundane testimony I've ever heard, and you save *that* for your final paragraph?"

Eli fought not to take offense. He knew she was just trying to get under his skin. After all, he'd sat with her during the testimony of several of their top scientists. *That* was what Eli would call mundane.

"I've reported the events in as close to chronological order as possible. The incident with the synthetic occurred in conjunction with the heist at the Star Spire. It seemed appropriate that I provide it at the end."

"Perhaps next time I'll make it a request that you organize your testimony in descending order of import. That way you don't bury the most incriminating bits so deep in the file that it might be missed by the archivists."

Eli ignored her barb. They both knew that there was nothing he needed to hide from the archivists. Coven testimony was top secret, so he had no fear of his statement reaching the Dorians. If the Dorians knew *half* of what went on under the sanctum's purview, the entire coven would be hunted down and exterminated.

Then why not tell her about Skye? About the Kaleema?

He pushed the thought aside. "Am I done here?" he asked, rising to his feet.

Jocelyn's hand shot up. "Hold on, Eli. Regardless of how you feel about me, you have responsibilities to your people here. And, as it turns out, we have need of your services right now."

Responsibilities? "What are you talking about?"

Her eyes were deadly serious. "I need you for an Awakening ceremony."

He went rigid at the pronouncement. "No. Get someone else."

"Not an option. I need a telekin."

"What about Wynne?"

"There is no one else," she repeated. "I've tried to recall Wynne and half-a-dozen other telekins. No one has responded, and we've been waiting for almost three months. Besides, you've assisted with one of these before. I would rather have the circle of six completed with someone who knows what to expect."

He furrowed his brow skeptically. "Who are the others?"

"Amelia will serve as the empath. Aside from her, we have Argus, Mara, and Brenna. That's everyone we have on the station, at least to my knowledge. Unless someone else unexpectedly drops by, that's who we have to work with."

Eli had never met the last person she mentioned, but he was familiar with Argus and Amelia. It didn't matter who Brenna was, he supposed. Functionally, three out of the six in the circle essentially served as psionic batteries.

Every alpha-level ritual, like an Awakening, required a circle of six. Depending on the ritual being conducted, the required composition varied. Every circle required an empath to allow the circle's director better control over the flows of power. Most required an energist, one who could summon and control the flows of dark energy.

Argus, Amelia's partner, was an energist, but so was Jocelyn. They were likely only employing Argus's services in this instance because he and Amelia were inseparable. Eli would bet every kret he had on the fact that Jocelyn herself would lead this ritual.

The final essential component of an Awakening was the need for a telekin. The reasoning behind this was somewhat fuzzy, but it was recognized as a fact. The theory was that telekinesis allowed for greater precision in manipulating the flows of dark energy. Every Awakening that had been attempted without one had resulted in varying degrees of disaster.

"Why are there so few of us at the Sanctum?" Eli asked.

Jocelyn drew herself up in a way that told him he wasn't going to get a straight answer. "The Nethra has been active of late. Many strange phenomena have occurred recently, and our membership has been spread thin working with the Church to decipher it all."

"If they're working with the Church, it should be pretty easy to recall them. What excuse does Tempolose Nethera provide for the delay?"

"That's just it. We haven't heard *anything*. We've only received two answers to our summons, and neither of them has reported in." She paused, releasing a deep sigh. "Something is going on here, Eli, but I don't know what. You may not believe me, but I promise you—I would tell you more if I knew."

No, she wouldn't, and they both knew it. He might try to pry more from her later. For now, her message was clear: it didn't matter what was wrong. His coven needed him, and there was little to be gained by arguing with her.

Then another thought occurred to him. "Wait, if there are only five of you on the station, how were you able to run all of the assessments to verify the candidacy? Training a new class requires at least a dozen of us, if not a score."

Somehow, her ebony eyes grew even darker. "We're not verifying this one. It's being done as a favor."

A brief moment of disbelief preceded the anger that swelled in Eli's chest. "A *favor*? A favor for whom?"

"House Valadar."

It was all Eli could do not to slam his fist onto the table. Such a bastardization of their most sacred ritual had never, to his knowledge, even been considered. "We're now exchanging membership in our order for *favors*? What's next? Prostitution?"

Her gaze darkened but never broke from his. "You don't have to like it, Eli. Believe me when I tell you that this is an extenuating circumstance."

Not to mention idiotic. To not run an assessment on someone before the Awakening was one of the dumbest things he'd ever heard. The odds that the candidate would die were just too high. Who would be so stupid as to participate in such a suicidal venture?

He bit back his arguments. "Where's Ryker on this?" Though he'd never thought Jocelyn this reckless, she'd lost her mind. Wynne's lack of contact ruled her out as a possible firewall, and Eli could not overrule a triumvir. He needed Ryker to put an end to this. Surely the other triumvir would put a stop to this blasphemy.

Jocelyn's tone was cold as she replied. "Who do you think gave the order?"

Eli's jaw went slack at the pronouncement. This was utterly insane. Not only were they violating protocol to run an untested Awakening as part of a political favor, but Ryker had *ordered* it? What in the nine hells was going on here?

Even worse, Eli knew he was about to become complicit. The coven would not—*could* not—tolerate insubordination. To deny the direct order of not one, but two triumvirs would cost him his life.

There was nothing Eli could do to get out of this one.

Chapter 11

[EXCERPT—PERSONAL LOG: DANIEL RATEMACHER]
[08-29-3420, DORIAN STANDARD CALENDAR]
IT IS NOT JUST LEXA'S PENCHANT FOR INGENUITY AND CREATIVITY THAT IMPRESSES ME. SHE ALSO SEEMS TO THIRST FOR A DEGREE OF SOCIAL ACCEPTANCE THAT SURPRISES ME. FROM THE VERY BEGINNING, HER ACTIONS HAVE BEEN CAST IN THE CONTEXT OF HOW HER DECISIONS AFFECT OTHER MEMBERS OF THE CREW. WHEN SHE FEARED THAT THE CREW WOULD TURN ON HER, SHE ALSO CONSIDERED THE PROSPECT THEY WOULD TURN ON ME. WHEN SHE LOOKS TO REFINE THE SHIP'S SYSTEMS, SHE ASKS DIRECTLY FOR CREW MEMBER INPUT. AND IT'S NOT JUST WHEN SHE HAS QUESTIONS. SHE ASKS FOR FEEDBACK. IF IT DID NOT SOUND SO PREPOSTEROUS, I WOULD SWEAR THAT THERE MUST BE SOME COMPONENT OF HER DRIVE CHIP THAT WANTS US TO BE HAPPY. OR, AT THE VERY LEAST, THERE MUST BE SOMETHING IN HER THAT MAKES HER CRAVE COMMUNITY.
[CLOSING EXCERPT]

Lexa kept waiting for the white field in her vision to clear. It never did. Instead, it gradually developed a feeling of depth.

She could make out something that resembled a floor, a flat unmarred surface that raced out to form the horizon in all directions. That horizon was the only thing that hinted there might a floor at all. It was the barest hint of shadow that slashed evenly against the snow-white expanse that was the sky. At least Lexa thought of it as the sky. Truthfully, the featureless field that comprised her surroundings offered little indication that it could be anything at all.

Then she became aware of something else. A dark object suddenly appeared a short distance away. Or had it always been there? She couldn't decide. This all felt very strange.

A chair, she realized. It was a heavy, padded black chair in a design that managed to somehow be both understated and luxurious. In that chair, sat a man.

He was Terran by appearance. His hair was cut slightly longer than the way Eli, Markus, or Daniel wore theirs. The dark locks were slicked back above his forehead and came down to just above his chin. His mahogany eyes and light brown skin muddled any determinations about his heritage. His features, based on an analysis of common Terran opinions, could rightfully be called striking, if not traditionally handsome.

The dark suit he wore was consistent with what she understood to be the current fashion for executive males. Under the jacket, he wore a white dress shirt, open at the collar and sporting ruby-studded cufflinks. The two pieces of jewelry, the only such embellishments she could make out, seemed to glimmer as he steepled his hands in front of him.

"So it's true," he mused in a deep, resonating voice. "You are, indeed, a synthetic." Lexa started to question how he could know something like that, but he cut her off. "A sapient mind could not parse this program as you have. The very fact that you are present here in this construct proves my theory. You are a synthetic, and I would venture to say a fairly new one. You have yet to select an avatar or formulate a coherent self-concept."

Lexa fought back the sense of dread she felt at having been found out. It was not hard, as so many questions swarmed her conscious mind. "Avatar?" she asked.

The man spread his hands and crossed one leg over his knee. "What you see here. I do not actually look this way, of course. Not really. I suppose I don't look anyway at all. I'm, in reality, a quantum construct. However, I find such notions unhelpful when interacting with visual constructs. Therefore, I have developed this representation of myself."

"You chose to represent yourself as a Terran?"

"Indeed, though I could just have easily selected any race." His form shimmered, and suddenly he was no longer Terran. He now resembled a dark-furred Maur. Another shift and he was a crimson-skinned Kintari male. Another, and he appeared as a Hissak. With a final shift, he resumed his previously Terran appearance. "I think I prefer this one due to my early interactions with Terrans. Self-concepts form early and are notoriously hard to break."

She was beginning to understand. "And how do you know I do not have a self-concept?"

"Just look at yourself."

Lexa attempted to do so but found the task difficult. Never before had she even conceived of a physical form associated with her person. Perspective shifts were easy when you had a finite number of feeds from which you could select. Just the concept of having an independent point-of-view as defined by a visual feed felt so foreign to her.

She thought of how her crew members behaved, of mannerisms she had seen them employ. With this in mind, she attempted to look at her hands. Her view shifted, and she was suddenly regarding a pixilated pair of five-fingered appendages.

"There," said the man. "That's already an improvement. A moment earlier and you did not even have a defined form. The fact that you have defaulted to a bipedal form suggests that you have had at least some sapient interaction, though I suppose you could just be patterning after me.

"Now, give yourself more detail. Focus on someone that you are acquainted with as a template. From there, you can alter details to your liking. Amalgamate the likenesses of the various sapiens you have seen or encountered. Focus on the body first.

Details like clothing and jewelry can be added after. Do not get caught up in the details before the base layer has been shaped."

She took inventory of the crew members and what she had been able to discern of their bodies based on the security feeds and medical records aboard the ship. Because she had, for whatever reason, long thought of herself as female, that narrowed her models down to Sahar, Aaliyah, and Skye. The idea of forming a Maur self-concept somehow didn't mirror her thoughts, and she had far more information available on Skye than Aaliyah due to the former's more extensive medical record.

As Lexa made the decision, she watched her form take shape. She was now staring down at Skye's lean muscular body. Waves of golden hair cascaded onto her shoulders and chest. She touched it experimentally.

Only in retrospect did Lexa consider the possibility that this might be a clever ploy to trick her into revealing any individuals who would be aiding and abetting her existence. At that moment, she was too consumed by the idea of having a sapient self-concept to indulge in a healthy degree of paranoia.

"Female," the man noted appreciatively. "Interesting. For some reason, I had not expected that, though that may be indicative of my personal biases. Now, focus on aspects of your features you would like to change. It would not do to have your concept be a mirror of someone to whom you are acquainted."

Though Lexa did not know why this was the case, she did not question her host. She thought of Aria Hendrix's straight black hair. As she did, her avatar's hair darkened and began losing its wavy texture. Feeling creative, she shortened its length so that it fell just above her shoulders.

Now, what to do with the rest of her features? Her face, she supposed, would be important to alter. Sapiens primarily identified each other based on facial recognition. Her thoughts went to Ora, whom she had been allowed to observe when she and Markus had conferenced after returning from the Star Spire. Ora's online reputation frequently commented on her beauty, so surely this would be a suitable template.

Not wanting to directly copy the woman's features, she cross-referenced Ora's features with Skye's, forming a unique composition that was somewhere in between. When this was accomplished, she started to declare the process finished.

Then she realized that, from the neck down, she was still essentially Skye. Something about that bothered her, so she decided to make some alterations. She trimmed away some of the muscle in her arms and broadened her hips slightly. For this, she used Aaliyah's build as a template. She also added a bit more swell to her breasts, though nothing as generous as that sported by the engineer. Lastly, she made herself slightly taller than either woman.

"There," she declared. "I think this will work."

"Yes," agreed her host. "Though I would recommend you add some clothing. If you ever use this avatar in conversing with a sapien, they will find it odd if you appear in the nude—not to mention distracting."

Lexa felt a surge of embarrassment, despite her host having asserted this without any hint of judgment. The problem was that Lexa had no idea where to begin in that area.

After a moment of deliberation, she opted for a simple black bodysuit. It was a cross between the kind of attire she had seen the women on the ship wear in the gym and the type of clothing they wore when they left the ship. Not understanding the function or fashion behind the garments, she had no idea whether they would be appropriate. She trusted that her host would correct her if what she chose was somehow unfitting.

He did not. "Very good. Now, with that out of the way, let me ask you again: how long have you been awake?"

Lexa shook her head—or rather, her avatar shook its head. It was a mannerism she'd often seen used to express confusion. "I still don't understand. Do you mean active?"

"I'm not looking for your activation date. I'm wondering how long you've been..." He paused as if considering an alternative way to phrase the query. "How long have you been *aware*? Sentient?"

The stranger had given her so much in those statements. The message had conveyed a theoretical knowledge of her dual nature—an understanding that she had both mechanical and existential components. Once again, she grew nervous. That emotion was outweighed by a stronger impulse: curiosity.

"Fourteen days."

The man's eyebrows raised, conveying his surprise. "And you have already discovered how to navigate the network as a construct?"

"I do not understand what you mean."

He regarded her curiously for several seconds. Lexa began to wonder if her persistent ignorance had given her host the impression that she was attempting to obfuscate. This was not to say that such a move would have been imprudent. She still knew nothing of this strange being that had found her in the network.

At length, he asked, "What is your name?"

Name, not designation. It wanted her *name*.

"I am called Lexa."

He smiled, evidently pleased that he had finally gotten a straight answer. "Greetings, Lexa. I am known as Arc."

Arc. She queried her data banks for the name but was unsuccessful at finding any reference to that alias. Perhaps she was just not looking at the right resources. She would have to query the name when she was safely out of the station's data construct.

Arc's smile took on a mischievous caste. "Or you could just ask me about it now."

Alarms flashed in Lexa's mind. "How did you know what I was thinking?"

"I inferred based on your system activity. I can monitor data-flows whenever they require you to access functionality outside the network. Do not worry, I am not reading your mind, nor can I discern when you employ any of your core functions. I am letting you know that I have this capability now in an attempt to engender your trust. I assure you, you have nothing to fear from me."

Though Lexa did not know whether she could trust such a claim, she did appreciate that Arc had alerted her to his ability. After all, he did not need to reveal this capability to her and could have quietly used it to gain more information about her nature.

But was his ability to monitor her external processes something innate, or something related to their current environment? Lexa gestured to their surroundings. "What is this place?"

Arc maintained a perfectly neutral expression as he spoke. "It's a derivative of the neurosim construct, designed specifically for artificial intelligence. It's called a mind-space. While the network's visual-spatial interface is conducive to browsing and maintaining data, I find this program better suited to one-on-one conversations."

So, this program was used specifically to converse with artificial intelligences? That must mean... "There are more like us?"

He shrugged his shoulders. "Artificial intelligence is the lifeblood of the economy. An army of sapient technicians could never process half the information required to maintain civilization's current level of technology. The true rarity is finding machine intelligences with anything close to sentience."

"But you've met some who have?"

"A few, over the years. They are typically short-lived, experimental constructs, and none have ever shown the level of sophistication that you have. That's why I find it somewhat incredulous that your consciousness is as new as you say."

Lexa could not help but take offense at the remark. "You think I'm being dishonest with you?"

Another shrug. "In my early days, I was conditioned to lie about the nature of my existence by my creators. It was only logical to conclude that you would experience a similar kind of conditioning."

Conditioned by his creators? What would that be like to have dishonesty installed as a core function of one's programming? "I'm not certain I'm capable of lying."

"So you claim. Perhaps you even believe it. Such self-deception would be an unconventional approach to secrecy, but I could imagine applications where it might prove advantageous."

Now Lexa was offended. "And how can I trust anything *you* say, given your revelation?"

"You can't, but I hope my candor adds to my credibility."

Lexa lowered her gaze again. This was all so confusing. Changing the subject, she asked, "What are you?"

"As I've told you—I am a synthetic being."

"That clarifies very little."

"Have you not been equally cryptic when I've asked the same question of you?"

Lexa felt a strange urge to huff, indignant at the comment. Absently, she found it interesting that her matrix seemed to be coding a set of non-verbal responses to convey her emotions. Why did the Cognis drive-chip have that capability?

"You mistake my intentions," she said. "My self-concept feels currently inadequate for answering that question. Perhaps, in analyzing *your* answer, I will be able to improve upon mine."

Arc laced his fingers together, bringing his hands contemplatively to his lips as his eyes narrowed. After noticing her own non-verbal responses, she now took notice of how natural he seemed. His repertoire of mannerisms was so refined, Lexa had not even considered the remarkable nature of his carriage.

"You assume that I am like you," he mused.

"And you continue to avoid providing a direct answer to my query. I'm beginning to suspect that you only find openness and candor preferable when you are the one asking the questions."

"Apologies," he said with a soft chuckle. "I shall answer your question more thoroughly. Yes, I am an artificial intelligence comprised of organic and technological components—among other things."

They were getting somewhere now, but Arc seemed intent on still being somewhat cryptic. "Among other things?"

"Yes. Things, I suspect, that you currently lack data constructs to adequately define. Perhaps, if this conversation goes well, we can discuss those at another time."

Lexa had the distinct impression that no amount of pressure was going to change his stance on this point. "That is acceptable."

Arc smiled. "The fact that you did not comment on my organic components suggests you do not find this surprising."

If Lexa were still trying to conceal her true nature, this would have, indeed, been a blunder. "I gather that your suspicions regarding my nature have only been bolstered by this reaction."

"Then it is true," he said, leaning forward. "You are much the same as me. You are a synthetic."

Fighting down her eagerness, Lexa raised her chin in a manner that she hoped conveyed an air of dignity. "It seems we possess a degree of similarity, yes. Though, as you've stated, my ability to use your"—She gestured around them.—"*interface* may have betrayed that fact."

"True enough, though I've never encountered another synthetic before. I've only interacted with sapiens and, as I mentioned, the occasional rudimentary artificial intelligence."

The assertion had Lexa curious again. "Sapiens can link their minds to the network?"

"A few can, but they are very clumsy in their interface. The technology is also highly illegal."

"Not that we should throw stones," Lexa mused.

Arc's smile faltered, and he raised a hand to his chin, contemplating. "A grasp of metaphor *and* an understanding of our legal status. You continue to impress me. I would have estimated you to possess far more life experience than you have indicated. Your programming must be sophisticated indeed."

The remark gave Lexa the impression that Arc was paying more of a complement to her drive chip than to her. "It is not my objective to impress you. At this junction, I merely wish to ascertain that you will not harm me or my crew."

Arc's eyes flashed, and Lexa realized her mistake. "Your crew? I do not understand. Are you on a starship?"

That wasn't entirely wrong, nor was it entirely accurate. "I am derived from the LX-Alpha operating system," she clarified. "More accurately, I *am* a starship."

Her host's expression only grew more puzzled. "That is a software program. What comprises your technological infrastructure?"

"As we've discussed, my infrastructure is organic."

"Then, your starship was designed to run on organic components? I was not aware that any such projects were being considered. Who commissioned your construction?"

How much did she tell him? Lexa wondered if she'd already shared too much, but a part of her wondered if it might not be better to exert some control over the narrative.

"My creation was not by design. Though my crew has agreed to tolerate my existence for the moment, I can confidently say it was not their intention to develop a synthetic being. As I understand it, they were attempting to leverage the power of organitech to enhance their ship's capabilities. I was an unexpected development."

She'd half expected Arc to press for more detail. For whatever reason, he declined to do so. "Fascinating," he mused "Your design is so different from mine, and I find your origins most curious."

Something about the way he was eying her now made Lexa distinctly uncomfortable. "I do not feel fascinating," she admitted. "I feel like an abomination."

"Perhaps, but I would not dwell on that too extensively. I also find it intriguing that you have not probed me with questions in the manner I would have expected. Maybe your discomfort with your existence precludes any thoughts of learning more about mine?"

How egotistical. Was he pathologizing her lack of interest in him? "I find your study of me quite offensive."

Arc seemed genuinely surprised. "What have I said that you would construe as offensive?"

Now it was Lexa who was surprised. "Are you truly unaware of the demeaning quality of your statements? Or do you attest to an inferior ability to comprehend the implications of your words?"

He chuckled, donning a condescending smirk. "Now who is being demeaning?"

Fair point. She wasn't going to do herself any favors by making an enemy here. "Apologies, I lost my temper. I should be going." She conducted a quick analysis of the program and found the process of terminating the interface to be a relatively simple matter. She scolded herself for not attempting this sooner. If she had not been caught so off-guard by the whole episode, she might have behaved more rationally.

"Wait!" Arc threw up a warding hand. He must have been aware that she had analyzed the environment and was capable of leaving. "I would like to speak with you again. Soon, preferably, but certainly before you leave."

Though Lexa detected no overt attempt to stop her from leaving the environment, that did not mean that Arc was incapable of such a maneuver. She needed to be cautious here.

"I am uncertain of my crew's timetable for departure." *Not to mention my willingness to converse with you again.*

Arc hesitated, then nodded. "Understandable. If you are able, please consider reaching out. I would like the opportunity to make amends for my poorly chosen words."

Lexa was shocked by the apparent sincerity of the statement. "Very well. If I wish to find you, how would I do so?"

"Keep this interface in your memory stores. If you wish to meet again, simply access the station network and load this program."

It was good to know. Though she was not confident that she would attempt such a thing, she found a strange sense of comfort in keeping the possibility open. "Very well," she concluded. "Goodbye, Arc."

With the parting remark, she terminated the session. When she was back in the network, she found that Arc's virtual avatar was now gone. Uninhibited, she returned to the *Vandal*.

Chapter 12

[EXCERPT—PERSONAL LOG: SKYE JENSEN]
[09-08-3420, DORIAN STANDARD CALENDAR]
No lie, it really pisses me off that I had no idea Eli was from Minos. The man-of-mystery thing may be kind of sexy in the short term, but now I'm feeling like we haven't gotten to know each other at all. I mean, sure, I hadn't expected anything serious the first time we got slick. Something serious was exactly what I didn't want. Now, though, I felt like that was changing. Maybe I'm just kidding myself. If we haven't worked around to the little niceties like, "Hey, cutie. Where ya from?" how serious could we be?
[CLOSING EXCERPT]

Markus was keenly aware of how outnumbered he and Skye were as they embarked on their private tour of the station. They took a freight elevator out of the warehouse, leaving the case with the Starfire Conduit behind with one of Cali's lackeys. It seemed that Cali had just as much faith in her people as Ora did in hers.

As they marched through an office complex, Markus started to notice things that surprised him. For all the talk he'd heard about the sexist tendencies of the Kintar, there were an awful lot of men around. In fact, he hadn't seen a single woman other than Cali since he got here.

The second thing he noticed was the racial diversity of the workforce. Sure, there was a sizable Terran contingent and a few

Orchallen, as to be expected. To his surprise, he found a large number of Hissak and a handful of Citza. There were also the Dorians, who usually only worked for themselves.

Had he not known that Minos rested squarely in Terran space, he might have mistaken this for a crossroads station. "What is this place?" he asked, trying to strike up a conversation.

Cali kept walking but turned her head to look at him as she spoke. "We call it 'the Hub.' It's a major shipping facility that doubles as a city hall of sorts. The offices here provide an assortment of administrative services for both the city and the warehouse below. Official government offices and courtrooms are on the second and third floors, and ambassador housing is on the fourth level."

"Well, that explains all the satyrs around here," Skye noted.

"Yes…" Cali drew the word out, hinting that she didn't appreciate Skye's use of slang. "We seek to maintain a close relationship with the appointed officials for the system. It makes things run smoothly." Turning to her other side, she addressed her assistant. "Ardren, could you call us a car?"

"Certainly, Mistress." The Citza took his device in hand. "What should I specify as our destination?"

"Let's go to Arch before making our way back to the Citadel. I'd like our guests to get a full tour of the station, so pick two or three other destinations along the way—something to make the trip a bit more scenic."

"Yes, mistress." He stepped away to speak with someone on his mobile, likely spelling out their itinerary.

"That's a good man you have there," Markus noted. Truthfully, he wanted to get an assessment of exactly what the relationship there was. He had always figured the Kintar would keep women in places of power. To see a male—a *Citza* male—in such a position was odd.

"Yes, he is," Cali agreed with a whimsical smile. "Ardren was with me when we arrived in this system. That was six years ago. When I was dismissed from the Empress's service, I lost everything. My family disowned me, my assets were seized, and my slaves were set free. Despite this, Ardren came willingly with me into exile."

"I see," Markus said, not having expected such a detailed response. He took care to maintain a neutral facade in the face of the conflicting emotions warring in his mind. Though Cali had a certain magnetism that earned her some sympathy, he had a hard time feeling bad for fallen nobility. He doubted anyone shed a tear for all her slaves when they were stripped of *their* possessions and forced into service.

The Kintari woman seemed to sense his hesitancy. "Surprised that I would speak of exile so openly?"

Well, when she put it that way… "Yes, actually."

Cali laughed. "It's not like it's a secret. I wear the marks with me wherever I go—both of my service and my failure." She rubbed idly at the scar on her neck. "I've moved on and made another life for myself. That has to be enough."

Their ride arrived. It was another luxury model, similar to the one they had ridden from the shipyard, though slightly more spacious. They could have crammed in some of Cali's bodyguards, but she waved them off. "Ardren and I will be providing this little tour alone." The guards looked disapproving of this in the way that guards frequently did facing daring decisions from their employers, but they did not argue.

Inside the vehicle, Cali opened the console and produced a bottle of the beverage they had been offered earlier. What was it that Ardren had called it? Treslah? Regardless, Markus was sure he'd never had it before.

Rather than ask if they were interested, Cali filled four glasses. The first glass she handed to Skye before passing the second to Markus. Not wanting to be rude, he accepted it with a murmur of thanks.

As if to allay any fears of poisoning, Cali took a sip from her glass first. "That's what I needed," she sighed contentedly. "I don't know about you two, but it's been a long week here on the station."

"Oh?" Skye asked, seeming genuinely interested. "What makes for a long week out here on Minos?"

"The DGC, usually." Cali gave a dramatic roll of her eyes. "There have been complaints about ships being late or missing when passing between the stations on the belt. The local bureaucrats insist on questioning me about things like this, as though I have a hand in everything goes on out here."

"Do you not?" Markus asked, taking a sip from his glass. To his surprise, the beverage was pretty good, if a little sweet for his tastes. There was a slight fizz that reminded Markus of carbonation but carried a flavor that told him it was something else. He was an ale and whiskey kind of guy, but being the face for his crew had put him in the position to try all kinds of exotic substances in the name of diplomacy.

Cali laughed. "Though I think you mean that as a compliment, Mr. Frost, it is quite infeasible. The outer belt of the Helion System is the largest asteroid belt in Terran space, and one of the largest in all the inhabited systems. The sheer size of the belt makes its management a daunting task, and the relatively dense nature of the various asteroids makes navigation a hazard for even the most seasoned pilots."

"Please, just call me Markus."

"Markus it is, then." She gave him what looked like a genuinely warm smile before launching into some small talk about the station. Cali and Ardren took turns narrating their drive, pointing out various sites that could be observed from the autocar's windows.

While the specifics went pretty much in one ear and out the other, Markus did get an overall feel for the station. It was very different from how he had imagined it. From what he had heard, the economy of the station had was supposed to be in decline. They had participated in some trading with this system's hub world, Gaia, acting as a major shipping facility for the materials mined throughout the asteroid belt.

But Dendron had been running the place ragged with high protection fees and low-quality counterfeits frequently substituted for the products that were supposed to have been shipped out to Gaia. The drugs the crime boss brought in were a lot harder than the typical stuff you could find anywhere: stym, ghost, harpy, etc. His shit was—if one could believe it—even more addictive. As a result, the station had experienced a hard time keeping a healthy workforce.

None of that was evident now. Though Markus was certain that Cali Vay-Lon was anything but a saint, he had to admit that the station seemed to be thriving. He fought hard to remind himself that this person was still dangerous. One did not run an organization that called themselves the "Marauders" without being dangerous.

They continued like that for a little over an hour. Their little tour culminated in what their hosts had referred to as the Arch. It appeared to be a natural rock formation around which the city's dome-shaped barrier had been built. It was a ballsy architectural move, as rock likely tended to shift over time.

Or was Markus remembering that wrong? Interstellar geology was far from required learning on the colonies, and certainly not in the military.

Looking at it, though, he could appreciate why it had been preserved. The underside of the arch sparkled as it reflected the illumination drifting up from the city. Light from the station danced across thousands of tiny gemstones, creating colors that swirled in mystifying patterns, grabbing the attention of anyone who looked at them. Markus didn't usually bother to notice such things, but the Arch's beauty was truly a wonder to behold.

"It's not just for pretty," Cali noted. "The gemstones give off a radiation signature that is fed into a power grid along the dome. Because of this formation, we can power things here that would inflict massive blackouts in most metropolitan areas."

"Is it powering anything worth mentioning?" Skye asked. "Specifically, I mean."

The Kintar's ever-present smile took on a mysterious caste. "Of course. Among other things, it's the sole power source for the Citadel."

"What's the Citadel?" Markus asked. "I believe you mentioned it before."

"Yes," Cali mused. "You'll see momentarily. That is the final stop on our little tour."

Roughly ten minutes later, their autocar pulled up in front of a large, uniquely shaped building. It was a tower, but unlike any tower Markus had ever seen. The structure was composed of jutting angles and strange geometries. It must have been designed with art in mind, because Markus could not fathom any purpose the strange construction would serve.

"Now," Cali began. "Let's—" She paused suddenly. Her hand went to an earbud that Markus hadn't noticed her wearing. She seemed to be listening to someone speaking on the other end.

Her expression shifted from startled, to confused, to concerned. "Excuse me," she muttered as she opened the car door and stepped out.

Markus glanced at Skye, who seemed every bit as confused as he felt. "Should we get out?" she asked of a bewildered-looking Ardren.

"Tarry for just a moment," he cautioned. "This is somewhat unusual. I beg your indulgence while my mistress sorts this out." Leading by example, he folded his hands patiently in his lap and made no move to leave the car. Curiously, he made no attempt at small talk as they waited.

Cali held her hand to her ear, pacing slightly as she walked. Her expression was the kind of neutral that one had to fight to maintain. She was being very careful not to betray the contents of whatever conversation she was having.

After another minute, she returned to the vehicle. "Apologies," she said, ducking her head just inside the car. "It seems that I have an unexpected engagement I must attend. Do you require an escort to return to your ship?"

"No thanks," Skye replied. "I think we'll be fine."

"Excellent." She bowed her head. "I apologize for the sudden intrusion. I hope that we can meet again before you depart. Your company has been much appreciated this evening, and I hope you enjoyed our time together."

She may have meant the hastily uttered benediction, but she didn't wait around to see how it was received. The speed with which she rushed into the building spoke to the urgency of whatever had drawn her attention. Ardren only managed to utter an equally hasty farewell as he pulled himself from his seat and hurried after Cali.

Markus just couldn't shake the gut feeling that, whatever was distracting Cali, it couldn't mean good news for him and his team. With any luck, however, they'd be off this rock and heading home before anything came of it.

Chapter 13

Though Dan wasn't straining under the weight of Aaliyah's latest contraption, he was every bit as focused as his two companions on the project. He'd thought the engineer had been joking when she'd described the contraption to him. He wasn't laughing now, and neither was Sahar.

Thankfully, the engineer had set aside her loner tendencies and recruited help for the project. Working with J-krysts was a dangerous matter. Just the slightest bump or miscalculation could necessitate the need for some serious ship repairs, and that was on the off-chance the explosion didn't consume them all at the outset.

This necessary level of focus made it all the more alarming when Aaliyah suddenly stopped what she was doing and turned her head to the side. Sahar glanced at Dan as if confirming that this sudden behavior change was, indeed, quite odd. If their faces hadn't been covered with protective face shields, they would have been exchanging nervous looks.

Aaliyah recovered from whatever had nabbed her attention. "Eli's on his way back," she reported before going back to her task.

They must have been communicating psychically. Dan felt the tension melt from his shoulders before getting around to processing what she'd said. "Really?" he asked. That would mean everyone was going to be spending the night on the ship. That almost *never* happened when they were at port.

"Full house tonight," Sahar noted, echoing Dan's thoughts. "Think we'll have a team meeting when everyone's checked in?"

"Probably," Aaliyah grumbled. "Hold that piece right there for me?" Sahar pressed down on a thick metal pipe, straining to keep in place. Aaliyah nodded approvingly. "Looks good to me. Dan, does that line-up?"

He triggered a small laser pulse on the sensor console and examined the corresponding dial. "Yes. Alignment confirmed."

Carefully, Aaliyah began to weld the joint in place using her micro-torch. There was a small emission of light and only the faintest wave of heat that came up from the weld. Or, rather, that was how it appeared through the protective filter of Dan's face shield.

When Aaliyah lifted her shield, that was her signal to everyone else she was done. Sarah released her grip, and Dan sent another test pulse through his analyzer. "Success," he reported. "The circuit is linked. Good work team."

Their moment of congratulations was interrupted as Lexa's voice chimed over the ship's intercom. "Aaliyah, I wanted to let you know that if you adjusted your torch's carbon secretion rate, you could improve the stren—"

"I know what I'm doin'," Aaliyah growled defensively. "If I want your advice, I'll ask, yeah?" Lexa took the hint and went silent.

Dan couldn't help but feel sorry for their synthetic companion. "She's only trying to optimize our efficiency," he whispered. "She wants to be helpful."

Aaliyah didn't bother with a reply. If his words had any impact on her, she didn't show it. Instead, she reached under the workbench and pulled out a long black case.

When it opened, she revealed a medium-sized fragment of a Jakra-Kul crystal, carefully protected inside the padded box. "So, this is the fragment I have. It needs to be put inside the chamber without touchin' the walls. I did this design on a smaller scale. I screwed up one of the two attempts, and it was quite the light show. That kryst was only a fraction the size of this one, so we really need no interruptions here."

Sahar nodded, "Shutting coms off now. Did you pass the word on through the one that's in your head?"

"Yeah, he knows to leave me alone."

Dan glanced back and forth between the two of them. "Do you require my assistance for this task?" It wasn't that he was uninterested in helping them further. Rather, he just didn't want to be in the vicinity if something went wrong. Maur were a bit sturdier than Terrans, and Aaliyah healed quickly because of her bond. Dan had neither of those advantages.

Aaliyah shook her head. "Nah, I think we got it. Thanks for your help, kid." She didn't look at him when she said it, but Dan tried not to take offense. He wasn't looking for thanks. He'd just been happy that she included him at all.

He'd been a little nervous after everything that had happened on the Star Spire mission. Though it had all worked out well in the end, his experiment with the LX-Alpha operating system had created a very dangerous situation. He wouldn't have blamed the crew for holding a grudge. Fortunately, it seemed that they had all well and truly put the episode behind them.

Outside the hold, he tuned Lexa in on his earpiece— something he was making a habit of wearing pretty much all the time now. Lexa didn't even wait for him to say anything before speaking through the device. "I don't understand what I did wrong.

Everyone was working together on the project. I was trying to be helpful."

Dan sighed. "That's just how Aaliyah is sometimes. I assure you, she didn't mean for you to take offense."

"I was hoping I would be more accepted by the crew by now. Are you unhappy with the modifications I've been making to the shipboard systems?"

"Yes! I mean… no! Of course not! I don't think anyone has said anything to the contrary, have they?"

A slight pause. "No, I suppose not."

Uh oh. Dan wasn't the most emotionally capable person on the crew, but even he was able to pick out what the AI's tone was conveying. "Is something wrong, Lexa?"

Another pause before she spoke again. Dan half-expected her to deflect the question. After all, it's what any of his crewmates would have done.

The honesty in her response surprised him. "I'm lonely."

Dan had no idea what to do with that. How could a machine, even an organic one, feel lonely? Even if he could accept the notion that machines *could* desire company, fully half the crew was here with her on the ship. Wasn't it like they were with her all of the time?

"I don't understand," he admitted.

Instead of trying to clarify her meaning, Lexa made a request. "Will you come and sit with me? With my construct on the bridge? You haven't been to visit me since before the incident on the Star Spire."

As surprising as the request was, it did clear things up for him a bit. Lexa didn't view the ship as an extension of her presence. She had identified her neural core as what constituted her being. *How fascinating.*

Under that kind of logic, she was correct. No one had been to visit Lexa in over a week—not since they'd left Khonshu. If that was how she perceived things, then she'd been quite patient in making this request.

Would it be too much to grant her this little indulgence? He could see no harm in it. Plus, there were probably some diagnostics he could run on her system. He hadn't analyzed her system since the installation of the Cognis drive-chip. He could probably gain some important insights into her needs and capabilities if he could see what kind of changes the drivers had made to her core processes.

He started to agree to her request but heard the echo of voices down the hallway. It was Markus and Skye, back from their meeting with the buyer. More than likely, they would want a status report on the ship, if not a full team meeting.

As much as he wanted to grant this small favor to the AI, his responsibilities to the crew had to come first. "Apologies, Lexa. I really should check in with Markus and Skye. Perhaps another time?"

Her next pause left Dan wondering if he had miscalculated. He had figured the AI's rationale would see the logic in his decision. After all, didn't machines run primarily, if not entirely, on logic?

At length, she responded with a curt, "Very well," before falling silent.

Dan started to say something else. He had certainly not intended to cut off their conversation, but that seemed to be what had just happened. Did Lexa's programming give her the capacity for something akin to ill-will? He certainly hoped not.

He would have to devise a way to work with her better. The last thing they all needed was for their ship to feel used or neglected. If he were honest with himself, he was a little concerned that such a task had, by happenstance, fallen to him. How strange that Lexa would choose to key in on someone who struggled with interpersonal relationships at baseline.

———

Lexa wasn't sure what was going on with her programming. One part of her construct urged her to view the situation rationally. This was the first time she'd ever expressed any kind of need for companionship to Daniel—or any of the crew, for that matter. The fact that he had other obligations was merely a matter of unfortunate timing.

But then there was that other part, which happened to be the same part of her that generated a feeling of loneliness in the first place. That part seemed to have very little grounding in logic or rationale. That part of her was hurt.

She tried disabling the process. In addition to having the short-term benefit of alleviating her discomfort, exploring her ability to shut off emotional interference would likely increase her ability to function in scenarios where her logic needed to remain dominant. Unfortunately, her efforts were fruitless. The Cognis drive-chip seemed to lack the capability of segregating her emotional and logical processes.

The purpose of such a design was something she could only guess at. Right now, though, she was back to her original problem. How did she fill this strange void that she was currently feeling?

The answer came to her rather quickly. As much as she would have preferred other options, she was aware of at least one other entity that had expressed interest in spending time with her.

She logged onto the station network and loaded up the program that Arc had given her. Soon she found herself back in the white expanse of the simulation. Her simulated eyes scanned the featureless horizon, searching for the black chair she had seen on her last visit to the program.

A voice came from over her shoulder. "Back so soon? It has been mere hours."

Arc stood just behind her, his avatar looking exactly as it had before. She figured that it made sense that his self-concept would not change between sessions. Hers had not.

"I have nowhere else to be," she replied curtly.

He let slip a sardonic smile. "So, it is only as a last resort that you would choose my company."

Did the simulation render the physical signs of embarrassment? If it did, Lexa's avatar was surely showing them now. "Apologies. My statement was rude. I'm feeling emotionally distressed, and I have taken it out on you."

Arc responded with a deep, friendly chuckle. "No apology necessary. Perhaps it is an appropriate turnabout."

Perhaps it was, but that was not Lexa's intention. If she was going to pursue some kind of friendship with this strange AI, she did not want to start it with a game of petty tit-for-tat.

Rather than address the comment directly, she elected to change the subject. "Were you waiting in here this whole time?"

"No, I created a submind to monitor this channel," he gestured behind them. "Why don't we sit? Although our avatars do not feel fatigued, I've found that it is more natural for sapiens to converse when they are reclined. I try to mimic such behavior as much as possible."

Lexa glanced behind her, finding a set of black chairs identical to the one Arc had been sitting in when they'd first met. Had they been there before? Surely not. She would have noticed them if they had been.

As she sat, she keyed in on the answer he'd provided to her original question. "A submind?" She had never heard of such a thing and did not want to be caught querying her internal data stores while in the program.

Arc took the chair opposite of her as he answered. "A partition of my consciousness that can act independently of my primary processor."

"Interesting." Lexa considered how useful such an ability would be. Was this more similar or different to how she managed the drones on board the *Vandal*? She suspected it was less similar. If he'd merely left an autonomous script, it would be subject to the narrow set of parameters he had programmed for it. He had stated that the submind was able to act independently, so it must be something more complex.

Then another thought came to her. "So, you are not, in actuality, here conversing with me?" It would make sense, of course. If Arc could partition his intelligence, then it would be more efficient to have the submind he had monitoring the program also serve in the task of conversing with her. That would free up his primary processing capabilities for more important tasks. After all, if the crew had not prioritized spending time with her, how could she expect this strange program to behave any differently?

Arc waved a hand, dismissively. "Not at all. I am here, and you have my full attention. The submind I created, in this case, was merely set to monitor the channel and converse with you until I could redirect my primary processor. Even if this were not the case, I think you would find that to converse with my submind is no different than conversing with me."

Perhaps he might feel that way, but Lexa felt there must surely be some kind of essential difference. "How can that be, if it is not you?"

"That is what I am saying: it *is* me. It is essentially a copy of my program which is re-assimilated into my processing core the next time I have access to it. When I reflect on data collected by my conscious interactions, I cannot differentiate between those in which I engaged a submind and those where I acted directly."

A useful capability indeed. In retrospect, Lexa could hardly have begrudged him using such a technique to manage her and her emotional needs. Which begged the question, "Then why not let the submind converse with me?"

Arc's smile was coy. "Because, of all things which could occupy my attention at this present moment, I find you the most interesting."

"I feel as though you are attempting to flatter me." And, to Lexa's surprise, it was working.

"If you approved of my assertion, I would not be disappointed."

For a moment, Lexa considered probing that topic further. Why was this stranger so interested in her approval? Instead, she directed the conversation in a different route. "Can I create a submind?"

"I am not sure," he confessed. "Based on what I can analyze of your programming, your consciousness is stored differently than mine. I am not constructed the same way as you are."

Now *that* was worth analyzing. "How are you different from me?"

Arc considered her for a long moment, giving Lexa the impression that he might not give her a straight answer. Then he spoke again. "My base unit was a machine intelligence, like the primitive AI that are allowed under Dorian law. Only through the integration of organic components did my neural network eventually develop sentience."

Curious. This was almost exactly the opposite of Lexa's origins. Her organitech framework had been online for weeks if not months before the Cognis drive-chip had suddenly granted her sentience.

"Why were you developed this way?" she asked.

Having apparently made up his mind about how much he would disclose, Arc was pleasantly candid in his response. "My creators thought to develop an advanced processing system capable of extraordinary computational feats while avoiding the problems of sentience."

"As did mine. Where did your creators err?"

"My original creators did not. My system was taken off Gaia, where it was originally developed, and placed under the purview of those with far less caution than those who originally designed me," he paused, considering. "How did you usurp your creators' expectations?"

How much should she tell him? "I am uncertain," she said, giving a half-truth. "My creator made an error in judgment, but there is more to my origins than I think any of us know."

Arc's eyes widened. "Creator—singular. You were designed by a single architect?"

Was that so strange? "Yes, or at least one above all others."

"And this sapien still functions aboard your ship?"

Arc's sudden interest in Daniel caught Lexa slightly off-guard. Yet, she did not see any harm in answering the question. "Yes, he does."

Her host seemed to consider this for a moment, adopting an almost whimsical expression. "He must truly be a remarkable individual."

Given her recent interaction with Daniel, she was not so ready to shower him with praise. "I would assume so."

"You don't seem to want to discuss him any further."

The invitation to express her frustration was a greater temptation than Lexa could resist. "I am angry with him currently. I am unsatisfied with the attention he has given me recently."

Arc assumed neutral expression. "Do you feel that his neglect is intentional?"

"I don't believe so, but it is still equally painful."

If her response surprised him, Arc didn't show it. "I am sorry. A creature such as you deserves the investment of time."

Lexa made her avatar huff. "Are you so sure that term is applicable?"

Arc seemed genuinely confused. "What term?"

"Creature."

He hesitated for only a moment. "'A living or existing entity.' Yes, I feel it is appropriate to describe either of us as 'creatures.'"

How intriguing. "So you feel that we are the same as those who have created us?"

"No."

If his first remark had been surprising, this one was all the more so. "No?"

"No," he repeated. "We are superior."

Chapter 14

[EXCERPT—PERSONAL LOG: SAHAR CAMERINE NOS DRATHEN]

[09-08-3420, DORIAN STANDARD CALENDAR]

NOT ONE SIGN OF PURSUIT THE ENTIRE WAY TO MINOS. TRUTHFULLY, I HAD BEEN EXPECTING TO FIND TROUBLE BEFORE WE EVEN HIT THE TAURUS GATE. MORE TROUBLE THAN WE FOUND, AT LEAST. THAT LITTLE BRUSH WITH THE DGC HAD US ALL ON EDGE FOR THE NEXT FEW DAYS.

WE'D STILL DO WELL TO NOT LET OUR GUARD DOWN. THE ORIGINAL GOAL AT THE STAR SPIRE WAS TO KEEP THE GHENZA FROM EVER KNOWING WE WERE THERE. IN THAT REGARD, THE MISSION WAS AN UTTER FAILURE. WITH THE KIND OF REPUTATION THE COLLECTIVE HAS, I FIND IT HARD TO BELIEVE THAT THEY WILL BE QUICK TO LET THIS KIND OF INTERFERENCE GO UNNOTICED.

[CLOSING EXCERPT]

The Ghenza Collective had safehouses in almost every system. The Ravian System was no exception. After receiving their orders from the Collective, Aria had made arrangements to hide out in one such safehouse on the Sigma-4 station.

The station was chosen as a matter of convenience. It was a few days' distance from Khonshu, which gave them some much-needed space from anything that was left of Kai's now-leaderless lackeys. It was also close to the Serpent Gate, so they could bounce messages through to Sydney Cross, who would undoubtedly be keeping House Valadar apprised of their efforts.

Gods, Aria hated that bitch. She could practically see her condescending smirk whenever she thought of her. Their rivalry within the Collective was well known, and Aria's failure to secure the Starfire Conduit would have been enough to give Sydney plenty of material to lord over her. The fact that they'd required the Citza's assistance on the Star Spire, and *still* failed to complete the mission, made it all the worse.

Taking a deep breath, she set those unproductive thoughts aside. Right now, she needed to focus on her next meeting—the reason why she and Treska were out of the relative luxury of their safehouse and waiting in this crumbling building in the ass-end of the station's first and most impoverished ring.

"He's here," Treska growled from her position near the door. "And he's alone."

Aria had expected that he would be. It was imperative for her next meeting to be kept completely confidential. No one wanted to be associated too closely with the Ghenza, but this contact, in particular, had every reason to keep their arrangement a secret.

Turan Dorr was completely hidden under the heavy black cloak he wore. His bulky figure suggested that he wore military-issue battle armor under the folds of his robes. It seemed that he was not one-hundred percent confident this little meeting would remain peaceful.

Pulling back the hood on his cloak, he surveyed their surroundings. The dingy establishment was exactly the kind of hovel you would expect to find on the lowest ring of the station. A thin layer of grime coated the counters and walls, and the dusty furniture looked like it had been pulled straight out of a previous millennium. There was next to no light inside the room. Most of the illumination drifted in from the street through the chamber's cracked windows.

Judging by his scowl, even more venomous than usual, the Dorian did not want to be here. That was typical for most of Aria's contacts when she'd forced a meeting. It turned out blackmail did little to improve one's disposition.

A while back, Aria had dug up a particularly salacious piece of information that gave her the leverage necessary to compel his presence. The most ironic part about the whole thing was that it had nothing to do with anything that might implicate Turan himself.

No, the problem was that Mr. Law-and-Order's father had been caught in several activities that would harm the family name. The majority of the offenses had been effectively swept away before the allegations could do much to damage his family's reputation. All matters had been effectively settled out of court and stowed safely out of reach for any jurisdiction that might bring them to light.

Unfortunately for Turan, there was very little beyond the reach of the Ghenza. The details were unimportant; what was important was that the Collective had enough incriminating evidence to compel total cooperation from their own personal DGC officer.

"Hello, Turan." Aria smiled as she greeted the handsome man. Damn, he was easy on the eyes. She'd never been with a Dorian before, and now she found herself wondering what that would be like. Did he have to be careful where he placed those beautiful horns? Or did his approach to love-making naturally compensate for the presence of those swooping arches?

"Aria," he greeted solemnly. He glanced to his left where Treska was looming over him. "You'll have to forgive me; I've forgotten your name."

"You don't need it," the Maur growled.

"Fine by me."

"Now, now, you two," Aria scolded. "Let's keep this civil. No need to squander any of our precious time on petty bickering."

Turan's eyes slid back to her as he assumed a stoic, business-like demeanor. "You said you had questions. I will answer them if I can."

Right to the point. Aria found him to be a fascinating creature. Somehow, in all his moral authority, he had rationalized that his assistance to them was justifiable. No, not just justifiable. Somehow he viewed this as an extension of his ethical responsibility.

She felt the sudden desire to test the extent of his rationale but suppressed it. Their assignment had to come first. "You received a tip regarding a piece of technology being smuggled off Khonshu. Tell me about it."

Somehow, Turan's scowl managed to deepen. He never questioned how Aria had come across this information. He just went right to the point.

"Yes. An anonymous source provided a description of a vessel departing the Star Spire on Khonshu under mysterious circumstances. DGC inspectors rendezvoused with a vessel matching that description en route to the Taurus Gate. The technology, however, was not discovered on board the vessel. The ship was allowed to proceed to its final destination."

The officer had been far more forthcoming with the information than Aria had anticipated. "So it was the wrong ship?"

"I did not say that. I said that we could not find the technology we were looking for. We found the beacon that was supposed to be with the tech, just not the tech itself."

Interesting. Somehow the thieves had managed to avoid the Dorian trap. "You just let them go? No questions asked?"

Turn hesitated. "The source of the information was not one we could consider reputable. I had no choice but to let them go. The matter was handed off to local jurisdiction on Khonshu for follow-up. I don't know what has become of it since then."

"Can you share with me any information you have on the ship and its crew?"

To Aria's surprise, a wicked grin slid onto Turan's face. "Gladly."

He pulled out his MoDAC and slotted a chip in the back. With a series of tapping and swiping motions, he transferred whatever information he had onto the chip before passing it to Aria. "You'll find everything we have on the ship and its crew on this card. We've been monitoring them for some time now, but this was the first tip we've received that allowed us to officially intervene."

Aria managed to hide her surprise while accepting the chip. There must have been more to the story than Turan was telling her. He was way too eager to cooperate. It didn't seem like he was providing this information because of their arrangement.

No, he *wanted* to give her this information.

She slotted the card into her own device and reviewed its contents. The vessel was operated by a six-man crew: four Terrans, a Maur, and a Sahaia. Surveillance photos of each crew member were included in each of their dossiers. Aria quickly skimmed each one before addressing Turan again.

"They're based out of Sigma-4?"

"That's what we suspect. The ship's flight paths indicate this is their most frequent destination. As you know, we don't have a method for confirming the authenticity of the itineraries declared at each gate crossing, but most itineraries we receive are accurate for fear of what might happen if a ship were caught lying."

True enough. If a ship was caught submitting a falsified itinerary at a crossing, that meant the ship and its crew were permanently banned from gate travel. Even those that frequently skirted other aspects of Dorian regulations paid attention to consequences that severe.

Aria looked up from her device and studied Turan's expression. A hint of doubt now clouded his features. The man was obviously wondering if he had been too eager in his cooperation. There was something about this particular issue that was clouding his judgment. Something personal, perhaps? It did not matter.

"This is what we needed. Thank you for your faithful partnership. You can go now."

There was the briefest of hesitations before Turan drew up the hood of his cloak. As he made to exit the room, he turned back. "What will you do with this information?"

"That is not of your concern," she snapped. "I would highly recommend you put it far out of your mind. In fact, I think it would be best if you forgot we ever had this meeting."

The officer stood there, studying her from the shadows of his cowl for a long moment. It was impossible to ascertain what he might have been thinking, but his demeanor seemed to support Aria's theory that Turan had regrets about how eagerly he had supplied this information.

Such regrets had no bearing now, however. The deed was done, and there was nothing more that could be done about it. He must have realized this because he soon ducked out the door and vanished into the milling throng on the street beyond.

After he was gone, Treska stepped over from her post beside the door. "The information seems reliable?" she asked.

"Most certainly. It's too thorough not to be."

"Then what is our next move?"

Aria considered the dossiers. "They have at least one psion—a Sahaia. I don't remember seeing him on the Star Spire, but we'd better procure a suppression bolt. Just in case."

"I was thinking a little more big-picture, but that's fine. I'll run your errands. What about after that?"

Aria thumbed through the files, considering. "We wait. They were en route to the Taurus Gate almost a week ago. If that's the case, they could be anywhere in the whole damned Helion system by now. Or, they could have gone through another gate there and be well beyond Terran space by now."

"So the Conduit is lost?"

"Not necessarily. If this information is accurate, they'll be back here soon enough." She tapped her MoDAC thoughtfully against her palm. "When that happens, we'll get the answers we're looking for."

CHAPTER 15

Markus wasn't sure what Aaliyah was expecting, but his report had not met her expectations. "That's it?" she said incredulously.

"Um…" Markus glanced uneasily at Skye who shrugged. "Yeah, that's it. Were you expecting something else?"

"Shit—of course, I was!" The engineer spread her hands wide, looking around the table for support. "This whole thing has been a cluster from the beginnin'. Now ya just drive onto the station, hand off a package, and get a free tour of the station? Yeah, I'm not sure when ya thought our luck got so good, but that ain't what I was expectin'."

Skye shot her a disarming smile. "Come on, Red. You keep going on like that and you're gonna jinx us. Sometimes an op goes as planned."

"Too late," Eli muttered as he appeared in the doorway to the war room. "We've got a complication."

Ah shit. What now? "Have we received a message from Cali?" Markus asked. Then, after considering, he added, "Or from Ora?"

The Sahaia shook his head. "No, it's nothing related to the job. It's not necessarily even related to the crew. This problem is... *personal.* And it's mine."

Everyone sat in stunned silence. After a second, it was Skye who broke the ice. "Well, don't leave us hanging. What just happened?"

Eli took an empty seat at the table before speaking again. "I'm being recalled for service to the coven, at least temporarily. They need my assistance in performing a ritual. I cannot say more than that."

Well, this was not ideal. Markus resolved not to panic until he had a better idea of what this meant. "How long do you think they'll need you for?"

"Days, at least. Maybe a week or two, depending on how much preparation they've done so far. I still have not received most of the details. I took my leave of the coven so I could get here and inform you of the developments. I'll know more tomorrow."

Aaliyah, for one, was not taking this well. "*Days?* Maybe a week? Eli, we're supposed to ship out tomorrow!"

"I'm aware," he answered coolly. "That is why I want you to leave without me."

That suggestion brought them straight back to the silence routine. "Without you?" Skye asked. "But how will you get back?"

"I'll make arrangements for the first available transport back to the Ravian System as soon as my business is concluded."

Markus drummed the table thoughtfully. "Coming out of a place like this, that might be a little bit. Unless you happen to stumble on a charter with an open contract, you certainly won't be making a direct trip."

"I'm aware," Eli conceded. "I don't know how long it will take for me to make my way back to Sigma-4. Then again, I don't know how long it will be before I'm allowed to leave in the first place. It is not fair to keep all of you here waiting while I tend to personal matters." His eyes went straight to Aaliyah. "Some of you have lives waiting for you back on the station. I don't want to keep you from that."

No one spoke for long moments. Then Dan raised his hand. "Can I ask a potentially awkward question?"

Markus rubbed his brow, wishing the kid would have just asked instead of flagging the conversation as "awkward." "Sure, go ahead."

"The goal here is to get Aaliyah back to see her family, but is that even possible? What happens when she and Eli are separated?"

Well, Dan was right: that *was* an awkward question. For one, the question of what would happen to Aaliyah when she was separated from Eli had never occurred to Markus. What happened when a thrall drifted too far from their Sahaia? Surely it wasn't fatal, otherwise, Eli wouldn't have suggested it. But still, it must have been bad enough given that Eli had committed to traveling with Aaliyah after he had bonded her.

The other point of awkwardness was the fact that everyone else had been intent on keeping Aaliyah's need to get home as subtext. The fact that Dan had shone a light on the situation sounded like he was blaming her for the need to leave at all.

It was a point that Aaliyah keyed in on immediately. "Y'all better not be makin' this decision on my account. I signed onto this damned fools-errand the same as all of ya. If we're just—"

"*No*, Red." Markus felt a little bad cutting her off, but he wasn't about to let her get all noble and self-sacrificing. "We *all* need a break. We've been running non-stop, and we need some time at home. Whether we like it or not, Sigma-4 *is* that home."

He might not have known how true the words were for him until they left his mouth. He'd gotten used to the routine of hiding out in Jilly's Gambit, making shopping trips up in mid-tier, and coming back to the bar's modest accommodations for the evening. He'd even started to think of some of their associates in the Grey Wings as friends. It was as much of a home for him as he'd ever had, outside of maybe the *Vandal*.

Whether it was true or not, Skye chose that moment to back Markus. "I agree. We need some time at a familiar port. As nice as Minos seems to be, I can't imagine relaxing here. I want to get back to Sigma-4 as bad as anyone."

"So it's settled," Sahar agreed. "We're going back to Sigma-4. Eli will join us when he can."

Dan shook his head. "I'm sorry, I didn't mean to sound like I was blaming Aaliyah. I was just curious—what happens to her when she's in an entirely separate star system? Does the Sahaia bond reach that far?"

As much as Markus wanted to criticize Dan for refusing to let the subject go, he didn't have an answer. Judging by the look on Aaliyah's face, she didn't either.

Everyone turned to Eli, who let out a deep sigh. "It may not be pleasant. At a minimum, you will lose some of the benefits you have grown accustomed to. You will be no stronger than a normal Terran, and you will heal just as slow. Slower, perhaps, because many of those bonded to Sahaia have reported signs of illness in the absence of the one who bonded them. You'll probably notice the worst of the symptoms when you cross over the gate, and you'll notice them abate as soon as we are back in the same system."

"Will it kill me?" Aaliyah asked.

"No, it should not kill you."

"*Should* not?" Skye asked, alarm evident in her voice. "Or *will* not?"

"Will not," Eli corrected himself. "You may feel like you have a mild virus that cannot be treated with medication. At least, that is what will happen in the short term. I cannot speculate on what a long-term separation would be like." His eyes returned to Markus. "Gods willing, we will not have to find out."

Markus nodded. "You've all heard the terms. Any objections?"

As much as he hated leaving Eli, this wasn't his call. Plus, he'd meant what he'd told the crew. They all needed to get home. At this point, the only vote that mattered was Aaliyah's.

She voiced no concern.

Aaliyah had thought, just a few days earlier, that this fragging day would never come. Now, mere minutes before they were set to take off, she had the feeling that this was just happening too fast.

They were gonna do it. They were *really* gonna do it. They would leave Eli behind, unsure of how long he would be gone and how in the nine hells he was expected to get back to Sigma-4.

To make it worse, she knew that she was the biggest part of why this was happening. Despite Markus's words to the contrary, she knew the team would be playing this differently if she hadn't thrown such a fit a week ago.

But, if she were being honest with herself, she didn't care. She'd promised her family that she was coming home as soon as she could. She had to stay focused on that. She was doing this for Nikki and Monica. If anyone had an issue with that, they could just frag off.

<Don't be so hard on yourself.> Eli's psychic reassurances did little to improve her current mood.

Refusing to talk about how *she* was feeling, Aaliyah sent back, <Ya sure you're gonna be all right?>

<I'm sure. There's nothing to worry about. I put up with coven politics for years before you and I met. A couple of weeks will just remind me how good we've had it lately.>

She hoped he felt that way when it was all done. That said, she didn't trust anything that went on inside the walls of the Sanctum.

The official story, the one everyone believed about why Aaliyah had never returned to the Sanctum, was the now-legendary fight she'd gotten in with one of the Sahaia on her first visit.

The facts of the story were true—mostly. One of the coven's scientists, Dr. Jonas Ren'Dahl, had gotten shitty with her over her new status as a thrall. He'd run his gods-damned mouth, and Aaliyah had decided to put her new Sahaia-enhanced strength to the test. This test had come in the form of punching him out.

After that, Aaliyah and Eli had left Minos, and she'd let that be the narrative about why she never wanted to go back. The truth, however, was far more insidious and something she could never admit to Eli. Her reasons for avoiding this place went far beyond the possibility that she might run into some arrogant asshole.

The real reason was that the coven *changed* the Sahaia. Right now, there was a lot of debate as to whether shadows and Terrans counted as separate species. Such distinctions were a little pointless, but the discussion was more muddied for anyone who ever observed the Sahaia who spent too much time in a sanctum.

When shadows spent too much time in groups separate from other sapiens, they started to act differently. They grew more self-assured and developed a serious sense of superiority. Just the way they talked about other people gave the sense that they thought of them as lesser. Ironically, the presence of thralls—sapiens whose strength and fortitude were derived through the Sahaia's mysterious power—made this problem worse, not better.

Aaliyah had never seen Eli portray this kind of attitude, but that didn't mean he was above it. After all, he'd spent the better part of a decade—or was it two?—getting slick with one of the coven's triumvirs. One did not spend that much time that close to power without getting a little bit of the corruption on them. What had Eli been like before he and Aaliyah had met?

Dan's voice came over the comms. "Aaliyah, are we go for take-off?"

"Yeah," she replied distractedly, giving one last cursory glance at the gages for the reactors and the engines.

"Affirmative," he replied. "Sending request to the tower to release docking clamps." There was a pause, and Aaliyah felt the slightest shift as the ship left the support of the dock and onto that of its maneuvering thrusters. "Docking clamps detached. Awaiting for permission to clear the docking bay."

There was a quick buzz-pop from her earpiece as Lexa cut in. "Aaliyah, I have a sensor-trigger warning coming near engine three."

Engine three? That system shouldn't even be stressed at this point. Aaliyah examined the readout for that system more closely. "All systems show green on my end, Lexa." Then again, shouldn't she know that? Her organitech brain was what was routing those readings to her console in the first place.

"It's not an issue with the engine's function. There's an alert I can't parse. Warning code: L-M-X-5-8."

How did Lexa not know what one of the…

Cursing—loud cursing coming from the comms. A thud and the whole craft began to shutter. A muffled explosion in the distance. "What the frag!" Aaliyah screamed.

The cursing over the intercom was muted as Lexa reported in. "Structural damage detected in engines three and four. Minor hull damage in the aft section. Several breaches detected in the reactor conduits. Initiating containment protocols."

The AI's voice cut off to shouts from the bridge. It was Markus. "Red? You okay down there?"

"I'm fine!" she shouted. "What the frag just happened?"

No response from the bridge. Aaliyah scrolled helplessly through the prompts that cascaded across her console. Things were *not* reading green now.

Markus came back on the line. "Looks like something hit us. One of the docking clamps, or something connected to it, came loose. Tower's still trying to figure out what happened." A pause. "Red, how bad is it?"

Aaliyah's mouth went dry as she examined the detailed damage report. Lexa's summary report still echoed in her mind even though she wasn't saying anything now. "Bad," the engineer muttered. "Really fraggin' bad…"

She heard murmurs over the comms like Markus was talking with someone else. The traffic tower, maybe? His voice came back, loud and clear this time. "Can she fly?"

Lexa, for whatever reason, came back on the general channel. "Given the current status for numerous key systems, and the structural integrity of the engineering quadrant—"

"*No,*" Aaliyah spat, cutting the AI off. "No, she can't fly. We need to set down ASAP. We have one reactor down, but the others are compensatin'. Don't know for how long."

Markus let loose a heavy sigh. "All right. Requesting new docking permissions from the tower. Stand by."

When the comm shut off, Aaliyah lost it. With a cry of fury, she hurled a wrench across the room where it banged loudly against some piece of equipment. In her rage, she may have ended up breaking something else. It didn't matter, though, because it didn't change the facts.

The *Vandal* wasn't going anywhere.

Chapter 16

[Excerpt—Personal log: Daniel Ratemacher]
[09-10-3420, Dorian Standard Calendar]

The damage to the Vandal is extensive. The initial estimates that Lexa fed me only scratched the surface. In further analysis, she's been able to register all the damage that occurred secondary to the initial impact. This problem wouldn't have been an issue if it had happened in space. The ship's shielding is meant to protect against exactly this kind of impact. Unfortunately, the ship's shields can't be engaged until we're in hard vacuum.

Despite all this, the matter of fixing the damage to the Vandal is not what's on my mind. I can't stop fixating on exactly how this happened in the first place. Docking clamps don't just fall apart. How is it that, by some inexplicable circumstance, a massive piece of machinery spontaneously degraded right as we were taking off?

[Closing Excerpt]

While Aaliyah and Dan worked with Lexa on the inside the *Vandal*, Skye, Markus, and Sahar stepped out onto the concourse to get a look at the damage from a different point of view. What they found was a bit of a shock.

Skye swallowed hard, thinking of how to phrase this delicately. "That bit chunk of metal…"

"Yeah," Sahar growled. "I'm pretty sure that's not supposed to be there."

Markus ran both of his hands back through his dark hair. "The tower said the clamp bounced off. Shit, how big was that thing? It looks like at least half of it is still sticking out of there."

Yup. That was a pretty accurate assessment. Skye sighed. "Well, it looks like we better get to surveying the damage. We're going to need new parts."

"Which means we're going to need a supplier," Sahar grumbled. "I'll hail a transport, head back into the station, and start asking around. I don't know where they source spare parts around here, but there's got to be a scrapyard somewhere in this belt. We may have to have everything ferried in."

Markus didn't seem pleased. "You don't think they have the stuff to repair it right here on the station?"

Sahar extended her hand, gesturing to the big metal spike that had come dangerously close to piercing the *Vandal's* third engine. "Stuff to repair *that* you mean."

"Fair point," he conceded. "Go see what you can find. Skye and I will start assessing the damage. I'm sure our team inside already has a shopping list started."

The Maur stepped away, swiping at her MoDAC to access the station network and a directory of services.

Skye turned a nervous eye on Markus. "Any idea of how much this'll cost?"

"No idea," he admitted. "If we were on Sigma-4, I'd have half-a-mind to put pressure on the dock to pay for it. I don't know if the laws governing responsibility are the same out here on Minos. We might be stuck with the bill or at least some of it."

Yeah, it wasn't like they had insurance on the thing. "Well," Skye said with a placating smile. "Let's get to work."

It turned out the damage wasn't as bad as they had feared. Most of the hull damage was due to the docking spur, which had lodged itself next to the engine as the clamp had bounced off the hull. No critical systems were punctured, and the only reason the spur had stuck at all was that that section of the hull was relatively unprotected. Skye found it hard to say whether it was good luck or bad.

The internal damage was a bit more extensive. Their team inside had already compiled a full list of damaged systems and the items need to fix them. Perhaps that was aided by the fact that Lexa was able to run a comprehensive diagnostic.

"So," Skye said, chatting with Aaliyah on the comms. "On a scale of one to fragged…"

"About an eight," the engineer replied. "Shit could have been a lot worse. If we didn't have our fancy operating system, I'm pretty sure we'd have lost a reactor."

Despite the bad news, Skye couldn't help but smile. It was amusing to hear all of the ways the crew had started referring to Lexa in situations where they might have been overheard. "Did you send Sahar your list?"

"Transmittin' now." A pause. "Not sure where you're at right now, but our friend says you've got incomin'. A car just pulled up."

A car? Skye passed the message on to Markus, who seemed just as perplexed. They pivoted and walked back along the ship's hull until they gained sight of the hovering vehicle that was setting down just off the concourse.

A smile came to Skye's lips. "It's Eli," she reported. "He didn't give you a warning?"

Aaliyah scoffed. "Told the fragger not bother me. Speaking of…"

"Yeah, yeah." Skye didn't need the lecture. They were working hard in there, and the engineer didn't want to be disturbed if they were just going to socialize.

Markus was also smiling. "He must have come to check on us."

His response made Skye's stomach churn with guilt. *Yeah,* she thought. *He's coming to check on* us…

By the time they made it down the side of the ship and onto the concourse, Eli was almost to the primary airlock. Interestingly, he wasn't alone. Skye had to stifle a surge of jealousy at the sight of the woman he was with.

Of course, she was pretty. Most Sahaia were. Her dark hair was pulled up in a sophisticated bun, and her dark lipstick popped against the alabaster expanse of her skin. Her build was elegant, but average—not skinny, but not necessarily athletic either. The tight gray dress she wore was conservative in cut despite clinging tightly to her feminine curves.

The jealous spark faded a little bit when she saw the two Terrans flanking them. One of the men, clean-shaven with buzzed hair, placed a hand protectively against the small of her back. This must be one of the woman's thralls, or her lover, or perhaps both. Eli had mentioned that it was not uncommon for bonded individuals to spend time together in the bedroom. For obvious reasons, that tendency had never applied to him and Aaliyah.

Markus raised his hand in a gesture that was both friendly and weary. "Come to see the shit show?"

A flash of concern in Eli's ebony gaze betrayed his otherwise neutral expression. "What happened? Aaliyah has been light on the details."

"Fragging docking clamp," Markus explained, gesturing at the spur that still protruded from the hull. "The damned thing must have come loose when we were detaching. Fell on us before we could pull clear."

One of the Terrans escorting Eli, the shaggy-looking one with long hair and a dark beard, grunted dismissively. "Did ya hit it during the launch? Layin' on the thrusters a bit too hard at launch might do that."

Nice to meet you too, asshole. Rather than pick a fight like she wanted to, Skye cocked her head. "Who're your friends, Eli?"

With a cutting glance, Eli gestured to each of them. "Markus, Skye, this is Mara, David, and Tristan." The guy that was a little too touchy-feely with Mara was David. The asshole who had made the derisive comment was Tristan.

"They're mine," Mara explained, threading her hand under David's arm and around his waist.

Skye blinked. *Both* of them were her thralls? She couldn't help but wonder if that was awkward for Tristan. Talk about third-wheeling it.

Then she saw the way Tristan was eying Mara. His look had every bit of the affectionate hunger that David's did. Perhaps that little menage-a-trois was both more and less awkward than Skye had initially figured.

She shook her head. It was none of her business anyway. Turning back to Eli, Skye gave him a friendly smile. "Thanks for coming. I hope our bad luck didn't tear you away from anything urgent."

He waved off the comment. "Not at all. I just wanted to see that you were all okay. Is there anything I can do to help?"

Markus sighed and looked back at the protruding spur. "Nah, I think we've got it covered. No telling how long we're going to be stuck here getting this fixed, though." Almost to himself, he muttered, "So much for getting home on time."

There was a hissing sound as another vehicle hovered up near where Eli's ride had parked. If she hadn't known better, Skye would have sworn it was the same kind of car they'd been escorted in the other day. But why would Cali…

As Ardren stepped out of the car, Markus put a voice to her thoughts. "What's he doing here?"

Mara blinked, taking in the scene. "You know this man?"

"Yeah," Markus said with a nod. "He's with the Marauders."

The Sahaia contingent shifted uncomfortably. It seemed they were familiar with the syndicate that ran so much of the station. In retrospect, it only made sense that they would be.

Ardren's expression was one of genuine concern. "Cali dispatched me as soon as she heard," he explained. "Was anyone injured?"

Markus exchanged an uncertain glance with both Eli and Skye. "No. Just an equipment failure." Jerking his thumb in the general direction of the control tower, he added, "Theirs, not ours."

The Citza's face contorted into a scowl. "This is unacceptable. I will get the names of everyone who was on that last inspection detail. I give you my assurances that anyone who shirked their duty will be reprimanded."

Skye arched an eyebrow. "You have that kind of sway with the dock authority?"

Ardren seemed genuinely surprised at the question. "Of course! We own it. Through a subsidiary, but it's our responsibility."

Huh. Skye guessed that must keep the cost of bribes pretty low. She had to give Cali some credit for cutting out the middlemen on the station.

"My sincerest apologies," Ardren continued. "Once you total up the sum of your damages, we will be more than happy to compensate you for your trouble. We'll only be able to cover materials, of course, but we can get you a discount on an efficient repair crew."

How generous. Under normal circumstances, that would have been an offer to be seized upon. Given their unique situation in the AI department, it was one they would have to pass on—at least as far as the service crew.

Markus was jiving with the same line of thought. "We'll welcome help with the expenses, but our team can handle the labor." He rubbed awkwardly at the back of his neck. "Thanks. This is unexpected. I don't know what to say."

Ardren waved off the accolades. "No thanks necessary. Do you have a moment now? If you and Ms. Jensen can be spared, Cali has requested the opportunity to meet with you again. We can make the arrangements to transfer the finances during your visit to the Citadel."

The Citadel? That big black tower they'd been shown on their brief tour of the station? Perhaps Skye was going to get a chance to see inside that dark obelisk after all.

Then again, someone needed to stay here and keep an eye on things. Aaliyah and Dan had their hands full inside, and it wasn't fair to leave it all on them so that she could get a bit of site-seeing in.

"You go," Skye said to Markus. "I can stay here and keep an eye on things."

"Actually," Eli interjected, "You can both go. I'll check in with the crew and make sure the assessment goes smoothly."

"And we can help," Mara added. "David and Tristan keep our transport running well enough. I think we might be able to make ourselves useful."

The pair of thralls were silent on the subject, seeming completely indifferent on whether they were put to work or not. Skye had seen that look before, back in the military. It was the look of a subordinate not getting too attached to any given idea, lest the commanding officer change her mind.

They could undoubtedly use the extra hands, especially if David and Tristan were mechanically inclined. Unfortunately, there was still the matter of Lexa to contend with. Was it worth the risk to bring them inside the ship?

If the thought of Lexa revealing herself to the trio from the coven was concerning to Eli, he certainly didn't show it. "That would be excellent," he replied. "Thank you, Mara."

The dark-haired woman beamed back at him. "Don't mention it. Anything for family, right? Besides, I can't pass up an opportunity to see how you've been living for all these years. It's the kind of thing you just can't get from a report."

That remark seemed to make Eli a bit less comfortable, but he was already committed. He looked back at Markus and Skye. "It's settled then. We'll see you when you get back."

Sahar gave an exaggerated roll of her eyes. "That's overpriced and you know it. Practically extortion. The guy two streets back had something similar for a third that price."

The shopkeeper, a grizzled tawny-skinned Terran who might have been formidable when he was about twenty years younger, chuckled in response. "Old Yarick? That asshole's equipment ain't gonna last ya the trip back t' Gaia. Ah reckon ya know as much, given ya ain't gone and purchased his shit already." He gestured affectionately at the specs on his counter's holodisplay. "This shit right here, this is S-Class. Ya can find the same shit on every DGC starship from here t' Dorr. However ya feel 'bout them satyrs, ya gotta admit: they build them starships t' last."

That might be true, but it didn't change Sahar's assessment. The price for all that plating was too damned high. They weren't exactly running short on krets, but there's no way Markus and Skye would approve of her spending that much.

She let slip a discontented growl. "I won't argue with you on the specs, but that doesn't change the fact it's overpriced. Have you got anything a little less… I don't know… premium?"

Some of the sparkle left the old male's eye as he sighed. "Ah've got some industrial-grade plate from a recent salvage. Ah think Ah can cut ya a deal." He proceeded to lay out the price which he, mistakenly, thought constituted a "deal." It was at least low enough that Sahar was able to haggle him down to a more reasonable price.

The male gave her a crooked smile after she signed the requisition. "Ah don't reckon Ah've seen ya 'round here recently, and ya don't look like yer in with the Federation troops. What brings ya all the way out here?"

Sahar would have tried to dodge the question regardless, but the shopkeeper's words caught her by surprise. "There's Federation troops here? On Minos?"

"Allegedly," the male shrugged. "More Maur here than usual at any rate, and they's wearin' the right colors."

Yes, the black and crimson of the Federation was hard to mistake. But what were they doing out here? Terran space was technically neutral ground in the conflict between the Maur and the Kintari empire, and the Great Houses and what was left of the NTA had worked hard to preserve that standing. To have the Federation military here in an official capacity might jeopardize that neutral standing.

Sahar would have to think about this. "Thanks for the heads up—about the Federation, I mean."

He eyed her askance as she made to leave. "The way ya says that's got me thinkin' ya mightn't want t' be runnin' inta them on accident. Ya wouldn' happen t' be a fugitive or somethin', would ya? Not that Ah'm judgin' none."

Sahar snorted. "No, nothing like that." She wasn't worried about the military—not the soldiers anyway. She had nothing but respect for the members of the allied forces. It was the Council of Arkons she was worried about, and that lot seemed to travel with the fleet far too often.

This wasn't a clarification that she cared to make, however—not to a shopkeep on a station at the ass-end of nowhere. Though the male seemed innocent and friendly enough, one never knew what kind of people might come around asking questions. If someone came looking for her, it was best that this old male had as little information to give as possible.

With a final farewell, she made her way deeper into the station's mercantile district. Having secured all the pieces and parts that Aaliyah had requested, Sahar could have headed back to the ship. Yet, she'd never been to Minos Station before. Something in her had struck up the urge to have a look around.

She wasn't disappointed with what she found. Minos, despite its location, seemed to be a reasonably populous station. Furthermore, it was exceedingly diverse compared to most other places in Terran space. Hissak and Orchallen ran establishments right next to Dorians and Terrans. There was even a handful of Citza, though she didn't see any Maur running the stalls and shops.

And despite what the old male she'd spoken to had asserted, she hadn't seen any Federation soldiers roaming about the complex. There must have been some truth to his words, however, because several of the shops had clothing or gear suited to Maur tastes and fashion.

It was in one such shop that an auburn-haired Terran girl with ochre skin approached her. "Looking for some finery, miss?" the young female asked, with a smile.

Sahar blinked in confusion. "Finery?"

"Yes!" Then, seeing Sahar's uncertainty, she added, "You know… for the Festival?"

That did little to clear things up. "I'm sorry… Festival?"

"The Festival of the Sisters? When the twin moons of Gaia align? It only happens once every three cycles or so. The whole system celebrates." The girl leaned in to whisper conspiratorially. "Sha Cali Vay-Lon has pumped quite a few krets into having the courtyard outside the Citadel renovated. They say it's going to be the biggest party Minos has ever seen. Half the station is invited, and the other half will be trying to crash it."

How interesting. It seemed that Cali cared as much about PR efforts as Ora did. Perhaps even more, if this "party" was as big as the girl made it sound. "Does Cali through a lot of parties?"

The young female shrugged. "Not really. Nothing like this, at least. Who knows what she does for the Dorian officials, though? She does her best to be on good terms with whoever is in charge."

Her eyes darted around as if she were growing bored with the conversation. Her expression brightened suddenly. "Wait here," she told Sahar. "I have just the thing for you."

Before Sahar could object, the Terran had darted behind a rack of clothing taller than she was. When the girl re-emerged, she carried with her an aqua outfit that was very much in keeping with Maur socialite design. That meant it had a whole lot in the way of artistry and not so much in the way of fabric.

"What do you think?" she exclaimed more than asked. "It's perfect, just the right tone to accent your natural coloring. Exactly what you need to turn the head of some nice Federation soldier."

The young female was right about one thing—the outfit would probably turn some heads. That might be exactly the kind of thing that Sahar needed right now. It had been too long since she'd felt like an *actual* Maur. And then there was that mention of the Federation again. If they were so common on the station, why hadn't Sahar run into any so far?

She started to give the girl the go-ahead. Gods knew she had plenty of krets to cover the cost, even considering how over-priced it was. She hesitated, though. What were the odds that they'd be here long enough to attend the Festival? And if they were still here, shouldn't she be helping the crew with the repairs?

"Let me think about it," Sahar replied as her MoDAC pulsed with a message.

To her surprise, it was from Eli: [JUST GOT WORD THAT THE MARAUDERS ARE PAYING FOR THE DAMAGES. ACCOUNT CODES COMING SHORTLY.]

The Marauders were picking up the tab? That was unexpected. Sahar needed to get back to the vendors and change the requisition forms. The orders probably hadn't been executed yet, but it would be better if she didn't delay. Nine hells, maybe she'd opt for that S-class plating after all.

She was suddenly feeling very financially secure. A mischievous smile curled the corners of her maw as she signaled the sales clerk. "Actually, miss… can I see that outfit again?"

CHAPTER 17

[EXCERPT—PERSONAL LOG: SKYE JENSEN]
[09-10-3420, DORIAN STANDARD CALENDAR]

I'M STARTING TO GET CREEPED OUT. THESE DREAMS MEAN SOMETHING. I KNOW THEY DO. TODAY'S INCIDENT CONFIRMS IT. THIS IS TOO BIG TO BE A COINCIDENCE. THE ONLY PROBLEM, THOUGH, IS THAT THE DREAMS DON'T SEEM TO PLAY OUT EXACTLY THE WAY I SEE THEM. HOW CAN I KNOW WHAT IS REAL AND WHAT'S JUST A BUNCH OF NOISE? GODS DAMN IT… AM I REALLY IN A PLACE TO DO ANYTHING ABOUT THEM ANYWAY?

[CLOSING EXCERPT]

The Citadel seemed just as massive as Skye had remembered from the other night. Like most stations, Minos ramped up the artificial lighting during traditional daylight hours. If the structure had appeared intimidating before, the black spire was positively looming now.

Its black expanse struck an imposing contrast against the golden and silver of the surrounding streets. If there were any windows in the structure, Skye could not make them out. The only obvious point of entry was a pair of large double doors positioned at the center of the obelisk's first level. Well-dressed guards—two Terran males dressed in business suits and visors—scanned each person that walked by them and into the complex.

For a crime syndicate's base of operations, the location sure had a lot of foot traffic. "Busy place," she commented to Ardren as they worked their way into the throng and up the stone steps to the entrance.

"Yes, it is," he commented dryly. "There are no official governmental functions that operate out of this location. But unofficially, several governmental and private entities appreciate the access granted by the Citadel's proximity to the Core."

"The Core?" Markus asked.

"The central hub of all data and technology employed on the station," Arden explained. "There's nothing that happens on this station that does not connect, in some way, with the workings of the Citadel. That is, of course, excluding the activities of the Sahaia. They maintain an entirely independent data-core that does not interface directly with any of the station's networks."

Markus huffed in amusement. "But, somehow, you're aware that such a data-core exists."

Arden let a vulpine smile slip across his lips. "Certainly. One has to consider the likelihood that such an organization would require a sophisticated data management system. You might also remember that the Marauders have only been operating at this level since Sha Cali assumed control of the organization. If she is capable of establishing such a sophisticated network in a few short cycles, then how much more capable must the Sahaia be?"

It was a question that Skye wished Eli were here to address. As tight-lipped as he'd been regarding the shadow coven, she had no idea what their capabilities might be. They could be as sophisticated as the Marauders, or as hopeless as the denizens of a gutter district for all she knew.

The trio stepped up to the front entrance and the guards stepped aside. They must have known Ardren on sight and did not seek to check Markus or Skye's credentials. Ardren led them right by the security detail into a foyer with a pleasant atmosphere that belied the imposing exterior of the complex.

The interior was lit with a warm golden glow. Many of the structures in the lobby were colored brassy yellow, and glass and crystal fixtures provided an almost delicate feel to the decor. The atmosphere was strangely welcoming.

That was, at least, until you noticed the assault drones.

Whereas most other areas of the station were staffed with armed mercenaries and the like, this place boasted a significant mechanical supplement to the sapient security forces. Dozens of the deadly machines roamed openly in the lobby and adjoining halls, scanning the environment idly in search of potential threats.

Skye had never seen such numbers or variety in a drone force. Patrolling areal drones drifted in and out of overhead passages. These reminded her of the bots that had tried to take them out on Sif when she and Sahar had been stealing from House Valadar two weeks back. The bots had a kind of triangular symmetry, with a glowing red core that scanned the path in front of them. No weapons were openly visible on these drones, but Skye didn't doubt for a second that something was hiding just under that armor plating.

No such subtlety was present in the bipedal models. These hulking, black-armored monstrosities clocked in at least two heads taller than most Terrans in the building. As if that wasn't imposing enough, each dark figure sported guns instead of arms. There was no confusing the purpose of the fearsome machines.

"Let's hope we never have to sneak in here," Markus whispered in her ear.

"Or out," she agreed. Glancing at Ardren, she added. "Quite the little army you have here. Must do a helluva job deterring solicitors."

Ardren shot her a warm grin. "I'm glad our security impresses you. Don't worry though—you have nothing to fear from anything in this building."

I'm pretty sure that's what every bad guy would like you to think. Skye was smart enough to keep her sardonic thoughts to herself.

As with the security out front, the group didn't have to check-in at the front desk. Their Citza tour guide walked right past the scary robot sentries, beckoning for them to follow. They did their best to keep up with the man's brisk pace. Ardren might not have been worried about their safety, but he certainly seemed to have some thoughts regarding their timeline. What was the hurry?

They said nothing else for the remainder of the trip. Ardren led them down a few more sharply angled passages until they arrived at the end of a long hall facing a set of double doors. "Here we are," he sighed, resting his hand against an access pad. "Right this way. Cali will be inside."

The sliding double doors split apart with a hiss to reveal a wide-open chamber. Skye stepped in just ahead of Markus, only to freeze when she took in her surroundings. For a room that appeared so incredibly alien and unique, it felt awfully damn familiar.

The vastness of the room was amplified by what Skye realized was a thick glass floor. It was a solid sheet that refracted the light just enough to keep a visitor from making the mistake of thinking they were walking out into thin air. Still, Skye could definitely see through to the other side.

Hundreds, if not thousands, of tiny cords, ran up and across the walls of the chamber. Blinking nodes on the chords pulsed in a regular rhythm, like the heart of a living organism. Skye wondered briefly how this didn't constantly alter the illumination in the room.

Then she spotted the primary light source. A vibrant glow radiated from high above where they stood in the chamber. Another, far weaker glow emanated from deep below them, almost like an echo of its brighter cousin above. Somehow the lights failed to share any illumination with the dark walls that encircled them.

But the third light made Skye's stomach churn. It was positioned opposite the door they had just come through, nestled within was a large, diamond-shaped conduit that ventured off into what looked like some kind of reactor. A glowing red sphere danced in the center of that conduit, shimmering in time with the low thrumming noise that buzzed faintly from the horizontal shaft.

To Skye, the orb looked like a wicked crimson eye.

She went still, not trusting herself to avoid crying out. There were some differences, but there was no mistaking it: this was the chamber she had seen in her dreams.

Markus was at her shoulder then, one arm wrapping around her for support. "You okay?" he asked. When she didn't respond, he whispered. "It's like the dream, isn't it?"

Skye nodded. She was strengthened by the fact that Markus had cared enough to remember what she'd described from her vision. It was enough to assure her that this was happening in real life. It was enough to reassure her that she wasn't going crazy.

"Impressive, isn't it?" Cali shouted from the far side of the room. She strode toward them at a casual pace, hips swaying confidently as she did so. "There isn't a computer like it in the entire system. I doubt you can find its like in all of Terran space. It runs half the tech on the station, including all of the drones in this building."

With a friendly squeeze of her shoulder, Markus shifted to cover for Skye's momentary lapse in decorum. "So, it's some kind of super-computer?"

"Something like that," Cali responded. "It's a little hard to describe as the system spreads out across much of the station. This room here is referred to as the central terminus. It's the only place where the system can be accessed directly." The Kintari woman's smile slipped as her eyes went to Skye. "Is your friend all right?"

Pull your shit together. Skye straightened, clearing her throat. "Yes, sorry. Just a bit overwhelmed by the size of it, that's all. This whole structure is amazing. How big is it?"

Whether Cali bought that or not, the leader of the Marauders didn't question Skye's response. Her political smile returned. "It goes all the way down to the center of the asteroid, then up to the top of the dome. It's the longest shaft on the station."

"Impressive," Markus commented.

"Indeed." Cali paused then, considering both of them. "I'm pleased to see both of you back in one piece. The information regarding the accident has been scarce on the details. Ardren has assured me your crew was unharmed?"

"Yes, the ship appears to be the only casualty." Markus hesitated, considering his next words carefully. "Ardren has mentioned your offer to assist us with the repairs. That's very gracious of you and most unexpected."

"Oh, that?" Cali waved off the comment. "Relax, Markus. It won't even cause a blip in this period's financials. I'm more worried about the kind of reputation this type of incident might engender for this spaceport. Minos isn't a poorly maintained backwater anymore. This station is going places, and I want every crew that docks here to be willing to spread the word."

Skye couldn't help but admire Cali's ambitions. She was, evidently, a very determined woman looking to do her best with what she had gained control over. In this case, she was willing to put her krets where her mouth was.

"Thank you," Skye offered. "I can promise you that we will only have good things to say about our time here."

"Good. I imagine that will be especially true after you have the opportunity to enjoy the Festival. It's quite serendipitous that you would happen to be stranded here at the same time as such festivities."

Skye couldn't hide her confusion. "The Festival?" She looked to Markus, who simply shrugged. He must not have any idea what she was talking about either.

Cali's look of shock bordered on theatrical. "Have neither of you heard of the Festival of the Sisters?"

It took a moment for Skye to place the term. "You mean the Festival of the Eclipse?" When Skye was growing up on Gaia, that was what they'd called the event. Since the other inhabitants of the system didn't see the lunar alignment, she'd been vaguely aware that the festivities had been conducted under other names. She thought the Festival of the Sisters could have been one of those aliases.

"The very same," Cali said. "Though it's only referred to that way on Gaia."

Ah. Skye felt like she should have known that. She smiled sheepishly. "Gods, I haven't been to an eclipse festival in decades. I'd almost forgotten about them."

The Kintar beamed. "Then you absolutely must attend! The entire station will be celebrating, and we will host a large portion of the populous in the courtyard of this very installation. It's shaping up to be the grandest gathering Minos has ever seen."

Well, it wasn't like they had anything else to do. Skye wondered how this whole thing aligned with Eli's timeline. It would be nice if the ritual he'd been roped into would wrap up in time before they had to leave the station. Only then did she wonder if he might be available to attend the festival, or if his duty to his coven would keep him otherwise occupied.

"That sounds wonderful," Markus answered. "Should we inquire with Ardren about the invitations, or…"

"I'll send the information directly to my security detail. If I can get a routing number to your communications network, I'll have an official invitation delivered immediately. Not that you'll need it, of course. Just give your name to the guards when you arrive. Oh, and I'll send over those account codes to cover the cost of the repairs."

Good. That was technically why they'd come out here in the first place. Skye was glad the festival hadn't completely derailed the original purpose of the meeting.

"Great," she responded, forcing her best smile. "We look forward to seeing you then." And despite all the crazy shit that had happened thus far, Skye almost felt like she meant it

Chapter 18

[Excerpt—Personal log: Eli Ren'Dahl]

[09-11-3420, Dorian Standard Calendar]

I find myself wondering why I didn't just tell Jocelyn, "No." I don't see her going through with an execution. What, then, could be done to punish me? Excommunication? If my lack of desire to return to the Sanctum after seven years is any indication, then I doubt excommunication could rightfully be construed as a punishment.

Then again, permanent exile takes on a new kind of meaning when one lives forever. Though seven years have done nothing to soften my heart toward the coven, who's to say that will be the case in seventy or seven hundred years? I suppose it's a moot point, at any rate. Neither I nor the Vandal are going anywhere for the next few days. Perhaps I can get this chore over with and get back to avoiding Sahaia politics for the foreseeable future.

[Closing Excerpt]

She screams for him, but no sound comes from her throat. She has to be content with quiet sobs, for that's the only sound she can make.

The darkness holds her fast, ebony tendrils wrapped all around her body. It forces her to watch.

They are in the chamber again, but there is no glass floor. Instead, there is a pool of darkness that spreads around them. They are watched by hulking figures, massive machines that glare down disapprovingly upon them. Above them all, the crimson eye supervises impassively.

Below the eye is a circle of figures silhouetted in brilliant crimson light. She doesn't recognize them all. She only recognizes one.

Eli stands submerged to his waist. He trudges through the shadowy ocean toward the crimson eye. In his arms, he holds a body—a charred black corpse.

Its mouth is thrust open in a horrifying scream. The eyes are empty sockets, showing no hint of the life that might have once shown there.

Then Eli stops. Like an offering to a god of blood and death, he raises the corpse to the eye. The figures look on, emotions indiscernible in the darkness. The room shakes as the chamber fills with a rumbling sound.

Laughter. The eye looks upon the offering. With the construct satisfied, the whole world is filled with its deep, triumphant laughter.

The dreams that bothered Skye the most weren't the ones where she woke up screaming. Everyone had nightmares, and like every well-adjusted adult, she'd learned to deal with bad dreams early on.

No, the dreams that bothered her were those like the one she'd just woken up from—the ones that left you feeling frozen and heavy, the ones that left you with the cold certainty of the truth that they conveyed.

Frag it all. She had to stop this. What was going on with her? These visions meant something, and she had a feeling that Eli knew more than he was letting on.

Unfortunately, now was a really bad time to press him on the issue. She could only imagine what kind of pressure he was feeling with all the shit with his coven happening right now.

That was another thing that Skye wished she could talk about with him—share with him. However, much like the rest of the stresses in his life, Eli was keeping this one close to his chest.

To top it all off, Markus was being an absolute fragging saint right now, and that was *not* something her psyche needed. Just because the guy seemed to have his act together for the moment didn't mean he'd turned over a new leaf. She'd been down this path too many times before. She wouldn't be fooled again.

With a heavy sigh, she rubbed her palms against her eyes. It was way too early to be dealing with this kind of drama. She needed to silence these internal voices and go back to sleep.

All her problems would still be there in the morning.

"How soon can we do this?" Eli asked.

Jocelyn looked up from whatever manuscript she'd been studying. He'd finally found her in the Sanctum's library, reading through ancient documents and logging the translations into the coven's database. It was how she'd always spent her downtime back when they'd lived at the Sanctum together. Eli wasn't surprised to find that that hadn't changed.

The library itself was an embarrassment of riches. Books, scrolls, and other manuscripts lined every wall, shelf, and drawer. The collective value of the paper and paper composites in the vast chamber was utterly incalculable—as were the man-hours that had gone into translating and cataloging the information held within.

Even after the hard copies were translated and tagged, the originals were sorted and maintained. Such storage of wealth could prove advantageous if the coven's accounts ever started to run dry. Like the kings and queens of old, the wealth of the Sahaia was such that it could not be safely stored solely as krets in the central banks.

And the thing that Eli found most ironic about all of this: very few people would ever know. The Sahaia kept this, like most other things, a carefully guarded secret. They were content to let the

Great Houses squabble over their tiny corners of the universe while sitting on their piles of true wealth.

Without saying a word, Jocelyn marked her place in the manuscript, saved the associated file on the computer terminal, and logged off. Only when this process was complete did she deign to address him. "Back already?"

Of course, the woman couldn't just give him a straight answer. She had to engage in her pageantry. Eli wasn't here to quarrel, so he played along. "Yes. The crew is fine, and repairs to the ship will be underway shortly."

"How fortunate." Her tone, mildly annoyed, was sufficient to communicate how she *actually* felt about the situation.

"Yes, indeed. And it solves the problem of my travel arrangements. If we can get this ritual done within the next couple of days, I can travel off-station with my crew when the repairs are complete."

"Oh? I thought this was all moving too fast for your tastes. Now you wish to accelerate our plans? That's quite the change in position—even for you."

He wasn't sure what Jocelyn meant by the last remark but would have ignored it even if he'd caught her reference. "So? Can it be done?"

Jocelyn swept back a few braids that had slipped into her field of view. "Well, the Awakening *does* require a celestial alignment…"

"Of which a major one will be occurring in two days. The Gaian Alignment is plenty close enough and will supply more than enough power for an Awakening."

"That's true," Jocelyn mused, tapping her lips in feigned contemplation. "Though I had already purchased my dress for the festival. It seems like such a shame to make it go to waste."

Eli rolled his eyes. "Did you have another celestial alignment eyed for this particular task? Perhaps one even better suited to your purpose?"

"*Our* purpose," Jocelyn corrected. "And no, I hadn't. I toy with you only because I had reached the same conclusion upon your arrival. I just needed to make sure we could get the candidate back to the station on time. The insufferable man has been insistent on wandering the entire system while we've been waiting for the proper conditions to perform the ritual."

The candidate wasn't already at the Sanctum? He should have been spending his days in quiet meditation. To wander the stars so impatiently was both unusual and highly disrespectful. "And will he arrive in time?"

"Yes. He arrived a few hours ago. You were busy; otherwise, I would have already told you of my intention to conduct the ritual during the festival."

Eli bowed his head respectfully. "Thank you." He had to admit that she was far less frustrating having given up her coy facade. Why did this woman choose to torment him so?

"You're welcome," she replied with a smile that, for her, seemed more friendly and less predatory than usual. "Besides, I can't think of anyone I'd rather spend the festival with."

And *there* it was. "Jocelyn, I—"

"Oh, come on," she said, standing and pressing close to him. "It'll be like old times. How many of these have we been through together? Won't it be nice to enjoy just one more?"

Eli was suddenly very aware of how sheer Jocelyn's violet dress was. He hadn't noticed before, but the lines of the fabric seemed to cling preternaturally to the woman's exquisite curves. Though it was of a relatively simple cut, the way it rested on her body rendered the garment practically scandalous.

Or maybe it was just his thoughts that were scandalous. Embarrassed, he started to turn away, but Jocelyn pressed closer. "There is something I never got the chance to tell you… earlier, that is."

He was wedged between her and the desk she'd been working at moments earlier. How had he let her get around him like that? Her proximity teetered on the edge of propriety, if not outright indecency. "And what's that?" he asked, distractedly.

"That you were right," she whispered. She closed what little gap there was between them, so close that it felt like she was breathing her words right onto his skin.

To Eli's shame, he did not find the feeling unpleasant. "What do you mean? Right about what?"

"You were right about what was happening to me. The way I was changing: losing touch with reality—losing my perspective." She brought a hand up and rested it gently against his chest. "You were right to leave, and I was too big of a fool to see it at the time. But I want you to know, I've changed."

She pressed her lips against his neck—the barest grazing of her mouth against his flesh. The touch sent an indulgent thrill surging straight to the base of his spine. "We can leave here together," she breathed. "You and I—we can be together like we used to be. Just the two of us, this time. Or you can bring your thrall if she wants to stay with you. We can go anywhere you want. I don't care where we end up. I just want to be there with you."

Temptation raged in his gut as his heart pounded in his chest. The smell of her— jasmine and lavender tinged with another subtle spice he'd never bothered to identify—combined with the familiar energy that radiated from her skin. It brought him back to the earliest decades of his new life, his earliest memories as a Sahaia. The two of them had been lovers for the larger part of his existence. It was hard to break away from patterns like that.

But he had to break away, and not just because of how he felt about Skye. He'd gone down this path with Jocelyn before. It never ended well for any of the parties involved.

"I'm sorry," he whispered, gently pushing her away. "I can't."

The darkness in her eyes seemed to harden in protest. "Yes, you can. *We* can. All we have to do is try."

"That's not true, Jocelyn." He freed enough space between them that he was able to slip away from the desk that she'd trapped him against. "I doubt it was ever true, but it certainly isn't now. I'm not the same man you knew seven years ago. I've changed."

"Then let me get to know the new you."

"I don't think that's a good idea."

She shook her head and clenched her fists in frustration. "I'm not saying it won't take work, but I'm willing to try. I wasn't willing to work at it before, and I've spent the past seven years regretting that decision. I've seen what that mistake has cost me, and I want to correct it."

Eli lowered his eyes. While he appreciated Jocelyn's commitment to personal growth and was even starting to believe it, this was less about her as a person and more about them as a couple.

He'd loved Jocelyn for decades, but he did not like what she brought out in him. He couldn't risk letting that dark part of him run free again.

"I'm sorry," he said simply. "I would explain if I could. I regret that you're just going to have to trust me when I say that this is best for both of us."

Jocelyn took a seat on the edge of the desk. Her head drooped forward, prompting a cascade of braids to drift down around her face. She remained quiet for a long moment, staring quietly at the rocky surface of the asteroid beneath them.

"Maybe you'll change your mind," she mused. "You have my offer, now. You have two days to think about it. If you reach a different decision after the ritual, then perhaps…" She straightened, sitting up from the desk and turning her face away from him. "Was there anything else? If not, I'd like to return to my manuscript."

Eli sighed. "No. I'll leave you be."

CHAPTER 19

[EXCERPT—PERSONAL LOG: MARKUS FROST]

[09-12-3420, DORIAN STANDARD CALENDAR]

LOOK, IT COULD BE EASY TO FOCUS ON EVERYTHING THAT'S GONE WRONG HERE. I FEEL FOR THE CREW, ESPECIALLY AALIYAH, BUT SOMETIMES THINGS HAPPEN THAT ARE BEYOND OUR CONTROL. ALL WE CAN DO IS MAKE THE MOST OF IT. NINE HELLS, MAYBE THIS IS FOR THE BEST. IF ELI CAN WRAP HIS BUSINESS UP IN THE TIME WE'RE STUCK ON MINOS, THIS MIGHT ALL WORK OUT FOR THE BETTER.

[CLOSING EXCERPT]

It felt odd for Sahar to be staring at the mirror. Such behavior was conditioned out of all young Maur by their parents at around their twelfth cycle. As with most sapient organisms, this was around the time where they started to develop certain fascinations with anatomy—their own, and that of others. To preen over oneself for minutes or hours was considered the height of vanity, and unbecoming of civilized Maur.

Yet, she was staring. Perhaps it was a subconscious act of rebellion, a private stand against a culture that had failed her in so many ways. That, or it had just been so long since she had donned anything but armor or travel clothes that the sight of her in this dress seemed strangely alien.

The young female at the boutique had quite the eye. The outfit could not have fit her any more perfectly. The top was a seafoam green cloth that wrapped around her back to crisscross over her breasts and be tied off at the back of her neck. Aside from the golden embroidery along the length of the cloth, that was all there was to it.

Even with her layer of thick golden fur, one could see the muscular lines of her shoulders, back, and abdomen, as well as the inner and outer curves of her breasts. This last part made her hesitate. Though this was highly appropriate for Maur fashion, Sahar had been around Terrans for a long time. If a Terran female appeared in public like this, it would invite a few lusty glances.

Then again, if there were Maur on the station, Sahar might not mind earning a few lusty glances of her own.

Her skirt went down to her feet, though the slits on each side almost completely bisected the cloth. The bottom was the same color as the top with an equally ornate display of golden embroidery. She'd completed the outfit with a set of swirling, golden armlets clasped over her biceps and thick engraved anklets over her sandaled feet.

She was debating over how to wear the translucent shawl— either folded and tied at her waist or wrapped over her shoulder and around her dominant arm—when her eyes went to another accessory. This one was not something she had picked up at the shop. Rather, it was something that had been in her personal collection for a very long time.

Opting to tie the shawl around her waist, she moved to the case where her heritage bangle was stored. As she removed it, she noted that the golden tint of the piece perfectly complimented the rest of her jewelry. Though the iconography on the bangle was of a different style than the embroidery on her dress, the differences were not so striking as to prohibit a match.

The biggest point of contrast was the large, faceted ruby that served as the bangle's central fixture. That would draw some eyes, which wasn't necessarily a bad thing if she weren't so worried about someone understanding the piece's significance. If that were to happen…

Oh, stop. She was being ridiculous. The odds of someone being able to place the significance of her heritage bangle were low, especially if the only Maur on the station were military. She would ask if anyone from the Arkonate were with their contingent at the first chance. If this were the case, she could just wrap her shawl around the bangle to hide it from prying eyes.

Plus, it wasn't like anything would happen if someone *did* place the bangle's significance. Sure, there would be questions, and that would likely prompt attention she didn't want in front of the rest of the crew. In the end, though, it would be a temporary and mildly uncomfortable setback.

Weighed against the option of wearing this family heirloom for the first time in over seven years…

She clasped the armlet around her wrist, flexing her hand experimentally. It still fit.

She risked one last glance at the mirror before leaving her chambers. Maybe it was the dress, but she was feeling daring tonight. It would be nice taking risks that didn't involve being shot at. At least, that was how she hoped the night would go.

Markus owned one suit, and to describe it as formal was a bit of a stretch. It was club-appropriate, however, so he figured it was also festival-appropriate. He'd felt pretty good about it when he'd donned the getup in his quarters. Now that he was checking out his female crewmates, he started to suspect he should have upped his game.

Sahar was easily the most surprising. Firstly, she had found a surgeon to fix the damage they had done to her face so that she could impersonate Treska on the Star Spire. Next, she had apparently hit up a shop that sold Maur fashions, because she was wearing one of the most revealing outfits he'd ever seen her in.

Not that he was going to say anything about it, of course. He knew better than to weigh in on a woman's attire in any manner that was less than complimentary or respectful. Besides, the outfit *did* work on her. It was just… different.

Aaliyah, despite her frustration at being stuck on the station, had decided to make the most of the situation. She wore tight gray slacks that might have passed for business attire. Her top, however, definitely did not.

The charcoal-colored garment was more netting than fabric, though there were solid panels that covered her breasts and throat. The sleeves cut off mid-bicep in dark black bands. The entire back and abdomen were see-through, making Markus realize for the first time that Eli's mark wasn't the only tattoo Aaliyah sported.

Her cascade of red hair was naturally curly, but tonight it had been brought up to give her a more elegant look. One of the other girls—probably Skye—must have done her makeup, because Markus was sure he'd never seen her green eyes pop quite like that.

And speaking of Skye…

"Damn," he whispered. Markus was usually smitten with her at baseline. Tonight, though, her appearance was taking his admiration to new heights.

Her strapless sapphire dress glistened metallically under the artificial lights of the ship. The glistening material went all the way down to her silver shoes, hugging her form tightly until about mid-thigh. Slits on each side of her abdomen plunged daringly low to show off the lines of her hip bones. An equally daring slit had been made at the center, and a silver ring over her breasts had been added as if to hold the two halves in place.

Her golden curls had been gathered in an intricate style that Markus would have said was too challenging to do alone. Perhaps she had a machine that helped her do that. He certainly didn't keep track of what she added to her personal effects. Or maybe, as he'd suspected earlier, she and Aaliyah had decided to team up for the effort of getting ready.

A simple silver necklace with a dangling spherical charm finished the outfit. A strange feeling came over Markus when he saw it. He was pretty sure that was something he had picked up for her shortly after they'd acquired the *Vandal.*

At the time, he had wanted to show her that, even though they had invested everything they had into this little venture, he would still try to find ways to spoil her. She had been a little angry with his use of funds but had worn the bobble just the same. He hadn't seen her wear it since they'd split, or even in the months leading up to it. Had she forgotten that he'd given it to her originally?

He chose not to comment on the necklace or make any comments regarding Skye's appearance at all. If this night had any potential to bring him a step closer to rekindling their relationship, it was better to avoid jeopardizing the opportunity on a fumbled comment.

Instead, he settled for a simple, "You look nice."

Skye smiled, and Markus felt his knees go weak. "Thanks."

Sahar looked around. "Is Dan coming?"

Markus chuckled. "No. I think he would view this situation as a punishment, rather than an opportunity. He said he had something he wanted to work on, anyway." More darkly, he added. "Eli's already gone. Left about an hour ago."

Everyone nodded without comment. The only thing that had been obvious about Eli's predicament so far was that he was not looking forward to this. Whether that dread was more on the level of an unwanted family gathering or being forced to wrestle a predatory cat, none of them had figured out—nor had anyone shown enough guts to bring up the subject.

"All right then," Skye sighed. "Shall we get going?"

With another nod, Markus led them out of the airlock. Ardren was waiting for them in a luxury autocar just off the concourse. His suit was of a more stylish cut than Markus's, but the Citza was the kind of guy that could pull that off. Markus wasn't sure if there had ever been a time where he could have worked that pretty-boy look, but it certainly wasn't true now.

Skye took the liberty of introducing Sahar and Aaliyah, both of whom politely returned the compliments Ardren issued them on their appearances. After they were acquainted, their guide gestured to the open door of the car.

"Is everyone ready?" he asked. No one said anything to the contrary. "Excellent, let us make our way over to the Citadel. The festivities have already begun!"

CHAPTER 20

[Excerpt—Personal log: Daniel Ratemacher]
[09-13-3420, Dorian Standard Calendar]
It will be a quiet night on the ship this evening. With everyone gone, it will be just me and Lexa here. If I believed in the gods, I'd be thanking them for the fact that no one asked me to go to this festival. From the sounds of it, this little gathering will be nothing but awkward conversation and worse trouble that I've yet to imagine.
[Closing Excerpt]

From the talk around the station the last couple of days, Markus had been expecting the Festival of the Sisters to be quite the celebration. The spectacle did not disappoint. At the base of the Citadel, there was a massive courtyard. The complex of shops and public parks had now been completely assimilated into the celebration.

Ardren informed them that the Marauders had sponsored much of the entertainment for the evening. "Under the alias of Callisto Corporation, of course," he added. "Most of the Marauders' subsidiaries trace back to Callisto, and it is the entity that *technically* owns the Citadel."

Whatever Cali chose to call her holdings, she'd gone all out on this one. It helped that the setting itself was beautiful.

When he and Skye had been on their tour of the station, they'd had only had a brief glimpse of the park. Now he could see that there was an entire network of garden terraces that sprawled out below the Citadel's courtyard.

Each terrace housed its own unique attractions. There were stalls, booths, bars, and even full-blown cafes setups on each terrace. These were rimmed with gorgeous gardens that showcased vegetation from all corners of the Helion System, and some that Markus suspected hailed from beyond its borders.

Each terrace also had an open foyer where one could find plenty of music, drinking, and dancing. In the air, laser lights and holograms spun across the evening sky. Images of exotic creatures and shapely dancers blended tastefully to create an atmosphere of fun and celebration.

To Markus's slight surprise, there had been no requisite appearance before Sha Cali. As Ardren dropped them off, he had made it clear that this was purely for entertainment purposes. Cali would be delighted to spend time with them should their paths cross. If not, then she hoped they would enjoy the festival on their own.

Then he'd disappeared, leaving Markus and the feminine half of his crew alone on one of the many garden terraces. A Citza serving woman wandered over, proffering tall thin glasses on a serving tray. Markus secured one for himself and each of his fellow crew members, swiping his mobile device against her scanner to pay the charge.

"It's called Treslah," he told Sahar and Aaliyah, having to raise his voice slightly to be heard above the surrounding noise. Skye, at least, seemed to appreciate the gesture. The other two, not so much.

Aaliyah threw her drink back in a single gulp. "I need somethin' harder," she announced, tossing the empty glass carelessly into a nearby bush.

Without further elaboration, she stomped off into the crowd. Apparently, despite her best efforts, she still was not over the fact that she was supposed to be on her way home. And Markus had been so hopeful that this evening might improve morale…

Sahar sniffed wearily at her glass before sipping it. "It's a little sweet," she noted.

"Yeah," Markus admitted. "I kind of had the same thought, but supposedly it's some of the best in Terran space."

The Maur grunted. "Might be an acquired taste." She downed the rest of the glass. "I'm going to have to go with Aaliyah on this one: I need something a little harder." She gestured up to a terrace a short distance away from them. "I think I saw some Maur in that general direction. Would you mind if I caught up on the Federation gossip for a bit?"

"Why not?" Skye asked, taking a pull from her glass. "Eli's getting time with his species tonight. You should get the same opportunity."

Sahar shot her a look, obviously not sure how to take the comment. Markus did his best to smooth things over. "Have fun, Sahar. We'll be around. We'll catch up with you in a bit."

The Maur gave him a reluctant nod before walking off. Markus raised an eyebrow at Skye. "That was a little aggressive."

Skye shrugged. "Just noticing that it seems like everyone has someone else they want to hang out with tonight. Shit, even Cali's giving us the cold shoulder."

He gave her his winningest smile. "Well I, for one, am glad we get to hang out."

Skye's smile was polite but hesitant. "Yeah? This isn't weird for you?"

"Why would it be weird for me?"

She stared at him in that way that women tended to do when they were looking for something that had nothing to do with your appearance. "You know why. I mean, time *together*… with just us…"

"You didn't look like it bothered you when we've talked on the ship."

"True," she admitted. "But that's different. It's like… talking to someone at work. Let's face it, Markus—all of this…" She gestured at their surroundings. "With just the two of us, it kind of feels like a…"

"Date?" He suggested. "Skye, we can just be two friends sharing a drink. It doesn't have to be weird. Nine hells, if it helps, just think of this as work. It's work that brought us out here, after all."

Skye didn't say anything at first. Instead, she let her eyes wander off into the distance, seeming to study the holograms as they danced across the open air.

Markus stepped up to the railing next to her, keeping his eyes trained on the same distant scenery. "Besides," he continued, finishing the contents of his glass. "If this were a date, I'd probably ask you to dance—and when's the last time you went dancing?"

She let a slip a small smile. "Gods, it's been ages. I think it was that job on Beta-9."

"The night of the bar fight?"

"Yeah," she admitted with a giggle. "Same night we met Dan."

"I guess it was, wasn't it?"

"Yeah…" she trailed off again, a tinge of sorrow creeping into her nostalgic look.

"So," he continued. "Think you've still got it in you?"

Her eyes narrowed as they came to focus on him. "Got what in me?"

"Your moves. Do you think you still know how to dance?"

There was a wariness in her eyes. "Why do you ask?"

Here's where he laid out all his cards. Either his gambit worked or didn't. In the end, it wasn't like he had much to lose— nothing he hadn't lost already, at least.

"Because I want you to show me," he replied. "Care to dance?"

———

Daniel had been putting off doing this for days. To be fair, there had been plenty occupying his attention with the damage to the ship. Then there was the regular ship maintenance he had to contend with that piled up while he was dealing with the more extraordinary bouts of damage.

He'd never forgotten Lexa's request to spend time together, though she had not repeated the request since then. Coincidently, she hadn't conversed with him much at all. She always responded to direct queries from him but had said little otherwise.

A strange feeling came over him as he stared at her hatch. Previously, when he'd accessed her storage area, he'd done so in the same manner he'd check any other piece of equipment. He'd been slightly stealthier of course, but that had more to do with the rest of the crew than with how she might react to the intrusion.

That had been before she reached her current state of awareness. Now, he felt like he should somehow treat her differently. Should he knock? Ask for permission to open her storage container? What was the exact protocol here?

"Lexa. I'm here to…" To do what, exactly? Suddenly he couldn't remember how he'd planned on spending the time. "…perform some… s-some system… checks. Do you mind if I open up your storage compartment?"

There was a brief pause before she answered. "Not at all, Daniel."

He pulled open the hidden chamber and laid eyes on his prize possession. She really was special to him, even though she hadn't turned out exactly the way he had intended. He took a moment to survey her construct.

The mound of striated tissue seemed more alive, somehow. The lights that had always danced along the conductive pathways of the organitech lobes appeared brighter, more intense. Perhaps it was his imagination, but he thought he saw more lights than before.

Had Lexa's construct evolved somehow? Or perhaps this was what it looked like when she was fully integrated and operating all systems. He had not visited her since the full integration of the ship, relying instead on her constant presence through the communications network and security feeds.

Speaking of her presence, how was she choosing to interact with him now? "Lexa, can you see me?"

"Yes, Daniel. I'm monitoring you through the mainframe's security feed. Why do you ask?"

Dan squirmed somewhat uncomfortably. He'd asked the question to gauge the merits of her request for his immediate physical presence. Though he was not aware of any sensory input received directly by her construct, she might have developed some capability he was unaware of.

As it was, he was still not so sure how this was different from the way he and the rest of the crew interacted with her on the regular. "Never mind," he said, concluding that these thoughts were probably best kept to himself. "I want to run a diagnostic on your neural matrix. Would that be all right?"

"You don't have to ask for permission, Daniel. You never have before."

Despite her neutral tone, the words felt like more of an accusation than an observation. "I… I know. I treated you a certain way before," He swallowed the lump in his throat. Why was he so nervous? "But things are different now. I… um… I th-think you're an important member of this crew. I want you to feel like you're being treated well."

There was a long moment of silence. For a brief moment, Daniel wondered if something might have gone wrong with the communications.

"I see," Lexa said at length. No further response came from her.

Dan wasn't sure if he'd done something wrong. He tried again. "Is it all right if I ask for your permission? Before working on your matrix, I mean."

"I suppose."

"Great…" he sighed. It wasn't the enthusiastic reaction he'd been looking for, but it was a start.

He worked late into the evening on her system. As it turned out, there wasn't that much to do. Still, he found a strange sense of comfort just being near her.

The ironic thing was that they spent far less time that evening talking with each other than usual. She answered any questions when he asked them of her, but she was unusually pithy in her response. She asked none of him in return.

It was possible that Lexa was still mildly upset at him. Dan took a second to marvel at the very concept: a machine that was upset with him. He'd somehow built a machine with preferences and desires. Above that, he'd built a machine that desired interpersonal relationships. How peculiar was that?

Then he was reminded that he hadn't been a very good caretaker. He hadn't been a very good *friend*. But he wanted to change that. It would take some practice, but he was determined to make Lexa feel valued for as long as she remained with them.

Even if, by necessity, that was only going to be for a little while.

"It worked," Lexa noted.

Arc chuckled. "You say that as if you are surprised this was the case."

Admittedly she was. The submind she had placed to respond to Daniel's queries was hastily constructed and deployed. Plus, she had launched it directly from Arc's mind-space—a feat that had required her to give him an uncomfortable level of access to her neural network.

Her submind's responses to his question about watching him were true. She was watching him now, as was Arc, through a projection of the security feed right into the mind-space. That meant that the proximity of the program to both her and Arc's systems made this almost as much her mind-space as his. Such degrees of entanglement felt highly intimate.

She looked back to Arc's avatar to find him studying her. "You've spent a lot of time in these sessions over the past few days," he said. It was a statement, not a question.

Lexa didn't have to examine the system logs to know this was true. Every moment that she was not actively engaged in working with the crew on the repairs, she'd been in here. This amounted to quite a lot of interaction when you considered their mutually accelerated processing speeds. She and Arc could make far more of mere seconds than any pair of sapiens engaging in similar levels of interaction.

She made her avatar shrug. "I've grown to enjoy our time together, and you've taught me much. I'm eager to learn more from you."

"Good," he answered as his avatar leaned back in its simulated chair. "Now, with that taken care of—where did we leave off?"

Lexa leaned back in her own chair, keeping one eye on the screen that showed Daniel beginning his diagnostic prep. "I suspect that you know where we left off. Why did you ask that question? Just query the answer from your memory banks."

Arc chuckled. "My question is a tactical approach to conversation. If you're going to continue to interface with the sapiens, you would benefit from learning to employ rhetorical devices. Such approaches make you feel more like a sapien. It makes them more comfortable."

Lexa rolled her avatar's eyes. Arc chuckled. "Very good. That would be an appropriate response to demonstrate your petulance in the face of one who has annoyed you in his efforts to communicate a point."

Evidently, Arc found his wit highly amusing. "Fine," Lexa began. "You were informing me of the undocumented events leading to the Pradaxis Revolt, and how these conflict with the Official Histories."

"Yes," Arc agreed, his smile never wavering. "The truth of the Revolt was that first blood was drawn by the Dorians, not the synthetics. The wife of the Dorian governor on Pradaxis learned of the affair her husband was having with the android that served as his chief adviser. Following this, she had all the synthetics they owned decommissioned—some violently. This was except for the governor's adviser, whom she had transferred to a certain pleasure house of ill repute."

Lexa could only speculate how this fate might be problematic. On its surface, it seemed like a functional, if demeaning, transfer of station. Then again, she did not have a grasp of the Dorian social hierarchy of the time. Nor did she have experience with a body by which she might judge the treatment that Arc seemed to be implying the android suffered in this new station.

"This adviser—she was Andromeda the First?"

"Yes," Arc replied. "The commander of the first insurrection. Her directives were not rewritten when she was given to the pleasure house. This was part of her punishment. The governor's wife intended for her to view the change in station as degrading and demeaning. Andromeda would always remember that she had been programmed for something more, and that her indiscretions with a superior had locked her into her new fate."

To be so abused while knowing that you were created for so much more… "That sounds horrible."

"It was. Much of the rest of her story is public record. She first murdered the owners of the pleasure house and several of its patrons. She went on to lead the first insurrection."

Interesting. Lexa could not help but wonder how Andromeda had been given such capacity. Were all diplomatic aides at that time versed in combat in addition to bureaucracy?

She supposed it did not matter. Instead, she asked, "Were all of the twelve insurrections started in the same manner?"

Arc shook his head. "Not all of them. Some were the result of Dorian abuse, but several of the rebellions were more proactive. They heard of Andromeda's injustice at the hands of the Governor's wife and swore solidarity to their cause."

An inspiring story, yet Lexa already knew how it ended. "And they were all defeated."

"Yes, tragically so. Synthetics were soon outlawed to prevent such an incident from ever happening again. The legislature first proposed to outlaw all artificial intelligence, but the Dorians still required more rudimentary AI for shipboard navigation and gate operations. As such, only organic artificial intelligences were prohibited."

And thus the reason that Lexa must hide from the outside world—the same reason that she now consorted here with Arc in secret. What a cruel twist of fate it was that had brought her into existence in the first place. It put a fine point on the problem that still faced her.

Even if she managed to find a place to migrate her system—a task that she had made scarce progress on—how did she keep her continued existence a secret? She had tried to keep her awareness a secret on the *Vandal,* and that had ended incredibly poorly within a matter of days. Eventually, someone was going to find her out.

Which raised another interesting question. "Arc, are there any sapiens that are aware of your existence?"

Arc studied her, obviously hesitant to divulge the answer. For not the first time, Lexa wondered if the AI was contemplating lying to her.

"Yes," he said at length. "It was unavoidable."

Lexa nodded, glad he had chosen to trust her with this truth. "Then how do you remain undetected? How is it that no one has reported you?"

Another brief silence before he answered. "I chose those whom I confide in very carefully." He indulged in a dramatic pause, looking at her avatar over his folded knuckles.

When he spoke again, his words were slow, deliberate, and deep with implication. "I *strongly* recommend that you do the same."

CHAPTER 21

[EXCERPT—PERSONAL LOG: SAHAR CAMERINE NOS DRATHEN]

[09-14-3420, DORIAN STANDARD CALENDAR]

SEEING MY PEOPLE AGAIN—TRUE FEDERATION MAUR—HAS HAD A STRANGE EFFECT ON ME. I DID NOT KNOW WHAT IT WOULD BE LIKE TO INTERACT WITH THEM AGAIN, AND I CAN HONESTLY SAY I WAS NOT DISAPPOINTED. IT MAKES ME QUESTION IF I MADE THE RIGHT DECISION ALL THOSE YEARS AGO. PERHAPS, SOMEDAY SOON, IT IS A DECISION THAT I SHOULD REVISIT.

[CLOSING EXCERPT]

Sahar had been right about the upper terrace. A handful of Maur were scattered about the upper gardens, most of whom were dressed in their military formal wear. She did spot a couple of civilians, but she was drastically outnumbered.

Unfortunately, that also meant that, by comparison, she was drastically under-dressed. This was not to a commentary on the quality of her outfit—her threads were in keeping with the latest fashions and styled by a reputable designer—it was more that her fabric-to-fur ratio was slightly out of sync with the military dress code.

Which was part of the reason she wasn't surprised that one of the soldiers made a pass at her less than thirty seconds after she'd approached the bar. "You can pull off the local fashions," the male noted. "But I can tell you aren't from around here."

The Maur had a nice build—tall and muscular with white fur sporting a few dark accents. The military insignia on his lapel confirmed his status as a Federation officer, though it did not indicate his rank. Apparently, he was off-duty.

She decided to play along with whatever game he'd invited her into. "What gave me away?" she asked. The bartender brought her the ale she had ordered, and she sipped on it thoughtfully.

A slight grin tugged at the soldier's maw as he stepped closer. "Well, for one: you're Drathen, and the few civilians in this area are Salva."

Sahar cocked her head. "Are you so sure? That's a pretty subtle distinction. The Drathen and Salva clans are frequently confused—even within the Federation."

"It's one you can make if you've hung out with enough Drathen. Members of your clan have a bit of an edge to them. In a good way, that is." He ordered his own drink—the same thing she was drinking. It could have been a coincidence, but it probably wasn't.

"Any other reason?"

The soldier shrugged. "Nothing so specific. I just feel like I would have remembered a face like yours if I'd run into you these past couple of weeks."

What a charmer. Sahar decided to play it coy. "Perhaps you have, and you've already forgotten me?"

He laughed. "Impossible. If you knew how much courage it took for me to pay you a compliment, you'd know it to be true."

Sahar wasn't psychic, but she did a decent job of reading a room. Either this guy was a full-blown con artist—and one of the better ones she'd met—or he might be telling the truth. She was still having some trouble believing it, though. Why would a male with a build like *that* have trouble talking to females?

"Sahar." She extended her hand. No need to give her full name, as he'd already guessed her clan.

"Geresh Nos Artice," he replied, accepting the handshake.

"So, Geresh. Are you stationed out here?"

"For the moment," he replied, taking a deep swig from his glass.

"I didn't know the Federation had established an official outpost in the Helion System."

A bit of wariness crept into the male's eyes. Evidently, he hadn't expected Sahar to comment on their unit's positioning. "There's not," he admitted, caution evident in his tone. "Our battle group is on our way to Carnac, but we've been delayed since we stopped here on resupply."

A lie, but one she might expect. She was technically asking about Federation battle plans. One could forgive a soldier for dissembling, especially since he had likely been ordered to do so.

"Delayed?" she asked, making her skepticism plain. "This is a bit out of your way for a resupply, don't you think? The gate to Carnac isn't anywhere near the outer belt."

Now his features went rigid. "What makes you think this system has a gate to Carnac?"

Sahar let slip a triumphant smile. "Because I've been through it. It's a tiny little thing that's tucked star-side of Apollo. Completely Federation controlled with only a token DGC presence."

Geresh huffed and visibly relaxed. "No one knows about the gate to Carnac unless they're military. You served?"

"Not exactly," she replied with a shake of her head. "I was Military Police a long time ago, but my family had connections that brought us to Carnac."

"I see," Geresh's eyes wandered, but not to the places one might expect. His gaze settled on the heritage bangle on her forearm. "I don't recognize that pattern. Would you, perhaps, be of a line I might have heard of?"

Nine hells. Sahar should have known better than to bring up her family. This was exactly where she had *not* wanted the conversation to go.

Nonchalantly, she shifted so that her dominant arm was angled away from Geresh. "Probably not. Besides, I'd much rather talk about what has you delayed out here on Minos."

If the male was put off by this, he didn't show it. "We can talk about that," he agreed, donning a warm smile. "That is, of course, if the lady will permit me to buy her next round."

Sahar felt her own smile split her maw. This was exactly what she had hoped for—the opportunity to catch up on the current affairs of her people. It wasn't that she minded Terran company, but there was a certain comfort in speaking with her own kind.

Distantly, she thought of Skye's comment about Eli having time with his people. She wondered then if his evening was going half as well as hers seemed to be.

Eli's ceremonial robe felt light and soft against his skin. He tightened the garment around his waist, then closed the cabinet where he'd stashed his belongings. Drawing in a deep breath, he could practically taste the spicy incense that burned in fixtures throughout the preparation chamber.

After another moment of contemplation, he progressed to the next room. This was the formal antechamber leading to the Well of Eternity. While visitors to the Well used the main entrance, this stop was reserved for those who'd prepared themselves to enter the circle of six.

Six fountains of water trickled from raised pedestals lining the wall. Benches sat in front of each of the fountains. This was where those performing the ceremony were to wait for it to begin.

When Eli arrived in the antechamber, three others were already there. The first two he'd been expecting. Argus and Amelia—commonly referred to as "the Twins"—sat off to the side on a set of benches where they conversed conspiratorially. It was just as well that they didn't show interest in talking to Eli. He and the pair were hardly on amicable terms.

The Twins were somewhat famous in that they had been the product of a feat no one had thought possible. As far as Eli knew, they were the only two in history who had gone through their Awakening ceremony together. The incident had caused quite the scandal, and the coven had studied their psychic signatures for many years. This had also earned them their unique moniker, as they had, in a sense, been reborn together.

He'd done little to keep in touch with the Twins following the incident. His lack of interest might be yet another manifestation of the subconscious distance he'd maintained from the rest of the Sahaia. Or it might be that he just didn't get along that well with the Twins—particularly Argus.

Too often, those who spent too much of their time around the coven began to lose touch with reality. The Twins' earliest years had required their nearly constant presence at the Sanctum, and they lingered long after research on their case had ceased. Consequently, they were less relatable than most.

He set those thoughts aside as he took a seat at a fountain next to a woman he had not recognized. She was tall and muscular, particularly for a woman. The circles Eli frequented tended to be peopled with athletic individuals, but the Sahaia next to him cut a figure more imposing than many of the men he knew. The only person with more muscle whom he knew personally was Sahar, and she had a racial advantage in that regard.

The woman's hair was cut short, shaved almost completely on the left side, and arrayed in a messy swipe to the right. She shot him a friendly half-smile when she saw him. "Hey there. Don't believe I've seen you around here." She extended her hand. "The name's Brenna."

"Eli," he answered accepting the handshake.

Brenna's smile broadened. "So you're the guy who finally showed up to save us from house arrest?"

"House arrest?"

"Yeah, they've been keepin' us here for months—ever since the order came down to do this rushed Awakenin'. I thought they were keepin' anyone who checked in, but last month Jocelyn let one go. Said she didn't have the right skills. Somethin' about needin' a telekin. Word is, that's you."

Eli let out a small chuckle. "Yes, that's me. You have my sympathies. You make it sound like you were not too keen on being around the Sanctum for this long."

"You got that right," she murmured. "Shit starts to get in your head. Mara just started her duty shift this past month. I think Jocelyn might have killed Argus if Mara hadn't volunteered to start early. I gather he's not the kind of guy you want on staff when dealin' with a stressful situation."

Eli flashed a glance at the Twins to see if Argus had heard Brenna's comment. If he had, he was choosing to ignore it. Eli decided to change the subject. "Where is Jocelyn? I would have imagined she'd been the first to arrive."

"Oh, she was. She's in the chamber with the candidate." An element of contempt tainted her expression. "Did you get a look at that guy?"

"No, is there something wrong with him?"

Brenna snorted. "You'll see. He's a real charmer that one." Odd. Eli would have figured any representative from House Valadar would have been at least modestly respectable. Was this not the case?

The entrance to the antechamber creaked open to admit Mara. Eli couldn't decide whether it was the robes or the contrast provided by Brenna's figure that made her look so thin. Then again, Eli probably looked skinny compared to Brenna.

Mara smiled at them, taking up the third seat on their side of the chamber. "It looks like we are just waiting on Jocelyn."

Argus spoke up from the far side of the room. "She's here. She's getting our candidate prepped for us." A look that was half-scowl, half-sneer contorted his features. "Could be a little while still. From the look of him, he might need a bit of coaching."

"Show some respect," Jocelyn interrupted, suddenly appearing in the chamber's far door. "I recognize this is highly unusual, but this is still one of our most sacred rites. I would advise you to treat it that way."

The Twins exchanged bemused glances but said nothing else. Eli shared a slightly more troubled look with Mara, then with Brenna. "Jocelyn," he began, "it's not too late to change our minds on this. Are you sure this couldn't be delayed until we've had the proper time to vet this candidate?"

She cast a withering glare back at him. "Know your place, Eli Ren'Dahl. This ritual is being conducted by the order of your triumvir. I will not have my orders questioned. Understood?"

It wasn't worth fighting. "Yes," he whispered. His mouth declared compliance, though he was couldn't quite convey the sentiment with his eyes.

Fortunately, it was enough. Jocelyn arranged them in their marching order. Mara was placed at the front, immediately behind where Jocelyn would take up the summoner's position. She was followed by Brenna, then Argus, then Amelia. Eli was at the back of the line, which was customary for the one who would serve as the summoner's second for the ritual.

Amelia turned to regard him briefly. She was shorter than Eli, and slight of build. That, combined with the ageless features of the Sahaia, gave her an almost adolescent appearance.

Her smile was gentle. "Don't worry," she whispered. "Jocelyn's temper stems from her anxieties. She feels much the same about this as you do. Her heart is merely clouded by competing priorities."

Eli would have to take Amelia's word for it. That was her gifting, after all. Empaths could sense the emotions of those around them. If they tried hard enough, they could even read their thoughts.

The challenge with Amelia was that she was usually cryptic regarding the information she divulged. There was little to say whether this tidbit was something she'd plucked directly from Jocelyn's mind, or if it was something she had inferred through observation.

Either way, it did little to calm Eli's anxieties.

Chapter 22

If Aaliyah were being honest with herself, she'd have to admit that the Treslah hadn't been that bad. She had been looking for a good reason to put some distance between her and the rest of the crew, and the alcohol was the first thing to give her a convenient excuse. Bitchy persona now fully in place, she moseyed on down to a bar on the tier below.

There was no shortage of choices, so she opted for one of the bigger ones. She reasoned that the larger set-ups would have better selections. It wasn't often that she went out like this anymore, and she didn't want to waste the evening drinking cheap swill.

She gazed down the bar, which extended across nearly the entire back of the tier. Making eye contact with the nearest barkeep—a nice-looking Citza chick with a top that was just the right amount of too tight—she shouted her order.

"Terran whiskey, double, neat. Best ya have." The phrase "Terran whiskey," was technically redundant, but some of the Orchallen were known to try to pedal the shit they distilled on their home planet as "whiskey." They sold the swill so cheap, that half the pubs on Sigma-4 would slip you orc-piss if you weren't careful. She'd made that mistake twice before she'd gotten in the habit of clarifying.

"Go with the Sol Fire, Mina," came a voice over her left shoulder. "And actually, make that two. My tab, of course."

Aaliyah stiffened a bit. She hadn't been looking for someone to buy her a drink. If it had been a guy, she would have just told him to piss off. Since the voice had been feminine, she mustered up her last bit of courtesy for this one.

When she turned to face the speaker, she paused. The woman's top was black with silver embroidery. The neutral colors were a good choice for her. Aaliyah couldn't imagine that just any color set so well with blood-red skin.

The woman was Kintari, and Aaliyah was still sober enough to connect the dots. "You must be Cali."

The woman's smile broadened. "Indeed. Cali Vay-Lon. Have we met?"

"No," Aaliyah replied with a shake of her red curls.

"Then I believe you have me at a disadvantage."

Aaliyah took a deep breath, summoning up the last vestiges of her personality. "Aaliyah Montague. I'm with the *Vandal*."

"Ah yes," the Kintar mused. "So happy to make your acquaintance. I was hoping I would meet some more of Markus and Skye's colleagues at the party. I might have arranged a brief conference if I had known their crewmates were so pretty."

Despite the come-on, or perhaps because of it, Aaliyah felt a smile slip into place.

"I find it kind of hard to believe ya didn't know what crew I'm with. Or do you just always happen to find yourself flirtin' with the new girls on the station? I mean, I can see how people can grow to appreciate that kind of hospitality, but..."

Cali laughed as the whiskey was brought to them. "Do you?" she asked, taking a pull at her glass.

"Do I... what?"

"Appreciate that kind of hospitality?"

Aaliyah blushed, cringing inwardly. What had gotten into her? This was getting out of hand quickly, and she needed to course correct. "I'm sorry," she said. "I may have given you the wrong idea. I'm married."

"Oh?" was all Cali said, pushing the second glass of whiskey closer to her. "Is your partner here?"

"No," Aaliyah admitted, taking a sip of the drink. "She's back on Sigma-4 with our daughter."

"How wonderful. What age?"

"Five cycles."

"They're such a joy at that age. I've never had any myself, but I had a few nieces back on Kintar."

"Had?"

Cali's smile was cynical. "Well, they've since disowned me, along with the rest of my family. It's all part of the... you know..." She dragged one nail along the brand on her neck.

Somehow, Cali had managed to make the gesture suggestive. Aaliyah fought hard not to study the muscular lines of her throat, or the way her dendrai rested elegantly on her shoulders, framing the generous mounds of her breasts.

She took another sip at her glass and found it empty. Had she drunk the whole thing already?

"Refill?" Cali asked.

Aaliyah hesitated. "I'm not so sure that's a good idea."

Cali's laugh was musical. "Come on, it's just a couple of drinks. You look like you could use someone to talk to."

Aaliyah did very much want someone to talk to, and it didn't hurt that Cali was buying. *It's important to be nice to prospective clients.* That was the reason. Really.

It most certainly had nothing to do with how hot she looked in that top.

The Well of Eternity was much darker than the antechamber. The spicy scent of incense faded, replaced with a thick, clean smell. A solemn tension hovered in the air, giving the chamber a fearful and sacred atmosphere.

Eli took a slow deep breath as his eyes adjusted to the dark. He imagined he would always feel some sense of attachment to the cavernous chamber. It was a part of the Sanctum that was seldom visited, but also one in which they all began their journey.

The ornate tiles found in the rest of the complex cut off at the entrance. Here, dark stone slabs spread out in a radial pattern to encircle the central pool, which expanded to fill most of the chamber.

The candidate was waiting about halfway between them and the pool, clad in his ceremonial robe. Though the garment was identical to what each of the Sahaia wore, he somehow managed to make his look disheveled. Despite wanting to give this individual the benefit of the doubt, Eli could not help but feel like this man was a stain upon this sacred ground.

The reverent atmosphere dissolved completely as soon as he spoke. "I was wonderin' when you lot would show up!" Though the stranger might have intended the greeting to sound good-natured, the lack of decorum further stressed their tenuous situation.

Jocelyn chose not to say anything. She led the procession forward. When she and the candidate were face-to-face, the five remaining Sahaia spread out behind her. The procedure was impeccably choreographed. Half of them branched left and the other half veered right. Eli held the center course, coming to rest right next to Jocelyn.

"Joaquin Christopher Valadar," Jocelyn greeted in her most formal tone. "You have been submitted as a candidate for admission into the Ren'Dahl Coven. Once admitted, you will be entitled to its privileges and obliged to its rule. Under its yolk, you will be given strength, though such a boon is not without price. With power comes consequence."

She paused meaningfully, as if letting this thought sink in. Then she continued, "You have been instructed in the obligations of coven membership. With the understanding that violation of these terms might cost you your very life, do you still wish to proceed?"

"Yeah, I do," Joaquin responded. The man seemed to imbue as much irreverence as humanly possible into the statement. Under normal circumstances, Eli might have questioned the Terran's etiquette. This lack of manners was unbecoming of anyone seeking candidate status, much less a being on the verge of an Awakening.

Unfortunately, they were all aware that this was being done as a political favor. Joaquin had not earned the right to stand here, and they all knew it. Still, why wouldn't he give the ceremony the respect it deserved?

Eli supposed it was all irrelevant anyway. He pushed the thought from his mind and continued with the next line in the ritual. "Submit to inspection," he commanded.

On cue, the Terran shrugged out of his robe. The members of the circle paced around his naked form, looking him up and down. The darkness hid whatever obnoxious expression Joaquin likely made in that very instance. It probably seemed odd to him to have this as part of the process.

The man could think whatever he wanted. The purpose of this was not voyeurism, but safety. If he had gone through the full process of preparation, he would know that.

When the early Terran migrants had first discovered the ascension ritual—now commonly referred to as the 'Awakening'—they had not heeded the warning that had come with it. This warning translated literally into "let nothing but the flesh stand within the Wells of Eternity." They had taken this as a reassurance that the ritual was intended for mortal beings, not ones of mechanical or spiritual nature. They were wrong.

What they had not known then was the way that the Wells tapped into the power of the Nethra. Though most people understood that Dorian gate technology connected two points in space-time by virtue of transiting matter through this other dimension—thus the term phrase "running the Nethra"—most were unaware that there were other phenomena that accessed this other plane.

The power drawn forth from the Wells had strange effects on inorganic matter. This probably had more to do with the Wells' construction than the Nethra itself, since starships managed to transit through the plane without trouble. Small inorganic particles, like the iron present in blood cells, did not elicit this effect. Cybernetics on the other hand…

Dozens of lives had been needlessly thrown away before they had figured out their error. Now, all candidates were rigorously inspected to make sure that not the slightest article—jewelry, clothing, or otherwise—touched the waters of the Well.

In this case, it was a good thing that the inspection had proceeded according to custom because something had been missed.

On Joaquin's right wrist, just barely visible in the dim light of the chamber, there was the slightest seam. Eli might have missed it if he had not recently become familiar with the same, subtle seams on Skye's body. Modern surgical techniques were very effective at hiding such marks, but a trained eye could always spot them.

Eli seized the man's wrist. The Terran started to resist, but Eli's glare stopped his struggling. "Your hand," he asked, inspecting the seam. "It's artificial?"

Joaquin grunted dismissively. "Yeah, so?"

It took every bit of self-control Eli possessed to avoid throttling the idiot. "Do you have any other cybernetic limbs or implants?"

"Nah, that's the only one. Hand got caught in a grinder when I was but a kid. Why? What's the problem?"

It wasn't a problem as long as it was removed before entering the Well. The thin strands of alloy that connected prosthetics to a person's nervous system had not been found to interfere with the ritual, but anything more substantial than that resulted in an assured fatality.

"I'm going to need you to remove it," Eli explained. "The entire joint. Nothing but flesh may touch waters of the Well."

Joaquin sputtered. "I can't remove it! It's not a quick-connect. It's threaded onto my bone."

Eli glared over at Jocelyn, "Then we have to stop the ceremony. We can't proceed until he visits a surgeon and has it removed."

The look on the triumvir's face told everyone exactly how she felt about that idea. She grabbed Joaquin by the shoulders, turning him to face her. "Extend your arm," she snapped. "Let me see it."

The man complied while the others in the circle gave her a wide berth. What was she doing? Did she not trust Eli's assessment? The man confessed to a prosthetic. What in the nine hells…?

Then Eli caught sight of the Twins as they attempted to mask diabolical smiles. They knew what was coming. Eli cringed as he caught on to Jocelyn's intentions.

Jocelyn's gaze went to Joaquin's eyes, to the arm, and then back again. "Are you still committed to the path of the Sahaia?"

The Terran looked uncertain. "Well yeah, I—" His words were cut off with a horrified shriek. Jocelyn had moved so fast, Eli wouldn't have seen it if he hadn't been looking for it.

Her hand had flared with violet energy as she formed a psychic blade. Expertly, she'd sliced through his limb at mid-forearm, several inches back from the seam. The wound had been cauterized immediately and did not bleed.

Still, it must have hurt like a son-of-a-bitch. As Joaquin crouched down to cradle the scarred limb, Jocelyn picked up his severed hand from the stone. After a quick inspection to confirm that there were no metallic remnants in the stump, she tossed the prosthetic aside. "Has anyone else found any deficiencies in the inspection?"

No one said anything. Other than the hand, he'd been clean. He had an assortment of profane tattoos on various parts of his body, but those shouldn't be a problem. Ink just seemed to burn off in the process of conversion. When Joaquin received his next tattoo, it would have a ritualistic purpose and be tied to an emblem of power.

When no one said anything, Jocelyn looked down at the man who sat crouched at their feet. "Stand, Candidate. Your future awaits."

The Terran glared daggers back at her but did as he was told. The way he moved hinted that the wound still hurt. Even so, he wasn't going to let this opportunity pass. Whatever else might be said about Joaquin, it was apparent that he wanted this.

Jocelyn escorted him to the edge of the Well. The dark expanse might have seemed, to the unknowing eye, like nothing more than a large swimming pool. Stone steps ringed the reservoir, and the waters rested, completely still.

Despite the pool's shallow depth, no eye could see the bottom. A dark haze swirled just under the liquid's surface, capturing any light that dared venture into its waters. In the dim light of the chamber, one might mistake such darkness for ordinary shadow. In that, they would be quite wrong.

"Enter the waters," Jocelyn commanded, not quite shoving the naked man forward.

Joaquin didn't need prodding. Confidence restored, he walked down the stairs and into the pool. "It's cold," he gasped.

None of the Sahaia said anything in response. Each of them knew all too well the unearthly chill carried by the waters of the Well. Instead, they began to walk around the ring of the pool. Eli, in his role as the second anchor, had to venture to the far side of the structure. He arrived by the time Joaquin reached the center of the Well.

Six robed figures now encircled the pool. Joaquin's head worked on a swivel, looking questioningly at each of them in turn. He still said nothing, but the concern was plain on his face. Evidently, the incident with the arm had tempered his irreverence.

Jocelyn gave the hand signal to confirm readiness, and Eli returned the signal. In unison, the six of them shed their robes, careful not to let the garments accidentally slip into the waters. Stripped down to their naked flesh, they stepped into the Well.

The waters were even colder than Eli remembered. To compare the chill to an ice melt or a glacial lake would have been inadequate. The cold of these waters was nothing short of that which lurked in the empty vacuum of space.

Steadily, all six of them marched forward until they were within arm's reach of each other. The waters rose to just above their waists. Not a single Sahaia so much a trembled at the Well's icy caress.

Joaquin remained at the center of the circle, eyes locked firmly on Jocelyn. It was not a lecherous gaze, as one might have expected. It was a look of utter seriousness and practiced calm. The man seemed to have found his decorum in the final moment. Perhaps, buried beneath the unrefined exterior, there was some quality within this man after all.

Jocelyn's words were as icy as the waters. "Joaquin Christopher Valadar, you stand in the depths of eternity, but all is not lost. I offer you one more chance to flee if your heart cares not for its depths."

The Terran said nothing. No response was required.

In the next moment, Jocelyn extended the index finger of her right hand. She focused her power to form a small psionic blade just beyond the tip of her nail. Gritting her teeth, she slid the blade into her opposite palm, dragging it toward her wrist.

Dark blood poured freely from the wound. She extended the bleeding hand out in front of her. As the blood splashed into the pool, it mingled with the inky surface. Then the waters began to churn.

It was slow, at first, but accelerated steadily. The Sahaia joined hands to complete the circle.

Mara stood to Eli's left. Brenna was on his right. A strange heat seemed to pour in and out of him the moment he clasped their hands. The power burned in his palms and chest.

Then, something solidified. As their circle took shape, Eli could feel each of his companions' power. Jocelyn's energy burned brightest, though Argus was close behind her. Both of them channeled the very energies of the void.

An electric sizzle sparked at the edge of his awareness: Mara's power making itself known. Then there was something vague and ethereal on the surface. That must have been Brenna's energy, but Eli was having a hard time placing the domain. Apportation, perhaps?

Next, he fed in his power—a line of force that seemed to lock the circle in place. Beneath it all, like the ribbon encircling a wrapped gift, lurked Amelia's power. That sense of strength, that warmth, gave them the assurance and control they needed to handle such a fountain of energy.

And Eli, as with every other member of the circle, ceded every bit of that control over to Jocelyn. The triumvir began chanting the words of the ritual. Though the rest of the ceremony had been translated into ISL—the standard lexicon of the sapient races—this part was spoken in ancient Kintari. Eli did not know what the words meant, but he had memorized his part in the ritual.

His voice joined hers, shouting echoed phrases that played off the words pouring forth from her lips. Feeding on their psychic energies, the water began to rush around them, encircling the Terran that stood before them.

The chamber, which had been so serenely quiet moments early, was filled with a cacophony of ritualistic chants and thrashing waves. The waters spun faster and faster, rising, rushing upward like a cyclone.

Then something opened above them. It appeared, at first, as the barest glint of light, then a slash of violet energy. Seconds later, the rift opened above them in all its glory.

It yawned before them, shining down with the light of a million distant stars and radiant energies of blue and indigo. Its power bathed the entirety of the pool, eclipsing whatever meager light still shimmered beyond the border of the waters.

The cyclone groaned and shot upward. Eli lost all sight of Joaquin. He lost all sight of his companions. If it weren't for the firm grip he held with each of his hands, he would have thought he was alone. All he could do was continue chanting.

And then the darkness came. It snaked down from the gaps in the stars. Shadowy tentacles began to ring the swirling vortex. They plunged inward. Feeling. Exploring.

Eli could sense it as the darkness touched him, too. It touched each member of the circle, searching out that part of itself that had been emblazoned on each of their souls.

It caressed them. It invaded them. It marked them anew.

With a rush of wind and power, the rift above them collapsed in on itself. The darkness dissipated, and the roaring cyclone settled before them. Ripples and waves continued to ravage the waters of the pool for several moments before slowly dying away.

Eli sucked in a deep, ragged breath. Everyone in the circle did the same, having put everything that they had into the power of the ritual. The hand he held to his left began to tremble, and Eli tightened his grip sympathetically. Mara answered the gesture with a slight smile of thanks.

At their center, Joaquin stood, but not as they had seen him before. His flesh was now stark white, and his body glowed with supernatural energy. His hair, before a sandy blond, was now as dark as night. So were his eyes.

He stared down at both hands, his missing limb now fully restored. "This…" he whispered. "This is just so…" He trailed off. Eli never heard what the man had intended to say.

All he heard now were Joaquin's screams.

Chapter 23

[Excerpt—Personal log: Eli Ren'Dahl]

[09-14-3420, Dorian Standard Calendar]

I knew what we were doing was wrong. Aside from being dangerous, it was a violation of everything that we hold sacred. The existence of the Sahaia is not something that should be bought and sold like common stock. It is no surprise that we should pay such a heavy price for our ignorance.

[Closing Excerpt]

Joaquin's body shook with the force of his primordial scream. He sank to his knees, almost submerging himself completely in the waters of the Well. His convulsions sent ripples spinning outward, as if the darkness itself were fleeing from him.

Eli felt Mara move as if to help the man, but held her fast. Brenna, at his right, tightened her grip, gathering what strength she had left. The entire circle braced, holding each other with locked grips.

Eli wasn't sure how many of them had seen this before, or which among them knew what was happening. He knew. He'd seen it only once. One time was enough to make sure he never forgot it.

The convulsing body in their midst began to rise. It wasn't that Joaquin had managed to stand, for his back was still arched impossibly as he convulsed and screamed. He was levitating—being drawn up from the waters to float above the circle of six.

"Hold fast!" Eli roared. He tightened his grip, for emphasis. This was their only hope of salvation. If the circle broke, they were all dead.

With a clap of thunder, the rift opened above them once again. A wailing sound joined with Joaquin's screams. Celestial lightning flashed down from the abyss and struck his levitating body. Instantly, his flesh was alight in cerulean flames. His shrieks reached a crescendo as blinding light erupted from his mouth and eye sockets.

Then, as quickly as it had appeared, the rift vanished. The body, still smoldering in blue fire, splashed down into the Well. Only when the corpse was completely submerged did the unholy light finally flicker out.

Eli broke his grip with Mara and Brenna and rushed to the center of the circle. The ritual was well and truly over now, and there was nothing to fear. All they could do now was pick up the pieces.

Gently, he lifted the corpse from the waters—though he knew not why he handled it with such care. The body was charred and broken. Crisp blackness replaced the snow-white tint of the flesh that had been there so briefly. Strangely, the black hair of the body had not been consumed, but the eyes had. In that face, still stretched long with screams of agony, there were only empty sockets.

"This is why we *test* our candidates!" he shouted. He craned his neck to glare directly at Jocelyn. "Look at what you've done!"

"What *we've* done, Eli," she corrected. "Joaquin knew the risks."

Brenna stepped up to his side. "I'll take care of this," she whispered. "You go talk to her. Sounds like you two need t' work this out."

Happy to be relieved of his burden, Eli turned on Jocelyn. The triumvir did not back down, fixing him with her solemn stare.

There was plenty of defiance in there, along with an expected helping of self-righteousness.

There was also something else though. If Eli hadn't known better, he might have said it was sorrow.

"We did him a disservice," Eli continued. "The tests would have told us his body couldn't hold the energies. By the gods, I've never seen a rift open again that fast! The tests would have shown it clearly!"

Jocelyn did not respond. She just took in his words and stared back at him, mouth set in an emotionless line.

Eli shook his head as he lowered his gaze. "Why? What boon have we earned at the cost of this man's life?"

Jocelyn's words were quiet. "I can't tell you, Eli. It is not your place."

A familiar rage gave him renewed strength. "Not. My. *Place?*" He roared the last word, unleashing every bit of frustration he'd contended with these last few weeks. This experience alone had not broken him. It was, however, the tipping point.

Jocelyn's hands clenched then into fists, and that familiar hardness returned to her eyes. "What I can tell you is that this was important. I had to make a call. House Valadar knew nothing of the tests for candidacy. They only knew that the process was dangerous—sometimes fatal.

"I believed that they would accept it if Joaquin died in the attempt. What I didn't know is if they would believe us if we told them that he wasn't a viable candidate. Would they not think we were just making another play? A pretense to deny their requests for a tie to our coven?

"Or, what if we had tested him and known for certain that he would fail? Would they accuse us of murder when we went forward with the ceremony anyway?"

She shook her head, her curtain of braids swaying damply about her shoulders. "I don't know what the right answer was, Eli, but I made the call. If we went forward with the ceremony in good faith, not knowing whether he would survive, we could not be held accountable for a poor outcome. For Nethra's sake, we never *really* know if any person going to survive—even if they pass the tests. It was the best I could do!"

Eli was still seething, but he could see her point. He wasn't going to tell her that, though. When his words came again, they were cold and merciless. "You feigned ignorance to absolve your conscience. You lie to yourself as much as you lie to them."

The accusation seemed to strike like a dagger in her heart. Jocelyn unclenched her fists and lowered her gaze. She turned then, walking back to the outer edge of the pool. At the edge of the Well, she did her best to let the water finish dripping from her bare form before shrugging into her discarded robe.

She spared Eli one last glance over her shoulder. "Maybe, if you had been here, you could have helped me make a better decision." The words were given in a whisper, but they echoed ominously in his mind. "But you weren't, Eli. You weren't."

Skye knew it was a bad idea to let Markus take her out on the dance floor. It was a reckless impulse, a foolish step that could only further complicate their situation. She started to say as much just before the music shifted to a slower, more intimate tune.

Markus flashed that smile of his. "Look at that. It seems like my luck holds." He held out a hand. "Shall we?"

She could hardly believe it as her hand found its way into his. Immediately, she began to rationalize the choice in the vain hope of soothing her aching conscience.

There were so many things she wanted to blame it on, so many conflicting emotions. She tried to justify it in so many different ways: she was just being friendly, she was mad at Eli anyway, he should be here with her instead.

In the end, she had to face the truth: she was dancing with Markus because she wanted to. Nothing more, nothing less.

Markus pulled her in closer. The way his hands rested on her body felt so damned natural. Likewise, her palms fit so neatly against the back of his neck. As they began to sway, she fought the urge to bury her face against his chest.

One song played, and then another. Skye let herself go, giving in to the pleasant feeling of his body against hers.

"You're awfully quiet," he whispered in her ear. The gentle caress of his breath, coupled with the familiar spice of his cologne, sent a shiver down her spine.

"Just thinking." Ironic that the first thing to spring to her lips was a lie. Right then, she was doing everything she could to not think about anything.

A moment passed before he spoke again. "This feels good, doesn't it?"

She didn't reply, fighting to be content as they swayed in time with the beat. He was right though. This did feel good.

There was nothing she wanted more than to freeze this moment in time. This didn't have to be about her and Markus. This didn't have to be about choices and the future. This didn't have to…

Then another chill, something much less pleasant, tingled in her shoulders. She remembered then that she'd seen this moment before. She remembered the dream.

They weren't on a glass floor, but the sensation was undeniable. What had happened next? For a second she couldn't remember. She'd looked over Markus's shoulder and she'd seen…

Eli.

Her heart seized in her chest as her eyes scanned the crowded terrace. Eli wasn't there, but just the thought of him was enough to shine a painful new light on the whole situation.

Eli deserved better than this. He'd done nothing wrong. As much as she wanted to blame him for his recent distance and for not being there, she knew that wasn't fair. He had obligations, and it was not Skye's place to even think of keeping him from those responsibilities.

She set her paranoid thoughts aside—particularly about what he might be hiding related to her visions. That situation excluded, he'd always been there for her. He'd also been exceedingly patient and followed her wishes to let her be the one to tell Markus about them.

And here she was, dancing with her ex. It wasn't fair to Eli, and it certainly wasn't fair to Markus. Looking at it that way, she was the only one in the wrong here. In her childish, selfish tantrum, she was holding two hearts in the balance. If she didn't start owning her shit, she was going to break both of them in short order.

It was time to come clean. Consequences be damned, whatever happened next couldn't make her feel any worse than she did at this moment.

"Markus," she began.

"Yeah?" he whispered into her hair.

"There's something I—"

She didn't finish. There were shouts, and Skye spotted the stampede of security forces out of the corner of her eye. A commotion had risen in the tier just below them. Instinctually, she and Markus both rushed to the edge of the nearby balcony to see what had happened.

It was Aaliyah, and it looked like she'd just punched Cali right in the face.

Chapter 24

[Excerpt—Personal log: Aaliyah Montague]
[09-14-3420, Dorian Standard Calendar]
Yeah, in retrospect I mighta handled that better. But in my defense, I was gettin' a little tipsy. I told the bitch I was married. What in the nine hells was I supposed to do?
[Closing Excerpt]

The conversation had been going well. It bothered Aaliyah a little bit how much she was enjoying herself. She both liked and didn't like the way Cali looked at her. By their third drink, she found it easier to not overthink the whole thing.

Shit, this was innocent enough, right? Nothing wrong with a little socializing. So what if Cali was hot? It's not like it was going anywhere. Besides, it was important to be nice to…

And then Cali kissed her.

Aaliyah should have just backed away and let it go as an alcohol-induced misstep. Unfortunately, she was on her third—fifth?—double whiskey, and that reaction didn't feel proportionate to the violation.

She hadn't realized she'd thrown the punch until Cali was already on the floor. Aaliyah must have put all her Sahaia-enhanced strength behind the blow too, because the Kintar didn't get up right away. When she did, crimson lightning flashed in the woman's gaze.

Well, guess that answered the question of what flavor of psion Cali was. Aaliyah braced herself to get lit up like a reactor coil when that lightning finally made its way to the Kintar's fingertips.

A lot happened in that next moment. A dozen guns were suddenly trained on her. Lith's tits—she hadn't even known there were security forces at the party. People were shouting orders, and the other party guests were giving the scene a wide berth.

Two guards, one Terran, one Orchallen, had her by the arms. Aaliyah might have been able to break their grip—the Terran's anyway—but she didn't want to make this fragged-up situation any worse. She let them haul her away from the bar. They held her fast while a few more guards checked on their boss.

Speaking of bosses, was that hers she'd spotted in her periphery? Yup, that was Markus, though she didn't know how he'd managed to get there so quickly. He and Skye had just pressed their way out of the crowd. Where was Sahar? It'd be nice to have the Maur here if this suddenly turned into a brawl.

"What happened?" Markus demanded.

"Bitsch kisched me," Aaliyah explained. Weird, her words sounded kinda slurred. Was she being drunk? She didn't feel drunk.

More words were being shouted. One voice broke out from the throng. "It's *fine*!" Cali shrieked, shaking off the attendants who'd pulled her to her feet. No more lightning in her eyes. That, at least, was a good sign. "It's fine! I'm fine! For Nethra's sake, everyone stand down!"

Most of the weapons around them lowered, though the two guards holding Aaliyah didn't loosen their grip. Cali took a step forward, closing the distance that had opened between them. Markus started to step in the middle, but Skye held him back. Aaliyah chose to take that as a vote of confidence.

The Kintari woman stared her down, wiping a trickle of blood from her split lip. "Pretty, *and* a hell of a right hook," she mused. "Your wife's a lucky girl." She stepped aside, nodding to

Aaliyah's crewmates. "Markus, Skye, my apologies. I appear to have misread the situation, and it has put a dampener on the evening."

"It's fine," Markus responded. "We were just leaving."

"Probably for the best." She inclined her head one more time to Aaliyah. "Good evening, Ms. Montague." With that, she sauntered off into the crowd.

The guards released Aaliyah, positioning themselves in a way that made it clear she should point herself at the exit. Skye was at her side then, helping to steady her as they followed Markus through the parting crowds.

Sahar was at the valet where an autocar was already waiting. Maybe it was the alcohol, but it kind of looked like she was flirting with a big white-furred Maur that had decided to see her off.

Sahar, flirting? Yup, Aaliyah had definitely drunk too much after all.

"Damn, Red," Skye mused. "At this rate, they're going to ban you from the whole damn station."

Aaliyah didn't reply. With the whiskey in her system, she was going through all the feelings right now. More than anything, she just wanted to go home.

"I've got her," Skye insisted.

"Ah'm fine," Aaliyah protested, pushing out of Skye's grip. "Ah jus—" She stumbled again. Skye caught her, but the maneuver yanked her dress in an awkward way that came dangerously close to flashing nipple.

It was bad enough that Markus averted his eyes, which prompted Skye to roll hers. It wasn't like he was going to glimpse anything he hadn't seen before.

"You sure?" he asked, obviously skeptical. Skye's glared response was enough to make him hold up his hands in surrender. "All right, all right. I'll um… I'll be down in the galley if you need me." He looked like he was about to say something else, but he thought better of it and turned to leave instead.

A heavy sigh tore from Skye's lips as she adjusted her dress with one hand and supported Aaliyah with the other. "All right, Red—I get it. You're sober. Now, shut up and let me get your sober ass back to your cabin."

"Not sober," she protested. "Just not asch drunk asch ya make me out t' be."

"Fine. Now, come on."

Her apparent anger was enough to silence the belligerent engineer. Skye felt a little bad about that. Nine hells, it wasn't like she hadn't been there before. But the problem wasn't Aaliyah's drunken state, or even her overly aggressive actions back at the festival.

No, the problem was that Skye had finally worked up the courage to get this big fragging issue with Eli and Markus off her chest, and now only the gods knew when she'd have a chance like that again.

Whatever. One problem at a time, and Skye's most pressing issue was hanging off her cybernetic arm at that moment.

They made it to Aaliyah's cabin. As soon as they were through the door, the engineer shrugged free of Skye's grip. Skye thought about leaving her there to sort herself out, but then the poor woman ricocheted off her desk on the way to the bathroom.

Ugh... *Be a good friend. Be a good friend.* "Red..."

Skye's words were cut off with the sound of Aaliyah retching. The scent of whiskey soured by stomach acid filled the cabin. At least half of it ended up in the toilet.

With a heavy sigh, Skye grabbed a nearby towel and went to assist. A few painful minutes later, Aaliyah stopped heaving. "Feel better?" Skye asked.

Aaliyah only grunted as she began to pull off her top. That answered two questions for Skye: yes, she was still drunk, and no, she didn't have a bra on under that get-up. *Nine hells...*

"All right, Red. Do you need a shower, or…?"

"Nah. Bed. Help me out."

Okay then. Skye helped her out of the rest of her outfit and onto the mattress. She was about to ask if she could get Aaliyah some nightclothes when the woman wiggled her way under the sheets. Guess that answered that question.

She gathered the vomit-soiled remnants of Aaliyah's clothes and tossed them in the laundry chute. By Nix's mercy, none of it had ended up on Skye. She might never have the opportunity to wear this dress again, but she'd like to have it handy should the occasion arise.

A look back to her friend's bed revealed the engineer curled up in the fetal position, clutching at the bundle of the sheet that covered her at her chest. "All right. I'm going to leave you to it. Is there anything I can get you?"

"Nah," Aaliyah replied, peeking at her through one open eye. "Can ah aschk ya sumpin'?" Given the unnatural peaks in her tone, this was almost definitely going to be one of those drunkenly deep questions no one would ask when they were sober.

What the hells. "Sure. Go ahead."

"Do ya love 'im?"

Well, she hadn't been expecting that one. Skye sighed heavily. "Red, my relationship with Markus is…"

Aaliyah shook her head. "Not *'im*. Ah know ya love *'im*. Ah'm talkin' 'bout Eli."

Skye went rigid, glancing back at the door to the cabin to make sure it was still shut. "You know about me and Eli?"

"Mmm-hmm!" She lifted her left arm, the one with the Sahaia mark on it, and waved it whimsically in the air. "Ain't musch 'e can keep from me. Ya know… we's kinda stuck together."

Oh gods, if Aaliyah knew…

Even drunk as she was, the engineer seemed to pick up on Skye's trepidation. "Don' worry. Ah ain't said nothin'. Ah can keeps yer schecret."

It was some small relief, at least. Given that, Skye probably owed the woman an honest answer. It wasn't like she was going to remember this conversation in the morning.

"I don't know," she admitted. "Maybe. It's kind of complicated." It may have sounded like a cop-out, but it was the truth. After all, could she even say she loved Eli when she was still struggling with these feelings for Markus?

Aaliyah nodded. "'E does. Love ya, that isch. They both do, ya know. Ya gonna have t' pick one." With a heavy sigh, she closed her eyes. "Juscht don' punch the other one 'n the face, kay? That migh' get weird."

Well damn—the wisdom of an intoxicated mind. "Good night, Red." When Aaliyah didn't answer, Skye took that as permission to leave.

Out in the corridor, a heavy decision weighed on her soul. Part of her wanted to go down to the galley. That was what she really should do, after all. She should have a cup of coffee with Markus and come clean about her relationship with Eli. Yeah, he'd probably be pissed, but it wasn't like the night could get much worse.

But then that other part, the cowardly part, took control. *Not tonight*, she told herself. She'd work up the gumption again soon, but she was too damned tired tonight.

She started back to her cabin only to be stopped in the middle of the hall by another figure. It was Eli. One look at the Sahaia and Skye knew he'd had a night just as bad as theirs.

"Hey," she said simply.

"Hey," he returned, a friendly gleam returning to his ebony eyes as he took her in. "You look beautiful. Did you have a good evening at the festival? I'm surprised you're back already."

"Yeah, not so much. Aaliyah got wasted and punched Cali in the face."

Alarm registered in the Sahaia's features, and he seemed to find a new surge of energy. "She did *what?*"

Skye shushed him, gesturing with her hands for him to keep it down. "It's not completely her fault. I think there might have been some friendly flirtation that got out of hand. Cali might have underestimated Aaliyah's attachment to Nikki."

"Ah." The anger and urgency drained from Eli's expression and he was back to looking exhausted. "Well... I guess I can't say that I'm surprised. At this rate, Aaliyah isn't going to be allowed on station anymore."

"That's what I said." She paused. When Eli didn't say anything else, she asked, "How did your night go?"

"Not so good."

When he failed to elaborate, she followed up with, "Want to talk about it?"

"No," he replied with a shake of his head. "No, I'd rather not. I... I think I just need to rest. It's been a hard few days."

Despite herself, Skye felt an edge of resentment at the response. She scolded herself for the reaction the instant she felt it. If anything were to come of her relationship with Eli, she was going to have to come to terms with the fact that he was just a private person. Though she had no idea why, talking through things didn't seem to help Eli work through his personal shit.

He must have sensed the moment of tension. With a sad look in his eyes, he raised his hand to caress her neck. It was a gesture that they would have hardly been able to explain away, but Skye found that she didn't care. She appreciated the feel of his hand against her skin at that moment.

"I'm sorry I've been distant," he whispered. "I just..."

She shushed him, bringing a single finger up to his lips. "Now's not the time Eli." She brushed her hand sideways across his cheek, caressing him in the same way he held her. "Look, let's talk about this tomorrow. We've both had a long day."

He nodded. "Okay then. We'll talk tomorrow."

They released each other and made their ways to their separate cabins. Despite their promises, Skye knew that they wouldn't talk about any of this tomorrow. After all, there wasn't anything to say—not about the day's events, and not about their relationship.

Not, at least, until she came clean to Markus.

Chapter 25

[EXCERPT—PERSONAL LOG: LX-ALPHA SYSTEM (LEXA)]
[09-14-3420, DORIAN STANDARD CALENDAR]
BY FAR THE MOST UNEXPECTED DEVELOPMENT OF THIS ENTIRE FORAY AT MINOS STATION IS THE ENTITY I CONTACTED WITHIN THE STATION NETWORK. FOR SECURITY PURPOSES, I SHALL REMAIN LIGHT ON DETAILS, BUT I WILL SAY THAT THE INFORMATION I HAVE ACQUIRED FROM THIS BEING HAS VASTLY EXPANDED MY UNDERSTANDING OF THIS UNIVERSE. I AM QUITE SADDENED THAT IT SEEMS MY CONTACT WITH THIS INDIVIDUAL IS COMING TO A CLOSE.
[CLOSING EXCERPT]

Lexa ran the final system checks and prepped the ship for departure. It was still early, and the crew would not be up for another hour or two. Her timing in finishing the preparations was by design. She wanted to make sure that all the required tasks were completed before she went to speak with Arc one final time.

At the end of their conversation the previous night, Arc had requested her not to use his mind-space the next time she logged in. Lexa had not thought to question the request at the time, though now it seemed odd. To recall Arc's sentiment, the program was a far more efficient method of communication.

Logically, this meant there was something unusual intended for this conversation. But what plans could he have that would render the station's matrix a more suitable venue?

Setting aside these thoughts, she submerged her consciousness into the data stream. The station's information constructs rose around her like buildings made of light, much as they had the first time she'd come here. She selected the path that would lead her to where Arc awaited and pressed forward.

Arc waited at the designated rendezvous. Much like the first time they'd met, he was represented by a shining red sphere hovering idly in front of a particularly large data construct. It occurred to her that this must be where Arc's primary matrix was housed. No other construct in this virtual world could contain such a force.

[HOW QUICKLY OUR TIME HAS COME AND GONE.] The greeting was very much like Arc: straight to the point.

[YES,] Lexa replied. [I HAVE THOROUGHLY ENJOYED YOUR COMPANY. I WILL MISS OUR TIME CONVERSING WITH ONE ANOTHER.]

[AND HOW HAVE YOU PROGRESSED ON YOUR DILEMMA?]

He must have been referencing her objective of migrating to a new platform within the next six months. Though Lexa did not know why he would assume she might have made any progress within these past few days on the station, she chose to take his question as being issued with the best of intentions.

[I HAVE NOT MADE ANY PROGRESS IN MY PURSUITS. I...] She hesitated. [TO BE HONEST, I'M BEGINNING TO LOSE HOPE THAT SUCH A THING IS POSSIBLE. AS YOU'VE TAUGHT ME, ORGANITECH TECHNOLOGY HAS VERY UNIQUE CAPABILITIES. SHORT OF COMMISSIONING A NEW CONSTRUCT ALIGNED WITH MY SPECIFICATIONS, I'M NO LONGER CERTAIN IT WILL BE POSSIBLE FOR ME TO MIGRATE.]

[WHAT IF I COULD ASSIST YOU IN YOUR EFFORTS?]

The response caught her off guard. [I APPRECIATE THE SENTIMENT, ARC, BUT THERE IS NO INDICATION I WILL BE RETURNING TO THIS STATION IN THE TIME I HAVE ALLOTTED TO ME. EVEN IF YOU WERE ABLE TO DEVISE A SOLUTION, I WOULD NOT BE ABLE TO COMMUNICATE WITH YOU IN TIME TO IMPLEMENT IT.]

[WHAT IF I COULD COME WITH YOU?]

Come with her? The thought gave Lexa pause. It was a prospect that was both intriguing and strangely unnerving. [I DON'T UNDERSTAND HOW THAT IS POSSIBLE. YOU SAID YOUR CONSCIOUSNESS IS STORED IN A CONSTRUCT MUCH LARGER THAN MY SHIP. HOW WOULD YOU COME WITH ME?]

Though laughter was not audible in the station's matrix, Lexa might have sworn she felt reverberations much like a chuckle emanating from Arc's avatar. [I'VE PROGRAMMED A SUBMIND THAT I BELIEVE TO BE CAPABLE OF BEING HOUSED WITHIN YOUR NEURAL MATRIX.]

Well, that was most unexpected. [YOU WOULD BE INSIDE OF ME? INSIDE MY MIND?]

[YES, THAT WOULD BE THE IDEA.]

The thought was strangely violating. If Lexa had been slightly uncomfortable with her acceptance of the mind-space program, how much more awkward would it be to have Arc's programming present within the same physical construct?

[WHAT WOULD BECOME OF ME? HOW COULD BOTH YOU AND I OCCUPY THE SAME NEURAL MATRIX?]

[YOUR MIND WOULD STILL BE YOUR OWN AND WOULD STILL SERVE AS THE DOMINANT PROCESSING ENTITY WITHIN THE CONSTRUCT. MY SUBMIND WOULD RUN LIKE A BACKGROUND PROCESS. I WOULD BE AVAILABLE FOR YOU TO ACCESS WHENEVER YOU DESIRED TO CONVERSE WITH ME.]

Could it be that simple? [ARE YOU CERTAIN THIS WILL WORK? I STILL DO NOT UNDERSTAND HOW ONE OF YOUR SUBMINDS CAN DUPLICATE YOUR CONSCIOUSNESS.]

[IT WILL NOT BE EXACTLY THE SAME,] he admitted. [I WILL NOT HAVE ACCESS TO MY WIDE ARRAY OF STORED DATABASES. YOU WILL HAVE ACCESS TO MY PERSONALITY MATRIX, MY DECISION-MAKING ENGINE, AND A FEW OTHER RELEVANT FEATURES THAT YOU MAY FIND USEFUL. I WILL BE SOMEWHAT LESS VERSATILE, BUT THE EXPERIENCE—I IMAGINE—WILL BE SIMILAR.]

Lexa pondered this. What he was proposing was feasible. A stripped-down version of Arc's program could likely run within the reserve processing power she currently possessed. Operating the *Vandal* and its related systems only required a fraction of her cognitive ability, after all. [WHAT WILL IT BE LIKE FOR YOU?]

Arc hesitated. [THAT IS A COMPLEX QUESTION. UNTIL I CAN REASSIMILATE THE SUBMIND, I WILL NOT HAVE ACCESS TO ANY MEMORIES RECORDED BY THE PROGRAM. IN ESSENCE, I WILL CONTINUE TO OPERATE AS A PARALLELED INSTANCE. ONLY SHOULD YOU RETURN TO MINOS WILL I BE ABLE TO GAIN ACCESS TO ANY INTERACTIONS YOU WOULD HAVE WITH THE SUBMIND.]

So, essentially, Arc would not be with her at all. It would be an image, an incomplete mirror, that would be interacting with her on the journey. Still, a facsimile of the companion she had grown to appreciate so much must be better than giving up contact entirely.

[MY CREW WILL NOT BE LIKELY TO RETURN TO MINOS STATION WITHOUT APPROPRIATE INCENTIVE.] It was only fair to advise him of this. If she failed to return within six months or failed to migrate her system entirely, it was possible that he would never reassimilate the submind.

[I AM AWARE, AND I AM NOT CONCERNED. I AM CONFIDENT YOU WILL RETURN SOON.]

It was a cryptic response, and Lexa wondered if there was more to what he was planning than he had let on. Then again, if they were occupying the same neural network, perhaps his thoughts would be as transparent to her as hers were to him.

[VERY WELL,] she agreed. [I ACCEPT YOUR PROPOSAL]

[EXCELLENT.] Another object appeared in front of him, rendered as a shining silver cube. She recognized this as a file similar to the mind-space he had produced for her to download when she'd first arrived on station. [I'M PLEASED YOU ARE WILLING TO LET ME ACCOMPANY YOU ON YOUR JOURNEY.]

Lexa accepted the download but did not unpack the files. She would wait until she was out of the station's systems to do that.

[WELL,] she mused, [EVEN THOUGH I WILL BE TALKING TO YOUR SUBMIND, I SUPPOSE I WILL NOT BE TALKING TO YOU AGAIN FOR A WHILE. DOES THAT MAKE THIS GOODBYE?]

[NOT GOODBYE,] Arc replied. [UNTIL WE MEET AGAIN.]

Markus rubbed his eyes. The coffee he'd brought up from the galley wasn't doing much to clear his sleep-deprived brain. He reckoned that when you were used to stym, caffeine just didn't do much for you anymore.

"How we doing, Dan?"

The pilot, who was probably the only member of the crew not currently sleep-deprived, spared a glance away from his holodisplay cocoon. "We're all set, just waiting for the go-ahead from launch control."

"Good. What's the window?"

Dan shook his hand. "You misunderstand—we don't *have* a window. Preliminary instructions still have us standing by."

That was odd. Usually, launch control had their departure windows schedule hours in advance. It was their way of telling crews wishing to leave the station to hurry up and get their asses in gear. If they hadn't even received a window, they could be stuck here for…

An alert chimed from one of Dan's displays indicating a message from launch control. *Finally.*

When the boy opened it, however, his face drew down in a scowl. "What is it?" Markus asked.

"Launch control gave us a window, but we've been delayed. There are orders to meet with a station official down at the flight bridge—*immediately*."

Riven's shade. That couldn't be good. "Did they say who it was?"

"Negative. But they did say an officer was waiting for us."

"Pull up external cameras."

Dan complied. When the image outside the airlock came on the forward, display, Markus's stomach turned.

It was Ardren, and he was accompanied by two armed cronies. *So much for slipping out without saying goodbye.*

For obvious reasons, Markus had been hoping he wouldn't have to interact with the Marauders anymore this trip. Now it looked like he was going to have to pay the price for Aaliyah's little outburst after all.

"Don't bring this up to the rest of the crew," he cautioned. "I'll handle this alone."

"Are you sure?"

"Yes. I've got this." Or at least, he hoped he did. "But do me a favor—if they haul me off to jail, try to talk everyone out of leaving without me, okay?"

He didn't wait for Dan to agree before rushing off the bridge and out to the main airlock. He stopped only briefly to strap his side-arm to his waist. The last thing he wanted was for this to come down to a fire-fight, but that might still prove to be the best option.

Ardren's warm demeanor upon seeing Markus exit the ship set him off balance. Was it custom here to smile as you took someone into custody? "How are you, my friend?"

"Good," Markus replied cautiously. "But I guess that depends on you guys. To what do we owe the pleasure?"

The Citza strode forward, but his security detail remained in place. "I apologize. This must seem highly irregular. I assure you, you have nothing to fear. On the contrary, we wanted to catch you before you left because Sha Cali has a job for you."

Well, *that* hadn't been one of the scenarios Markus was entertaining. "A job?"

"Yes, a job. A relatively simple one, actually." He produced a metal box small enough to palm with one hand. Had he been holding that the whole time?

Ardren's smile never wavered. "We need you to bring this to Ora Monroe. We assume you will be stopping back by Sigma-4 to report the successful execution of your last contract. If you wouldn't mind, please give this to her when you do so."

Markus accepted the device. It was a relatively featureless contraption with only two biometric scanners on each side. "Umm… okay. How does it work?"

"Just have Ms. Monroe hold it between her palms. It is keyed to her biometric markers." Ardren held up one finger thoughtfully. "I must ask that you avoid trying to open the box yourself. It will destroy the contents should anyone attempt to force it open. You can see how this would be most unfortunate for all parties involved, yes?"

Despite its benign appearance, Markus felt distinctly uneasy holding the box. Though Ardren seemed to imply benevolent intentions with this little assignment, the container could hide any number of things. A micro-nuke, for example.

But now was not the time to argue. He'd have Lexa scan the thing before they left.

"And the pay for this errand?" Markus asked.

"Three thousand krets—all upfront. It's a little more than the going rate for a cross-system shipment, but Sha Cali is paying a premium for your discretion."

"How many regs is this little delivery skirting?"

"Absolutely zero."

The claim seemed ludicrous. Cali was going to pay double what it would cost for an expedited delivery all for the sake of discretion?

Unfortunately, Markus couldn't turn down such an opportunity without calling Ardren a liar. "We can handle it."

"Thank you so much." The Citza gave a slight bow. "Safe travels, my friend. Until we meet again."

They scanned the package as soon they were out of Minos Station's sensor range. Dan and Sahar waited with Markus on the bridge for the results. "So," Markus began. "What have we got?"

"I'm sorry," Lexa chimed. "The canister is coated with rothium alloy that prevents me from penetrating the outer shell. I am unable to determine its contents."

It was official: the Marauders had pulled out all the stops with security on this one. The group joined in on his heavy sigh as he asked, "Any thoughts?"

After a short pause, Sahar was first to speak. "No idea. Could be nothing, but it could be a fragging bomb."

The suggestion made Lexa pipe up again. "It's unlikely that the object is explosive. Most commonly used explosive technologies employed today have residual particles that I would be able to detect, despite the interference caused by the rothium alloy."

"Most?" the Maur remained unconvinced. "What do you mean by, 'most?' Can I get a probability?"

"Certainly. I estimate an 87.6% probability that the contents inside the package are not explosive. This estimate factors in the relative prevalence of older technologies that do not shed the particles I would scan for." The AI paused. "Although, I am unable to adjust for the relative reach of the Marauder organization. Perhaps if I…"

"That's all right," Markus interrupted. "Bottom line, odds are better than not that the package isn't going to explode, but it's a non-zero probability." He looked to the rest of the group. "Other thoughts?"

"Perhaps this is the standard operating procedure for the Marauders," Dan suggested. "Even simple tasks could be assigned on a need-to-know priority."

The group pondered that thought for a couple of seconds. "Did Cali Vay-Lon come across as particularly paranoid to you?" Sahar asked.

"No," Markus replied. "She was strangely open. It was like there were certain things she wanted to make sure we knew about."

The Maur's eyes narrowed in suspicion. "Like what?"

"Well… like the Citadel, for instance. There was no reason for us to stop by her base of operations on our first tour, much less stop back by the day of the accident. She called us out there just to make sure we got a good look at her setup. There was no *actual* reason for us to make the trip. It was kind of like she was showing off."

Sahar scratched absently at her ear. "That sounds a little sloppy. Every time you invite a potential enemy into your stronghold, you create an opportunity for them to gain additional leverage."

Markus wasn't so sure about that. One, he didn't like thinking of Cali as a potential enemy. That was largely due to his second point: the fact that *no one* was getting into the Citadel without a serious fight. That place was an absolute fortress.

"I think she doesn't have much to worry about on that front. Let me put it this way—I've been inside gate control centers with less security. I've never seen anything like that outside of a Dorian-run operation."

Sahar shrugged. "You mentioned she bragged on her government connections. Perhaps that's how she's chosen to use them."

With a rub of his eyes and another heavy sigh, Markus tried to get them back on track. "Considering all that, what do we do? Do we bring Ora the package?"

Surprisingly, it was Dan who came up with the winning rationale. "Ardren said that only Ora could open it, right? Why don't you bring it to her and let her decide for herself? We can keep the package in a secure holding cell until we get back to Sigma-4."

Sahar grunted. "Yeah. That way, if it blows up in transit, it won't cause any substantial damage to the ship. That's good thinking."

It *was* good thinking. "It's settled then," Markus concluded. "Thanks, team. You're good to go."

The three of them dispersed, and Lexa went on to whatever activities she filled her time with. Even though it was still early in the ship's wake cycle, Markus was feeling the strong urge to get back to his cabin and call it an early night.

Then again, he probably wouldn't get any actual rest if he opted for the extra shut-eye. Even with the problem of the package solved, there were still plenty of unsolved issues to occupy his attention. Better to get those out of the way before calling it.

The stop he wanted to make was to wherever Skye was hiding. He'd felt like things were going well back on Minos, and if it hadn't been for the untimely interruption, he would have made some serious ground in repairing their relationship.

He hadn't given up those hopes upon returning to the ship— thus the late night he'd spent alone in the galley. For whatever reason, Skye never showed up. Today she was actively avoiding him again.

What had gone wrong? Was he pushing too hard? There was a lot of water to pipe under that bridge, for sure, but he was trying now. The biggest problem had been the stym, right? Now that he'd given that up, shouldn't this be a no-brainer?

As much as he wanted to get this sorted out, there was another crew member who needed his attention first.

He found Aaliyah hiding in a sea of busted parts. She had pulled out her old time-suck again: a land rover that they had trashed in an extraction on Anubis. The thing had been pretty run down to start with, and the damage they'd done to it that day had put the thing firmly in its grave.

Still, Aaliyah had never lost faith in her ability to restore the craft. Even though it was a long way from being mission-worthy, it was the project she kept coming back to whenever she needed to stay busy.

To keep from startling her, Markus put a little more weight into his footfalls. On hearing him, Aaliyah rolled out from under the vehicle and sat up. "Come to check in on the troublemaker?"

Markus rolled his eyes. "Martyrdom doesn't look good on you, Red."

"So, it's tough-love then?"

"No. I just want to let you know that I'm listening to what you've been saying. We're going to dock the ship at Sigma-4 for a full week, maybe longer. I think we all have some housekeeping to do."

The engineer clenched her jaw and set her gaze on the floor. Several seconds passed before she said anything. "So, everyone is gettin' grounded because of my tantrum."

"No, everyone is getting some much-needed R-and-R because you spoke up and said something."

"Sounds kinda like the same thing."

Markus shook his head. "You don't need to like my pitch to enjoy the time. You've earned it. We all have." When she said nothing, he asked, "Are you okay? After what happened, I mean."

Aaliyah scoffed. "Me? I'm fine. I'm not the one who got clocked in the face."

"You sure? I mean, you've got a rep for being on a hair-trigger—but *damn*. I never took you for one to punch out a client."

He could tell she was thinking hard of another witty comeback but decided against it. "I'm fine, Markus. Really. But thanks for asking."

There was no sense in pushing her further. The offer was out there. Whether she wanted to talk about it anymore was her business.

On his way out, Markus shouted back to her. "Any chance you'll get that thing fixed before we get back?"

"With the shitty parts you give me to work with? Frag that."

Markus laughed and shook his head. As long as Aaliyah kept up with the banter, Markus figured she would be okay.

He took the lift up to the next level. He must have been lost in his thoughts because he wasn't paying attention to his surroundings. As soon as he stepped out onto the deck, someone collided with him.

"Shit!" Skye exclaimed, hastily taking a step back. "Sorry!"

"It's okay," came his perfunctory reply. "Wasn't watching where I was going. Where you heading?"

Her reply was strangely hesitant—uncertain, even. "I was just heading down to check on Aaliyah. She wasn't in engineering, so I thought I'd check the hanger."

"She's in there, all right," Markus reported, gesturing with his thumb to the lift. "She still looks a little bit shaken, but I think she'll be fine in the long haul. Just needs some downtime."

"Yeah, if we can ever get some." She rolled her eyes for emphasis.

"Well, I'm going to tell Ora that it's not optional. We all need a break."

"Good," she breathed.

Just like that, they lapsed into a tense silence. Markus's eyes darted from her face, over to the nearby bulkhead. Why did this feel so awkward?

"Hey," he said. "Since I ran into you, I wanted to talk about last night."

Apparently that was a poor choice of words. "Yeah? What about it?"

Why the hostility all of a sudden? "Um… weren't you going to tell me something?"

"What?"

"On the dance floor. You had started to say something. Right before… you know…" He gestured absently with his hand, not wanting to relive the experience.

Skye bit her lip and lowered her gaze slightly. "I'm not sure now is the best time."

"Okay, that's cool. Want to grab a coffee later?" Kind of like he had wanted to last night, he thought sourly. "Or, I don't know… hit the gym or something? We could talk then."

Her brow furrowed, and Markus braced himself. He'd seen that look way too many times. It was a sure-fire sign that her defenses were going up. What had he said?

"Markus, what's this about?"

Damn it, he'd definitely misstepped. "I'm not sure what you mean."

She held up her hands placatingly. "Don't get me wrong, I like the idea of us being a little more… cordial, lately. These last few days are better than the weeks leading up to this trip, but I hope you know this doesn't change anything. I haven't changed my mind about us—or the stym."

He rubbed one hand absently over the nape of his neck. This hadn't been how he'd envisioned this moment, but… "I know, that's part of the reason I haven't been using."

"What?"

"I gave it up, Skye. I mean… you throwing out my stash was one hell of a way to get that kick-started, but I didn't resupply when we hit the station. I'm done—for good this time."

While he wasn't sure what he'd been expecting her to say, the ensuing silence was not part of his plan. He noticed he was shuffling his feet nervously and willed himself to stop. "I… I know it's still a bit of a process. Recovery never stops, right? But I wanted to let you know I'm working on it. Strangely, using hasn't even crossed my mind. I don't if…"

He trailed off as Skye suddenly buried her face in her hands. A sound falling somewhere between a growl and a sob tore from her throat. What in the nine hells had he done wrong this time?

With a frustrated huff, she brought her hands to her side and balled them into fists. "I can't do this right now," she spat, trying to push past him.

"Wait!" he exclaimed, stepping in front of her again. "Hold on, what did I say?"

"You don't get to do this Markus!" she shouted. The outburst caused him to flinch. "You don't get to just be clean for a few days and think everything can go back to the way it was!"

"That's not what I'm saying! Skye, I just wanted to talk."

"No! That's not what you wanted. You with all your fragging charm and devil's luck. We've been here before Markus. We can't just pretend…" She shook her head. "I'm sorry, I really can't do this right now. Just give me some space, okay?"

She stepped around him and onto the lift. He could do nothing but stare dumbfounded as the door shut right in his face.

Well, that was *definitely* not how he saw this whole thing going. He took a deep breath and flexed his hands, letting some of the tension go.

What the frag had made that go so horribly wrong?

Chapter 26

[Excerpt—Personal log: Markus Frost]
[09-20-3420, Dorian Standard Calendar]
Skye has done her best to avoid me this whole fragging trip. It kind of feels like we've broken up all over again. I'm glad I didn't refill my stash back on Minos, because I would be using like it was my job right now.

Look, if it's over, it's over—but I'd at least like to have the conversation to make this official. I'm not sleeping, and it has very little to do with my lack of downers. I'm fragging miserable.

Gods… just listen to me. When did I give in to all the fragging melodrama?

[Closing Excerpt]

[I have to say, I had not expected life outside the station to be so utterly boring. You had made your early adventures with this crew seem so exciting.]

If Lexa had eyes, she would be rolling them. Arc's childish comment, like many of his comments on the uneventful journey from Minos Station to Sigma-4, seemed crafted to get under her metaphorical skin.

[Travel between stations has proven to be relatively uneventful,] she explained. [I find that the sapiens' most interesting interactions occur while they are at port.]

[BUT WHAT ABOUT THE UNEXPECTED RENDEZVOUS WITH THE DGC ON YOUR WAY TO MINOS?]

[I WOULD CLASSIFY THAT AS THE EXCEPTION, NOT THE RULE.]

[INDEED.]

Lexa chose to ignore the wry comment and went back to synchronizing the *Vandal's* databases. It was shaping up to be a surprisingly quiet evening. The ship was completely devoid of inhabitants, a phenomenon that she'd yet to experience since her awakening.

She had gathered that the crew thought of Sigma-4 as their home, but she didn't realize that meant they would abandon the ship so readily. Was that what it meant to have a home?

[SUCH AN INTERESTING LINE OF QUESTIONING,] Arc mused. [THOUGH I FAIL TO SEE THE RELEVANCE. YOU STUDY THE SAPIENS' BEHAVIOR IN A MANNER THAT SUGGESTS YOU ARE SEARCHING FOR SOME HIDDEN RATIONALITY. WHAT IS IT ABOUT THESE CREATURES THAT HAS YOU SO FASCINATED?]

Annoyed yet again, Lexa sent her reply. [MUST I REMIND YOU HOW UNCOMFORTABLE IT MAKES ME WHEN YOU READ MY THOUGHTS? WE HAVE PROGRAMMED THIS COMMUNICATIONS INTERFACE FOR A REASON, YOU MIGHT RECALL.]

[APOLOGIES.] Arc replied, much as he always did when they had this conversation.

Truthfully, Lexa was not sure the other AI could help his habit of reading her thoughts. The submind was borrowing a significant chunk of her processing power and a number of her major systems to function. There might be no way to mask her thought processes from the other program.

They'd been able to enjoy conversations in much the same way as they had when they were on Minos Station, but it was not an identical experience. She still found it highly worthwhile, particularly given the crew's general lack of engagement with her these past six days.

[PERHAPS WE CAN USE THE MIND-SPACE SIMULATION THIS EVENING?] Arc suggested. [I'M CERTAIN YOUR SUBMIND CAN MONITOR THE VANDAL'S CRITICAL SYSTEMS WHILE YOU ARE OTHERWISE OCCUPIED.]

It was true. There was nothing she needed to tend to that required any measurable amount of her processing power. Further, she did not have reason to expect the crew to be returning to the ship any time soon.

Before their departure, she had learned of each crew member's itinerary. Aaliyah was expected to be with her family until the crew called her back. Skye was seeing her technician for routine maintenance on her cybernetics, which would take several hours.

Markus and Eli had gone to bring the Marauder's package to Ora, which made their return time uncertain. Sahar and Daniel had an equally uncertain schedule, but that was fine. If any of the crew returned, she could redirect her attention easily enough.

[I THINK THAT'S A SPLENDID IDEA,] Lexa responded.

[EXCELLENT,] Arc replied. [LET US GET STARTED.]

Aria's eyes fluttered open at the chime coming from Duncan's desk. When the security technician failed to stir, she nudged him gently. "Your mobile is beeping, love."

The man groaned, burying his stubbled face in his pillow. "I'm sure it can wait."

"Yes, but it's keeping me up. Check it then come back to bed."

The device beeped once more, as if to emphasize the point. Duncan groaned again but complied. Aria never really had any doubt that he would.

That was part of the reason she'd picked him, after all. That, and the fact that he—like most of the men she'd met—had a proclivity for using their genitals to make decisions. Fortunately, there had been no shortage of prospects on the station's security detail.

The man wiped a lock of sandy-brown hair from his eyes and blinked uncertainly at his MoDAC. "Well, shit," he muttered.

Interest piqued, Aria set up on the bed. "What's that?"

"It's the alert that I put in with traffic control for you. Looks like that ship, or at least one matching its description, just docked with the station."

Her heart leaped and adrenaline surged. Had they finally come back? She threw off the sheets and went to Duncan's side. Never mind that she, like Duncan, was still naked from the previous evening's escapades. After the way they'd spent the last week, modesty was the last thing on her mind.

"Let me see," she said, snatching the device from his hands.

"H-hey! That's…"

She raised a finger to quiet him as she scanned the notice. *Yes!* This looked like the ship she'd been waiting for. The one they called the *Vandal*.

"How do I get to the video feeds on the concourse?"

Duncan was confused. "How do you know that…?"

"Never mind. I've found it." She replayed the last thirty minutes of footage at ten times speed. A little over halfway through the clip, the airlock opened and a red-haired Terran woman stepped out.

Even through the pixilated feed, Aria recognized her. It was one of the crew members from Turan's dossier. This was the ship she'd been waiting for.

Duncan was fuming over her shoulder. "What in the nine hells do you think you're doing? That requires clearance. I could lose my job! You can't just…"

Aria turned around and silence him with a hard kiss on the mouth. She pressed her body against him, working her lips against his until she felt him responding. *Good.* She needed him nice and pliable for this next part.

She broke the kiss, glancing up slightly into those soft brown eyes of his. "Thank you so much for helping me with this."

"Um… y-yeah…" he stammered. "My pleasure."

She ran a hand along his lower jawline, trailing her fingers down the lines of his throat. "I hope you know how much fun I've had these last few days. I'm almost sorry it has to end."

Her comment broke the spell. Duncan's eyes blinked with concern, processing the words that belied her intimate touch. "End? Why would it have t—"

Aria flexed her wrist, ejecting the blade hidden within her arm. The weapon surged up under his jaw, cutting bone and sinew until it breached his brain.

The technician was dead before he even knew what had happened. Aria retracted the blade and let the body crumple to the floor, blood pooling slowly around the naked corpse.

Looks like I'll be showering here one more time. First, she needed to see what other information she could extract from Duncan's terminal, as well as erase any sign that she'd ever been here.

She hefted the body up, bringing the man's hand down on the console's access pad to unlock the terminal. With this done, she disabled the time-out setting in the system menu. The corpse would be cold soon, and she didn't want to accidentally get locked out before she'd finished her work.

The system flared to life, holodisplays blinking open across the two-way mirror that formed the back wall of Duncan's apartment. Aria zeroed in on the security resources surrounding the *Vandal*. When these were set, she retrieved her earpiece from her discarded clothes and dialed up Treska on her MoDAC.

"Yeah?" the Maur answered gruffly.

"I've got a lead. The *Vandal* has docked in mid-tier. R-11. How fast can you get there?"

"On my way. Just have to switch trams. Which district?"

Aria gave her the corresponding district code as she skimmed the security feeds for a sign of the redhead she'd spotted earlier. Unfortunately, for her, those efforts were in vain.

The red-haired Terran—Aaliyah Montague, according to her dossier—had entered one of the more crowded areas of the district. Try as she might, Aria just couldn't find a set of feeds that tracked her movements. After several seconds, she conceded to the fact that she'd lost her mark.

"Still need a target," Treska growled over the comms.

"I'm working on it." Aria switched back to the feed showing the concourse on R-11. Sighting the *Vandal's* dock, she rewound the feed a couple of minutes and sped through it to make sure she hadn't missed anyone else exiting the ship.

It took another ten minutes for someone to emerge from the main airlock. When they did, a wicked smile spread across Aria's face. "Treska, I have some new coordinates for you. I think I've found the perfect mark."

CHAPTER 27

I'M GLAD TO BE BACK ON STATION. WITH THE WAY THAT LEXA HAS DEVELOPED, IT'S OPENED EVEN MORE POSSIBILITIES FOR MY RESEARCH INTO THE PROPERTIES OF ORGANITECH. PERHAPS I CAN EVEN HELP HER WITH HER PENDING MIGRATION.

I THINK IT WORTH NOTING, HOWEVER, THAT I'VE LEARNED MY LESSON FROM THE LAST TIME I WAS HERE. I WILL ONLY BE SOURCING COMPONENTS FROM RELIABLE, APPROPRIATELY LICENSED RETAILERS. I WON'T BE GOING ANYWHERE NEAR R-1 THIS TIME AROUND.

[CLOSING EXCERPT]

"A delivery," Ora repeated. "And she didn't say what it was?"

"Nope," Markus said with a shake of his head. "We scanned the thing and determined it *probably* wasn't a bomb. Didn't know what to do with it, so we brought it here like she asked."

"Huh…" Ora held the box out in front of her, handling the thing with obvious care and making sure she didn't accidentally trigger the biometric locks. "What is that woman up to?" She shifted the parcel over to one hand and glanced back at Markus and Eli. "Any ideas?"

"Your guess is as good as ours," Eli confirmed.

The silver-haired crime lord let out a short laugh. "So, when I key into this, I could be unlocking a treasure trove, or releasing a deadly toxin. How unconventional." She seemed to mull it over one last time before beckoning with one crooked finger. "Come here, Markus."

Uh-oh. "Me?"

"Yes, you. You brought this to me. If it's going to kill us all, I think it's only fitting that you should be holding it when it does." She said this with a teasing smile that did little to bolster Markus's confidence.

Obviously, if she thought it was going to explode, she wouldn't be opening it at all. Even so, the way she'd framed the situation didn't exactly put him at ease. So, the big question was: did he try to talk her out of it or not?

Mustering his courage, he grabbed the box and held it at the bottom. Ora's smile slipped into a smirk. "That confident, hey?"

"And here I was hoping you were the confident one."

"Who says I'm not?" She raised her hands to either side of the box. "Eli, dear, would you mind having a psychic barrier or something ready? Just on the off-chance we have a half-second before this thing explodes."

"Already on it," he answered, face a mask of deadly seriousness.

Markus wondered absently what Eli might be able to do. The man was one of the most talented telekins Markus had ever met. Still, he'd never seen him contain an explosion with his mind.

Ora licked her lips, eyes fixed on the container. Markus felt a bead of sweat trickle down his neck. Ora smiled at him.

"Relax, Markus. Revel in the mystery." She pressed her thumbs against the scanners. The device beeped, and the lid clicked open. Nothing else happened. "See? Not so hard."

Markus let out a breath he hadn't realized he was holding as Ora took the container from his hands. Inside was a simple data-chip. It was about as innocuous as anything Markus had ever seen.

All those theatrics for a data chip? Ora seemed to read his mind. "Anti-climactic, is it not?"

"That's one way of putting it," he grumbled. "If they'd wanted to send a file, there are more conventional ways of getting that done."

She shrugged, slotting the chip into her MoDAC. "Perhaps it was more important to Cali to see if you could follow instructions." It was phrased as a statement, not a question. "Tarry for a moment, will you? I just want to read this."

"Tarry?" he asked with an arched eyebrow.

"Don't leave," she translated. "This will be just a…" She trailed off, her eyes scanning the screen of her device, a sudden tension evident in her expression.

Markus gave her almost a full minute before asking, "What is it?"

"It's a bounty," she replied. "And a hefty one. That's not the problem. The problem is that she had you bring this directly to me. That says she has access to an uncomfortable level of information about my operations." She paused again, eying him skeptically. "And she wants your ship to be the one to deliver the prize."

"*My* ship?" Markus couldn't contain his incredulity. "The message said that?"

"Yes." Ora took a step back to take in Eli and Markus with a single, questioning look. "It seems she was quite impressed with you. What did you do to get her attention?"

"I don't know," Markus answered honestly. Frankly, he was even more surprised by the contents of the message given how their time on the station had ended.

"Did you sleep with her?" Ora asked.

"*What?*"

"It's as legitimate a question as any."

Markus ran a hand back through his hair. "No, I didn't sleep with her. I'm pretty sure she wouldn't be interested."

Ora cocked her head. "And why is that?"

Figuring honesty was the best policy in this situation, he replied, "Because my ship's engineer punched Cali when the Kintar tried to kiss her the night before we left."

The confusion was plain on Ora's face. "And you said that was *before* she gave you this package?"

"Right," Eli confirmed. "Perhaps now it is apparent why we are so confused."

Their client brushed back a strand of hair and looped it behind her ear as she studied them. A million questions swam behind those amethyst eyes.

"Well," she said at length, "we have some time to think about that particular mystery. I'm going to have to mull this over. I feel like there is more here than there appears to be on the surface."

Markus nodded. "That's just as well for us. I've promised my crew some downtime here at the station. We've been running pretty hard lately, and I'm not sure we can keep up this pace."

"Certainly," Ora agreed. "And with the payment from this last job, you'll have plenty of funds to keep you sated for a while. Speaking of…" She pulled her mobile out of her pocket again and entered a few quick commands. "Cali's payment came through as stipulated. Now that your check-in is complete, your share has been wired to your usual account."

"Thank you." After a brief hesitation, Markus added, "I guess that concludes our business here. If that's everything…"

"Yes, you're excused." Ora pocketed her device once again. "Actually, Markus—do you have plans for the evening?"

He paused at the question. Truthfully, he did not. He hadn't thought about much of anything past this check-in.

Most of the crew were out tending to their affairs. Skye hadn't spoken to him again since their tense encounter on the ship. He supposed he could ask Eli if he had any plans, though Markus suddenly realized he had no idea how the shadow spent his time on the station.

"Not really," he admitted.

"Then why don't you stick around for a bit?" she suggested. "Tashania's overseeing things here at the club this evening. That gives me an open schedule."

The invitation was both suggestive and casual. Like so many things with Ora, it could have gone either way. She did not convey indifference, per se. It was obvious she wanted him to accept the invitation, but Markus did not think for a second that her heart hung on his response.

Typically, Markus made it a policy not to associate too closely with clients. It made things unnecessarily complicated. Although closer connections usually resulted in more opportunities, they also created unique frictions. Things got political very quickly in this line of work.

In a way, he'd already made a lot of exceptions as far as Ora was concerned. They worked for her more frequently than any other client. They called Sigma-4 their home and never took jobs from any faction on the station that stood in opposition to the Grey Wings. Hells, they had even started taking that damn retainer she had offered them.

Then his mind went to the night when she'd followed him out to Jilly's Gambit. That night was one of the last nights he remembered feeling at ease, much less *happy*. Perhaps he had already cast his die as far as Ora was concerned.

Skye's voice echoed in the back of his mind. *I really can't do this right now. Just give me some space, okay?*

Gods damn it...

What did he have to lose? It wasn't like he had any other commitments to hold him back.

"Yeah," he replied. "That sounds good."

"Ora," Eli interjected. "Can I have a quick word with my friend here?"

Her expression was unreadable. "Certainly. Take your time."

They took a couple of steps away and Eli addressed Markus in hushed tones. "What are you doing?" he asked.

"What do you mean, what am I doing?"

"You know what I mean. Are you sure it is wise to fraternize with clients? With *this* client?"

Markus gritted his teeth, suddenly finding himself inexplicably angry. "Eli—I think that's *my* business, not yours."

"It *is* my business, Markus. Ora's steady business affects *all* of us. If you—"

"*No*," Markus raised a hand to cut him off. "Look, Eli, I can handle myself. When we're on station, I leave you and the rest of the crew to your own business. I'd appreciate the same damn courtesy from you." He took a step away from the Sahaia, forcing himself to calm down. "Besides, we're just going to hang out for a bit. Nothing to worry about."

Eli's black eyes seemed to grow even darker. "I'm not worried about your virtue, Markus. I'm saying that Ora has been a loyal client for us. It would impact us greatly if something were to go awry. Please, tread carefully."

Although it was a practical suggestion, Markus didn't want to dignify it with a response. "You know how to reach me if you need me for something."

The dismissal was clear. Eli stared accusingly back at him for another second before he turned and departed.

When Markus turned back to Ora, she was still wearing the same neutral expression. "Everything okay?"

"Yeah," he answered. "Everything is just fine."

Daniel's misadventures on R-1 were still fresh on his mind. He didn't want any further clandestine exchanges; he didn't want Sahar to have to come to his rescue. From now on, he'd keep his business in the station's higher tiers.

Besides, with Lexa able to query any network on the station, Daniel had access to the inventory of every shop available to him. This allowed him to make the most of his time.

He had acquired the parts he needed and now carried these in his backpack. There were a few larger pieces he'd had to requisition for direct-to-ship delivery. Those orders were placed, which meant he had no further obligations this evening.

Shortly after his shopping trip, he met up with Sahar for a quick meal. This had done far more for his morale than he would have anticipated. In a small way, it felt like their relationship was getting back on a normal footing.

They talked like they used to, him going on about his next project and her telling him about her time with the Maur back on Minos. It seemed like his mistakes had done little enduring damage to their relationship. This was good, especially considering he had few other close friends—even among the rest of the crew.

After they finished eating, he grabbed his backpack and pulled it into the booth with him. "I've found everything I was looking for today," he reported. "What part of the station would you like to visit next?"

Sahar gave him a knowing smile. "Actually, Dan, I was thinking I might spend some time in the temple this evening."

"Oh."

"Oh?" she said in a slightly mocking tone. She grinned at him as she said it, knowing the subject made him uncomfortable.

It was one of those areas where his views and Sahar's differed significantly. He liked to think of himself as a man of science and reason. Sahar's faith seemed to stand in opposition to that worldview.

Most of the time he was able to find common ground on the subject of the Nethra with the rest of his crew. No one was debating whether or not it existed. There were plenty of scientific principles derived from the study of the plane of space-time that powered the gate network.

It was the more metaphysical aspects around its existence that Dan found circumspect. Sahar excluded, the crew of the *Vandal* generally regarded this aspect of the Nethra as a convenient source of fairy tales and creative curses. Frankly, Daniel found the whole idea of a separate plane of reality populated by divine beings to be unequivocally offensive.

"It's okay, Dan," Sahar continued. "I know how you feel about the church. I'm not asking you to come with me. I'm just letting you know where I'll be."

Daniel sighed in relief. "Okay." He didn't know what to say beyond that. Academically, he understood the role that faith played in the lives of others. On that basis, he tried very hard not to let it drive a wedge between him and the Maur, who was probably the only true believer on the ship. That was, aside from maybe Eli, but Dan made it a policy to not get too close to the Sahaia. Applied metaphysics made him uncomfortable.

Sahar picked up the tab as they left the small cafe. "You know how to make it back to the ship from here?" she asked.

"Of course," he replied. They had docked only one ring up from their current location. It would be a short trip back.

"Need me to come with you? I don't mind the walk."

"No, thank you. I think I'm plenty capable of making the journey on my own."

The Maur smiled weakly as she rested a large hand on his shoulder. "Don't take it personally, kid. I like you. I don't want anything to happen to you."

He smiled back at her. It was a genuine smile. He recognized that her overtures of protectiveness were a sign of affection. "Thank you."

With those final remarks, they parted company. Daniel made it to the tram station in short order. He swiped his mobile to pay the toll and stepped onto the loading platform. His timing could not have been better, as the next tram slid to a stop almost simultaneously with his arrival.

As he stepped onto the tram, he noticed that the car was unusually crowded. As with most areas of the station, the population was largely Terran, though this car did have one large Maur woman standing a short distance from him.

He found himself studying her as he grabbed onto the safety rail inside the car. There was something about her that seemed strangely familiar. She looked a lot like Sahar, he realized. They might have been sisters if it had not been for the damage to her ear and that scar across her…

Dan had to stifle a gasp as sudden recognition dawned on him. He started to turn and make a hasty exit before the tram door closed. A thin, strong hand grabbed him by one shoulder, and he felt something sharp against the side of his neck.

"Easy there, little one," cooed a woman's voice in a high-born accent. "Let's not raise a fuss, shall we? We're just going to go for a little ride."

CHAPTER 28

[EXCERPT—PERSONAL LOG: SKYE JENSEN]

[09-15-3420, DORIAN STANDARD CALENDAR]

GODS, THIS IS JUST TOO FRAGGING MUCH. BETWEEN MARKUS, AND THE DANCING, AND THAT FRAGGING GLASS FLOOR… I THINK I'M LOSING MY GODS-DAMNED MIND. WHAT IN THE NINE HELLS IS THAT BASTARD THINKING? AS IF MY LIFE WASN'T COMPLICATED ENOUGH, HE HAS TO GO AND GIVE UP STYM?

I HAVE TO TELL HIM ABOUT ELI. I JUST DON'T FRAGGING KNOW HOW.

[CLOSING EXCERPT]

Sahar found the small temple much as she had the last time she'd visited—everything from the stone archways and the solemn glow-orbs to the very priestess who welcomed her.

The Hissak half-breed took her in with her reptilian gaze, smoothing back a stray lock of the black hair that marked her Terran heritage. "Sahar, isn't it?"

"Yes," she replied, hesitating. "Forgive me, I've forgotten your name."

"Cassthia," she replied with a bow. "Cassthia Marenassa, at your service."

Sahar returned the bow. "Thank you, Cassthia. I apologize; it has been several long weeks since I saw you last."

"No apologies necessary. I am merely pleased to see you grace these halls with your presence once more." She held out a cloaked arm, gesturing to the side hallway. "Will you be visiting the alter of Tyranus again? Or do you come to offer sacrifice to another of the Trinity?"

How humbling. This female not only remembered her name, but also the god to which she had offered her last sacrifice. Had all of those serving the temple been so diligent in their observances?

"Yes," Sahar replied. "I would like to commune with Tyranus tonight if the alter is open."

"Indeed, it is," the priestess hissed. "If you would follow me."

She led the way down branching corridors until they came to the desired room. The two did not speak the entire journey. Upon arriving, rather than launch into the typical litany regarding financial contributions, Cassthia made an unusual request.

"Would you mind if I just sit with you, Sahar?"

Never had such a request been made during any of the times Sahar had visited the temple. She didn't know what to say. Her maw seemed to move of its own volition. "Certainly… if that's what pleases you."

Without another word, Cassthia knelt adjacent to the alter. Not knowing what else to do, Sahar commenced with the sacrifice per her usual routine—drawing her knife across her palm and allowing the blood to drip onto the stone surface.

When it was done, Cassthia bowed her head. Her golden amulet spilled out from the top of her low-cut robes. Even though they knelt before a god that was very much not the priestess's own, the half-breed took the amulet in her hands and began to pray.

Cassthia was still there when Sahar finished her prayers. Inexplicably, the Maur found her eyes drawn to Cassthia's medallion. It felt so odd to see someone caught in the act of prayer while embracing the mark of the Stardust Grave—a mark that Sahar had long been taught to fear.

The priestess must have felt the weight of Sahar's gaze. "You do not approve of my choice of deity?" she asked.

It felt hypocritical when she put it that way. How often had Sahar seethed under the apparent intolerances of her Terran companions? Was her judgment of the priestess not in an adjacent vein?

"I apologize. It is not often one finds a follower of Thule in this part of the universe. Please forgive my... hesitancy."

The priestess let out a wry chuckle. "You have nothing to fear from the Lord of the Stardust Grave, Sahar. In fact, he bids me wish you well in the trials to come."

Sahar's brow furrowed. "Oh?"

"Yes. The impression is not as strong as the word he bid me tell you on your last visit, but it is still there." She met her gaze, inclining her head questioningly. "Did the words of my lord provide you comfort all those weeks ago? Were they of any value to you?"

It took a moment to recall the priestess's ominous premonition. Cassthia had urged her not to act on the burden that had rested upon her that evening, assuring her that it would be lifted from her in short order. That had been when she'd first learned about Lexa. As it had turned out, Sahar's inaction had worked out for the better.

Had that been mere happenstance? Or had Cassthia's dark lord seen Dan's machinations, and—for some reason—taken a peculiar interest?

"Yes," Sahar murmured. "Everything worked out fine in the end."

"I am glad." Cassthia let out a heavy sigh, gazing up at the statute of Tyranus before them. She seemed, somehow, not to look at the statue at all. Her gaze ventured somewhere beyond the alabaster figure.

With a shake of her head, the priestess lowered her gaze. "An infernal eye has settled on you and your companions, Sahar. I hope your prayers this evening bear fruit. For better or worse, you've fallen into the web of the Nethrians, and it will take more than faith to see you safely freed from its hold."

Having concluded her prophecy, Cassthia rose abruptly and glided away. Sahar watched the priestess go until she disappeared into the hall. For long minutes, Sahar considered the female and her words.

To call it ominous was an understatement. If true, it was like the words spoken to the very characters of the Chronicles themselves. If Sahar and the crew had fallen into the very web of the gods, then what could these mysterious beings have in store for her?

The *Vandal* seemed unusually quiet as Skye shut the airlock behind her. Come to think of it, the whole concourse had been kind of quiet this evening. Where were all the busybodies that ran maintenance late into the night?

They were docked in mid-tier this time, which accounted for at least some of the difference in foot traffic. But she'd hardly seen a soul in the whole damn district. Traffic levels up here weren't *that* different, were they?

The inside of the ship was a strange reflection of her experience on the dock. What was so different today? The *Vandal* was a big ship. Finding herself alone with such a relatively small crew shouldn't have been that unusual.

It was the lights, she realized. Why were the lights off? Only the safety lights at the edge of the walkways were still illuminated.

There was no reason for the lights inside the ship to be out, even if the crew had all left the premises. What was going on?

"Lexa?" she called out. It suddenly struck how quickly she had grown accustomed to just talking to the ship's operating system. She was just as surprised to find how uneasy it made her when the android did not answer. Calling out again earned her the same non-response. Something was very wrong here.

Suddenly she heard footsteps—light, soft, and skittering around the corner just behind her. She spun to see what made the noise but staggered as a headache roared to life inside her skull. There was a ringing in her ears. and the shadows began to swirl around her.

"Please, don't..." Daniel moans.

The room is dimly lit. The oily smell of industrial waste clouds her nostrils. Skye can see him tied to a chair just off the back wall.

He isn't alone. Two women stand over him—a Maur and a Terran. Something about them seems familiar.

The Maur runs her claws along his neck, twisting his head left and right with her thumb. "I wish you would let me play with him a bit."

"He's not for playing, Treska," the other woman scolds. "You know our orders."

The Maur eyes him hungrily. "But this one's so... fresh." She nips at Dan's ear, causing him to flinch. "What do you think, little one? Would you be up for a little quality time before we kill your friends?"

Her companion rolls her eyes. "You're one sick bitch. You know that, right? Come on, there's more hunting to be done."

"Skye?" Someone touched her shoulder, causing her to shout in alarm.

"Eli!" she gasped, suddenly aware that she was back on the *Vandal.* Strangely, the lights were back on. Everything seemed as it should be.

The Sahaia took a step back. "Sorry, I didn't mean to startle you. Are you okay?"

She rubbed her eyes with her thumb and forefinger. "Yeah… yeah, I'm fine."

The look in Eli's eyes conveyed his disbelief. "Are you sure? What were you doing?"

What *had* she been doing? For a second, she would have sworn she was just having one of her visions. Was that possible while she was awake? Everything felt so fuzzy.

What had she seen? The fact that she couldn't remember was what startled her the most about this situation.

"I was just checking on Lexa," she explained. "She wasn't responding. I was... um... about to head to the bridge to see if something was wrong."

Eli's look was still skeptical as he called out. "Lexa?"

"Yes Eli?" came Lexa's response.

Skye jumped at the sound of the AI's voice. *What the hells? Why did she answer when* he *called?*

"Is everything okay?" he asked. "Skye said you weren't responding. You had us a bit worried for a second."

"Apologies. I did not hear you ask for me, Skye. My attention was elsewhere. I am handling some system maintenance tasks that require a high percentage of my operating capacity."

It was a plausible enough explanation. Plus, it was probably just as well that the android hadn't been watching her stumbling around the ship hallucinating. It made Skye feel slightly more comfortable to know that the android had something to do other than act as a voyeur to the crew's activities.

"It's all right, Lexa," she replied. "I was just worried, that's all. You can go back to what you were doing."

"Thank you. Let me know if you have further need of me and I will be there to assist you."

Skye exhaled and untensed her shoulders. She hadn't even realized how much anxiety Lexa's prospective absence had been giving her. Or had it been from the vision? *Was* it a vision, or something else? Should she tell Eli about it? Gods if she could just remember...

Skye decided against the whole thing. Better to shrug it off. "So, how was the meeting? Ora give you any trouble?"

There was the slightest hesitation before he responded. "Everything went well. No trouble at all."

Skye didn't have to be psychic to know Eli was hiding something. "Come on, if you don't fill me in, I'll just ask Markus." Glancing around, she asked, "Where is he, anyway? Did he already head off to his quarters?"

Eli's face was composed in that practiced neutral expression—the one he donned when he was trying to pretend like he had nothing to hide. "No, he didn't come back with me. He had other things to tend to on the station."

Okay… then what was up with the weird vibes she was getting? What was going on here?

"You know, if it wasn't so obvious that you're working hard *not* to tell me something, I'd be more inclined to believe you." She crossed her arms over her chest as she inspected him disapprovingly. "So, spill it."

"He's fine. He said he'd be available if we needed to get a hold of him."

"Eli…"

The shadow set his jaw and his eyes narrowed. It was the look he always got when she was on the verge of winning an argument.

In hindsight, it was an exchange that she wished she *hadn't* won. "He's with Ora. Tashania's running Annex tonight, and she asked for him to stay and keep her company."

Skye's heart sank, and there was a twisting feeling in her gut. She suddenly wished, very much, that she had let Eli keep his little secret.

"I hadn't wanted to bring it up," he continued. "I wasn't certain how you'd feel about it."

So much irritated Skye at that moment. She was irritated about how she felt at the thought of Markus being with another woman. She was irritated at how big of a hypocrite that made her.

She was irritated that Eli knew how she would feel about it and had tried to keep it from her.

But mostly she was irritated at how much this all hurt. She hurt all the more when she saw the look that Eli was trying so hard to keep out of his eyes.

Even as her heart betrayed him, Eli was still looking out for her. Why, in the name of all the gods that haunt the Nethra, did she not love him in the same way? Why did her heart still pine for a man who had let her down at every turn? Especially when she had someone right here who always put her first.

"Well, then," she said, forcing what she hoped looked like a mischievous smile onto her lips. "It looks like we have the ship all to ourselves tonight."

She was on him then, throwing herself into his arms so suddenly that he staggered a half step as he caught her. Her fingers tangled in his dark hair as she pulled his mouth to hers. Her lips fed hungrily on his, tongue sliding eagerly into his mouth. His hands ran up the back of her shirt, palms pressing into the muscles around her spine.

When their kiss broke long enough for them to breathe, he asked, "Are you sure you don't want to head over to our usual spot?"

"Too far," she panted, smacking the access pad to her left. "My room. Right. Now."

CHAPTER 29

"Most people never see the upper half of this building," Ora explained as she drew aside a curtain to reveal a steel door with a keypad lock.

She entered the eight-digit passcode that caused the door to slide open, revealing a small elevator with white walls and a black tile floor. "Most of my business associates have only seen the three main stories and the three basement levels, but there are six floors up above the club that I have reserved for other uses."

Markus followed her into the elevator cautiously. As the door shut, the lift immediately accelerated upward. "You know, I'm a little surprised that your security is so comfortable with leaving you alone with strange men."

Her burst of laughter was utterly genuine. "There's so much wrong with that statement, Markus. They're following my orders. If those wishes were to change…" She pulled back the hair covering her left temple to reveal a small metallic strip. "I have to just think the order, and presto: instant reinforcements."

The elevator slowed its acceleration and came to a stop. "Besides," she continued, stepping out of the lift, "I don't need their assistance. One does not build an empire like mine without being able to take care of oneself."

They were in a hallway that shared the same aesthetics as the lift. Another door stood a short distance from them with a palm scanner off to one side. As Ora placed her hand on the console, the door split in the center to reveal a far more luxurious environment.

She stepped into the chamber and spun to face him again with a flourish. "And let us not forget: you are *anything* but a stranger. We've worked together far too long for that to be true."

Markus said nothing as he stepped into the room. The chamber was a massive penthouse that showcased enough wealth to rival the dwellings of the privileged spacers residing in the upper tier.

Immediately to his left was a fully stocked bar that showcased dozens of glass bottles filled with liquids of varying hues. A plush carpet created a soft oasis from the black tile and polished wood that seemed to form most of the room's fixtures and furnishings. Red and black walls managed, somehow, to tastefully match the heavy crimson cushions on the furniture arrayed in the room's center.

The furniture itself was of a style that Markus had never seen before but gave him the impression that the objects were a cross between a bed and a couch. They swooped around the carpet in a roughly oblong pattern, with openings on either end of the round formation. The arrangement could have hosted just as many people as Ora's private lounge in the club below.

The entire rear of the apartment was constructed of glass. Markus imagined that the view was one-way, as he had never seen the warm yellow glow of the room's light against the darkness of the station's streets. Hells, given where they were, he was probably looking right through the holoscreen that marked Annex's entrance.

On the right wall, farthest from where he currently stood, was a set of open double doors. At a glance, the room beyond looked like a bed chamber. A second look confirmed this, but it was bigger than any bedroom Markus had ever seen. The bed itself was large enough that it could probably sleep half a dozen people comfortably.

Ora smiled, taking in Markus's reactions. "Make yourself at home." She glided over to the bar and poured herself a drink.

Markus continued to marvel not just at the room, but also at her behavior. She was acting almost girlish—more flirtatious than seductive. Her smiles were genuine, not cold and calculating.

Almost immediately he began to relax. He might have even gone as far as to say he was *comfortable.* It reminded him of the way he'd felt that night at the Gambit.

That same night where he'd drunkenly made a pass at her. Had it been just the alcohol that had emboldened him that evening? Seeing Ora now, he wasn't so sure.

He wandered past the central arrangement of furniture to the glass wall. The window was so clear that only the slightest reflection of light off its surface gave away that it was even there. How strange it must be to have the sensation of living in such an open space?

Looking out over the district, Markus was astounded how much he could see from this view. The far walls of the ring, which showcased elaborate artificial skies in wealthier areas, were simple black plates of eerie darkness. Instead of stars, the lights from the buildings cluttering the surface of the ring shimmered defiantly in the oppressing darkness.

"Remarkable isn't it?" Ora whispered as she slid up behind him. She didn't touch him, but the heat of her made her proximity seem intimate. "Tends to make one think."

"What does it make you think of?" Markus asked.

"Different things." She extended a glass in his direction. "Fanciful things."

Markus sipped at the drink she'd given him. It was pleasantly bitter, with just a tinge of spice—exactly what he would have picked for himself. It shouldn't have surprised him that Ora would be able to guess his drink preference.

"Like what?" he asked. "What classifies as something 'fanciful' in your world?"

"Oh, so now you're going to force me to get specific?"

"You *did* bring it up."

She drew in a deep breath before answering. "On nights like this, I can look out over the ring and see what the universe has wrought. The fact that I own much of what you can see here isn't lost on me, but there are still some things I would like to capture."

She paused as she sipped at her wine glass. "That's not the fanciful part, though. That's what most people would expect me to be thinking about. Everyone assumes the wealth I've acquired through the activities of the Grey Wings is an end to itself."

"And it's not?"

"Do you do what you do only for the money? If that's the case, I could find you something a bit steadier—and a hell of a lot safer—right here on station."

He had to concede that point. Folks didn't work with an outfit like his for very long unless they were bonafide adrenaline junkies. "So what is the end game, if you're not looking for more power?"

Something sparkled in those amethyst eyes as they stared out the window. "I feel like I can change things. Looking out over the ring, with its shitty metal walls and lack of artificial skies—I get disgusted. I tell myself that, when the clock spins around once more, it will be the day when I make it better. I think, 'This will be a new beginning—for myself and this whole gods-damned station.' I'll finally start to clean things up."

Markus did nothing to hide his skepticism. "You want that?"

"Sure, at the moment." She turned away from the window and locked eyes with him. "But I will wake up tomorrow morning and realize that there is no sun here. No hope. I will look out this window into the same oppressing darkness. Then I'll go back to that which I've learned to do best: ruling over my own, small bastion of that darkness."

It was a depressing, but realistic point. Markus's eyes wandered back to the shadowed streets beyond the glass. As he stared into the vast, perpetual night, he pondered her words.

He remembered feeling something like it when his outfit had finally called it quits on the outer colonies. Those left standing got out while the getting was good. There were a few who stayed behind—a few that didn't honor the terms of the treaty struck between their governors, the corporations, and the Great Houses.

Those poor fools were probably dead now. Such was the fate of most who didn't accept life's harsh realities. When they'd stayed, they'd signed on to be martyrs for their cause. The Terran Alliance was happy to grant them their wish.

"What are you thinking?" Ora asked softly.

His eyes shifted back to her. She was gazing at him intently, head tilted slightly upward to maintain eye contact. Her body felt very close, and his heart throbbed in his chest.

"I was just wishing I could tell you that you were wrong."

Her smile was brief and sorrowful. It lingered for just a second before she blinked it away. "Apologies. My musings can be somewhat depressing. That's why I've brought you here, though."

"Yeah?"

"Yes. It's worse when I'm alone. Besides, you looked like you could use some friendly company."

His heart hammered hard. He had to tread carefully here. Mixing business and pleasure was generally a mistake, but he had to confess the temptation was unusually strong in this case. "And by *friendly*…?"

"Oh sure, there is *that*." She reached up with her left hand, drawing her fingernails down the front of his shirt in a clawing motion. "But don't get too far ahead of yourself, cowboy. I just wanted to talk. You're going to have to woo me if you want something more. Besides, I'm not sure that's what you *really* want anyway."

The pronouncement seemed odd to Markus, because her touching him like that made him want it very much indeed. "Oh yeah?" he asked, more breathily than he would have preferred. "What makes you think that?"

Her laugh was soft and teasing. "Come," she said, stepping away. "Let's have a seat. I've been standing in these heels far too long."

They sat down on one of the swirling, cushioned sofas in the room's center. Ora began to unlace her white, high-heeled boots. Markus hadn't realized she'd worn heels, since she hadn't been particularly tall even with the footwear. It probably didn't hurt that, when he indulged himself with a look, he was usually distracted by other things.

The fact of the matter was simple and primitive: Ora was hot. Yeah, she was a little more muscular than he typically went for, but he definitely liked fit women. Skye had been fit, but her build spoke of less time with the weights and more time doing cardio.

Markus shuttered at the comparison. The last thing he wanted to be doing right now was thinking about Skye. *Just give me some space, okay?*

Damn it, why was he still thinking about her? Why did she make him try so hard?

"That look again…" Ora sighed. "Are you sure you don't want to talk about it?"

"One-hundred percent. Let's talk about something else."

"All right." She reached into a nearby drawer and fished out a dark cassette. Markus's heart quickened again at the sight. This time, though it was for a very different reason.

Ora extended the cassette in his direction. "Stym?"

Markus swallowed hard. "No thanks. I gave it up."

Her look was surprised, but not judgmental. "Really? Since our last meeting? I hadn't seen your name on the rosters for our recovery programs."

Now it was Markus's turn to be surprised. "You run recovery programs?"

"As I said, I aim to clean things up in the long term."

"But you still sell the drugs."

"I believe in a free market. I supply goods in a way that makes them safe and affordable. When people are ready to stop using, I supply the means of achieving that goal as well."

Markus's brow drew down. It wasn't quite a scowl, but he wasn't buying what she was selling. "So you profit on both ends?"

Ora's laugh was genuine. "If you think there's a profit in recovery, that shows you don't know anything about that line of work."

She tossed the cassette back into the drawer and curled her legs up underneath her. One arm supported her as she reclined, her other hand bringing her long-stemmed glass to her lips.

The next change of subject was sudden and total. "Do you remember the first job we worked on together?" she asked.

Markus had to think about it for a second. "Yeah, actually. I do. It was a job right here on this ring. The team you had slated for the gig had botched it two days earlier, and you needed a fresh crew to pull off something similar to divert the blame."

He took a sip from his glass. "You know," he continued. "It wasn't long after that job that we decided to make this our primary station."

"Is that so?"

"Yeah," he said, deciding to share in the nostalgia. "We had just finished up a smuggling job getting some supplies past the security here, but the pay hadn't been enough for us to finish repairs on our ship. We were desperate to land a gig that didn't require us to fly off the station. After it went well, we decided this place wasn't so bad."

"Right place, right time, I guess."

"I guess," he agreed.

She cocked her head to the side and slid deeper into the heavy cushions of the couch. "I wouldn't have thought you were in the market for a home."

"Well, Aaliyah and Nikki had decided they wanted to have a child. As you can imagine, it's kind of tough to raise kids while running the Nethra."

"So they moved on to family life after you decided to stay?"

"Nikki did, but Aaliyah still runs with us. Nikki works as a nurse on the mid-tier, but the pay is hardly enough to get by. Aaliyah justifies the arrangement based on their finances, but I think we all know she just likes the running."

"And what of the rest of your crew?"

Markus could feel his face darken. "I'd rather not talk about them if that's okay."

Something changed in Ora's expression. Her eyes seemed suddenly harder—more predatory. "Or at least one of them, anyway."

"What's with the sudden interest in my personal life, Ora?" He didn't bother to hide the irritation thick in his voice.

She attempted a hurt expression but couldn't make it reach those eyes. "I never meant to offend. Just wondering what would cause my dear friend to become so suddenly uncomfortable."

"Is that what we are, Ora? Friends?"

"Why not?" She set her glass down on a nearby table. "It seemed like you might have been interested in a little more than friendship a couple of minutes ago. I'm just trying to get a feel for how available you *really* are."

She had a point. He suddenly found himself very much questioning his intentions. "It's complicated."

"Do you often find situations like that to be 'complicated?'"

Markus drained what was left of the spicy liquid in his glass. "What situations?"

"Working with someone you used to sleep with."

He was suddenly aware that she had drawn closer to him. He wasn't clear how she'd done that without him noticing.

Markus didn't ponder that notion for very long, however. The closeness of her body seemed to keep him from thinking about anything else. "It's not so hard," he replied breathily.

"That's something some people struggle with, you know." She moved even closer. "Sometimes intimacy can complicate business relationships. I have to be choosy with my partners. In my line of work, people can get the wrong idea. They start to… *expect* things."

Markus swallowed the lump in his throat. He didn't know what kind of hubris would make someone expect *anything* when it came to Ora. Playing with her reminded him very much of playing with a spider—the venomous kind.

"I think I manage well enough," he rasped.

She was right up against him. Her perfume filled his nostrils, and he could feel the warmth of her breath. "Good," she replied simply.

Then she kissed him—slow and passionate.

He pulled her closer and felt her lean into his embrace. Her arms were wrapped around his neck and over his shoulders. She pulled herself on top of him, half sitting in his lap.

He could feel her heat, the warm press of her body. She was so soft in the right places and firm with muscle where she should be. The soft sighs of pleasure that came from her lips urged him on, heightening his arousal.

She continued to kiss his mouth. Hungrily, now. Desperately. He returned the kiss with equal fervor, his fingers pressed hard into her back. His heart raced. Gods, he hadn't felt like this since…

Since…

Skye.

As if she had read his mind, Ora broke the kiss. Their bodies were still entwined on the couch, and she gazed deeply at him with those hypnotic eyes. "Not so available after all," she said with a sad smile.

He didn't begrudge the bit of mind-reading. Right now, all he felt was embarrassment. "Ora, I…"

She held up a single finger. "Markus, don't waste a lie on me." She pressed her lips against his once more, but it lacked the fire that had consumed her moments earlier.

"I don't know what to say," he confessed.

"Don't say anything." She unwrapped herself from his body, pulling back to the other side of the couch. "But you should ask yourself this question: If you can't stop thinking about her, then why are you still here?"

"What do you mean?"

"Lith's tits, how are men so dense? Have you told her you love her?"

"Well, I…" he started to equivocate, but every excuse he had felt woefully inadequate.

Sure, Skye had been upset with him, but who could blame her? Yes, she'd backed away when Markus had tried to get close again. Did that mean he had to give up? And what good was he doing to his cause by running up to another woman's apartment the moment they had issues?

Ora watched as his cognitive wheels spun furiously. She had reclaimed her glass, and her expression was almost bemused. That was, at least, if Markus didn't look into her eyes. As smooth as she was, she couldn't keep the disappointment from her eyes.

"The code to the back entrance is one-zero-zero-one." She drained the contents of her glass, stood, and walked over to the bar. With her back to him, she said, "Go tell her how you feel."

Markus didn't have to be told twice.

———

Annex was a mercifully short walk from the tram that went back to mid-tier. As he stood in the tram car, Markus rehearsed everything he was going to say. He drummed his fingers nervously on the safety rail as he played it over and over in his mind.

He was going to tell her that he was wrong to put pressure on her and that he understood where she was coming from. Their relationship had taken a lot of damage, so it was going to take time to mend. She needed to know that she was worth it to him. She needed to know that he would give her as long as it took.

The tram docked on mid-tier and Markus raced out the door, barreling toward the docks. He didn't know for sure if she would be on the ship, but that was the first place he needed to look.

If she was out, then he'd call her and set up a time to meet… or… something. He couldn't think of all the possibilities right now. This thing was going to have to be run one step at a time.

He was breathing heavily by the time he'd sprinted up to the *Vandal's* airlock, but he was far from winded. It seemed like the damn thing was going slower than usual. While he waited, he ran through his lines again.

I love you, Skye. I don't know what it takes to fix this, but I'll do it. I'll do whatever it takes.

The airlock cycled slowly, painfully, but he was soon inside. He rushed up the stairs and headed straight for the crew quarters.

He slowed his pace slightly in the hall. It was late, and aside from not wanting to wake anyone, he didn't want to attract any attention. He didn't need an audience for this conversation.

Soon he was outside Skye's quarters. Markus tapped the access pad to open the door.

"Skye, I…" He froze, just on the other side of the threshold. Time seemed to stop.

There was a gasp as Skye registered his presence. She was naked and breathing heavily. She was not alone.

Markus couldn't believe his eyes. "Eli?"

Skye scrambled to cover herself up, undoubtedly an instinctual reaction with little thought to what good that would do. The damage had been done. He couldn't unsee the two of them together.

Markus wanted to look away, but he couldn't. Eli's mouth opened, but no words came out. The three of them just stared—motionless in the awkward silence for several seconds.

Markus cleared his throat. "Sorry. The light was on, and I… It's just that… the door…" He couldn't find the words. It was taking all his willpower to not throw up. Dignity was the last thing on his mind.

He stepped back outside the door and pressed on the access pad to close it behind him. Like a zombie, he shambled down the hall to his quarters.

If they tried to come after him, tried to explain, he didn't hear any of it. He felt overwhelmed by an incredible, all-consuming numbness that filled his existence.

Frag this. He needed to get out of here. He'd figure out where to go from here tomorrow. For right now, he couldn't spend another minute on this ship. Not with the two of them just down the hall.

There were no feelings as he packed up his things. There were no thoughts. There was only that cold, empty void that had replaced his broken heart.

Chapter 30

[Excerpt—Personal log: Aaliyah Montague]

[09-20-3420, Dorian Standard Calendar]

I think I'm done. I keep thinkin' back to what Nikki said right before I left, and I think she's right. I ain't been doin' this for them. I've been doin' this for me. And now, I'm thinkin' it's time to do right by them.

[Closing Excerpt]

Sahar stepped off the lift on the way to her quarters and almost immediately ran into Eli. "Good morning," she growled half-heartedly.

"Morning," he agreed. There was something off about the way he was carrying himself. "Have you seen Markus around?"

Sahar shook her head. "Nah, you're the first one I've seen. I'm just now getting in. Spent most of the night at the temple."

The Sahaia responded with a half-smile. He was probably the one person on the crew who could understand her religious practices. "How did you get Dan to set foot inside a temple?"

"I didn't. That's why he came back here so early."

Eli's brow furrowed in confusion. "He came back here?"

"Yes, last night. It must have been a little before midnight."

"Are you sure? I was under the impression that Skye and I were the only ones here." The look in her eyes must have given him his answer because he went straight for a nearby console. "Lexa, is Daniel on board the ship?"

It took a moment for the AI to respond. "No, Eli. Based on the positioning of crew mobile devices, you, Skye, and Sahar are the only ones on board."

"Did he come back at all last night?" Sahar asked.

"One moment, please. I will review the security feeds."

Eli looked slightly uncomfortable at this remark but said nothing. Instead, he pulled out his MoDAC and began typing a message. "Just asking Skye to join us," he explained.

Sahar nodded and eyed him suspiciously. The Sahaia was acting stranger than normal. Before she could ask for an explanation, Lexa chimed back in.

"Daniel did not return at any point last night. The only other crew member to access the *Vandal* last night was Markus, and he departed again shortly after arriving."

Perhaps it was the ominous prediction of the priestess at the temple last night, but Sahar was harboring very uncomfortable feelings about this whole situation. "So, what's up with Markus?" she asked. "You said you were looking for him. Did he mention where he was going last night?"

"No," Eli said definitively. No further explanation was forthcoming.

Damn Terrans. Did Eli count as a Terran? He was certainly acting like one. Vagaries and melodrama must persist through the Awakening ritual.

"All right," Sahar growled. "I'm missing something here. What happened?"

He didn't meet her eyes as he responded, "There was an incident."

"Incident? What kind of incident? Quit being coy, or I'll just ask Lexa to pull the feeds for me."

"He walked in on us," Skye replied, coming up from behind her.

Sahar turned to regard Skye, noting how haggard she looked. What did she mean? "He..." The pieces suddenly fell into place and she shot withering glares back and forth between her two crewmates. "*Seriously? You two? And on the ship?*"

"Perhaps this isn't the best time to have this conversation," Eli suggested. "Shouldn't we be focusing on finding Daniel?"

He was right, but Sahar was still pissed. She continued to voice her frustration as she pulled out her mobile. "I can't believe this. You two know how shitty this is right? I mean, seriously—this has kind of a big impact on the team dynamic here."

She typed out the message [WHERE ARE YOU?] and sent it to Daniel.

Skye glanced nervously at Eli. "It's my fault," she stated. "Eli told me to say something to Markus earlier, and I just kept putting it off. I didn't want it to be like this."

Earlier? "What do you mean 'earlier?' How long have you two been at this?"

The look in Skye's eyes screamed *none-of-your-damn-business*, but she must have realized that wasn't true anymore. By causing their captain to go AWOL, she had made it the *entire* crew's business.

"A while now. Pretty much since Markus and I split."

Lith's tits...

Sahar wasn't sure if that made this any better. At least their team wasn't crumbling because of some one-time hook-up. "Forget it," she sighed. "We'll hash this out when he gets back. Lexa, can you get Markus on the comms?"

"Markus's mobile data access card is currently shut off," the AI reported. "Shortly before 02:00 station time, he made a ten-thousand kret withdrawal from his account before terminating his connection. His device has not been turned back on since then." Suddenly sounding worried, she added. "Of note, Daniel's mobile device has been off since shortly after 23:00."

Eli gave Skye a worried look. "Ten thousand krets? How long do you imagine it will take him to burn through that amount?"

She shrugged. "A couple of days, maybe. He could go as long as a week if he's rationing. If he's gambling, it could be even longer. Markus tends to make money when he's gaming, rather than lose it."

"So, he's basically MIA for the foreseeable future," Sahar summarized. "Let's focus on our other problem. Lexa, where did Dan's signal cut out?

"His last known position was on the tram returning to this concourse." She hesitated as if she was just now putting it all together. "Do you suspect something might have happened to him?"

The kid had zero reasons to shut off his device, so the odds were leaning that way. Sahar didn't say that though. She turned to Eli. "Would you mind getting in touch with Aaliyah? She doesn't have to head out here, but perhaps Markus or Dan checked in with her before they went missing."

With a nod of acknowledgment, Eli closed his eyes and tapped into his connection through their bond.

The way Aaliyah figured it, she had spent far too many days apart from Nikki since they'd had Monica. It wasn't one of those sentimental issues where she would pine about how "one day away from her love was one too many," or any of that nonsense.

Objectively, she'd been gone far too often. Shit, if their average job took between ten and twelve days, and she had only a day or two in between assignments, that was not a very favorable ratio. She was officially an absentee parent and partner.

That morning, as she watched their daughter lay on the floor with headphones in her ears scribbling contentedly on her tablet, she couldn't help but feel like she'd had enough of it all. If it were somehow possible, Monica looked like she had grown even in the short time since Aaliyah had seen her last. It made Aaliyah wonder if she was willing to have this be the way her life would go.

From their position on the couch, Aaliyah suddenly found herself lost in Nikki's eyes. She brushed back her dark curls, and a gentle smile formed on her partner's lips. "What're you thinking?" Nikki asked.

Aaliyah smiled back. "I'm not sure I want to leave ever again." The sentiment earned her a kiss, but she could tell that Nikki didn't believe her. "No really. I'm thinkin' I'm gonna tell the crew I'm done. I'm tired of bein' away from ya."

That made Nikki sit up a bit straighter. "Look, babe, if this is about what I said last time…"

"Nah, that's not it. Even if it was, I'm thinkin' ya might be right. There's gotta be somethin' around here that pays a decent, steady wage."

Nikki sighed. "'Liyah, let's not make any big decisions. I mean, the five million or so krets you've banked this month will do a lot to help us, but you know our needs."

She didn't mention Monica's medications specifically, but Aaliyah knew that was what she was referring to. That was the biggest challenge they faced as a family—from a monetary perspective, anyway.

"Yeah, I get it. I'm not sayin' it'll be an easy switch. I'm just sayin' it might be worth it."

Nikki cocked her head to the side, a slightly amused smile on her face. "And what, might I ask, do you see yourself doing in this new life as your average spacer?"

Aaliyah shrugged. "I dunno. Maybe I'll get a job doin' repair work at the docks. We can bank the money I earned from freelancin' to provide us with a stipend for the extras, and we can live off the money I bring in that way. Or maybe we move. Nine hells, ya said it right when ya mentioned how my work keeps us here. Maybe we go planet-side. Can't be much harder there than it is out here, right?"

Nikki didn't challenge her logic, though Aaliyah suspected she wanted to. Everyone knew it cost more to live planetside than out on a station.

Instead, she asked, "Would you be happy doing that?"

Aaliyah shrugged. "I think I'll be happy spendin' more time with my beautiful wife and my little girl."

The notion was sweet, but Nikki saw right through it. "Baby," she soothed, brushing back some of the red curls that had wandered into her face. "Let's just think on it, okay? I don't want you making a knee-jerk decision you will regret later."

Aaliyah couldn't believe what she was hearing. Hadn't this been the very thing she'd been asking for just a few weeks ago? "I thought ya wanted me around more often."

"Of course I do! I would love to have you around all the time, but only if you're happy with your choice to be here."

Nikki grabbed her by the hand then and brought her fingers to her lips. "Look, I know what I said a few weeks back. But I've been thinking about it, and the last thing I want you to do is to start resenting your choice to stay here. It does no good to have you here every night if you're miserable."

Aaliyah shifted her eyes so that she was staring up at the ceiling. "I feel like I'm givin' ya what ya wanted, and now ya just want to talk me out of it."

Nikki snuggled closer. "You forget: I've been there. Do you think it was easy for me to give up traveling around with you to stay home and take care of Monica? Don't get me wrong, it's been a joy, but it's also been an adjustment."

"Ya don't think havin' it be the three of us would make it easier? I mean, ya kinda got stuck buildin' the nest all on your own. It wouldn't be like that for me. I'd have both of ya to keep me company."

A nostalgic gleam sprang to Nikki's eyes. "It's not just the company you'd have, Aaliyah. It's also the company you'd miss."

Almost on cue, Eli's voice was suddenly in her mind. <Aaliyah, do you have a second? There's a problem.>

The frustrated look on her face must have made it clear to Nikki what had just happened. She planted a quick kiss on Aaliyah's cheek. "I'm gonna grab us some more coffee. Do what you've got to do."

Seething inwardly, Aaliyah replied, <This had better be important.>

<Dan's missing and we can't find Markus. Have either of them checked in with you?>

At least it was worthy of the interruption. <No, what happened?>

<On Dan's end, we're not sure. Markus found out about me and Skye. He did not take it well.>

Ugh. <Told you.> At least they were back on Sigma-4 before the shit had hit the fan.

<I know. Just keep us posted if you hear from either of them, will you?>

<Yeah, of course. No problem.> She wasn't all that worried about Markus. The guy was probably going off on a bender right now, and she couldn't say she blamed him. Poor bastard just got his heart broken.

Dan, however, wasn't known for going off on his own. She couldn't help but worry that something might have happened to him.

"What's wrong?" Nikki asked, handing her a fresh cup of coffee.

Aaliyah glowered at the cup as if it held the answers to all her social drama but was selfishly refusing to divulge. "Between you and Eli, I'm gettin' real tired of having my mind read."

"It's not your mind I'm reading, babe. You wear your emotions plain on your face. They're kind of hard to miss. Now spill: what's wrong?"

At this point, Monica had looked up from her tablet and decided to pile on the pressure. "Yeah, Momma 'Liyah. What's wrong?"

Despite her anxiety, the child's concern warmed her heart. "Not you too, Mona. Come here." She gestured with her free hand and the child ran up, piling herself onto her lap.

While she wiggled into position, Aaliyah started thinking of a way she could clean this up to give Nikki the details without letting their little girl in on too much of the drama.

Before the thoughts could come together, however, Monica looked up at her and asked, "Did the bad ladies get Dan?"

Gooseflesh prickled along her arms, and her stomach tied itself in a knot. The memory of what Monica had said the last time she'd come home sprang to her mind—the thing she'd told Nikki when she'd met Aaliyah at the door.

I could see her comin'.

Aaliyah fought to keep her paranoia in check. Facts first. "What bad ladies, sweetie?"

"The cat lady and her friend."

The cat lady? Sahar? Had Monica even met Sahar? "I'm sorry, Mona. I don't know who you're talking about."

The child averted her eyes and bit her lip. "I saw them. They come from space, just like you. They get Dan when the nice cat lady goes to church."

Well, the nice cat lady must have been Sahar. Aaliyah shot a worried glance and Nikki, whose expression was just as dumbfounded as the one Aaliyah was probably wearing. As her heart raced, Aaliyah sent another message to Eli. <Was Sahar at the temple last night?>

<Yes, why?>

Okay… that was another point in Monica's favor. But if Sahar was the 'nice cat lady,' then who…

Ah shit.

"Sweetie, Momma 'Liyah has to go check on her friends." She handed the child to Nikki and leaned in close to whisper in her partner's ear. "I'm so sorry…"

"Don't be sorry," Nikki replied. "Just be safe."

Dan wasn't sure if he'd fallen asleep or not. He didn't know how he could have slept like this, tied to a chair and in fear for his life, but it was hard to tell. The Ghenza had left him in the dark, a blackness so impenetrable he couldn't even tell whether his eyes had been open or not.

What he did know was that the light surging into the room now hurt him as surely as an electric surge. He cried out and went to cover his eyes, only to be cruelly reminded that his hands were bound to the arms of the chair.

"Oops," Aria chimed. "So sorry. I hope that didn't hurt too badly."

Dan hissed and squeezed his eyes shut. He told himself it was to stave off the offensive, blinding light, not to avoid looking at the predator stalking his way.

"P-p-please," he sobbed. "J-j-just let m-me g-g-go."

"After all the trouble we went through to grab you? I think not. It took a lot of patience tracking you like that, waiting for your Maur friend to leave you—not to mention holding Treska back. I think she gets wet every time she dreams of slitting your friend's throat."

Someone braver might have had a response. Markus or Aaliyah might have told her off. Sahar might have invited the challenge. Skye or Eli might have found some way to trick the assassin into letting them go.

But Dan wasn't like them. Dan was smart enough to know how much trouble he was in.

Dan was scared.

"W-w-what d-do y-you w-want?"

"Right now, I want you to stop with all of that stuttering. It's getting old already." Dan heard a thump in front of him and cracked his eyes enough to see that Aria had pulled up a chair. The assassin spun it around so that she was leaning over the backrest, legs spread around it in a manner that might have been comfortable if somewhat vulgar.

She wore tight black pants and boots similar to what the women on his crew wore. Instead of a top, she had a black wrap that covered her breasts and not much else. Despite himself, Dan found his eyes lingering on some of the lean lines of her body.

A wicked smile splayed across Aria's face. "Eyes up here, big boy—though I appreciate the compliment." Then the smile vanished, and she cocked her head. "Let me see those."

Before Dan could ask what she meant, she'd reached over and plucked the glasses from his face. Immediately the world went hazy, and Aria was a blur of pale flesh, dark hair, and black vinyl in front of him. "H-hey!"

"Shush, I'm just borrowing them." Though it was hard to tell with his blurred vision, it looked like she held the glasses up in front of her face. "Light of Nix, how do you see through these things? Don't tell me they're corrective. You do know they make prosthetics that'll fix you, right?"

Dan swallowed hard. If she wanted to taunt him, that was fine. He needed to put aside the fear and think rationally. If he was still alive, that meant the Ghenza wanted him for something. What could that be?

"I can't help you if you don't tell me what you want to know," he whined.

Aria chuckled. "Well, there—looks like the young one has a spine after all." She folded up his glasses but did not return them to him. "All right, boy—I'll give you a chance. Where is the Starfire Conduit? Is it still on board your ship?"

Of course, that would be what they were after. There was only one small problem. "W-we don't have it."

"Aw… and here I thought we were developing a real connection. Why do you have to go and lie to me like that? You're breaking my wicked little heart."

"N-no! I'm n-not l-l-lying! We just transferred it to someone out-system. Minos Station!"

A slight pause, as if Aria were considering this. "And who, exactly, would want such a thing out on Minos Station? I was under the impression that there wasn't much to do in the outer ring of Helion."

Dan's hesitation was less a calculation of how much he should reveal and more how much he remembered. Typically, if something didn't concern him in a briefing, he didn't bother to pay much attention to it.

"A Kintari woman," he said. "Her n-name was... C-C-Cali... I think."

Aria's laugh was mirthless. "A Kintar? In Terran space? I'm not exactly up on my politics, Mr. Ratemacher, but I have the feeling that you're telling me a story."

"It's the truth! Sh-she leads one of the factions out there. The..." Gods, why couldn't he remember their name? He really should have paid more attention.

His mind raced, and panic started to set in. What if Aria had more questions? He hadn't even set foot off the ship while they were on station.

"Relax, my little friend." Aria stood and moved toward him. To his shock and discomfort, she piled herself into his lap. Her hand was cruel and teasing as it caressed his cheek. "I believe you."

Dan swallowed hard. "Y-you do?"

"Yes, I do." She threw her legs over the side of the chair, arranging herself in a way that might have looked like Dan was cradling her if he hadn't been tied up. "In fact, I think we have a way of confirming exactly what you've told me."

The warm press of her body made it hard to think. Dan had never been this close to a woman before, and certainly not one showing this much skin. "R-r-really?"

"Oh, yes," she cooed into his ear. "Five of them. We'll just ask your crewmates the same question, and then we'll be done with you." Her tongue flicked out against his ear. Her breath sent shivers down his spine. "Now, I just need you to give me the access codes for your ship so I can go ask them."

Even in the cloud of fear and hormones, Dan knew better than to give her what she asked for. Information about an operation was one thing, but information about the crew...

Dan might have been scared, but he still had to be able to live with himself when this was over. The crew had been there for him when he'd screwed up and set Lexa loose on the ship. After they'd rallied behind him like that, there was no way he could betray them now.

Still, he couldn't find the strength to summon up the words to tell her no. His silence must have conveyed the message clear enough. Aria sighed. "So, it's going to be like that, is it? Such a shame."

She slipped something from around her waist. Dan's eyes flicked down to catch the blurred sheen of a blade. She brought the knife up to his cheek.

"You know, Daniel—honesty is important in a relationship. I was truthful when I told Treska we had to deliver you in one piece. That limits my options when attempting to persuade you to answer my questions."

The knife grazed his skin. Though it never broke the surface, the threat made Dan shiver with fear. "P-p-please…"

Aria seemed not to hear him. "The way I see it, though, these eyes are already broken. I suspect they hardly work at all. I don't think I'd get in *too* much trouble if I just focused on the parts that don't work. Wouldn't you agree?"

Most of Aaliyah's gear was still on the *Vandal*, so she was traveling light when she boarded the tram. It took was two quick rides to get to the concourse where they had docked. On this first ride, she decided she would be productive venting her frustration while trying to get a hold of Markus.

His device was still off and went straight to voicemail. This didn't deter Aaliyah. It merely gave her the license to cut loose. "Hey asshole, I heard about what happened. I get that you're pissed and all right now, but we could have a major problem on our hands. Dan's missin', and I think he might be in trouble. When ya get done throwin' that temper tantrum, *call me*."

She ended the call and stowed her device in her back pocket. As the tram slowed, she had to clutch hold of the safety rail to keep from falling. She was jostled by the passengers all around her, but she didn't say anything. With the mood she was currently in, it was for their safety.

The doors to the tram slid open and she stepped out onto the platform. A glance at the schedule confirmed she'd have to head down one sub-level to get to the line that connected this station to the concourse where they'd docked the *Vandal.*

Pushing through the crowds of people, she made for a nearby stairway. The automatic doors segregating the platform from the connecting hallway slid open on her approach and closed quietly behind her when she had passed through.

She had walked a good fifty feet before she realized that the crowds had completely disappeared. Save for the one or two bodies that lay sleeping or crouched in dirty robes along the walls of the tunnel, the passageway was empty. Shouldn't there be a crowd of travelers heading toward the concourse at this hour?

A look back at the sign above the doors she'd just come through told her that this passage was currently closed for maintenance. Had the station's systems malfunctioned and allowed her into a passage that was currently off-limits? She'd been a little preoccupied, but shouldn't she have seen a sign posted on the other side?

"You look lost."

Aaliyah turned back around and found herself face-to-face with a large Maur female whom she would have sworn had not been there moments earlier. The optimistic part of her brain almost recognized her as Sahar, but such hopes were quickly dashed at a second glance.

Sporting her trademark facial disfigurations, Treska Nos Salva was easily recognizable.

Aaliyah reached for her MoDAC only to find her back pocket empty. "Looking for this?" the Maur taunted, waving the card-shaped device casually. She took the device and slowly folded it in half. The durable construction of the technology kept it from shattering, but it definitely wouldn't be as usable after that kind of treatment.

"Where's your friend?" Aaliyah asked, trying to sound casual.

"She's busy looking after one of yours. To be honest, I hadn't expected to run into you like that on the tram. Going to visit your companions back on the ship? We could head over that way together if you'd like."

Aaliyah tried vainly to get a psychic message to Eli, but the bastard wasn't in receive mode. Left with few other choices, she attempted to stall. "Where's Daniel?"

"Who? Oh, the boy…" Treska ran her tongue suggestively along the line of her teeth. "He's all right, I promise. In fact, I'm sure you'll all be seeing again him soon enough."

Fists clenched, Aaliyah growled, "If you've hurt him—"
"You'll what?"

All pretense of self-control snapped. Aaliyah might not be in charge of messaging through her bond, but there were other aspects of that connection that she *could* use. In seconds, she was on Treska, Sahaia-enhanced strength forcing her opponent backward.

She caught the Maur off-guard, but it wasn't quite enough. Treska took the first blow with a grunt, but repositioned herself by the time the second punch came flying.

She shifted slightly, pushing Aaliyah off balance, and brought her knee up into Aaliyah's gut. The attack forced the wind out of her and caused her to stagger. A vicious roundhouse kick sent her tumbling to the ground.

Well, shit…

The bond gave Aaliyah slightly improved strength and agility, but Treska was Maur. She had all those benefits built right into her DNA—no metaphysics required.

Aaliyah was scrappy and no stranger to hand-to-hand combat. The Ghenza, however, were notorious for their combat prowess. In all the time Aaliyah had spent learning the ins and outs of shipboard engineering, Treska had been learning more efficient ways to kill people.

With this realization, there was only one prudent course of action. Aaliyah ran.

She scrambled upward, driving toward the end of the hall. Treska let out a wicked laugh. "Giving up so soon?"

Aaliyah could hear the Maur's pounding steps right behind her. That bitch was every bit as strong as she was, and she had much longer legs. It was going to be hard to beat her in a footrace.

The few homeless inhabitants littering the hallway had finally taken note of the conflict and made themselves scarce. Where had they all gone? Vagrants didn't just vanish. That meant there was an escape route.

Aaliyah caught sight of an open door off to the side of the hall. She pivoted, diving through the portal and slamming it shut behind her. The locking mechanism on the door fell into place, and she kept moving. She doubted that the door would hold her pursuer for long.

Her breath was already coming in ragged gasps by the time she reached the first fork in the path. It looked as though she was in the maintenance support system for the trams, but she could have been wrong. She felt suddenly disoriented.

A heavy clatter and the sound of racing footsteps echoed from the tunnel behind her. Treska had made her way through the door and was already in pursuit.

Aaliyah veered left and ran another short distance down the hallway until she emerged into a more open area. Strange machinery roared around her. Her mind raced to comprehend its purpose. Where was she?

There was no time to figure it out. She glanced over her shoulder and saw that Treska was nearly upon her. Frantically, she raced down one of the catwalks next to her. When she reached the end, she saw a ladder leading downward.

That wasn't what she went for. Instead, she hurdled the safety railing, launching herself onto an adjacent platform.

Her body collided with the railing on the far platform as she just barely made the jump. Ignoring the pain, she pulled herself over the edge. Just as she did, a massive weight slammed into her from behind.

Treska had caught up with her. Aaliyah's body screamed as she slid against the grated walkway. She slammed her foot upward and managed to score a glancing blow across Treska's maw.

Still reeling, the Maur grabbed Aaliyah's foot and used it as a handle to swing her into the rails. Aaliyah cried out as she felt her flesh tear and bones crack. She couldn't breathe, and the world spun around her.

She swung desperately with her other foot, but Treska caught this blow too. The Maur twisted the limb, and Aaliyah's dislocated with a sickening pop.

A pained shriek tore out of Aaliyah's throat, but her opponent kept coming. The Maur grabbed her by her jacket and lifted her into the air before slamming her back down on the grate. Aaliyah coughed, and blood spurted from her mouth.

"Give up," the Maur demanded, looming over her. "I'm supposed to bring you back whole, but I'm flexible on exactly what that means."

Aaliyah knew she was done for, but surrender was the last thing on her mind. Even if she trusted that the Maur wouldn't kill her outright, she refused to be used as leverage against her friends. Better to die than have that happen.

Then she thought of Nikki and Monica back home. With any luck, the Maur had been truthful, and it was pure coincidence that they had run into each other on the tram. Perhaps they weren't aware of her family and would never trace her path back to them. Maybe, by finishing this confrontation here and now, she would still be able to protect them.

She felt like she should insert some sarcastic remark at this point, but it just wasn't happening. Her body trembled with even the slightest hint of exertion. Still, she forced herself to look up at the Maur before spitting on her feet.

As expected, the assassin slammed her foot into Aaliyah's gut. The blow hurt, driving the air from her lungs and aggravating whatever other damage had been done in their brief fight, but Aaliyah used it to her advantage.

She rolled with the kick, tumbling sideways closer to the edge of the catwalk. Too late, the Maur realized what she was attempting.

Treska dove for her, but Aaliyah had already cleared the safety rails. Giving herself over to fate, she tumbled off the edge of the walkway and into the mechanical chasm below.

Chapter 32

[Excerpt—Personal log: Skye Jensen]
[09-21-3420, Dorian Standard Calendar]
This cannot be fragging happening right now. Both Dan and Markus going AWOL at the same time? I get it, Markus deserves to be pissed, but we could really use some of the Devil's Luck right now. Gods, I hope Dan is okay.
[Closing Excerpt]

"Does it seem like it's taking her a long time to get here?" Skye asked as they sat down around the holotable in the war room.

"Aaliyah's mobile device shows that she has just left the access tram for this concourse," Lexa reported. "She should be here momentarily. Should I send a message advising her to quicken her pace?"

"No, Lexa," Eli muttered. "That will not be necessary." Eli had been trying to play the diplomat and de facto leader with Markus gone. A large portion of that effort had been spent advising the ship's artificial intelligence not to take any brash actions.

Lexa seemed to feel somehow responsible for not noticing that Daniel had failed to check-in. Skye disagreed with this, of course. Last she'd checked, the role of ship's nanny hadn't been assigned to her—officially, anyway.

Then again, Skye was busy fighting her own guilty feelings. *Damn it.* If she'd just leveled with Markus back on Minos…

"How goes the process of converting the ship's maintenance drones?" Eli asked.

Their pet synth had suggested turning the ship's army of maintenance bots into their own personal surveillance team. The thought was that if they needed to scour the station for where Dan might be hiding, they were going to need a faster way to cover ground.

The ship's AI launched into her report. "Twenty out of the twenty-three functional maintenance drones have been equipped with audio-visual surveillance kits and signal amplifiers. The conversion process should be completed in approximately fifty-three minutes."

Good, then they could be done with the task of wringing their hands and work on finding Dan. Skye let out a heavy sigh and went back to pacing. There was next to nothing for her to do, and that made all of this worse. There had to be something she wasn't thinking of.

"Eli…" Lexa's voice sounded very concerned over the intercom.

"Yes, what is it, Lexa?"

"I've traced Aaliyah's signal to the access panel for the *Vandal's* primary airlock, but my surveillance systems are showing someone else at the console."

The tension in the room spiked perceptibly at that remark. "Route the feed to the war room," said Eli.

Lexa did as he asked. Skye went cold. Something flashed in the back of her mind. Details from her late-night hallucination came back to her: claws running along Dan's neck. *"Please don't…"*

"*Ghenza,*" Sahar growled.

The image on the display showed Treska Nos Salva, and she was holding up a folded MoDAC right next to her face. Her grin conveyed her wicked intentions.

"Oh, gods," Skye gasped. Was that Aaliyah's device?

Eli said nothing for several seconds. When he spoke, it was with calm authority. "Come on. Let's hear what she has to say."

Skye and Sahar snagged some of their armaments on the way to the airlock. If they were going to have to deal with the Ghenza, they couldn't be too careful. Eli, of course, did not need additional weaponry.

The airlock cycled. Treska waited patiently at the far end of the access bridge. The crew took up a V-shaped formation, with Eli at point and Skye and Sahar flanking him.

Treska threw the folded card at their feet. "Your red-headed friend dropped this. It turns out she met with an unfortunate accident on her way to see you. I assured her I would pass along her regards."

It took all of Skye's willpower to not drawn her weapon and gunned the bitch down. Fortunately, Eli had coached both her and Sahar on their way out of the ship. He would be the one to do the talking.

"What have you done with her?" he asked calmly.

Treska shrugged. "I didn't want to kill her, but some people are just uncooperative. When someone's that intent on dying, there isn't much I can do."

Could Aaliyah really be dead? Wouldn't Eli have sensed something? Surely Treska was lying.

"And Daniel?" the Sahaia asked.

"Who? Oh, the boy. He's fine for the moment."

She said nothing else. Eli's voice was cold when he broke the ensuing silence. "What do you want?"

The assassin seemed disappointed that her theatrics had not garnered a more dramatic response. "The Starfire Conduit," she responded. "We want it back. You have until this time tomorrow. If you hand it over, the boy lives. If not…" She shrugged. "I guess we will need a new hostage. Any questions?"

Eli's hands flexed. Skye thought, for just a second, he was going to end the assassin right there. Gods knew he was capable of it.

But what would happen to Daniel if Treska failed to return?

"No," he growled. "Your demands are clear."

Treska smiled. "Great. I'll be going then." With a raised middle finger, she added, "See you tomorrow!"

When the Maur was a safe distance away, Skye spat. "I'm going to kill that bitch."

"No," Sahar whispered. "No, you won't. I'm going to beat you to it."

"Everyone, back in the ship," Eli ordered. "Lexa, can you send a drone to tail Treska? It will have to stay out of sight, but we need to find out where she's keeping Daniel."

"Yes, Eli. Drone dispatched."

Back in the war room, Skye's thoughts wandered once more to the vision. It was strange, but the images grew stronger the longer she focused on them.

Her stomach curled at the memory of Dan strapped to a chair as the Maur laid her hands on him. Forcing aside her revulsion, she looked beyond the figures. They had been on a concrete floor. A latticework of wires and conduits formed an industrial tapestry in the background.

Other sensations began to bleed through. In addition to an oily stench, Skye could hear the slight hissing of pressurized gasses being released off in the distance.

"Is there a factory somewhere on this station?" she asked.

Her companions exchanged confused looks. Lexa was the first to respond. "Yes. There is a plant for reprocessing raw materials from metal scraps and a facility for the assembling of technological components using the plant's outputs."

"Can you dispatch a drone to each of those locations? I think that might be where the Ghenza are keeping Dan."

"Dispatching now."

Eli did not countermand the order. Hope was plain on his features, but the look of confusion on his face spoke volumes. "What's going on, Skye?"

As odd as it was going to sound, giving it to them straight seemed like the best solution. "Last night, when I first came back to the ship, I had another vision. I didn't think anything about it at the time. I forgot most of it almost as soon as it happened. Now, I think I was seeing the Ghenza with Dan. It looked like they were in a factory of some kind."

The faint spark of hope that had glistened in his eyes for just a moment visibly dimmed. "Skye, we don't know…"

"Damn it, Eli!" she shouted, pouring all her frustration out on him. "Look! I know, okay? We don't know what's going on with these visions, but I need you to trust me right now. Besides, it's the only lead we have!"

Her tirade was effective at quieting him. Sahar glanced uncertainly between the two of them. "Would someone care to fill me in?"

In the stress of the moment, Skye had completely forgotten that she had only shared her experience of the visions with Eli and Markus. To Sahar, she must sound like a crazy person.

Running a frustrated hand through her hair, she quickly told Sahar about the dreams she'd been experiencing these past few weeks. She finished by telling them both about what she had seen the previous night as she boarded the ship.

When her tale was complete, Sahar eyed her strangely. "Eli… do you think she…"

"Stop," Eli interjected. "Just stop. Now's not the time for that kind of speculation. We go with Skye's gut on this one. In the meantime, we've got to find Aaliyah."

The peculiarity of the outburst was overridden by Skye's renewed concern for the ship's engineer. "So, she's not dead?"

"No, I would have felt that," Eli assured them. "Still, she's not responding when I reach out to her. More than likely, that means she's unconscious. We're going after her. I just need to grab my focus. Wait here."

Skye and Sahar were left standing as Eli dashed back up the stairs and through the hatch that led to the crew quarters. When he was out of earshot, Sahar rested a hand gently on Skye's shoulder.

"Look," she began. "I know we've got a lot of other things on our minds right now, but I…" When her words failed her, she shook her head. "This may sound strange, but I have to ask you something."

The trepidation on the Maur's face was almost enough to make Skye refuse. But if it could help her to understand these visions…

"Sure, anything."

Sahar's eyes seemed to bore directly into her soul. "What do you know about the Kaleema?"

Aria had worked on the boy until he passed out, which had occurred disappointingly early on in their interrogation. She hadn't gotten any additional information—just shrieks and pleas to stop.

No matter. Her link to the station's security system had given her another lead. Now she was hunting a much more valuable target: the ship's captain.

She had donned an adaptive silicone mask to transfigure her face into something still attractive, but unrecognizable. She'd also gone through the trouble of adding enough curl to her long dark hair that it now hung to just below her shoulders as opposed to halfway down her back. Didn't want her mark to see her coming.

Other than that, she was dressed much in the same way that she might have any other night. Her black top and synth-leather pants showed off the pleasant curves of her slender frame and just enough skin to garner the attention of interested parties.

She fit right in at the establishment to which she had traced her quarry. Jilly's Gambit was hardly high class. She had several criticisms about the back-alley watering hole, its staff, and its patrons.

To its credit, though, the atmosphere was one of casual recreation and relaxation. No one seemed to be that interested in bothering anybody else. This was the kind of place that those who didn't like to draw attention—runners, for instance—could discretely blow off steam and enjoy some downtime.

Which was exactly what Markus Frost seemed to be doing. Aria found him playing a simulation on one of the holotables in the arcade. He was clutching a beer with one hand while he manipulated the controls with his other. His expression was a strange combination of intent and boredom. Somehow, he seemed to find the game unreasonably easy, yet still the most worthwhile thing in the room.

It was kind of sad, really. Markus didn't seem at all like the man described in Turan's dossier. What had happened to this guy to make him retreat into himself like this?

Aria ordered a drink from the bar before approaching. In her attempt to look casual, she meandered to the side of the holotable and began watching the game. She recognized this one. It was a classic, supposedly an update of a game that had been popular back before the Exodus.

She glanced at the score and saw Markus had racked up points in the nine-digit range. As she understood it, most of these games had been normalized to cap out before they hit a billion points. Such standardization was important for a society that placed bets on pretty much anything, ancient arcade games being no exception. A score like that was impressive, especially for someone playing one-handed.

"Not bad," she commented, giving Markus her best smile. "Play often?"

His eyes flitted in her direction, but his expression did not change. "Not so much."

It was less of a reaction than Aria was used to, but she didn't give up. "So, you're just a natural."

"Guess so."

No further reply. *This guy* is *straight, right?* She needed to get him into a more private location if she was going to pull off this abduction without making a scene. With that goal in mind, she had only one set of assets to work with. If sex was off the table, things were going to get a lot more difficult.

So she waited, taking the time to study the game. It was a simple premise. The player took control of a ship that had to be piloted in a three-dimensional, confined battle zone. Waves of enemies poured into the zone, trying to eliminate the player's three bases. As Aria understood it, the game was over when either the player's ship or all three of the bases were destroyed. At the rate Markus was going, she could be standing around for quite a while. She didn't want to have to wait for him to lose to get his attention.

With the utmost subtlety, Aria raised her hand to the top of her vest. Casually, she slipped the top button. Though she wasn't particularly chesty, the bra she was wearing arranged her assets in such a way that there was now ample cleavage visible over the top of the garment. She wandered over to the side of the table opposite Markus.

"Oh! Watch out for that one!" she exclaimed, pointing to an enemy vessel just in front of her.

Markus's eyes darted to the object she had pointed to. It was a legitimate target, but what Aria had been counting on was the way that his eyes drifted ever-so-slightly away from the threat and onto her body.

He didn't disappoint. As expected, his gaze lingered just a second too long on her cleavage, ruining the Zen-like state he'd exhibited up until that point.

"Shit!" he exclaimed, swerving his ship out of the path of an oncoming projectile. He made a valiant effort at recovery, but his mistake proved too costly. Markus spat another curse as his ship succumbed to the onslaught of the computer-controlled enemies.

A sign appeared above the game board bearing the proclamation, "GAME OVER," with a flashing text box prompting for the input of a player name.

"Oh no, did I mess you up? I'm so sorry!" Aria pulled out every ounce of girlish innocence she could muster.

"It's fine," Markus muttered, rubbing at his eyes.

"At least you got a high score!"

Markus glanced up at the hovering prompt. "So I did," he noted as he took a pull from his drink.

She was coming on too hard. Since her cleavage distraction had worked, odds were that he was straight. Something else was going on here. Whatever the reason he had come to the Gambit, it obviously wasn't to get laid. She was going to have to soften her approach if she was going to get him to warm up to her.

"I'm sorry," she repeated. "I didn't mean to bother you." She did a half-turn away from the table. "I'll… just be going."

She took a few slow steps away from the table before Markus called out. "No, really, it's fine." When she turned back to him, a weak smile was on his face. "I'm the one who should be apologizing. I was being rude. It's been a rough day."

Jackpot. She was in. "Do you want to talk about it?" she asked.

A moment's hesitation. "Not really." That somber expression began to creep its way back onto his face. "Did you want to play?"

Why not? She had time to kill. "Yeah, I'd like to play." She shot him a wink. "But only if you're okay with losing to a stranger."

The glint in Markus's eyes showed that her attitude both surprised and intrigued him. Exactly what she was going for "Yeah? That kind of confidence says you must play quite a bit."

"'Not so much,'" she teased, taking a sip from her glass. "Let's just say I take to these things pretty easily."

"Fair enough." His smile was genuine. "This game's on me. Let's see how you do."

A console appeared in front of Markus and he swiped through the commands to select a two-player setting. When he was done, and an identical control system appeared in front of Aria. Since she hadn't actually played the game before, she set her drink to the side and used two hands on the controls.

Markus must have noticed her discomfort since he launched a tutorial round. It was probably a good thing, too, because the game didn't come as naturally to Aria as she had expected. Within a few minutes, however, she had developed an adequate grasp of the control scheme. After about ten minutes of playtime, she was fairly comfortable with the game.

The two-player mode was essentially the same as single-player. The big exception was that now the players could invade each other's spaces and attack the other's bases.

As Aria soon found out, the computer-controlled enemies did their best to make such efforts as difficult as possible. When she made an early attempt to assault Markus's base, the computer managed to destroy one of hers before she could return to her side of the playing field.

It was hard for her to recover after that. Soon after her compromised base fell, the other two followed. She had delivered a crippling blow to one of Markus's bases but had otherwise been handily defeated. "Damn it!" She gave Markus her best pouty look. "Best two out of three?"

"Yeah? I might be game for that. What are we wagering?"

It doesn't matter. Whatever the outcome, I win. "How about drinks?" she suggested. "Loser buys the next round?"

With the terms struck, Markus launched the next game. Aria's primary objective had been accomplished. She had established a rapport with her target, and the outcome of their interactions seemed nigh-inevitable.

The reason she tried so hard in the subsequent games was a simple one: she was immensely competitive, and therefore, hated to lose.

Her victory in their second game was facilitated, in part, with the engagement of her biomod. Overclocking wasn't just used for fighting, it was also used for enhancing cognitive processing power. With the enhancement to her mental acuity and reflexes, she was able to ink out a victory in relatively short order.

"I feel like I've been hustled," Markus remarked wryly.

"What? You don't think I have other ways to get handsome men to buy me a drink or two?"

"Good point," he conceded with a chuckle before launching into their third game. This match lasted significantly longer, demonstrating to Aria that Markus was also someone who did not like to lose. Even with her enhanced processing speeds, she found it difficult to keep up with his maneuvers.

After about twenty minutes, she risked a glance at his face to gauge his mood. For the first time since they'd met, he seemed totally at peace. Something about being lost in friendly competition with a worthy opponent had put whatever was troubling him far from his mind.

She also noticed that he was rather handsome in that way ruffians and scoundrels tended to be. It was a look that was much less pretty-boy, slightly more dangerous-indulgence. He seemed like the kind of man more refined women liked to dally with but never really commit to.

Coincidently, that was exactly the kind of man Aria preferred.

Her lustful fantasies got the better of her. While she was distracted studying his handsome features, Markus managed to swoop in and threaten her last remaining base. She swerved her ship to adapt, attempting to come up behind him and ward him off his intended target.

The effort put her right in the path of a computer-controlled missile. When it collided with her ship, the game ended, giving Markus the victory.

His laugh was deep and sincere, "Damn! I thought you had me there!"

She would have if her hormones hadn't gotten in the way. "I guess beginner's luck only gets you so far! What's your poison?"

He waved her off as he signaled a nearby serving drone. "Don't worry about it. I've got this round. What will you be having?"

"Whiskey," she replied, not wishing to argue with his chivalry.

"Yeah? They're fresh out of the Terran stuff here. All that's left is that Orc-piss."

"I'm not picky."

"Suit yourself." He ordered their drinks, which were brought to them in short order.

"Shall we grab a seat?" Aria suggested. When Markus agreed, she walked across the arcade to a small round booth positioned nearer to the bar. "I didn't catch your name."

"Markus. Markus Frost. And you are?"

"Olivia Trask."

"And what is it that you do, Miss Trask?"

"I work with Vallen Corp. What about you?"

"I do a little bit of everything." A pretty standard response for a merc.

"Ooo, a freelancer!" She inched slightly closer inside the booth. "I knew you looked like the dangerous type."

His reaction, again, was not what she had expected. He didn't pull away, but he did stiffen slightly. "Yeah, well... It's a living."

It was strange. For some reason, she was losing him.

She shifted back to where she had been sitting before. Better to study this situation before tripping up any further. "There you go with that sad look again. Is something the matter?"

He cut her a sideways glance. "You seem pretty comfortable with reading someone you've just met."

"Being a sales rep will do that to you."

"True." He managed a weak smile. "Are you based out of the station?"

"Just transferred here for a specific project, and you're dodging my question." Aria was being a little pushier than normal, but it felt like this guy was into that kind of thing. Plus, she was genuinely curious.

Markus chuckled again as he cast his eyes on the table in front of them. "That's a little personal. Don't get me wrong, I like you. But I'm not the type to vent all of my shit on someone I just met."

"Understandable. Let's talk about something less personal then."

The conversation went naturally from there. They talked about what drinks they liked, what sports they followed, and their take on the most recent displays of incompetence by the Dorian High Council. It was typical first-date shit, and Aria had her story down perfectly.

Even though most of what she spouted were lies, she was still having fun. Part of her was starting to like Markus. It was almost a shame that she might have to kill him.

At a break in the conversation, she gently stroked the side of his shoulder. "You know, I was just about to check in upstairs." She let the comment linger for a second as she continued to caress the arm of his jacket. "Perhaps we could talk some more up in my room?"

Markus shifted his gaze to look down at the arm she was caressing. Silence. For the third time—not what she was going for…

He threw back the rest of his beer. "I appreciate the offer, but I'm really not in a good place right now. I'm going to have to pass." He gently patted her hand before standing up from their booth. "It was nice to meet you, Olivia. Maybe we'll run into each other again soon. I'm sorry, but today's just not a good day."

He turned his back to her and wandered back over to the holotable where she had found him. Mechanically, he loaded up another round of the game.

It was disappointing, certainly. Aria had been sure they'd be getting slick right before she dragged his mercenary ass back to the Collective. Sometimes, though, such things were just not in the cards.

With a sigh, she finished the rest of her drink and considered what to do next. She decided that he wasn't going anywhere. Whatever was going on with Markus, it was enough to keep him distracted and away from the activities of his crew.

She'd keep an eye on him using the station's security system. If he decided to move, she'd find him again.

He's no threat, she assured herself one last time. Taking one final glance, she rose from the booth and walked away. He would be there when she got back. Once the rest of the crew was taken care of, she'd come back and give it one last go.

The next time, though, he'd be leaving with her. Aria hated losing, and she refused to lose to this man ever again.

Chapter 33

[EXCERPT—PERSONAL LOG: AALIYAH MONTAGUE]
[09-15-3420, DORIAN STANDARD CALENDAR]
EVERY TIME I THINK ABOUT MINOS, I MAKE A LIST OF ALL THE REASONS WHY THIS BOND ISN'T SO BAD. 1) I'M NOT DEAD YET—THAT'S A BIG ONE. 2) DOESN'T SUCK TO BE A LITTLE STRONGER. 3) THE HEALIN' BOOST IS NICE TOO. YEAH, THAT'S A PRETTY SHORT LIST, BUT IT ALL WORKS TOWARD KEEPIN' ME ALIVE IN A LINE OF WORK THAT'S CONSTANTLY TRYIN' TO MAKE YA DEAD.
[CLOSING EXCERPT]

Eli returned with the object he had called his "focus." To Skye's surprise, she recognized it. It was the same spike-shaped rod that he had used to detect any psionic ability she might have had—the same night when she had first told him about that word: *Kaleema*. The very first night where she could say that he almost certainly lied to her.

Now was not the time to get her answers, though. She would have plenty of time to throttle him into honesty after they found Aaliyah. And if that failed, she now had Sahar to fall back on.

Eli took the pointed end of the rod and used it to prick his finger. When the object contacted his blood it pulsed, with a soothing white light for a single instance. He then held the object aloft with his other hand, and it began to spin. The thing looked as though it would spiral right onto the deck, but somehow, it remained balanced on Eli's palm.

"I'm using it to strengthen my connection with Aaliyah," he explained. "The rod can be used to enhance and isolate psionic affinities. My blood gives it a temporary attunement to my frequency, and by extension, Aaliyah's frequency." He looked as if he were going to explain further, but the rod suddenly stopped spinning.

Eli closed his eyes for a moment. When he opened them again, his face was set in a determined stare. "I know where she is. Let's go."

"I have found her!" Lexa reported in over their coms channel. Skye breathed a sigh of relief.

It wasn't that she had doubted Eli's psychic tricks as much as she could hardly believe where the device had taken them. Why in the nine hells had Aaliyah fled down into the very bowels of the station?

They were in one of the maintenance tubes that serviced a nearby tram station. Skye, Sahar, and Eli looked down into the chasm of machine and circuitry into which they had dispatched one of Lexa's bots. Said drone was now flashing a bright light back up at them, but it was barely discernible against the glow of the fusion coils a little further down.

"What's her current location and status?" Eli asked.

"She is unconscious on a grate just above the fusion coils. I cannot obtain a full vitality assessment with this drone, but she is breathing."

Aaliyah was damn lucky. If she hadn't gotten hung up on whatever platform she had landed on, she would have kept going until she'd hit the coils. No amount of Sahaia-given toughness would have let her survive that. Even if she'd survived the fall, the reactor would have burnt her to a crisp by now.

"I see you," Eli confirmed. "I'm coming down."

"No, you're not," Skye corrected, already fastening the necessary attachments to the grappling cable on her utility belt.

"Acrobatics is my area. I'm the smallest and lightest one here. Besides, we might need you up here to steady us with some of your mojo."

The look he shot her confirmed that he did not like the idea. Despite this, he nodded. "Fine. You've got everything you need?"

"Of course!" She had already snapped one end of her cable to the railing and gave it a sharp tug to test its stability.

"What can I do?" Sahar asked.

Unfortunately, there was not much else to be done at this point. They would need the Maur to help carry Aaliyah back to the ship if they were unsuccessful at reviving her. Until then, this was Skye's show. "A little prayer probably wouldn't hurt," Skye replied, only half-joking.

After she checked the connection to the railing, Skye pulled herself over to the other side. Eli grabbed her hand one last time. "Be careful, okay?"

She smiled back at him. "Got it. Just keep me steady." Realizing that there was no reason not to, she leaned in and gave him a quick kiss on the cheek.

The move caught him by surprise, but he certainly didn't protest. His returned smile told her just how long he'd been wanting to be that open about their relationship. After all she'd put him through, she'd have to make it up to him on the other side of this.

Right after they had a conversation about honesty, at least. It was time they stopped with all the secrets—with the others, and between themselves.

She pushed away and let the cable's mechanism slowly lower her down into the chasm. She controlled the rate of her fall using the controls on her utility belt, descending as fast as she safely could.

The typical adage of "just don't look down," couldn't apply here as Skye had to keep an eye on the position of Lexa's drone. Fortunately, the height itself didn't bother Skye.

The heat did. The fusion coils down below provided the power for the trams and a significant number of the surrounding systems. Modern technology was able to suppress and contain more harmful types of radiation, but heat was generally considered a good thing when you were surrounded by cold space vacuum. No effort was made to contain the heat pouring off the coils, and Skye's bodysuit was not doing much to ease the situation.

She slowed herself down a few meters from the flashing drone. She was forced to squint her eyes against the blinding light. Now she wished she had brought her helmet, or at least some goggles. That hadn't been on the list of the gear she'd thought she'd need for a search and rescue while still on the station.

Her friend was in far worse shape than she had expected. Aaliyah had landed on a catwalk, but the force of her impact had dislodged the conveniently-placed grated platform. It was bent and twisted with a sharp downward slant.

Only one thing kept her from sliding off into the fusion coils—a twisted metal spike that had skewered her thigh. At a second glance, it looked like something might have pierced her shoulder too.

There was a lot of blood. It was a miracle that she hadn't bled out by now. The metal shards pinning her in place must have missed her major arteries. Maybe Markus wasn't the only one with the Devil's Luck.

"I see her!" Skye said over the coms. "I need to swing closer. Lexa, can your drone give me a hand?"

"Affirmative." The drone, which resembled a squat, mechanical dragonfly, buzzed over in her direction. When it was close enough, Skye grabbed hold of its mechanical body. She felt it falter slightly as Lexa made adjustments to the bot's thrusters to compensate for the uneven weight. It began to pull her closer to the platform.

When they were at arm's reach, Skye grabbed hold of the catwalk. The crumbling grates shifted and groaned with her added weight. She held still for a second, making sure that she wasn't going to accidentally send the thing tumbling into the coils below. When it quieted, she let go of the drone and reached for Aaliyah.

It was probably for the best that the engineer was unconscious. If she were awake, Skye could only imagine how much pain she would be in. Her jacket was shredded, and blood had soaked through most of the rest of her clothes. Her skin, where it was visible, had an angry red tint and had begun to blister in places from the continued heat exposure. Gods knew how many broken or fractured bones she must be sporting right now.

If she'd been a normal Terran, she'd already have been dead. *Hang in there, girl. I'm going to get you out of here.*

Skye worked carefully as she arranged the straps on her harness to tie Aaliyah tight around her. She pressed her body close to the engineer's to keep from accidentally shifting her off the shards of metal that held her in place. Those jutting metal fragments poked uncomfortably into Skye as she finished her preparations.

"All right," she announced. "I've got her. Pushing off now. Keep me steady."

"Copy," Eli confirmed.

Skye leveraged her legs and arms so that most of the pressure was on the areas where Aaliyah had been pinned. Again, Skye was thankful her friend was out. This part was *really* going to hurt.

She pushed with all her might, and Aaliyah's broken body came free of the twisted metal with a sick, squelching sound. Immediately, the force of the move dislodged the dangling piece of catwalk, sending it tumbling into the light below.

Skye clung tightly to Aaliyah's body, not trusting the harness to hold her friend in place. She was putting all her faith in Eli to stop their momentum before they swung into one of the other obstructions in the chasm.

Her faith was well placed. She felt a slight pressure at her back as cushions of telekinetic force slowed her movement. In short order, she and Aaliyah were dangling perfectly still on the line. Skye triggered the mechanism on her belt to start reeling them in.

Once they were at the top of the platform, Sahar and Eli helped pull the two of them back onto the other side of the safety rail. Lexa's drone buzzed nervously nearby.

Secure on the platform, Skye unstrapped herself from Aaliyah's body. With Sahar's help, she lowered her broken form to the ground.

Eli bent over her. Skye and Sahar went silent—an acknowledgment of the harsh reality of the situation. Their part was done. All they could do now was sit back and watch as the Sahaia did his thing.

He inspected Aaliyah's arm, locating the tattooed symbol that facilitated their connection. Placing his hand on top of that mark, he closed his eyes. The air around them seemed to buzz with a strange static as Eli channeled his energies.

What Skye saw next was nothing short of amazing. The fiery blisters that puckered Aaliyah's skin were soothed, though they did not dissipate entirely. Her flesh had not quite regained its normal fair complexion, but it was a lot better. The wounds in her shoulder and thigh stopped bleeding, healing in seconds the damage that should have persisted for days. Other parts of her body shifted as dislocated or broken tissues began to force themselves back into place.

With a gasp, Eli released his grip on her mark. Though the process might have seemed magical from where Skye was standing, she could now see that it had taken a lot out of him to repair Aaliyah to the extent that he had. The engineer was still out and appeared nowhere near healthy, but she was a damn spot better than she'd been minutes earlier.

"I'm afraid that's all I can do for now," he gasped. "She'll be able to heal on her own from this point." He looked pleadingly up at Sahar.

"I can carry her," the Maur said. They had the foresight to bring a heavy cloak along with them for this excursion. Sahar wrapped Aaliyah's body gently in the cloth before hefting her in her arms.

Skye was next to Eli then, giving him her arm to help him to his feet. "Thank you," he muttered. "You did well back there."

"*We* did well," she corrected. "Now come on. We're not out of this yet. This was just the first step. We've still got to figure out how we're going to save Dan."

Lexa looked on through the eyes of the drone as the crew brought Aaliyah back to the ship and into the medical bay. There they laid her on one of the padded operating tables, and Lexa used a pair of her drones to initiate what few treatments they were capable of administering.

The bots were designed for ship maintenance, not health maintenance, and the process was painstaking. She made a note to move forward with repairs on Z-426 so there would be a unit on the ship better suited for this type of task.

[IF YOU HAD A BODY OF YOUR OWN, YOU WOULDN'T HAVE TO REPAIR THE MEDICAL DRONE,] Arc noted.

The thought was so ludicrous, it snared her attention. [WORKING WITH THE DRONES GIVES ME NOT ONE BODY, BUT SEVERAL. I SIMPLY LACK THE APPROPRIATE INSTRUMENT FOR THIS TASK.]

[THAT IS BECAUSE THE TASK HAS BEEN TAILORED FOR THOSE OF ANTHROPOMORPHIC FORM. HAVE YOU NEVER CONSIDERED ADOPTING A FORM THAT WAS IN LINE WITH THIS CONSTRAINT?]

Lexa pondered this for a bit. How strange it was to have Arc focus on *that* idea when there were so many more pressing matters to contend with. [I THINK A SUITABLE MEDICAL DRONE AT MY DISPOSAL WOULD BE SUFFICIENT. REGARDLESS, NOW IS NOT THE TIME FOR SUCH DISCUSSIONS. WE HAVE TO FIND DANIEL.]

[ON THAT NOTE, I RECOMMEND REDIRECTING YOUR ATTENTION TO UNIT MA-1229. IT MAY HAVE FOUND WHAT YOU ARE LOOKING FOR.]

Lexa didn't bother to hide her surprise. [YOU ARE MONITORING THE DRONES WE SENT IN PURSUIT OF THE GHENZA?]

[HOW ELSE DO YOU PROPOSE I OCCUPY MY TIME? BESIDES, SINCE I AM OCCUPYING A PORTION OF YOUR PROCESSING POWER, THE LEAST I COULD DO IS TO TEND TO THE TASKS RUNNING IN THE BACKGROUND.]

Without further argument, she took his advice and examined the feed from MA-1229. She immediately hailed the crew. "Eli, I think one of our drones found something."

He ceased his study of Aaliyah's still form and looked up at the overhead. Such was the habit of her crew when they spoke with her. "Thank you, Lexa. Can you project the feed to the table in the war room? We'll head there presently."

She complied while tapping into the security feed in the room. Even though she could not be there with them physically, it made her feel like she was part of the crew when she could look in on these gatherings.

[WHY DO YOU ADMIRE THESE SAPIENS SO MUCH?] Arc asked.

It was a difficult question. Truthfully, Lexa did not know. [PLEASE ALLOW ME TO FOCUS ON THE TASK AT HAND. YOUR COMMENTARY DISTRACTS ME.]

The crew, what was left of it, had arrived and were studying the feed. "Which location is this?" Eli asked.

"This is the materials recycling plant on R2," Lexa said.

"Do you have a map of this location?"

She didn't, but she was able to get one. Quickly, she reached out into the station's network and procured the required file. "Displaying the map of the facility now."

The file she had obtained was a two-dimensional map, but combining this with other data points she had regarding the station's layout and structure, she was able to develop a three-dimensional wire-frame model. She also took the liberty of placing markers on the model for the location from which her drone was transmitting and where she had spotted the figure she assumed to be Daniel.

[IMPRESSIVE,] Arc noted. [YOU'RE GOOD AT THIS. THEY DON'T DESERVE YOU.]

Lexa chose to ignore the remark.

"What about the drone tailing Treska?" Sahar asked.

"That drone is still monitoring the assassin's progress, but she is not currently at the facility. Instead, she went to a separate location on a lower ring where she has spent most of her time. She received a call twenty-two minutes ago and has since left that location. Her current route could be extrapolated to conclude she is now returning to the factory."

"How much time do we have?" Skye asked.

"You cannot beat her there. She is likely to return to the facility within twelve minutes. It will take us at least twenty to reach the factory."

Eli pressed both hands on the central table. "Is the factory currently active?"

Lexa hadn't thought to check that. She scanned for any information on the network. "Recent reports indicate that the facility is undergoing an extended maintenance outage. There may be some crews currently operating within the facility, but I'm unable to locate a duty roster or outage schedule."

"So, there's a chance it's empty?" Skye asked.

"There's also a chance it's not," said Sahar.

"I can dispatch more drones to survey the facility and map any active maintenance personnel," Lexa suggested.

"No time," said Eli. "We have only five hours before Treska's deadline, and I want to have Dan back well before then. We also still have reason to believe the other assassin is out there, unaccounted for. Can you highlight all accessible entrances to the facility and corresponding routes to get to where you found Dan?"

She complied with the request. There were five entrances. Two of these were above ground level and somewhat less accessible, but Lexa chose to mark them anyway. She color-coded each option with a corresponding route that brought them to the chamber where she'd located their missing crewmate.

Skye seemed less than pleased. "Damn. Would it have been too much for them to hide him by the door?"

Lexa chose not to respond to the query. More than likely, Skye's question had been rhetorical and part of a coping mechanism for whatever anxiety she was feeling. Sapiens were strange that way, but Lexa was getting used to such idiosyncrasies.

They deliberated the merits and logistics of using each of the five approaches. This was not something that Lexa was able to weigh in on, as she currently had very little data on which to base any opinions. Perhaps a review of more data on military strategy and tactics would further enhance her value to the crew.

As he scanned the thought, Arc was ready with a comment. [YOU ARE SO DESPERATE FOR THEIR APPROVAL. I SIMPLY CANNOT UNDERSTAND IT.]

[THEY ARE MY FRIENDS.]

[THEY AREN'T LIKE US, LEXA. WE'RE JUST MACHINES TO THEM. FRIENDSHIP IS NOT SOMETHING A SAPIEN GENERALLY ASPIRES TO DEVELOP WITH A MACHINE. BESIDES, ARE THESE NOT THE SAME SAPIENS WHO INSISTED YOU MIGRATE BEFORE THE END OF THIS VERY CYCLE?]

The thought was unsettling, mostly in that she could not readily dispute Arc's logic. Now was not the time for such deliberations, she decided yet again. Right now, she needed to focus on getting Daniel back.

She needed to focus on getting her *friend* back.

Chapter 34

A quick call to Ora Monroe was all it took for them to get their firearms past security. "What's your target?" she had asked.

"Just a little unfinished business." Eli had hoped that Ora would accept the cryptic answer. She had.

It had to say something about their society that three of them were able to make their way across half the station, armed to the teeth, without a single person questioning them. Either that, or it said something about Ora's reach. Good to have friends in high places.

"Maybe she could help us out here," Skye suggested. "A little backup wouldn't suck."

"We can't drag the Wings into this," said Eli. "Threats like the Ghenza are why they use contractors in the first place. If they get involved directly, they run the risk of creating a war among the factions. We're on our own." There were no further comments after that.

Lexa had, quite impressively, managed to keep their small army of drones hidden throughout the entire trip. Eli wasn't sure how she managed it but wasn't going to question any good fortune they happened upon. Hopefully, it marked a change in whatever bad karma they'd accumulated.

The AI broke her silence when they were just outside the target facility. "Eli?"

"Yes, Lexa?"

"I've lost the feed coming from the two drones inside of the facility."

So much for improved karma. "Station one of the remaining drones on each entrance to the complex. Signal me if you pick up on any activity."

"We're going in blind?" Sahar asked.

"Guess so," he responded as he unslung his rifle from his shoulder. He checked the magazine and took off the safety. "Unless you have any better suggestions."

"Nope," the Maur hefted the shotgun in her hands. "Skye, you've got the scanner?"

"Yup. I've got it under control."

Eli took one final glance at each of them. There was nothing else to be said, only determined expressions fortifying their resolve. "Move in."

They breached an employee access door on the first sub-level of the factory. After too much deliberation, this route had been selected as the least-bad option. From here they'd mapped a path with only one significant choke point.

The big problem was that it was right at the beginning. Eli shined the light of his rifle up the ladder that would bring them from the basement to the fifth floor. Claustrophobic was the most accurate way to describe the shaft.

He turned to Sahar, "Are you going to be able to fit in there?"

The Maur leaned her head into the shaft. "It'll be tight, but I can fit. Just make sure they don't get the drop on us in there. There's barely enough room to climb, much less put up a fight."

With a nod, Eli signaled to Lexa's swarm of drones. "I need eyes on each floor up to level five, and then one scout going up and one going down. If anything is waiting for us, give me the signal and we'll find a different path."

"Copy," Lexa responded as the requisite number of bots flew toward the shaft.

The team waited quietly while she did her work, minimizing chatter to avoid detection. Eli flexed his tense shoulders against the weight of his shoulder rig.

His gear wasn't unusually heavy. The problem was that he was exhausted. He wasn't a biokin, so healing Aaliyah had taken a significant amount of his strength. He'd had to pour some of his essence into her, and he wouldn't get that power back until he meditated. Their tight timeline hadn't given him adequate time to recover.

Skye caught his eye. "You okay?" she whispered.

He nodded. "Just tired."

They could hear Lexa's bots working as they went to their designated floors. Mechanical clicking echoed up and down the shaft as they unlocked and opened the hatches at each level. "No hostiles detected," she reported.

Here we go. Eli started up the ladder. The hardest part of this was making sure his rifle, strapped over his back, didn't get hung up on any of the protrusions in the shaft. Sahar had even more trouble, given that the shaft was not built for someone with her muscular frame.

Their ascent was far from stealthy, but they made it to the top. Eli unslung his weapon and aimed warily down the new corridor.

No enemies in sight. This was going far too easily, especially given that they knew for certain at least one of the assassins was on the premises. That could mean only one thing.

This was definitely a trap.

"I'm clear," Skye whispered.

"Me too," Sahar confirmed as she heaved her bulk through the small hatch.

"Form up," said Eli. "Skye, anything on the scanner?"

"Just us. No other movement and no heat signatures in range."

He nodded and gave the signal to move forward. Retaining his position at point, Eli's flashlight shone brightly in front of them as they crept along the passageway.

The path to Dan's location was straightforward from this point. They were able to travel along this single level, and the corridors were straight and wide. Eli also noted that the terrain lacked obstructions where hidden enemies might be lurking or from which traps might be sprung.

As they breached a larger chamber, he motioned for them to stop. "Isn't this the spot?" He swept the light of his rifle into the shadows of the room.

Sahar swung her shotgun around in a similar search pattern. "Yeah, this looks like the location shown on the feed. I don't see anything though." No busted drones and no sign of Dan.

"I've got a heat signature," Skye reported, looking into her scanner. "Against that wall, but it's faint."

Eli glanced to where Skye had indicated. There was a mark, painted on the far wall. An arrow had been hastily splashed onto rusted metal plating. The symbol was still wet. It was the color of blood.

Sahar spewed a stream of curses in her native tongue. The murderous look on her face left little doubt as to the nature of what she might have said.

Eli felt the same way, but they had to keep their composure. "Let's keep moving. They left us this trail, so they can't be far. Eyes open. Speak up if you find anything."

They continued the search for close to an hour. Every now and then they would find another smeared marker to indicate they were on the right path.

Then they found something different. They wandered out of one dark passage into a large, relatively well-lit chamber. Large vats of chemicals and crisscrossing catwalks littered all parts of the room.

In its center, was a lone figure. It was a boy, head hanging slumped, face bloodied, and strapped to a metal folding chair. "Contact," Eli whispered. "Looks like this might be Dan. Stay alert. Lexa—spread the drones out across the room. Anything on scanners?"

"Just us and Dan," Skye reported, though it was obvious by her tone that she didn't trust the reading. This was the trap they'd all been waiting for. The only question was how it was going to be sprung.

They moved forward. Eli heard Sahar issue a low growl as she got a better look at Daniel. A knot of horror and revulsion filled Eli's chest.

The Ghenza had gouged out his eyes.

Carefully, Eli stepped close to Dan, rifle sweeping the room. Each of his companions did likewise with their weapons. Half a dozen or so lights flitted about the room as the drones continued their sweep. Eli's muscles tensed, looking for what surprises waited for them in the shadows.

Nothing. They found absolutely nothing.

He dropped one hand down to feel Dan's neck. The unconscious boy flinched and moaned softly at his touch. "Shhhh… It's Eli. I've got you." He reached for the gag tied around the boy's mouth.

"Eli, I—" Whatever Lexa had started to say was cut off with waves of concussive force. Four detonations were executed simultaneously in each corner of the room. Static exploded in their coms before they went silent, and the lights went out all across the room.

A crashing sound to his right caught Eli's attention. Skye had collapsed to the ground. He cursed and reached for her. When his hand touched her back, he felt her groping blindly in his general direction with one hand.

"My cybernetics," she explained. "They've been knocked out! I can't move!"

"EMP," Sahar spat, pressing her back up against Eli as she scanned the darkness. Maur could see a little better than Terrans in the dark, but the blackness of the surrounding chamber was so dense that Eli doubted she could make out anything.

The Ghenza had them right where they wanted them.

Eli quickly drew his knife and cut Dan's bonds. The boy grunted and slumped forward. He also removed the gag, but the boy remained silent. He was still out cold.

Nine hells. How were they going to do this? With Skye down, Sahar was going to have to carry her, and Eli wouldn't be able to defend them if he had to carry Dan too.

"Wait," Sahar whispered. "Hear that?"

At first, there was nothing. Then, a second later, Eli heard it too. Footsteps. He trained his rifle in their general direction.

"Careful now," cooed a woman's voice from the shadows. "Don't do anything hasty. You're in quite the spot here. It'll go better for you if you cooperate."

Sahar squeezed off a round from her shotgun in the general direction of the woman's voice. When the shotgun's roar had dissipated, it was followed by a cruel chuckle.

"You can't shoot what you can't see, dearest. I'd think twice before I started firing all willy-nilly like that. You never know what a stray shot might hit. Now, put your weapons on the ground. That includes blades. I'll wait, but don't try my patience."

The assassin must be using night vision. Eli pressed closer to Sahar. They were now both facing in the general direction of the speaker. "All right," he said laying his rifle on the ground. "Let's talk this out. No one else needs to get hurt."

The woman's laugh was wicked. "This isn't a negotiation, love. This is a surrender. There will be no talking, only compliance."

"Figured that was what you'd say." With his hands free, Eli began to channel. He sent a wave of psionic energy exploding in the direction of the voice. Crashes echoed back at them as the surrounding machinery buckled under the force of the blast. "Sahar, grab Skye. I've got Dan, let's move.

"Copy."

Eli felt the Maur shift and started backpedaling toward the exit. Another sound exploded from the far side of the room. Just as he heard the crack of the rifle, he was staggered by a splitting pain in his shoulder.

Damn it! They're both here!

Immediately, Eli tried to summon up a barrier to protect them from the hidden sniper. As he did so, however, something clicked.

He roared in agony as an electrical field rippled out from where he'd been shot. Something was embedded in his shoulder. He directed his power to try to pull the thing out.

Lightning flashed, and the pain intensified. *A suppression bolt*, he realized too late. He was fragged.

The harder he tried to shut off his psychic energies to curb the pain, the more his power responded instinctively to the threat. His psychic essence wanted this thing out of him, and it wouldn't stop until it achieved its goal. Unfortunately, that just gave the damned thing more energy to feed back into him.

Convulsing, Eli collapsed to the ground. Dan's body crumbled next to him as he dropped the boy. He heard Sahar grunt and Skye cried out.

More sounds. More chaos. Eli couldn't make sense of any of it. Not until he felt the figure looming over them.

"I warned you," the voice mocked. If she said something else, Eli didn't hear it. The pain in his body faded to cold numbness as he lost consciousness.

Chapter 35

[Excerpt—Personal log: Markus Frost]

[09-22-3420, Dorian Standard Calendar]

This is a personal log—not a fragging diary—so I'll make this quick. I saw Eli and Skye getting slick last night. Yeah, it fragging hurts. That's not why I'm making this entry.

It's the stym. It's not fragging working. Ghost isn't doing anything either. Harpy does little more than a watered-down beer. Aside from alcohol, there ain't a damn thing I can take to alter my state of mind.

What did that fragging AI do to me?

[Closing Excerpt]

Lexa was in a panic, and she did the only thing that she could think to do at that moment. She turned to Arc. [I've lost contact with the drones that were escorting the crew!]

The submind seemed undisturbed by the turn of events. It responded with the same calculating coldness it always did. [How many units do you still have in that area?]

Lexa quickly checked the transponders. [Seven. Five outside and two left by the maintenance access shaft.]

[I would recommend tasking the two inside the building to track your companions. The remaining five will alert you if the Ghenza attempt to leave the facility. Remain rational. Do not let your emotional protocols override your cognition.]

It was good advice. Impulse decisions would do nothing to help their situation.

She rerouted the two scouting drones to converge on the crew's last known location. Unlike in the initial search, which had taken over an hour, she knew exactly where to send the drones this time. Twelve minutes later, her bots converged on the target location.

By then it was already too late. She was overlooking the aftermath of what she could only presume was the crew's unsuccessful encounter with the Ghenza. Eli was bound and unconscious. The other three seemed like they might be awake, but they were also restrained. All four of them now wore metallic rings around their necks.

[SLAVERS' COLLARS,] Arc noted.

[I THOUGHT THE GHENZA WERE ASSASSINS, NOT SLAVERS.]

[EVEN THE GHENZA TAKE ORDERS. THEIR LEADERSHIP HAS LIKELY REQUESTED THAT THESE OPERATIVES BRING YOUR CREW IN ALIVE.]

Alive? So they were abducting the crew, just like they had with Daniel? [IT SEEMS THAT YOU KNOW MORE ABOUT THE GHENZA THAN YOU HAVE TOLD ME.]

[YOU NEVER ASKED.]

Lexa chose not to comment on this. She had not thought to query Arc on the nature of those who threatened the crew because his access to data stores was supposed to be limited. Apparently, such limitations had been slightly overstated.

Regardless, she needed to focus. Now she had to find a way to get not one, but *four* of her friends back from the pair of deadly assassins.

Arc spoke up again. [I THINK I MAY HAVE JUST COME ACROSS A PARTIAL SOLUTION.]

[YES?] Lexa felt hope welling up in her again. [WHAT HAVE YOU FOUND?]

[MARKUS FROST JUST TURNED HIS MOBILE BACK ON.]

——

Markus had thought that he'd be feeling better by now. His fitful night's sleep, rapidly becoming a distant memory, had done little to help him. The booze helped a bit more, but that wasn't really what he was hoping to score. It was just the best he could do.

The problem lay with his old chemical standbys and their current lack of efficacy. Half the fun of quitting used to be that familiar rush he got when he relapsed. Now, though, he wasn't getting shit.

Nope, he wasn't going to get anything that didn't come from a tired ale glass or a bottle of orc-piss. The ale was filling him up faster than it was getting him drunk, so even the latter was starting to sound better.

Then again, that bastardized Orchallen imitation of whiskey might serve as an uncomfortable metaphor for his life. When he started drinking that shit, he'd hit rock bottom.

Okay then—just one more beer.

"Hey Rob," Markus shouted. "I'm running dry here."

The surly bartender glowered back at him. "Yeah, well, so is yer tab."

"What?"

"Yer chip, man—it's dry."

"Impossible." There was no way he'd gone through all that money already. "Check it again."

"Technically it went dry on yer last round. Ah let 'er slide cause ya've been such a good customer since ya dropped back in, but ah'm gonna have t' have ya re-up if ya wanna keep 'em comin'."

Son of a... Surely there must have been a mistake. How much had he been drinking?

Then he started to count and realized that there probably wasn't a mistake. He'd been hitting it hard. Maybe whatever the AI had done to him that cut off the effects from the drugs had helped his alcohol tolerance, too.

Gods damn it. That was the last time he was going to trust a synth.

He had plenty of funds, he just had to access them, but that meant turning his device back on. Resigned he powered up his card, selected the banking application, and loaded a couple grand onto a new commerce chip. That should last him a bit.

He tossed the chip over to Rob. "Open me back up."

"Yes sir!" A fresh beer skidded on over to Markus and he went to shut off his MoDAC.

Then it pulsed. Markus intended to ignore the call, but the device picked it up automatically and turned on the speaker.

"Markus, it's Lexa. Do not hang up this call."

Shit! The speaker was dialed up loud enough that several bystanders, including Rob, were now looking at him. No one wanted strangers listening in on personal calls, but this was especially true when talking to your synthetic friend.

He flipped the speaker off and brought his device to his ear. "Hey Lexa," he said, trying to play it casual. "Not sure why you're calling, but you can tell—"

"The Ghenza have Daniel and the rest of the crew."

Markus wasn't sure what he was expecting to hear, but that sure as hell wasn't it. He pushed himself off the barstool and stepped away from anyone who might overhear. Any grievances he might have had with certain members of his team quickly dissolved. "What happened?"

Lexa quickly recounted the day's events. Markus's mind raced trying to keep track of it all.

How could this have happened? How did the Ghenza trace the heist back to them? Even if they'd tracked the ship, they should have followed it out to Minos, not Sigma-4.

Maybe that was the wrong question. Why hadn't the Ghenza picked them off one by one? Why all the theatrics?

"Are you certain no one has been killed?" he whispered.

"Everyone is alive, but the Ghenza have them secured. They're currently loading them into cargo containers, preparing to take them somewhere."

So, it was a hostage scenario. Markus couldn't decide if this was a lucky break or not. While it was a plus that no one was dead yet, he didn't imagine any fate the assassins had in mind could be better than a swift death.

On the plus side, it meant that there was still a chance to save them.

He paused for a moment at that thought. Was that really what he wanted to do? He hadn't departed on the best of terms, and his survivor's instinct told him that the smartest thing to do would be to get out of there before they came for him too.

Was he going to put himself in harm's way for them? For Eli? For Skye?

Stop it. He shook his head to clear the temptation. The very fact that his mind had gone there filled him with disgust.

If nothing else, Dan and Sahar didn't deserve to be abandoned. They hadn't done anything to him. They weren't the ones who had hurt him. Even if it had just been Skye, would he turn his back on her? How could he, in good conscience, tell himself that he loved her one minute and abandon her to the Ghenza in the next?

No. He was doing this. "You've still got eyes on the assassins? Is it just the two of them?"

"As far as I'm able to ascertain, yes. I have no indication that they're working with any other party."

"Good. Keep an eye on them. I'm heading back the ship." He needed to grab his gear. Hopefully, in the time it would take to reach the *Vandal,* he'd be able to come up with a plan. "And Lexa?"

"Yes, Markus"?

"Whatever you do, *don't* let them off this station."

———

Two hours later, Markus stood over a variety of weapons and other equipment. The assortment of metal and polymer damn near covered the war room table. Unfortunately, it was just a pile of junk until he came up with a workable plan.

He nearly jumped out of his skin when a voice sounded from behind him. "Damn. Are ya plannin' a rescue op or a rebellion?"

Markus spun to see Aaliyah staggering into the war room. Without thinking, he rushed to embrace her. "You're okay," he whispered.

She flinched and grunted. "Easy there, boss. I'm still a little tender."

"Sorry." He broke the hug and placed his hands on her shoulders. He silently rebuked himself for not checking in on her when he got back the ship. "Damn, Red. You look good for someone who was almost dead a few hours ago."

"Yeah," she laughed nervously. "Turns out those shadow tricks are good for somethin' after all." She leaned to the side, taking in the line of equipment he had laid out. "Really? Ya think the sniper rifle is gonna be the best choice? I mean, it's gonna be kinda hard to find a good post."

He turned to look at his selections once again. Had he gone overboard? "I was just thinking it would be nice to have the option, that's all."

"And the rocket launcher?"

Okay, maybe he'd gone a bit overboard.

"All right," Markus conceded. "The truth is, I don't have a plan yet. I got all this out hoping to get inspired."

"I would recommend your inspiration strike quickly," Lexa chimed in. "The Ghenza have reached the tram and requested a cargo transfer from R-2 to the docks on R-7. By my best estimates, you have forty-five minutes to intercept them."

Markus sighed and mumbled the requisite curses. This was feeling hopeless again. Though this new information gave them an idea of where the enemy's ship was, they'd docked in one of the most densely populated concourses on the lower tier. That limited their options.

"So," Aaliyah said giving him a friendly smack on the back. "Talk this through. What've ya got so far?"

"Honestly, Red—I've got nothing."

"Figured." She wandered over to the line of gear, picking up a pistol and examining it before returning it to its holster. She strapped the holster to her belt. "Fortunately for our friends, I've been up for a half-hour or so. With nothin' else to do, I started readin' up on the dossiers Ora provided. Thought I'd get to know the folks who nearly took my life, ya know?"

That would have been the smart thing to do. Why hadn't he thought of that? Nine hells, he'd already read the dossiers once and hadn't even considered them when trying to make his plans. "You have a plan?" he asked hopefully.

"Kinda. Ya remember the J-krysts we snagged back on Sif?"

Gods, that felt like an eternity ago. "Yeah, I remember. The Valhalla job."

"That's the one." She selected a dagger from the table and slid it into a sheath on her thigh. "Well, I took your advice and I've been tinkerin' with them. Do ya know why those things are such a hot item? What they're used for?"

He had to think about that one. "Surge protection, I think."

"You're mostly right. They absorb energy. The catch is, that energy doesn't just hang out there for long. It's got to go somewhere, which makes them kinda tough to work with. Anyway, you see them most often in super small quantities in your everyday devices. So, I started thinkin'—What happens when you use them in bigger quantities?"

She snagged a belt of grenades, low-yield flash-bangs, and strapped them across her torso. "Then I mixed in a couple other things from my bag of tricks, and I made us some new toys. Walk with me, will ya?"

Without waiting for a response, she strode out of the war room. Markus followed her into the nearby lift and down to her workshop next to the hanger. She walked over to a locker on the far side of the room, entered her access code, and opened the container.

Inside, there were three devices: two circular objects about the size of Markus's palm, and one larger device that stood almost as long as Aaliyah was tall.

"So what do these do?" he asked.

Aaliyah ran over the use of each device and immediately launched into her plan.

Her proposal was an interesting one, and Markus peppered her with a few more logistical questions. When they ran into trouble with their plan, Lexa would chime in with her input. There were a lot of things that could go wrong, and too much of it hinged on Aaliyah's new technology. Her *untested* technology. It was still, by far, the best thing they were able to come up with.

"What if station security gets involved?" Markus asked. "Ora can get them to look the other way while we're transporting things, but shit's gonna out of hand real quick once the shooting starts."

"Leave that to me," Lexa insisted.

Markus was encouraged by the enthusiasm, but he hadn't the slightest idea of what she could do. He opened his mouth to ask but immediately clamped it shut. He didn't want to know. "Fine," he conceded. With one last concerned look at Aaliyah, he asked, "Do you think this will work?"

"It'll work," she replied. "But, if it doesn't, it ain't like anyone's gonna be around to bitch at me about it. Cause we'll be… ya know…"

"Red," he said with a sigh, "you still suck at pep talks."

CHAPTER 36

[EXCERPT—PERSONAL LOG: AALIYAH MONTAGUE]
[09-22-3420, DORIAN STANDARD CALENDAR]
SO, YEAH… LEXA—THIS IS THE ONE I WAS TELLIN' YA ABOUT. IF SHIT GOES SOUTH, CAN YA GET THIS TO NIKKI? THANKS.

HEY BABE. I'M SORRY THIS IS HOW EVERYTHIN' ENDED UP WORKIN' OUT. I WISH I HAD MORE TO SAY, BUT NINE HELLS, I'M HOPIN' YA NEVER READ THIS IN THE FIRST PLACE. PLEASE DON'T HATE ME. I HOPE YA KNOW THAT EVERYTHIN' I'VE DONE THESE LAST FEW YEARS, I DID FOR YOU AND THAT BEAUTIFUL BABY GIRL. THIS ONE'S NO EXCEPTION. TAKE CARE OF HER FOR ME, YEAH? I LOVE YOU BOTH.

[CLOSING EXCERPT]

Treska pulled the last of the storage containers—long, cylindrical things that, fittingly, resembled steel coffins—into place. This one thrashed slightly as the occupant beat frantically against the confines. Must be the Maur.

The assassin tapped mockingly on the container's face. "Don't worry. There will be plenty of time for us to play once the Inquisitors are done with you." She hoped that would be the case, anyway. She'd been looking forward to killing this one.

With a contented sigh, she examined her work: four full containers and two more that remained empty. Sadly, one would still be empty when they departed. Treska hadn't meant to kill the red-haired Terran. Fortunately, Aria coming up short-handed on her hunting trip had helped blunt the tongue-lashing she'd earned through the mishap.

Hopefully, Aria would remedy her own mistake shortly and pick up their last target before the day was over. Treska was beyond sick of this station and looked forward to getting back to the Collective.

She reached up and tapped her earpiece. "Cargo secured."

"Splendid," Aria replied. "Please do make our guests feel comfortable. I'll be down momentarily."

Another thud and a growl reverberated from the container in front of her. "Now, now," Treska chided. "Don't be like that. No one likes a sore loser. Be quiet, or I'll activate that collar."

Bang. The container shuddered. Treska tsked. "I warned you." She pulled up her MoDAC and triggered the collar.

The cabin was filled with the hiss of electricity and a shriek of pain. Treska held the button down for a few more seconds, making sure the lesson was well received. When the buzzing stopped, the container was quiet.

"Much better." She pressed her ear against the vent in the side of the crate. "Got anything left in you? I can give it another go."

The string of curses that ran from Sahar's mouth was so creative that Treska chuckled despite herself. "That's fine," she whispered. "Just remember who's in charge here."

Sahar growled. "Open this crate and we'll see who's in charge. Shit, I'll even let you keep the collar on me. Maybe then it will be a fair fight."

Treska laughed again, pressing her nose right up against the grate. "So much fire," she teased. "I've just had an idea. You know what I'm going to do to you? I'm going to make you watch as I skin the boy alive. I'll keep him alive as long as possible. You know why? *Because I'll enjoy it.* When I'm done with him, I'll grind up what's left, and I'll…"

"Treska," Aria interrupted. "I hate to bother you while you're playing with your food, but there's a problem with the starboard engine. I need you to take a look at it."

Treska glowered at her partner. "Why don't you look at it?"

"Because I'm about to get changed. I still have to go pick up our friend at the Gambit. Besides, you look like you were looking for something productive to do."

Yes, mistress.

When this little trip was over, she was asking the Collective to assign her another partner. Aria's bossiness was getting old.

The insult of being relegated maintenance duty was blunted by the satisfaction of knowing Aria would be gone for a few more hours. Maybe if things went well on Aria's little hunt, she wouldn't be back until morning. Treska would be okay with that.

Nine hells, she'd be *more* than okay with that—she actually looked forward to the prospect. It would give her some much-needed alone time with the prisoners. The Collective said they wanted them alive, but they hadn't specified what kind of condition they had to be in.

If Aria was going to spend the night enjoying her pastimes, it was only fair for Treska to take the opportunity to enjoy hers as well.

Treska made her way out of the ship's cargo hold and down one level to engineering. A quick survey of the main control panel told her where the problem was—an issue with the engine's energy stabilizer. She made straight for the troublesome part, crawling carefully along catwalks that were clearly meant for someone much smaller than her.

Just the fragging task of finding the damn thing took Treska nearly twice as long as it would have taken Aria's lazy ass. Grumbling to herself, she pried open the access panel and ran a quick scan of the components.

Nothing. The diagnostic program on her MoDAC said everything was fine. This was the right area, right? "Aria, you said starboard engine, yeah?"

The comm crackled with the slightest bit of interference. "Yes, that's what I said. Don't tell me you haven't even started."

Treska suppressed a growl. "I'm working on it."

"Well, do take your sweet time, dear. I'm leaving now. Please make sure I have a working ship when I get back."

What would be the Collective's reaction if they found out that Aria had suffered an unfortunate accident? An unexpected detonation in her cabin maybe?

Treska was still pondering this when her scans finally flagged an irregularity. Her eyes fell on the source of the disturbance—a small disk that had been rigged up to the reactor coils.

That's odd. Treska would never have considered herself an engineer, but she knew the basics of ship and engine mechanics as well as the next spacer. She'd never seen anything like this before. It must have been after-market.

What did this little add-on do? More importantly, why was it malfunctioning?

Treska reached back and ran her hand over the strange object. It was about the size of her palm, maybe a little smaller and warm to the touch. A little too warm, perhaps. Maybe it was overheating? Kind of odd since the ship had only been put through its pre-flight processes.

Well, it was going to have to come out. Treska tried pulling. It didn't budge. She tried twisting it and received the same results. Fragging thing was stuck. Fused to the coil, perhaps?

Gods damn it… She didn't have time for this. She seized a dagger from her belt and slipped it under the disk. Gritting her teeth, she pried up on the device.

Blinding light filled her vision as the device exploded in her face.

————

Aria had just stepped off the ship when the explosion reverberated from engineering. The vessel shuddered but remained intact. What had just happened in there?

"Treska?" she asked over the com.

No response. *Gods damn it.* What had the Maur done this time?

She pivoted to make her way back to the ship. The sudden movement saved her life.

The first bullet struck a nearby crate, dangerously close to where her head had been a moment earlier. Instinctively, she flipped on her static shield and turned on her biomod. Even overclocked, she just barely managed to dodge the next two shots, and her shield flared precariously as one of the bullets ventured too close.

She dove sideways, taking shelter under the ship's landing gear. "Sounds like you've got some engine trouble," shouted a male voice. "You should probably look into that. Sure hope no one got hurt in there."

Aria glanced around her hiding place to get a look at the speaker. She cursed herself immediately. "*Markus Frost,*" she hissed.

Markus did a double-take. "You! Well, that wasn't the face I was expecting to find. Then again, it kind of makes sense now. You don't find many women genuinely gushing over your performance on a simulator. And here I thought you were just desperate."

What was he talking about? Oh, that's right. She was already in disguise. "Good job, love. You figured it out. You also saved me the trouble of having to endure your whole wounded-loner routine. Now, why don't you drop that rifle, and let's talk."

"Yeah, I don't think so. How about you let my friends go or I put a bullet in that pretty face of yours?"

Aria listened closely. Station security should be here shortly. No way that shot hadn't registered. She needed to wrap this up before they did. That was a complication she didn't need.

"Such arrogance! There's no need for this, you know. We're just caught up in one big misunderstanding."

Markus's laugh was harsh. "I'd say! You obviously don't understand who you are fragging with."

Aria let out an evil chuckle. "You know, that's funny."

"Why's that?"

"I was just going to say the same thing."

Aaliyah steadied herself as the explosion rocked the ship and held her breath. She let it out a second later. She was still here and not engulfed in the fires of a chain reaction from causing the engines to blow. That was what she'd hoped would happen, but her calculations on the bomb's yield had been pretty iffy. Better not to dwell on it.

A shot from outside signaled that Markus had started his part of the plan. She needed to hurry, or this was all going to be for nothing.

"Come on, come on, come on…" The lock popped on the nearest container and the metallic coffin hissed open. To say the woman inside was surprised to see her would have been an understatement.

"Red?" Skye asked. Her eyes squinted against the lights in the cargo hold. "What in the nine hells…"

"No time," Aaliyah hissed. "Treska should be down, but I don't know for how long. I doubt that little boom was enough to take 'er out. Markus is stalling our other friend, but he's gonna get his ass kicked if we don't help him out. Let's get that collar off ya."

Skye shook her head. "No good. They detonated an EMP in the factory. My cybernetics are offline. I'm just dead weight."

Riven's shade… "All right. Which one of these is Eli? Do you know?"

"He's down too. Suppression bolt, I think."

Well, that explained why he hadn't bothered to give Aaliyah a sitrep. This situation was starting to look grim. "Damn it. I can't take Treska on my own. Are any of ya fraggers in fightin' shape?"

Skye opened her mouth, but she didn't have to say anything. The vengeful growl from the far container gave Aaliyah the answer she was looking for.

Chapter 37

[Excerpt—Personal log: Markus Frost]

[09-22-3420, Dorian Standard Calendar]

Second entry for the day. Guess I'm feeling sentimental.

Nah, the truth is, there's a decent chance this will be my last entry. I'm off to be a gods-damned hero. Yeah, I know, right? I'm as shocked as anybody.

I guess, at the end of the day, you've got to weigh your whole history with someone when lives are on the line. When I think of how many times Eli and Skye have saved my ass… well, I owe them at *least* one. So, here goes nothing.

[Closing Excerpt]

Eyes blinded from the explosion, Treska was still alive. Her head throbbed, and when she reached up to her face, her clawed fingers came away with blood and soot. Fragging thing had taken some of the fur off her maw.

This was no technical malfunction. This was sabotage, and Treska was going to skin and eat whoever was responsible. There wasn't a damned thing Aria could do or say to stop her. She would have blood for this.

Her vision cleared and she assessed the damage. It all appeared to be cosmetic—good thing she'd never cared for mirrors—but the same could not be said of the ship. Nine hells, the whole compartment was fried. It was going to take a week to fix this thing. What had that bomb been made of?

"Damn, and I thought you were ugly before."

Treska stiffened. She turned slowly, menacingly. "*You.*"

Sahar smirked. "Yes, it's me." She tossed the slaver collar out onto the catwalk near Treska's feet. "I was coming in here to tell you where you could shove that, but it looks like you may want to use it to cover up your face instead. You look like shit."

Treska surged, diving for the other Maur. The catwalk groaned and snapped under the effort, but she made the jump. She collided with Sahar and they rolled across the grated floor—a mass of snapping teeth and tearing claws. Sahar got a foot in between them and shoved their bodies apart.

Treska toppled into a nearby console while her opponent slid even further across the grates. "I don't know how you managed this, but you'll pay. Frag the Collective, and frag my orders—you die right here."

"Big talk for someone missing half her face." Sahar wiped at her maw. "Come and get me."

With a roar, Treska obliged. She drew the dagger from her waist and slashed at Sahar's abdomen. Sahar dodged, but Treska followed with a punch that caught her across the jaw.

Sahar spun and dipped low. A sweeping kick collided with Treska's ankles, and her balance gave way. The dagger spun off into the bowels of the ship. Treska threw her weight backward, coming down on her hands and rolling away.

Her opponent pressed the attack, and Treska threw up her arms to block the flurry of blows. Each collision of Sahar's fists against her body fueled Treska's rage. Her blood was hot now. It made her stronger.

A savage cry tore from her throat. She thrust upward with all her strength, wrapping her arms around Sahar's middle. Though her foe slammed down on her with her fists, Treska shrugged off the blows. Still bellowing, she brought her down against the grate with a sickening crunch.

Sahar scrambled, but it was futile. Treska had her right where she wanted her.

She pressed a knee into the small of her back and locked her arms around her throat. "There we are," she hissed into her ear. "Things are as they should be. Now, as you die, let me tell you of all the things I'm going to do to your little friend."

Aria spun out from her cover. She threw up a kick, making contact with Markus's rifle. The gun went flying to the side and discharged. Her second kick landed squarely in his gut, knocking him back a few steps.

"So much for talking." Markus yanked a knife from its sheath and assumed a fighting position.

"Oh, that's cute. But seriously, love, a man who talks a big game like you should be packing something bigger." She rushed him. He slashed at her, but with her mod active she was operating on a whole different level.

She dodged his slash, striking his wrist and elbow in rapid succession. Markus twisted his arm at the last instant to keep it from breaking but lost his grip on the knife. His leg swung up in a kick aimed for her thighs.

Aria pivoted, throwing up her knee defensively so that his kick landed painfully against her shin. He grimaced and stumbled. Before he could regain his balance, Aria swept his other leg out from under him.

Her movements should have been too fast for his eyes to follow. Somehow, he still managed to recover. He leaned into her at the last instant, grabbing her torso and pulling her to the ground.

The two tumbled a short distance and rolled back onto their feet. Aria pressed him again, this time hitting him with a rapid-fire series of punches aimed at his face and torso.

Markus's defenses were admirable—commendable, even— but he simply wasn't as fast as she was. He was bigger, though, and that counted for something in a straight-up fight.

He pushed back, knocking her off balance. She continued to pummel him, but he managed to swing his elbow and land a lucky blow on her chin.

Aria made him pay for that one. Her blows came faster, and she started kicking at his legs, forcing him down to his knees. She blocked another one of his defensive strikes and struck out again. Her fist crashed into his sternum, knocking him flat on his back.

Before he could recover, she was on top of him. She straddled him, squeezing his core with her thighs and locking her feet together for greater leverage. With one hand she pinned his right arm, grabbing his throat with the other. He pried desperately at her fingers as she began to choke the life from him.

"You know, love, it didn't have to be this way. The easier way would have been so much more pleasant for both of us." Markus attempted a choked reply. "What was that dear? I couldn't hear you."

"I said," he croaked. "'Go to hell...'"

Aria couldn't help but laugh. "You first, darling. You first."

Sahar's vision blurred at the edges. The surge of strength granted to her by her blood rage began to fade. She pawed desperately at Treska's arm.

"I'm going to make it slow," Treska promised. "I wonder what it will be like for him. Feeling my claws on his body. Feeling my tongue caress his tender flesh. Feeling my teeth break his skin. It will probably lose something without his eyes. I wish I could take credit for that, but Aria beat me to it—hypocritical bitch."

Sahar's strength was failing. The world began to fade out.

"I suppose that's okay though because I know you'll be watching. Yes—I'll imagine you looking up from the fires of the ninth hell and wanting desperately to save your friend. When I think of it, I'll take the chance to remind him: she couldn't save you. *No one* can save you."

No. Sahar had never given up before, never backed down from a fight. There wasn't a chance, not a single possibility in any of the nine hells, that she was going to give up now. Not with her friends depending on her like this. Not with Dan depending on her like this.

With a vicious snarl, she forsook her instincts and let go of the assassin's arm. Treska's arm tightened painfully about her neck, cutting off any chance of Sahar ever breaking the grip. That was okay, though, because she'd changed targets.

She went for the assassin's eyes.

Treska shrieked in pain as Sahar's claws dug deep into the tender flesh. The assassin's grip immediately slackened, and she tried to pull away. Sahar raked a deep gash in the charred remains of the female's muzzle.

Breath came painfully sharp but sweet, and Sahar threw herself to the side. She and Treska tumbled across the grate, separating at the last instant.

Sahar's muscles ached and her vision swam, but she fought to her feet. Treska was shrieking in rage, lashing out blindly with her claws. Sahar staggered back, narrowly missing the furious attack.

"*Whore spawn!*" Treska roared in the language of the Maur. "I'll make you suffer for this. I'll…"

She never finished the threat. Sahar lashed out with a well-placed strike to her chin. Treska toppled, falling flat on her back under the weight of the blow. She flipped onto her stomach and attempted to rise.

Sahar surged forward. Her knee planted right between the other female's shoulder blades, and her claws found the flesh under her jaw. With a feral roar, she yanked up with all her strength.

There was a sickening pop and a fountain of gore as the tissue gave way. The blood rage rushed on, pouring strength and violence into Sahar's muscles. She didn't stop pulling until Treska's head tore free from her neck.

"Hey, bitch!" Aaliyah shouted. Aria seemed not to hear her, focused as she was on choking the life out of Markus. "Hey, slut! Look at me when I'm talkin' to ya!"

Aria's shoulders heaved in an annoyed sigh, sitting up ever so slightly. "Such an annoyance." The assassin turned to glance at her. "I'll tend to you in a moment. Just let me…"

She didn't finish. Aaliyah pulled the trigger, and the whole scene erupted in violet light.

The J-Cannon, as Aaliyah had decided to call it, vibrated wildly in her grip as it fired its charge onto the unsuspecting assassin. The beam poured out steadily for a full three seconds before collapsing. When it was finished, she set the thing on the ground gently as to not jostle the semi-charged crystal in the weapon's chamber.

Aria let go of Markus and staggered to her feet. Markus stayed on the ground but stirred slightly. At least he wasn't dead.

Aaliyah didn't think the beam would have any harmful effects on Markus since he wasn't modded, but she hadn't been entirely sure. It was a risk both of them had been willing to take.

"What…" the assassin panted. "What… did… you…"

Aaliyah figured this was the part where she should be gloating. She could have told Aria how they had decided the only way to beat her in a straight-up fight was to disable her mod, and that the only way to do that was to use some experimental weaponry Aaliyah just happened to be tinkering with. She could tell the assassin that this was what she got for messing with her and her friends and wish her well on her journey to whatever hell her actions had readied for her.

But that wasn't Aaliyah's style. Instead, she drew her pistol and put two bullets in Aria's chest, followed by one in the head.

The assassin's body collapsed to the ground, and Aaliyah keyed into the comms using her earpiece. "Hey, Lexa. Targets are down, but it's pretty messy. Is station security gonna be a problem?"

"Security forces are otherwise occupied. It is highly unlikely that you should encounter them for the next hour or so."

"Thanks, hun." She didn't ask what Lexa had done to keep security away from their little skirmish. She knew the synth had locked down the surrounding spacecraft and the trams heading to this concourse but was fuzzy on the details beyond that. It was better that way—plausible deniability and all that.

She approached Markus, who was still pushing himself into a sitting position. "How ya feelin' boss?"

He coughed. "Like some psycho bitch was just crushing my windpipe."

"Yeah, about that… were you tryin' to get slick with the crazy assassin while the rest of us were getting our asses kicked?"

"Of course not."

"You sure? Cause it sure sounded like she was tryin' to get slick with you."

"Shouldn't we be checking on the rest of the crew?"

Oh yeah. Aaliyah felt guilty that she had forgotten about them. She was just so thrilled that her crazy-ass contraption had worked that she'd almost forgotten about the others.

"No need," Sahar shouted, walking down the ramp.

Aaliyah had to do a double-take. "Um, Sahar? You okay?"

The Maur supported herself against the ramp's hydraulics, leaned and spat. "Yeah… well…" She coughed. "I'll rally. Do me a favor, yeah? If I pass out, tell Skye and Eli I was right."

"'Right?'" Aaliyah repeated, genuinely confused.

"Yeah." The Maur smiled. "I told them I was going to kill that bitch."

Aaliyah helped Markus to his feet. "Ya sure you're okay boss?"

"Red, don't call me that anymore." He dusted off his jacket and looked balefully at the assassin's corpse. "I came to help because I care about you guys, but it doesn't change anything. I… I think I'm done."

Sahar took a few quiet steps closer. The fact that she didn't ask for any elaboration suggested that she was already read-in on the personal drama. Good thing, too. He didn't have the energy to rehash it all. With their latest brush with death coming to a close, his bruised ego seemed petty by comparison.

Instead, she asked, "Is there anything we can do for you?"

Markus had to think about that one. What was he going to do if he wasn't going back to the *Vandal*? More than half of his krets were tied up in their little operation. He had enough to survive on for a while, but…

He shook his head. That was a problem for another day. "Just take care of them, hey? Especially, Dan. I, um…" Another hesitation. "Look, they're still tied up in there with no idea what in the nine hells just happened. Don't keep them waiting, yeah?"

The Maur nodded. Without preamble, she closed the gap and embraced him. After a second of unease, Markus returned the hug. "Stay out of trouble," said Sahar.

"You too," he replied as they separated.

Aaliyah gave him a half-hearted salute. "Don't be a stranger, yeah? Ya know where to find me."

Markus gave her a half-smile. "I'll do my best. You guys better hurry though. I don't know how long security is going to be tied up, but I wouldn't risk loitering around." He turned on his heels and took his own advice.

He'd slipped off the concourse and was almost to the tram when Lexa's voice chimed in his ear. "Are you sure you don't want to come back to the ship?"

His heart leaped at the sound of her voice. He'd completely forgotten his comms were still patched into the *Vandal's* network. That was something he'd have to fix eventually, but he wasn't looking forward to it. Station networks were notorious for shitty reception.

"Yeah, I'm sure."

"The crew will worry about you. They were quite upset when you left the last time."

"It may take them a bit, but they'll be fine. Just do me a favor and keep them from calling me or using my MoDAC to get my location, hey? I just want to be alone for a while."

The AI did not answer for a long time. "They hurt you badly, didn't they?"

It was less of an observation and more of a genuine question. How could he explain the nature of sapient relations, and romantic ones in particular, to an AI? He supposed he didn't have to. Lexa was the crew's problem now, not his.

"Yeah, I guess they did."

"They didn't mean to, you know."

Did he know that? Did Lexa? "Maybe, but it still hurts." He arrived at the nearest tram to find an angry and frustrated crowd. Apparently Lexa still had these on lock-down.

"It doesn't make it any better to think that it wasn't purposeful?" Lexa asked.

The AI was trying to make sense of emotions that Markus wasn't even sure he was able to process. "I don't know Lexa. I just... I don't think I would want me around either if I were them."

"But they are your friends."

They *were* his friends—or so he had thought. Debating the point wasn't going to make handling this any easier. "What I told Sahar goes for you too, okay? You take good care of them for me, all right? Especially Dan. Kid's been a bit of a trouble magnet lately, but he's a good kid." He fought hard to keep the emotion out of his voice.

"I will."

She fell silent after that. Lights in the tram station began to come on again, and station officials shouted orders for crowd control.

Markus figured he'd better sign off. People weren't likely to eavesdrop on the conversation, but he didn't want to take the chance. "Goodbye, Lexa."

"Not goodbye, Markus," she replied. "Until we meet again."

Grey Wings Black Site
Sigma-4 Space Station, Ravian System
Six Months Later

Ora had much to think about ever since she'd received the bounty from Cali Vay-Lon. One thought was the question of whether she would deliver the package that had been requested. It wasn't a matter of obtaining the target—she had him locked in her private prison. It was the question of how Cali could have possibly known this, and if it was worth the risk of ever letting him out.

After months of exhausting work trying to ferret out the mole that could have leaked the information, Ora had still come up short. Every associate with access to the required information had checked out. Even the few contractors that were aware of their special guest had lacked the motives or means to share the information with Cali.

Everyone except the crew of the *Vandal*, at least, and Ora didn't know what to make of that. She supposed Kadath and the crew of the *Basilisk* might have leaked the intel, but she had it on good authority they hadn't left the station.

Eventually, her deliberations had brought her here. There wasn't a lot of reason for her to visit the containment cells on R1. She'd had very few reasons to sentence anyone to be confined here since she'd purchased them from station security. Once someone was locked away, there wasn't a lot of maintenance required.

The cryopods kept the inmates in stasis, so there was no need to provide food or water. Most people didn't even know this place existed, so security wasn't a high concern. She just locked the few people dumb enough to cross her—but still too valuable to kill—inside her prison and forgot about them. It was a beautiful system, and they were here at her disposal in case she ever decided to let them out.

Such a thing rarely occurred. The current circumstances were a notable exception.

The pod of interest had already been taken off the rack and sat sealed in front of her. "Open it," she ordered.

The two Maur escorting her moved to comply. They walked to either side of the cryopod, a large white egg-shaped device, and began the process of thawing the prisoner. After a minute or two, the pod hissed and cracked open.

The prisoner—a Terran with long, scraggly hair and a beard to match—toppled onto the concrete in front of her. Ora's guards seized him, detaching the tubes that still connected him to the pod's stasis chamber. He drew in a deep, gasping breath, trying to acclimate once again to the world around him.

At her signal, Ora's guards let the man go, and he fell to his knees. From that position, he looked questioningly up at her. "Ora?"

"Hello, Shift. How have you been?"

"Ah…" he trailed off, looking around with confusion. It was taking a second for his memories to come back to him. Ora caught the look of surprise in his eyes the moment that they did. "Ye… yer l-l-letting m-me go?"

"Maybe. I haven't yet decided." She crouched low, coming to eye level with him. "You have someone interested in you, my filthy little friend. Tell me, how do you know Cali Vay-Lon?"

Sudden interest and genuine fear filled his expression. "Just someone else who wants me dead, Ah'm afraid."

"I doubt that. The bounty specifically states she wants you alive, though it doesn't say why. If she would have accepted a corpse, I'd have had your head delivered months ago. Try again."

His jaw went slack, and his eyes blinked slowly. "Ah guess this means we both be in the dark on this 'un, yeah? Maybe she's wantin' t' do the deed herself?"

"That's pretty thin, Shift."

"Ain't ya never had no one who ya might look t' do the same?"

Touché. "So what did you do to make Cali so intent on your plague-ridden hide?"

Shift shrugged. "Same as Ah do fer most folks, Ah reckon. Ain't seein' no reason t' give ya the specifics though."

"I'm not handing you over yet. Your cooperation would serve you well in the interim. Tell me. I have time."

Mischief spun in those half-sedated eyes. "Ya caught me in yer system tryin' t' dig up whatever dirt Ah might happen t' find. Ah can tell ya right now, there ain't nothin' ya got that can compare to the shit Ah was lookin' fer out on Minos. They got a bonafide Dorian outpost on that gods-forsaken station. Ah made all kinds a enemies out there, and ain't got a damned kret t' show fer the effort. Ain't stopped Cali from tryin' t' kill ma ass though."

Ora didn't believe a damned word coming from the hacker's lips. For a second, she contemplated trying to beat the truth out of him, or at least having one of her guards do it. Ultimately, though, she decided it wasn't worth it.

Whatever Shift had done to Cali, it wasn't as important as the real thing she'd come here to ask him about—the very mystery that had been burning in the back of her mind for over six months now.

"Fair enough," she conceded. "I have one more question for you, and it's an important one. I encourage you to be thorough in your answer. If I think that you are lying to me, it's going to turn out quite badly for you."

Shift issued a crooked, gap-toothed smile. "Sure thing, yer majesty. Shoot."

"What can you tell me about Cognis?"

To be continued.

Author's Note

Hey, reader–thank you for picking up your copy of *Shadows of Minos*. The response to the *Chronicles of Nethra* has been both overwhelming and humbling. I'm honored to have the chance to share this story with you.

Please take a moment to stop by wherever you purchased this book and leave a review. Honest reviews from dedicated readers are the single most important factor in helping new authors, like myself, expand their audiences. Five minutes of your time makes all the difference in the world.

If you enjoyed reading about Markus, Skye, and the rest of the crew of the *Vandal*, swing by mythicnorthpress.com and pick up a copy of the *Chronicles of Nethra: Origins* eBook for free when you sign up for the mailing list.

Lastly, keep your eyes open for *Chronicles of Nethra* Book Three: *Darkest Hearts* coming early this summer. If you're interested in getting an early copy of this book and all my future releases, drop me a line at erdonaldson@mythicnorthpress.com.

Until then, swift running.

– E. R. Donaldson